El Camino del Rio

Winner of the 1997 Frank Waters
Southwest Writing Contest

EL CAMINO DEL RIO

JIM SANDERSON

University of New Mexico Press Albuquerque

First paperback printing, 1999

Excerpts from this novel have appeared as short stories
in the following publications:
"Año Nuevo." *Portland Review* 43:1 (spring/summer 1996): x–x.
"Cleburne Hot Springs Resort." Conference of College Teachers of
English Studies LIX (1994): x–x.
"Contrabandista." *Atom Mind* (spring 1998): in press.
"Machismo." In *Gulf Coast Collection of Stories and Poems*, edited by James White.
Texas Center for Writers Press, 1994.
"Ocotillo." In *Semi-Private Rooms*. Youngstown, Ohio: Pig Iron Press, 1994.

Library of Congress Cataloging-in-Publication Data
Sanderson, Jim 1953–
El Camino del Rio / Jim Sanderson.
p. cm.
ISBN 0-8263-1990-4 (cloth)
ISBN 0-8263-2159-3 (pbk.)
I. Title.
PS3569.A5146E4 1998
813'.54—dc21
98-17138
CIP

for Truet and JoAnn

I would like to thank Lamar University,
particularly its faculty senate, for granting
release time to partially research
and write this novel.

And you know it's too late to change your mind
'Cause you paid the price to come this far
Just to wind up where you are.

—Ry Cooder, John Hiatt,
and James Dickenson,
"Across the Borderline"

El Camino del Rio

MOJADOS, WETS, MULES

Chief Deputy Sheriff Raul Flores pried open the dead wet's stiff fingers and pulled the glass vial out of the palm. Raul Flores held the vial between his forefinger and thumb and raised it up to the wind and sunlight. It was the same type of vial I had clutched, four years before, as I tried to press my guts back into my body. "Let me see that," I said, and Deputy Sheriff Flores flipped it to me. It was filled with the same silver blue metallic liquid as my vial.

I had been gut shot and was dying. I was up a canyon trail seven miles away from the river. Because of the steep canyon walls, I was in a dead zone, so I couldn't radio for help. Sister Quinn found me, gave me a vial, and told me to press the vial against my chest and pray. As I held the vial and tried to keep my teeth from chattering, she grabbed me under my shoulders and drug me down the trail. She grunted and strained, and I felt her sweat drip into my face. After a mile or so, out of the dead zone, she radioed for help on my walkie-talkie.

Fellow agents said that it was a miracle she had found me, but some of the locals along Texas Highway 170, El Camino del Rio, weren't surprised. She was magical, they said. She always showed up when someone needed help. Some called her a *buena curandera;* others said she was a saint. Some said that during the night, Sister Quinn could turn into an owl, just like the souls of the dead could, and perch on tombstones. They said she was probably flying overhead, returning from a tombstone, when she saw me dying.

Now here was another blue vial, only Sister Quinn hadn't been around to save this wet. I unsnapped the chin strap, then pulled off the motorcycle helmet and held it by the strap. The wind cooled my sweaty face and hair, and I felt a chill. Though you doubt you could ever get used to the summertime heat, you do, so the winters, pleasant to the snowbirds, sometimes chill you. I rubbed at my forehead and felt the dust smear into the sweat; then I pulled up the collar on my nylon jacket to keep the wind off my neck. My partner, Pat Coomer, Chief Deputy Sheriff Raul Flores, Deputy Sheriff Freddy Guerra, and I stared at the dead man. We had all seen the circling buzzards and wondered if something had happened to the wets we were chasing. I had spotted the mule just as the buzzards landed and started picking at his eyes and crotch. They lit out when I walked up. The flies didn't go away; they still buzzed around the neat .22 bullet hole in his head.

The six wets that Pat Coomer and I were tracking squatted together around a mesquite. The mama held her smallest kid while the other shivering kid cried. A woman held her bloody leg. One man stared at the ground. A second man smiled at me. All of them glanced up now and then to look at the dead man, as though he were some evil sign—*muy mal, un maleficio.* They had their plastic jugs filled with water and their extra clothes or bedding rolled into tight bundles beside them. It was the childless woman who had stepped in the lechuguilla.

Earlier, as I rode the motorcycle through and around the wash, dodging the cacti, I had seen the bloodied spear of the lechuguilla. The night before, agents had dusted the dirt levees on our drag that paralleled 170 to Ruidosa. This morning, with the sun in my eyes, I had tracked for signs and spotted the footprints. If the wets had stayed on the old ranch road, they'd hit the sensors that we had up in San Antonio Pass and they'd be easier to find, but they'd do less harm to themselves if we caught them before they went through the pass. Then the checkpoint on Highway 67 picked up signals from the magnetized, bugged bridge we had put up over one of Raymond

Kohlmeyer's fences. They had made good time; they were into the canyon.

So I had headed up 67 on the motorcycle, and Pat Coomer let himself in the northeast gate of Raymond Kohlmeyer's ranch and drove west. Kohlmeyer's ranch was just a lot of creosote and cactus southwest of the Chinati Mountains, but it was part of the only flat spot between the Rio Grande and the south rim of the Davis Mountains. Anywhere else this side of 67 was rough, ravine-filled territory; the other side of 67, the El Camino del Rio side, was even worse.

I had radioed ahead to Pat, who found no signs. I'd guessed that they would follow a dry wash, and I tried to track them. As I drove down the wash or along its caliche banks, I struggled to keep the motorcycle from fishtailing out from under me and away from lechuguilla spears. I noticed rolled pebbles, dust stomped off rocks, and eventually blood on another lechuguilla.

Raul Flores gave orders to Freddy Guerra, who was filling out the necessary Presidio County and state of Texas forms. Marfa was the county seat and Abe Rincón was the elected sheriff, but Raul Flores ran county matters around Presidio. Two years before, Joey Latham, who looked the part, was sheriff, but when we busted a pickup truck full of marijuana, the Anglo driver told us about the cocaine stashed in Joey's horse barn.

"Goddamn it," Flores said loudly to be heard above the wind, "I guess you better put gunshot as cause of death."

"No shit," Pat Coomer said. "What gave you that idea?" Red-haired Coomer had his usual give-a-shit grin, and now, even in winter, his fair skin blazed red in the sun and the wind.

"What are you going to do about it?" I asked Flores.

"Ask some questions."

"To who?" I asked.

"I've got my sources."

"What about this?" I held up the glass vial. "Doesn't this make you suspicious?"

"What the hell is it?" Coomer asked.

"*Curandera* shit," I said. "Medicine, luck, miracle juice."

"We'll question her," Flores said, then turned to his deputy, Freddy Guerra. "Better get that Baggie out of the truck and wrap this *vato.*" Freddy left, and I pulled off my sunglasses to look at Flores. Flores glared at me. "Christ, what the hell else you want me to do?"

"Why don't you just wait for that crazy bitch to turn herself in?" Pat asked through his chuckle.

"Why don't you search her *templo,* question her, scare her a little?" I asked.

"Christ, she's a nun. How's it gonna look if the Presidio County Sheriff's Department is hassling a goddamn Catholic fucking nun?"

Quiet Freddy Guerra came back with the body bag and unzipped it.

"Before we bag him, look at his boots," I said.

"What the hell?" Flores said. "You want 'em, pull 'em off."

"How many wets or even mules with the money they get packing dope you seen with Red Wing boots? And those are genuine Levi's, not some off brand. And look at his hair: long but well cut."

We'll compliment his mama or whoever else dressed him before he was shot," Raul said.

"Try a little harder," I said. Raul gave me a dumb look. "He's working for some people with money. And they're bad fuckers, real *broncos,* and he's a *bronco* too."

"So let's bag this bad fucker," Raul Flores said.

Pat shrugged just to me, then grabbed the man's feet to steer him into the bag. Flores lifted the dead wet's shoulders and looked up at me. "You too important to help, Mr. Senior Agent?" So I helped Flores with the dead man's shoulders so that Freddy Guerra could pull the bag over the body.

"At least it's not summer. They don't go ripe as fast in winter," Pat said.

As the deputy zipped up the bag, I sat down and looked at the huddled aliens. The wind gave me a chill that shook my shoulders. One man smiled; the other man stared at the ground; the woman with the children pushed the younger child's face into the soft spot of her shoulder and held the older child's hand; the woman with

By the time Pat Coomer pulled the truck into the Border Patrol station in Presidio and I pulled in behind him on the motorcycle, the wind had gotten stronger and cooler. The gas signs at the Presidio gas stations swung on their hinges, and trash and tumbleweeds blew down the dirt streets and caught on curbs or picket fences. The starving dogs that wandered over from Ojinaga looked for a place out of the wind to lie down.

The Border Patrol station was a cinder block building surrounded by a high fence, on the juncture between the only two paved streets in town, 170 and 67. During high winds the Border Patrol station caught its share of foam cups, old newspapers, greasy napkins, and tumbleweeds. Several of the starving stray dogs liked to dump over the station's large trash cans and scrounge for food. Even this isolated part of the world, with fewer people than most anyplace in the USA, had its share of people's trash.

As Pat Coomer stepped out of his truck and I walked up to him, two joggers in expensive Gore-Tex jogging suits loped past the station and into the north wind. Pat said, "Crazy Yankee bastards. Running in this kind of weather." I waved to the joggers, our newly hired city administrator, Ben Abrams, and the other "Yankee bastard," Father Jesse Guzmán from St. Margaret Mary's Church. Guzmán and Abrams were as close as we had to yuppies. They were headed for the recently bulldozed track a quarter of a mile north of the station. The high school track team used the rough gravel pit for practice. In this weather, Guzmán and Abrams would be choking on the dust.

Pat opened the back door of the truck to let the wets out; I held open the door to the station, and Consuelo and Arturo led the other man and woman and kids into the Border Patrol station for processing. Pat followed the wets in, but before I went in, I glanced up at Guzmán and Abrams, fighting against the wind.

The station was empty except for the secretary, Carmen Lopez, and Patrol Agent Dede Pate sitting at one of the desks, filling out her reports. Then the door to Major R.C. Kobel's office opened, and R.C., the patrol-agent-in-charge of the Presidio station, looked at the wets filing in. Without looking at me, he said, "Dolph, once you get these guys cleared up, stop by."

We pulled some chairs around a desk next to Dede and had the wets sit around us. "Hey, Carmen," Pat said. "How about some help typing?"

Carmen barely lifted her eyes from her own typing. "I plan to finish this just at quitting time."

"You know what it does to my nails," Pat said. Carmen didn't smile, didn't look up, just kept punching the keys in front of her.

So Pat and I, with Dede looking on, tolerated the stink of these people, took whatever names they decided to give us, checked them against names of people somebody in the country might want detained, filled out the forms to be filed up in Marfa at sector headquarters, signed everything, then looked through the forms for mistakes. Throughout, the woman with the cut calf repeated her refrain, *"Yo no soy pollita. Estoy un politíca."*

"Yeah, yeah," Pat mumbled to her.

Arturo courteously answered all our questions. The kids rubbernecked the room, and their mother, looking a bit worried, pulled at one, then the other to keep them seated politely and quietly by her. Maybe she had heard the rumors about kids being kidnapped to be sold to rich, childless gringos.

When it was over, Pat stood and said, *"Hasta mañana."*

With the wets looking on, I said, "Whoa! Who's gonna escort 'em across the bridge?"

"I got to get home," Pat said as a plea.

I raised my hand to my lips and motioned like I was drinking a beer. "Later?" The two men and Consuelo smiled at me. Then Dede chuckled.

"No," Pat said. "Like to. Goddamn, I need to, but the wife's been bitching. And you know how mean a Mexican woman can get." After four years in Presidio and no transfer, Pat met a local woman with a missing husband. She filed, and Pat married her and moved into her mobile home with her and her three kids. We'd both been up since dawn, so I let Pat get in his pickup and drive home.

As Pat left and let the screen door bounce closed, as Carmen slipped the cover over her typewriter and a sweater over her shoulders, as the Mexicans slumped in their seats and the two kids drifted off to sleep, I stretched my arms, rubbed my eyes, and got ready to beg R.C. Kobel for a transfer.

I heard a chair scoot across the floor, then turned to see Dede almost sitting on my lap. "Dolph," she said. "I hear you found another dead one."

"Yeah," I said.

"Shot?"

"Yeah."

"Scares you, doesn't it?"

"Especially since somebody is getting away with it."

"You going to do anything?"

I squared to look at Dede and smiled. Three weeks before, our newest and youngest agent had found a mule with a hole in his head and drug the body out of some Rio Grande cane and salt cedars. "What kind of boots did yours have?" I asked.

"What?" Dede stared at me and wrinkled her nose, making her look even younger. "You gonna start working on a Border Patrol *GQ*?" From beers and lunch with Pat Coomer and me, Dede was getting better with her jokes.

I smiled and said, "No, I'm thinking about going into the desert fashion-consulting business. What about his hair? What do you remember?"

"He had on good boots, no tennis shoes or hand-me-downs. His hair was long, in a ponytail." Dede's eyes started to brighten.

"And so?" I waited.

Five-foot four and small framed, she was the only Presidio agent shorter than me. And like most of the rest of us fifteen agents in Presidio, Dede was single, with no immediate plans to be other than single until she got transferred the hell out of Presidio. Since she had first appeared a year ago and got the male agents whispering about her young body, lines had etched themselves into her eyes and chin and her once long, permed, brunette hair was baked and frizzed and cut into a short, dirty pageboy. I patted her shoulder and kept myself from hugging her. “You get better after you’re here ten or fifteen years.”

“As old as you,” Dede said.

“Come on,” I said, and got up and headed toward Major Kobel’s door.

“What about them?” Dede jerked her head toward the wets.

“Where are they going to go?” Then I raised my voice. “Consuelo,” I said. The woman with the cut in her calf didn’t look up. “Consuelo,” I said again, and this time, realizing what name she had given herself, she looked up at me. “Watch them,” I said. Arturo nodded and smiled.

Dede raised her hand, but before she could knock on R.C.’s door, I opened the door and stepped in. When I walked in, R.C. sucked in on his Lucky Strike, then held it under his desk, but I could still see the smoke around his head and trailing up from under his desk. “No smoking in federal buildings,” I said.

“Goddamn you,” R.C. said. “This concern for our health is gonna kill some of us old farts.”

I walked up to R.C.’s desk and sat across from it. “You hear?”

“Another dead one.” Kobel’s head swung to Dede. I motioned to the other chair in front of his desk, and Dede sat.

R.C. grabbed a pad on his desk and shoved it toward me. As I tore the paper off the pad, R.C. said, “That’s some kind of Mexican Colonel So-and-so, working for the Ministry of Defense of Coahuila on special assignment to Chihuahua to track down some enemy of the state—or some such. Sounds like a crackpot, but he mentioned drug enforcement—not DEA bozos,” he added, referring to the Drug Enforcement Agency. We had constant battles with other agencies or other feds over turf.

“Customs or Feebies?” Feebies were the FBI.

“No, Mexican something or other. Maybe he can help you.”

“Yeah, wonder what the *mordida* is?” In dealing with Mexican officials, the “bite,” a kickback or bribe, was always involved.

“Well, then fuck him,” R.C. wrinkled his brow, then looked at Dede. Dede’s face remained frozen. She didn’t make it to R.C.’s office as often as I did.

"Ever get tired of detaining wetbacks and looking for drugs?" I asked R.C. "Ever want to really track something down?"

"I once caught a Czech, or at least he claimed he was," R.C. said. "He was planning on sneaking into this country by way of Mexico. What a poor dumb, lost, misguided bastard he was." And he told us that Border Patrol story. The R.C. Kobel story, like my getting gut shot, that had worked its way into the Border Patrol lore, was the one about Kobel's favorite horse getting gunned down. Kobel was riding down several wetbacks and cutting across ranchers' land up around Marfa. One rancher, who was feuding with a neighbor, shot at Kobel, but Kobel's horse raised his head and took the bullet between the eyes. Before the horse had even fallen, Kobel had drawn his pistol and put two bullets in the rancher. Legend has it that he walked to the wounded rancher and told him that the second shot was for the horse.

When he finished, R.C. raised his cigarette to his lips and took a drag, looked at Dede, then crushed his cigarette in an ashtray that he pulled out of his drawer. Kobel had been the agent-in-charge for two years. He had put in time at Del Rio, El Paso, and Marfa and wanted to ride a desk and the accompanying salary until he retired. This post was a gift to him for his past services.

"Dede, tell him about the boots," I said.

Dede swung her head between me and Kobel. "Good ones."

"Mine had Red Wings and this." I pulled the vial out of my pocket and held it up between my thumb and forefinger. "Sister Quinn's medicine," I added.

"Crazy bitch," Kobel said.

I put the vial back in my pocket and held up one finger. "One, the guys are dressed alike." I held up my middle finger. "Two, Dede's guy was less than a mile from the river, right?" Dede dutifully nodded. "So?"

Dede looked at me. Kobel said, "Quit being cocky. You're the hot shit senior agent who doesn't knock anymore."

"They're probably both with the same outfit. Probably some bad fuckers with some management problems, so they're shooting employees. But why would they shoot Dede's so close to the river, probably before he could deliver his dope?"

"Go on," Kobel said, but I looked at Dede.

"Because they were finished," Dede said. "They're taking something across from our side."

I smiled at Dede, then turned to Kobel. "Let me free to scout the river. A drug bust would look good for us."

Kobel nodded. "Okay, you want to investigate, go ahead." He looked at Dede, then back at me, and said, "I heard from Nogales."

Dede caught the hint. "I guess you won't need me."

I smiled, and Kobel said, "Thanks, Dede." Dede caught the handle of her pistol on the arm of her chair as she got up. She tilted the handle down and swung her butt to clear the arm of the chair, smiled, and left. "Probationary is up on her in how long?" Kobel asked.

"A year."

"How's she doing?"

"She can hang. What about Nogales?"

"Advanced degree, good record. Definitely supervisory material. The word is you have the inside track for assistant field office supervisor or agent-in-charge."

I leaned back in the chair and smiled. R.C. frowned. "But I've got a different suggestion." He hesitated while I leaned toward him. R.C. continued, "I think you ought to stick around awhile."

"Why should I stay?"

"What's so bad about this place?"

I looked out the window in R.C.'s office. Kobel's gaze followed mine, and we saw one of the stray, starving dogs digging through the trash. I didn't need to say anything, so Kobel did. "Mandatory retirement age is fifty-seven. I've got seven months. Sometimes that seems too long what with goddamn budget cuts, sensitivity training sessions, quadruple forms. Remember when we tried flying those silly ass blimps? Hell, the locals would just call the bad guys across the border when we'd pull 'em down, then the bad guys would fly the drugs over in their planes. Jesus."

R.C. had a way of trailing off. "Your point is?"

R.C. focused on my face. "You take my place."

"Why should I? Why should I stay here?"

"You ever seen Nogales?"

"It resembles America more than this place."

"You want McDonald's hamburgers?"

"I want to be someplace besides the third world."

"Look, you go outside and you ask some Presidio citizen what lawman in the area they can trust. What do they say? Dolph Martinez, goddamn it. They like you here. You know the people, the area. You're the best tracker I have. You know how hard it is to learn that shit? You could train the new people. Look what you've done with Dede."

"Goddamn, R.C., I can die happy now."

"Well, shit." Kobel tried to think. "This place ain't so bad. Great dove hunting."

"I don't like shooting God's defenseless creatures."

"Good climate," R.C. said, and I looked up at him. "In the winter," he added. "Great for golf."

"How far do you have to go to play golf?" I asked. Kobel didn't answer. "Where does your wife live?"

"Alpine," Kobel muttered.

"Where you going to retire?"

"A lake in central Texas."

I leaned back in my chair and laced my fingers behind my head. Presidio had no doctor, no drugstores, no paved streets except for the intersecting highways, no dry cleaners; it was a hardship station. You could put in for a transfer after two years, but transfers were slow. I had been here seven years. "You're goddamn right, I want to eat McDonald's hamburgers. I want to speak English more than Spanish."

I started to rise, but R.C. interrupted. "Why the hell are you in the Border Patrol, anyway? Why not a lawyer, a politician? You've got a goddamn graduate degree, for Christ's sake."

I stared down at the toe of my boot, then shrugged. "Jobs are tough to come by, especially cushy government jobs."

"Get them wets outa here. It's quitting time," R.C. said, and I pushed myself out of my chair and went back into the station. Dede and the wets were waiting for me.

The sun was setting and making cold shadows when Dede and I loaded the wets back onto one of our vehicles and got them to the crossing station at the new international bridge. We escorted them through customs on our side, then sent them across. Arturo's smile dropped—back in Mexico and no green card from a kindly *la patrulla* agent. The mother carried the sleeping child and pulled the older one by the hand. Her shoulders seemed to droop with the weight of her child. And Consuelo-María limped behind everyone and jerked her head over her shoulder to stare at Dede and me, hoping that maybe we'd call her back across.

"She's not from northern Mexico," Dede said. "Her accent is different. I'd guess Guatemala. She kept saying that she was a political refugee."

"I heard her," I said.

"You think she was lying?"

"Who knows?" I shrugged. "I hope I'm not the one to catch her next time. Let's go home." Home for Dede was a rented house built in the middle of what used to be a gravel street, so that now the unpaved street split at her gravel front yard. For me, home was Cleburne Hot Springs Resort.

CLEBURNE HOT SPRINGS RESORT

The muffler of my Toyota station wagon started its rattle as I turned off paved 170. I had busted oil pans, torn off mufflers, and broken struts by bouncing over dirt roads in my car. But the Ojinaga repairmen, without computers or high-tech equipment, could beat, weld, or file almost anything into a tight fit. I'd have bought a truck like everybody else, but I wanted to drive something other than a truck just because everybody else had a truck.

The last six miles to my home at Pepper Cleburne's Hot Springs Resort were over a dirt road, and even with my windows closed, I choked on the dust. I made the turn down the slope to Pepper's fantasy and stopped my car under the willows growing along the creek that was formed from the draining water of the hot springs. The wind made the willows' limp branches slap my face when I stepped out of my dusty station wagon.

I hunched my shoulders against the wind and walked along the line of small, squat stucco cabins, built in the thirties when Pepper Cleburne's uncle first got the idea of turning a desert hot springs into a tourist resort. A nice hot bath was just what somebody wanted in the middle of summer with the temperature up around 110 degrees.

I could taste the desert dust on my tongue, feel the grit in my teeth, but tomorrow the wind would die and it would be a cool, bright desert winter day. I squinted against the purple-and-orange glow on the undersides of the low, thin clouds to the west. The sun's streaks of light almost matched Pepper's two-tone, orange-and-white 1955 Chevy, with the restored engine and white leather interior. It was parked next to the ranch's rusted pickup in front of the "entertainment complex," Pepper's bar, pool, and dining room. Next to Pepper's car was one of those long, wide, aircraft-carrier-looking cars: a Pontiac from the early seventies. It had Chihuahua license plates and probably belonged to some of Pepper's Ojinaga whores.

As I circled the empty, cracked pool that couldn't hold water, scrawny, dried Ignacio, sitting on the steps up to the bar, lazily waved, moving with as little effort as possible. I nodded to the man Pepper called his "pet Mexican." Ignacio, my other roommate, a ranch hand on Pepper's daddy's ranch, helped raise Pepper. And in moving from one family property to the next, Pepper always took Ignacio as his handyman. He paid for Ignacio's dentist and doctor bills, bought him a color TV, and gave him a Christmas card every year.

Ignacio scooted to one side as I stepped up to the door and lifted his head to squint at me. *"Putas,"* he said, and shrugged.

"What about you?" I asked.

"Catholic," he answered.

I pushed open the door and walked into the bar, game, and dining room and saw several empty cans of beer on a table. I could tell which were Pepper's cans: the ones with the tops peeled off by an old-fashioned can opener and filled with Pepper's snuff-stained spit. The game room and bar were Pepper's attempts to create, as cheaply as possible, what he imagined the lost tourists driving to Cleburne Springs thought a motel bar should look like. Pepper had found an antique wooden bar in Juarez and had some guy claiming to be a coppersmith nail copper to the corners. I had torn several of my shirtsleeves on the rough edges of the copper. Pepper hung some ferns over the bar and bought the cheap iron tables in Ojinaga. He got the green indoor-outdoor carpet from a friend of a friend of an investor in Chihuahua City. The lamps hanging over the pool table came from a remodeling Holiday Inn in Pecos. The unsteady

Foosball table was a leftover from the student center at Sul Ross State University, up in Alpine, back from the time when that game was popular the first time.

The cabin Pepper lived in, the biggest one, had its own bath and phone. For three hundred dollars a month, Pepper let me live in his failing scheme. For three hundred dollars a month, though, I couldn't expect to have my own hot bath; the remaining room with baths was the "bathhouse," and it was for the tourists who seldom came.

I went to the large, industrial refrigerator behind the bar and pulled out a beer. As I popped it open and felt a bit of the beer's spew, I read the note tacked to the refrigerator with the magnetized plastic carrot. I had a telephone call from someone claiming to be a colonel working for the Coahuila Ministry of Defense. It was an Ojinaga telephone number. Pepper's cabins didn't have their own phones. Besides the public phone that didn't work anymore and the one in Pepper's cabin, we all shared the phone in the kitchen and the one in dining room/bar. I bought the answering machine but was the only one to pay any attention to it.

Ignacio walked in and said, "We got chili."

"Again?" I asked. "Doesn't Pepper know how to cook anything else?" Pepper took pride in his chili. Since the first chili cook-off in Terlingua in 1974, Pepper and Ignacio had been trying to concoct the best chili recipe. He'd gotten as far as third place. With a pool, a bar with a game room, and prizewinning chili, Pepper figured that the tourists would have to come. He and Ignacio made different batches of chili twice a week.

I pulled the telephone out from under the bar, punched the number, and asked the hotel clerk to ring the room of Colonel Henri Trujillo. As I waited and listened to the static that the Mexicans couldn't get out of their telephone lines, Ignacio watched as though he were still amazed at how a telephone worked. I jerked my chin to motion Ignacio away, but Ignacio jerked his chin right back at me.

A curt but polite, high-pitched voice answered the telephone. I spoke in Spanish, but when he learned who I was, Trujillo politely switched the conversation to English. "It is my pleasure, Mr. Martinez. Your captain, excuse me, major, speaks highly of you."

"He speaks highly of everybody."

"But you seem to be the man I need."

"What about *la mordida?*" I asked, and waited for a response.

Trujillo seemed to wait too. So we both listened to the static over the phone. "I can offer a fee," he said hesitantly.

I dropped my head. "Maybe we better just forget whatever it is that you have in mind."

"No, no, no. Please. This is legitimate. It sounds confusing because of our various bureaucracies, but the Mexican government is behind me."

"That's what scares me," I said.

"Please, we have had problems in the past, I admit, Mr. Martinez, but this is a matter of concern to the states of Coahuila and Chihuahua, and we have the cooperation of the PRI."

"Look, the Border Patrol doesn't give money to informers; we don't take any *mordida*."

"Fine, fine, just the way it should be." He said the words faster, like a salesman.

"Go on," I said.

"You found some bodies?"

"Yes."

"Would you be willing to help me, help the Mexican government, find the killers? Especially one man, Vincent Fuentes, a former priest. Have you seen him? Heard anyone speak about him?"

"Like I said, I can't take any money. Officially we don't have much to do with Mexican officials."

"I'll be staying in Ojinaga. Meet me for a lunch."

"Can I call you back?"

"The Mexican government will cooperate fully. Call the *comandanté* office at the garrison in Ojinaga. He'll know where I am."

"I'll be in touch."

"Remember. Vincent Fuentes," I heard as I pulled the phone from my ear, hung up, and congratulated myself on getting rid of "Colonel" Trujillo. From his voice, from other "colonels" I had met,

I guessed he was somebody's rich, pampered boy or some drug lord's bought stooge. He or his daddy had probably paid a sizable chunk for the "colonel" title. Now somebody legit or illegit but surely corrupt probably paid him to stay a colonel.

I would have to get up early in the morning, so I needed sleep, but I was restless. After a bowl of chili (one of Pepper and Ignacio's better attempts), I joined Pepper and his whores in the big bathhouse.

Vapors of steam rose from the hot water flowing from a wide-mouthed pipe into the large cement tub. The steam warmed the cabin, and the candles around the tub lit the place and gave it large shadows. The tub, planted in the middle of the floor, was nearly as large as Pepper's swimming pool. With the bathwater already up to his beer gut, Pepper was holding a can of beer above the steam. As he cocked his head to squint through his middle-aged eyes that needed bifocals, his diamond stud earring sparkled in the candlelight, and water dripped from the two twisted ends of his long, handlebar mustache.

To one side of Pepper, lying on the flat ledge that hung over the tub, was a mutilated beer can with his snuff spit and a round can of Copenhagen. On either side of Pepper were the two Ojinaga whores, crossing their arms over their breasts. Pepper's Ojinaga whores delivered, just like pizza dealers.

The younger whore startled when I waved; after all, I was still in uniform, *la migra*. The older one, who was Pepper's favorite, slapped at her and giggled. *"Su compadre,"* she said to her cohort.

"You, Dolph, peel off them clothes and jump in," Pepper said. "You know Alice Kramden here," Pepper said, and pointed to the older whore. "And this is Wilma Flintstone."

Alice Kramden leaned back against the edge of the tub and reached for a pack of cigarettes. She nonchalantly lit one up and said, "*Hola,* pretty boy," to me.

"Jump in, 'pretty boy,' " Pepper said, and giggled. He set down his beer, picked up his peeled beer can, and spit brown juice into it.

"Go to hell," I said to Pepper because Pepper had heard other Mexican women call me "pretty boy." I had heard the term most of my life. It was a Chicana term for a good-looking, bright, promising Chicano boy. My mother, an Anglo, called me "pretty boy"; she would face me at a mirror and say, "Look at my pretty boy." My mother's angular Anglo lines and complexion made my face. And my father was light skinned, *un güero.* I got my mother's green eyes and my father's thick black hair, now with some gray. But though I was now past forty, I remained the "pretty boy" to Chicanas because of my size, muscular but short, and maybe, as my ex-chicana lawyer girlfriend said, because I had a young person's aching want. She said it showed in my eyes. But I figure that was just bullshitting from a time when she still wanted me around.

I unbuckled my holster and held it away from me like it was a snake, then walked to the king-size bed and dropped the belt and holster on the pillows. I slipped out of my uniform; shivered in the cold room with the dancing shadows, gold light, and steam; saw Pepper and the two whores staring at me, Pepper's gut and the whores' titties floating in the hot tub.

Pepper and I sometimes used to have girlfriends, usually teachers from the Presidio Independent School District rather than whores in the tub, but lately Pepper preferred the whores. When Pepper and I first started bathing with whores, I had asked myself what the hell I was doing; I asked myself about the trouble he and I could get into, but I soon stopped asking. The whores Pepper picked out were as much for female company as for hormonal relief (after all, we were middle-aged men getting used to declining testosterone levels).

As I eased into the hot water, Alice Kramden looked at Wilma Flintstone, then at Pepper. "Take your pick," Pepper said. "No hard feelings here."

"Cogelo ese," the older whore said to the younger one, and the girl swished across the large tub to me and rubbed my back. Pepper smiled, then stretched out to completely submerge himself in the hot water. The young whore laughed and slapped the surface when he reached up from under the water to pat her ass.

Pepper came up laughing and shaking his head, drops of hot water flying from the ends of his mustache and his diamond stud earring sparkling. The older whore wrapped her arms around him and pulled him closer to her, and the hot water steamed off Pepper, and some dripped from his nose into her large cleavage.

"Comó te llama?" I asked the young whore.

"Wilma Flintstone," she said.

"Alice Kramden," Pepper's older whore said, and jerked her thumb toward her chest.

Pepper tossed me a beer, then leaned into the arm that Alice Kramden had around his shoulders. She reached around to the side of his head and twisted the end of his wet mustache. Pepper spit into his can, the juice just missing Alice Kramden's arm. "They've got this new sort of fiberglass thing that they can make a pool out of. They reinforce it with steel."

"Jesus, Pepper," I said as Wilma Flintstone started running a finger down my chest.

"Listen, I tear up that piece of shit pool I got and put in this fiberglass thing."

"Where you going to get the money?"

"My relatives."

"Pepper, who is going to drive to the middle of nowhere to go to a hot springs in a desert?"

"That's why I need the pool and the bar."

"Why don't you just leave this place as it is and rent to the few people who know about it?"

"Because those fuckers in Lajitas with the fake-looking Western town did a million worth of business last year. I wish I had a beer-drinking goat like Tommy Lawler's goddamn Clay Henry down at Lajitas."

"They're also next to a national park with just a few cabins for lodging."

"Ojinaga has a park." Pepper looked at Wilma, then Alice, and spoke what went through his mind. "If I could just peddle gambling and prostitutes, I'd have the best resort in Texas."

Wilma circled her finger on my chest, and I forced myself to smile at her as her finger moved down to my stomach to touch my long scar. *"Qué paso?"* she asked.

"A war hero," Pepper said. *"Buen hombre. Muy macho."*

I pushed myself up, and Wilma Flintstone looked at the scar. She smiled up at me, then she bent and first licked the hot water on the scar, then kissed it.

Four years before, I was sweating even more than I was in Pepper's hot bath, only I had on my uniform, and my gun belt was rubbing against my back and sides, chafing me. Sweat knotted up my clothes under my arms and crotch. I was tired. That was usual for summertime in Big Bend country. I thought I was tracking a wet and just walked up on the backpacker eating a can of pork and beans and smoking a joint.

I was on a steep trail that the Comanches had used in their raids on Mexico. And with the high walls around me, I couldn't make radio contact with Pat Coomer.

So at first I wasn't even going to stop and annoy the kid, but I saw the green trash bag. The kid probably couldn't even wait to get his dope home. When I asked him what was in the bag, he said, "Nothing."

"Show me," I said. And the college kid on a backpacking trip pulled one of those cheap .9-millimeter automatics out of the plastic trash bag and shot me in the gut. I took a step back and looked down at my stomach, but I couldn't fall. It felt like a wasp sting.

I guess my hand started reaching for my own pistol, instinct or training taking over; I don't remember. Then I felt another wasp sting as the kid shot again, again in the gut; I rubbed at the stings but still didn't fall like the movies say you're supposed to.

The kid was trembling; he pointed the gun at my head, but he didn't want to be a deliberate murderer or didn't want to see my brains splatter, so he pointed the gun at my gut and shot me twice more. This time my teeth clenched, and I fell to my knees. The barrel of the gun was even with my head, and the kid was shaking. Fall, you stupid son of a bitch, I said to myself, and fell face forward.

I knew the signs, the landscape, the weather, the locals. I could handle a horse, a motorcycle, a three-wheeler, knew all the trails, but I let people get the drop on me. The rancher that nailed R.C.'s horse probably would have killed me. No one ever caught the back-packer.

When I woke up in the hospital, I still had the glass vial with the silver blue metallic liquid in my hand. A couple of the nurses at the Alpine hospital said that they had seen other people go into surgery clutching such vials, especially "Hispanics," so they stuck it back in my hand after the operation.

It stayed in my hand all through intensive care, with Sister Quinn's and some Odessa donor's blood pumping into me. I don't want to believe that the vial gave me my dreams about being a lizard or a puma. And they weren't really dreams. I could feel my lizard's belly against the hot rocks and the soothing heat warming my cold blood. I could feel the tight, knotty muscles of my shoulders and hips as I sniffed for the crippled deer, then slowly crept up on it. I could see in the dark. My *dreams,* or whatever they were, made me a better tracker.

Throughout intensive care, Sister Quinn came to visit me. While I was still semiconscious, Sister Quinn told me that she could dream herself into being an owl and fly over the area. She told me that she had "felt" my pain and went out looking for me. And when I gained enough consciousness to thank her and to hear her tell me what happened, I threw the glass vial at her and said, "Take back your voodoo shit, *tu brujería. Es santería.*"

"The cure doesn't matter," Sister Quinn said. "Only your strength and your belief. You don't need to believe in that potion."

"I don't."

"But you must believe in something."

I looked through the steam vapor to see Pepper kissing his whore. Then I closed my eyes, felt Wilma's lips on my belly, and wished, no, wanted, like a young man wants, like a "pretty boy" wants, for some woman other than a whore to be kissing and licking my scar.

I woke up automatically as usual, at 5 a.m., and felt Wilma Flintstone's gentle snoring on the side of my face. I pulled my stiff arm, full of pinpricks, out from under her head and rolled away from her. Then I got up and slipped into some sweats and went outside to my weight bench beside my cabin. I always lifted my weights early in the morning because in the summer, by 10 a.m. the iron is too hot to touch and doesn't cool until 10 p.m.

As I finished my reps at the bench press, my scar seemed to tighten under the streak of sweat darkening the front of my gray sweatshirt. And when I looked at the sunlit, blue-and-pink, flattened peaks of the Chinati Mountains, I could see in that distance between my weight bench and the Chinatis a puff of dust—somebody driving fast over a dirt road, too fast, I reasoned, to be a coyote.

My weight bench was under one of Pepper's trees, and even when I wasn't lifting, especially in the summer, I liked to sit on my bench, drink a few beers, and stare off into the desert. The best part was to be in some shade. Just a little could cool the air by ten degrees. So of course something as comforting as shade was rare in the desert.

When I got back into my cabin, Wilma Flintstone was still asleep, so I took a shower and shaved. My wadded-up, dirty pants were wrapped around my gun belt, so I searched in my closet for another uniform. With pants and a T-shirt on, I pulled my gun belt out from the dirty pants and watched Wilma sleep. With some makeup rubbed off her, relaxed, she showed her real age: nineteen or twenty. I wondered if she ever tried to cross the river, headed for some American city in her mind where she could be something besides a whore, maybe a waitress or a maid. If she ever did decide to cross and got caught, I hoped that I wouldn't be the one to bust her.

Dressed, I passed by my hat rack and picked up the dirty felt cowboy hat rather than the standard-issue baseball cap. I liked to keep the sun off my face and neck, so I usually wore the straw hats that I bought across the border in summer and felt hats in winter. I opened my cabin door and walked toward Pepper's bar to catch the smell of Pepper's coffee and eggs. The wind had died down, the sun was up; the weather was pleasant. It would be good to be outside or driving the back roads.

Ignacio sat on the steps of the bar, throwing small pebbles into the pool. "Stop that," I said. "You'll fill that thing up."

"Good," he said. "Someday somebody going to fall into that *pendejo* hole and crack a *cabeza*." Pepper had rented a bulldozer, hired two Mexicans who snuck across the river at Candelaria (both of them claiming that they had built pools in the interior), and, with them and Ignacio, scooped out some dirt and poured some concrete.

"Breakfast ready?" I asked, and Ignacio just shrugged. Ignacio, Pepper figured, had gotten his attitude from his family history. His people had been in the Big Bend area longer than Pepper's. They had tracked Victorio's Apaches for the Mexican *federales*. In fact, Pepper figured that his grandfather had stolen some land from Ignacio's people. Somewhere around the turn of the century, one of Ignacio's relatives had killed a Texas Ranger and was then hanged when he came back from Chihuahua to get his wife. After that, Ignacio's people stayed in Mexico. Ignacio was the first to sneak back across to look for ranch work.

I pushed in the door and walked into Pepper's bar. Seams of sunlight came in from the east window in shafts of light. Pepper—dressed in boots, boxer shorts, and a velvet robe—came out of the kitchen with a steaming, hissing frying pan filled with bacon and its grease. His boot heels clicked against the linoleum floor. The kitchen was thick with the smell of bacon grease, and that smell followed Pepper into the bar. Pepper put the pan in the middle of a table next to a plate of stacked, thick-sliced, homegrown tomatoes and said, "Grab a plate." Pepper's whore, Alice Kramden, came out of the kitchen with another frying pan full of fried eggs and smiled at me as I scooted past her for a plate.

I got a cup of coffee from the drip coffeemaker on the bar and sat across from Pepper, and Ignacio came in to sit across from Alice Kramden. "You sleep any?" I asked Pepper. He hadn't waxed his mustache. The twisted ends drooped down.

"Couple of hours. Hell, all you public servants think about is sleep. A businessman doesn't have time for sleep." Since his last wife left him, Pepper had trouble sleeping; that was why he liked the whores to spend the night. Me, too. Some nights it helped to sleep next to a whore.

I looked up from my plate at Alice Kramden. She was all smiles. She seemed to dote on Pepper the mornings after she came over, but by midmorning she was always back in Ojinaga. She was the nearest thing either of us had to a steady woman.

"You ought to quit that silly-ass job," Pepper said as he sucked in on some coffee. "Get that retirement and go in with me."

"So I could throw money into an empty pool."

"Throw rocks into it," Ignacio said.

"You got to have dreams." Pepper shrugged. "I've got some people with reservations for today," he said. "Doing good."

I moved in with Pepper just after his third wife told him how much she loved her lover, the Alpine real estate developer. As near as I can guess, based on what he told me and what I saw, Pepper sort of imploded when a woman left him. With his last wife, he started to shake and continued to shake for several weeks. He shook so bad that his bourbon splashed out of his glass. And because he just drove around his pastures late at night and woke early in the morning to stare out of sore, red eyes at the sunrise, his ranch started losing even more money. So Pepper slid down the hierarchy of his family's landholdings until he became the proprietor of Cleburne Hot Springs.

Pepper wasn't just some dumb West Texas country boy. His family problems started when he pissed off his daddy and got a degree in philosophy at Sul Ross State University rather than in animal husbandry. His daddy couldn't figure him. Pepper was the most happy in his life teaching sixth through twelfth grade in Valentine, Texas, but then the state closed the school and bused the students to Marfa just as the family needed someone to turn Cleburne Hot Springs into a moneymaker.

But Pepper began substitute teaching in Presidio for extra money. And up in Candelaria, when the old rancher's wife who taught in the one-room schoolhouse got sick, Pepper took over for her and finished out the school year. Because he was good, because he was available, he could teach almost every day in Presidio, Terlingua, or even Ojinaga. And all the schoolchildren knew him, and they told their friends or relatives across the border about the funny cowboy with the hot Chevy. Both sides of the border, kids would chase after his car and follow him around when he got out.

The teachers liked him too. They were a wild crowd: other Texans looking for a little adventure in a wilder place or Yankees looking for a desert. They were the type that used to join the Peace Corps, and some of them, particularly the Hispanics, weren't sure about me since I was a part of *la migra* and the opinions in the textbooks about *la migra* were changing. Still, Pepper and I had some wild parties and got drunk on sotol with the staff of the Presidio Independent School District. I figured that Pepper would be better off sticking to teaching, teachers, and kids. They made him forget his family, his ex-wives, and his own ambitions.

Pepper was small like me, never grew up as tall as his six-foot brothers. He developed a drinker's nose, the bulbous kind with busted blood vessels lining the tip. And because he got still and rarely moved around when his wives or girlfriends left him, he grew a beer belly.

Of course, as a Border Patrol agent, even as a "pretty boy," I never had much luck with women either. One woman in El Paso, my pretty Chicana lawyer, the one who told me about the look in my eyes, made my hand start shaking my bourbon. So I asked for a transfer and got sent to Presidio and thus rented a cabin at Pepper's resort.

Alice Kramden stuck a piece of jelly toast into her mouth, started to chew, then turned to kiss Pepper on the cheek. Pepper smiled at her, gave a slight nod, pulled at one end of his mustache, and said, "This is the life, ain't it, Dolph."

And this is basically what we did every morning, except we didn't always have whores join us for breakfast. After breakfast, after I left, whether I was on duty or not, Ignacio would drive the old pickup out to some remote spot on the property to "fix" something, or he putted around in the cabins, cleaning them up. Likewise, Pepper left town once a week or so on "business trips." I suspect that Ignacio just liked filling up time and that Pepper liked drinking somewhere other than in Ojinaga and chasing women other than Ojinaga whores.

EL TEMPLO

I cut for signs out toward Ruidosa, tested the sensors in San Antonio Canyon and up toward Favor Peak, then met Pat Coomer for lunch at the Three Palms Inn Coffee Shop. I asked him if he wanted to drive out to Sister Quinn's *templo* with me.

"Goddamn, it's lunchtime, Dolph," Pat said, and stuffed a soft flour taco in his mouth. "At lunch you don't work." But he scooted out from the booth and followed me. Although we both had enough seniority to have the weekends off, even on weekends we'd usually meet up at the station, then drop by the Three Palms for lunch or coffee, and Pat would bitch about not having enough time off. But today was a workday.

Sister Quinn's place was down a dirt road that dissected one of Reuben Alamendariz's onion fields. In June, when the migrant teams from the south Rio Grande Valley came north and west to pick the crops, Sister Quinn's *templo* smelled almost like a hamburger. Now, though, in December, Reuben Alamendariz had some unemployed locals laying pipe for an irrigation system. Most of the locals were unemployed.

As we drove by they rested on their hoes, dropped their pipe, and waved to us. I looked across at them from the wheel, and Pat lazily waved. "Anybody look like a wet?" he asked me.

"Reuben keeps it legal," I said. People along the river had to keep it legal, with *la migra* cruising their farm roads. So poor Americans made a living picking crops along the border. The wets usually went farther north.

"Yeah, but what about Sister Quinn? Any wet looking for a place to stay can camp out in her *templo*."

As we passed, one lone man with a hoe suddenly raised a fist and shot the finger at *la migra*. He dropped his hand and stood defiantly, and Pat raised both fists to the window and rapid-fire, like he was shooting twin pistols in an old-time Western, gave his fingers to the Mexican. "Stop the fucking truck," he said.

I slowed and checked in the rearview mirror; the other workers were moving toward the belligerent Mexican. Generally the locals liked us here. They didn't make a distinction between us and the sheriff's department or the volunteer fire department. We got calls to get cats out of trees, requests to drag the river for drowned kids or wets, and reports of burglaries. We did it, so the locals called us *la patrulla* instead of *la migra*. The other workers would probably beat the shit out of the Mexican, so I drove on.

"What the hell you doing?" Pat said. "Did you see him? Let's bust his ass."

"For what? He's probably just read one of those Marxist comic books in Ojinaga."

"Still, we need all the respect we can get."

"Calm down, Pat. This is our lunch hour. We're off duty, remember."

We rounded the curve the road made through the field and drove into the salt cedar and mesquite that sloped toward the river. This was where Sister Quinn constructed her *templo*. Sister Quinn lived in the tar paper and ply board shack connected to the *templo*. At first the chapel looked just like the shack, but Sister Quinn conned her friends, or followers, into transforming the chapel into a sloppy mortar-and-stone building. Some highway construction worker brought in a state-owned bulldozer and, since Sister Quinn didn't want cars spoiling the environment around her church, cleared a "parking lot" some yards back from the small shack and chapel. I pulled up beside Gilbert Mendoza's truck, the one that he gave to "the church," and a red convertible Mustang.

Pat got out with me and said, "Holy shit, where do you think that crazy *curandera* got those wheels?"

"Maybe she's into chopping hot cars now."

"Car parts for misbegotten, mistreated, misused wets, huh?"

We walked through the brush toward the *templo.* As we rounded a mesquite, we saw an open lounge chair with a long sleeping blonde spread out the length of it. Her hair fell through the plastic slats of the chair and touched the dust beneath her. "Holy shit," Pat said. "A fucking goddess."

She rolled her head toward us and squinted. When she got her eyes focused on us, she immediately rolled away from us, but not before we saw her bare breasts roll from one side of her body to the other. "I've died," Pat said.

"Sorry." I put an arm in front of Pat. He stopped but stared at the woman's bare back. "Turn around, Pat," I said.

"What?"

I pulled his arm to make him face the opposite way with me. "Okay?" I said, loud enough for her to hear.

"Are you fucking nuts or what? How often you see a woman like that? Especially with her tits hanging out?" Pat whispered to me.

"Okay," we heard the woman say. And this time I turned before Pat to see her rise out of her lounge chair with the top to her bikini refastened. Her gold hair dropped behind her shoulders; her nose, a little too large, divided her face unevenly; her legs made her stretch above both Pat and me. As we walked to her she reached behind her, pulled a sweatshirt off the reclining lounge chair, and wriggled her butt and shoulders as she pulled it over her head.

"Shit," Pat whispered. The sweatshirt, with George Mason University stamped on the front, just barely covered the tops of her hips, and she walked toward us, trying not to place her bare feet into cactus or mesquite thorns, and held out her hand. Both of us shifted our glances from the arch of her left foot, which had either a birthmark or a tattoo, to the rest of her. "Ariel Alves," she said, and even bent toward us, her head was still above ours.

Pat shook her hand first. "You're Mexicano?" he asked.

Ariel dropped her head. "Alves is English. But my boss thought it sounded Hispanic when he first called me. It didn't hurt to have him think so." She smiled out of that slightly crooked side of her mouth. That long nose that seemed to command her mouth to twist into a crooked, mischievous grin was the imperfect detail making the whole of her face beautiful.

"Well, Ariel is one of those Greek goddesses, isn't it?" Pat asked.

She cocked her head to the same side of her face as her crooked smile, and I said, "It's from Shakespeare, *The Tempest,*" and held out my hand. As she shook my hand Coomer turned to stare at me. Ariel's hand was sweaty.

"Actually I looked it up in *Webster's.* It said an *ariel* is an Arabian gazelle."

"Fits," Coomer said.

"Six feet," she said, almost proudly. "Good for business." Coomer couldn't do a thing about the look on his face, and she couldn't help but notice it, so her smile took over her face, and it showed the playful meanness that took over her mind. "But all men want is some petite, small woman."

Pat's face flushed red, not from embarrassment but from consternation. "What are you doing here?"

"Sunbathing." For a desert rat to sunbathe at all was unusual (we cooked enough), but as though we had regulated ourselves to the seasons farther north, we never thought of shedding clothes in the winter, not even if it was eighty degrees. Only the snowbirds, who thought of this part of Texas as tropical, sunbathed in the winter.

"I mean, why are you at this place, Sister Quinn's?" Pat asked.

"I'm new in the area. I help out sometimes."

"Look, we're sorry," I said.

"No, I'm sorry," she said.

"Is Sister Quinn around?" I asked.

"She's in the chapel." Pat cocked his head at hearing Sister Quinn's *templo* called a chapel.

"Thank you," I said, and pushed Pat toward the *templo,* but not before I shot a glance over my shoulder. Ariel smiled, and I stopped. I turned away from Coomer and walked toward her, pulling my eyes from the arch of her foot way *up* to her face. "What do you do here? I mean, why are you in the Big Bend area?"

"I'm executive manager at Lajitas." As confused and flummoxed as Pat, I must have dropped my eyes or my mouth, and Ariel pushed her smile all to one side of her face. She was too cool, too careful, too refined to giggle. "I've paid my dues. Walter Bean himself sent me to work on profits."

"You're a troubleshooter."

"I'm supposed to kick ass, as Walter said."

I hesitated, then stuck out my hand again. "Dolph Martinez."

"Dolph?" she asked. "Funny name."

"My father's joke on my mother and me."

"We'll probably meet again," she said.

"I'm sure—not many people here."

Her smile faded, and she said in a serious, neutral tone, "Drop by the Lajitas hotel. My office is there. Lunch will be on me."

And because I had nothing left to say to this natural-born saleswoman, I walked back to Pat.

"*Muy mas macho.* If you ain't the cocksman," Pat said to me when I got to him.

"You're a married man."

"I didn't promise to go blind."

"I think she runs that whole goddamn Disneyland at Lajitas," I said.

"I wish she would have joined the Border Patrol," Pat said. And I hoped that I was still enough of a pretty boy for this tall, blond, all-American woman to watch me go. But unlike Pat, I didn't look back over my shoulder to check if the woman we had just spoken to was really a mirage, a psychosomatic trick of the desert.

We picked our way through the mesquite and creosote to Sister Quinn's front door. Azul, Gilbert Mendoza's runt of a boy, stood in her doorframe leaning on a broom. Gilbert Mendoza, always trying to get his two small fields to grow enough onions or cantaloupes to make him a living, was too much of a practical farmer to believe in the Catholicism or voodoo that Sister Quinn preached, but he worried about her, so he lent her his truck, and he sent his youngest child, Azul, to help her with the upkeep of her chapel. In a way, Gilbert must have figured he and his wife owed Sister Quinn for Azul's life. Azul stuck his head into the shack and shouted, "*La hermana* Quinn."

His parents called him Azul because he had been born a blue baby. Sister Quinn along with two women from Redford had helped deliver him since the doctor from Ojinaga arrived too late. We sent a patrol vehicle to drive the blue baby, his mother, and Sister Quinn to the clinic in Ojinaga. The doctors there said that it was a miracle he had lived. Some of Gilbert Mendoza's relatives said that it was a miracle he had been blue. This, they were sure, was a sign from God.

"Azul, *'ón' 'tá* Sister Quinn?" I asked. And he stepped to one side as she filled the doorway. As usual, her white tennis hat was squashed down on her head, pasting curls of her sweat-wetted red hair to her forehead. She tilted her head as she looked at Pat Coomer, then shifted her gaze to me and smiled, the hat making a small shadow across her face. Sister Quinn's white Irish skin blistered in the sun, the same as Pat's.

"Agent Martinez," she said. "How are you?" She stepped out of her doorway and extended her hand to me. When I shook her hand, the flab under her arm quivered, and her breasts shifted under the thin, worn cotton shift that she wore. You couldn't tell much about her shape; she was just round. She didn't shave her legs or wear makeup. You could mistake her for a small, round fat man; even her breasts looked like the titties a fat man gets.

Sister Quinn straightened, raised her hand, and looked beyond me. I turned around to see Ariel Alves standing behind us. "You've met Ms. Alves?"

Pat giggled. Ariel Alves, now with a pair of sandals on her feet, stepped up to us, and I could see that the silk-screened George Mason University was just beneath my chin.

"Come in, come in," Sister Quinn said, and motioned toward her shack. "I have coffee, ice water, and cookies."

"Got any wets in there?" Pat asked.

Sister Quinn and Ariel both shot mean glances at Pat. "Could I see you on a private matter, Sister Quinn?" I asked, and looked at Pat, who frowned, and Ariel, who suddenly looked puzzled.

"I'll just talk to Ms. Alves here," Pat said, and smiled.

Sister Quinn looked from one of us to the next, then jerked her head toward her shack. Ariel's smile twisted, and I tried to smile at her to show her that I'd rather be talking to her than Sister Quinn.

"In the *templo,*" I said. "This is sort of like a confession."

Sister Quinn looked suspiciously at me, then made a gesture, some private sign to Azul, and he ducked inside and returned quickly with a key. And she and I followed him to the door of the templo and waited while he unlocked the lock on the chain running through the door handles.

Meantime Pat went to work. "Well, Ariel how long have you been at Wally World?"

"Three months," I heard her say.

I stepped into the *templo* and pulled off my hat while Sister Quinn kept her tennis hat on, as a Catholic lady should, her only concession to gender. I adjusted my eyes to the dim light sliding in through the slats in the wooden shutters.

Sister Quinn opened a shutter, and the sunlight made the pews and the pulpit of the *templo* golden brown, and a slight breeze rustled the vestments on the altar, and I squinted into the light. After kneeling at the altar and crossing herself, Sister Quinn struck a match and lit the candles at the altar. She turned to face me. "Only a priest can hear confession."

"I want your confession." The flickering candle made shadows dance on the wooden statues of Christ and Mary. The Ojinaga artisan who had carved the statues had emphasized the pain. Sister Quinn was big on pain.

Only the front wall was for Christ and Mary's suffering. On the side walls she had hung small statuettes and pictures of saints, and on the back wall she had a reproduced photograph of Don Pedrito Jarmillo, the old nineteenth-century *curandero.* He stared out of his milky, cataract-covered eyes that didn't focus on anything. Sister Quinn said you could see his power, his faith, and his suffering in his eyes. He held his neatly folded white handkerchief, which he had used for his cures, over his heart and stared back at Christ or Mary or any parishioner who got in his gaze.

I reached into my pocket and pulled out the vial of silver, metallic liquid and held it up to the light. "We found that on a guy with a bullet in his head."

Sister Quinn stepped closer to me and squinted to see the vial. "You can get those in Ojinaga."

"I got one from you." I hesitated. "You're the only *curandera* in the neighborhood."

"I'm a nun."

"The Church doesn't like what you're doing. People say that Father Jesse Guzmán has written to the bishop."

"Come on, Dolph. Jesse Guzmán is an altar boy."

"I hear that when Lupe Rodriguez had cancer, you spread her out on a white sheet and burned candles on each corner. Then when the evil spirits got scared of the fire and ran out of her body, you folded them up in the sheet and burned it."

"You forgot about the praying. Lupe believed that the praying pulled the spirit that made her sick out of her body and onto the sheet. Then the candles scared the spirit and kept it confined to the sheet."

"What do you believe?"

"Faith."

"Lupe died two months later."

"Of course she did; she had cancer," Sister Quinn said, turning her back to me, then just as quickly spinning around to face me, as though she were doing a pirouette, a very quick and graceful one for a fat lady. "But Lupe felt better while she waited to die and didn't spend the money she needed for medicine on the *curanderos* in Ojinaga." Sister Quinn smiled at me. "I get a lot of my 'cures' at the *herbería* in Presidio. Whether you have a stomachache or the clap, you can find some desert root, berry, or leaf that cures it. Do you still feel yourself as a desert animal?"

I stared at her, felt myself smile, and hoped she would look away, but she wasn't about to give in. "Do you still turn into an owl and fly around at night and perch on backcountry tombstones?"

"Sometimes I feel my arms become wings. When that happens, especially late at night, I can feel flight. But with it comes"—she stared away from me—"comes a sympathy, a feeling of pure soul, a feeling of the spirit in everything, even the rocks."

I looked at the sunlight streaming in from the window and squinted against it. I wanted to bust her for this crime and so show her up in front of the locals, but I didn't want to hurt her. "Barbara," I said. I was one of the few people who even knew Sister Quinn's first name. I took a chance: "Vincent Fuentes is in trouble." She looked at me, her lips slightly parted, giving herself away. I smiled to myself because I had finally won one from her and because I had confirmed part of Trujillo's story. "These are some bad people, *broncos.* They smuggle dope."

"The people I help are sponsored by a priest." Sister Quinn hesitated and looked at me. "They are refugees, part of the world's dispossessed. You commit the crime by sending them back to their political and economic misery."

I almost said, "Shit," but instead I said, "Two of them were shot by their own people. One of them had some of your voodoo."

"He could have gotten it anyplace. The killers are not my people. Not the women and children whom I help."

"Look close at your friends."

"Look close at what you do."

"Who are you with? Who's helping you—on this side?" Sister Quinn's jaw drooped, but then her mouth turned into a smirk. "They're using you," I added. Sister Quinn backed up to the candle at the altar while she kept her stare on me. "I could bust you again. We've found a couple broken sensors. Destroying federal property is a crime, you know. And this time the bishop will excommunicate you. Nuns shouldn't go around breaking US law."

"Whether the church sponsors me or not, this is still my *templo.* I help the people with faith."

"What about the law?"

"Faith is law." Sister Quinn pulled her gaze from mine just for a moment to look at the lit candle. She then gazed back at me with a sick smile. Never pulling her eyes away from me, she held her hand over the flame of the candle and then lowered it until it touched the flame. Her hand, then her mouth started to quiver, and she quickly pulled her hand away from the flame. "Until you fully feel the universal suffering of poor people and then become a part of that suffering, until you can feel adequately punished for being either white or rich in a world where most are poor and dark, mere pain will have to do."

"So us *güeros* are out of luck?" I felt that if I didn't keep smiling at her, I'd end up roasting my knuckles over some goddamn fire because of a stupid dare. "Besides, how about a little wisdom? I can start with just plain information."

"You better know what you believe, Dolph," Sister Quinn said. "Then wisdom will come."

"Tell me who and when," I finally blurted, knowing that it would have no effect on her.

"Find your God, and you will know when."

"When they divorced, my mother wouldn't let me speak to my father because he was mostly a drunk. But when I was around thirteen or fourteen, I would go see him after school. He was usually drunk, but a couple of times he took me to see this *curandera,* not because he believed anything she said, but so he could piss off my mother. And sometimes, when he'd walk home with me, just far enough toward home so my mother wouldn't see him, we'd pass a church, and he'd make me cuss the church and then God. Meanwhile my mother sent me to Episcopal Sunday school because most of the rich Anglos were Episcopalians," I explained to her and myself. The first time I said the awful *f*-word that my mother told me never to say, I said it just before the word *Jesus.* My father, Miguel Martinez, said, "See there, what did God do to you?" I didn't feel like I would be struck down by a bolt of lightning or roast in hell, but I felt ashamed that I had said a nasty word my mother wouldn't approve of. After that, the words *goddamn, motherfucker,* and even *chinga tu madre* entered my vocabulary, and I made more friends with the boys at school.

I pushed my hat back on my head and slowly backed toward the door. "There's my confession," I said. "What about yours?"

"If I can help you, please come back."

"Thank you," I said. "Eventually you'll have to tell me what you're up to. If not, I'll bust you."

Her face didn't change. She didn't pull her gaze away from me, but she was out of words, as though her mind, independent of her eyes, had drifted off somewhere, perhaps to a perch on top of some tombstone.

So I turned away from her and walked across the chapel floor. When I stepped back outside and the sun burned my eyes, I bumped into Azul. *"Dispénsame, por favor,"* I said to him. He smiled at me, then ducked into the *templo.* He ran to Sister Quinn and stood by her side, and she put an arm around him. Whether inside Sister Quinn's mausoleum, her dedication to her own demons, or outside on her property, Azul followed Sister Quinn around like a puppy. Ariel and Pat were gone. I looked around and thought about calling for her before I called for Pat, but then I saw Ariel coming through the brush toward me. I walked to meet her.

"Your friend can get rude," she said.

"So can yours," I said. And she wrinkled her brows.

"What are you doing with her?" I asked, and jerked my thumb back toward Sister Quinn's place.

Ariel looked down at her feet. With her sandals on, I could see that her feet were long and slender. I pulled my eyes away from her feet to find her looking at me and pushing that smile into one corner of her mouth as though she had caught me once again staring at her body parts. "I like her."

Like a jerk or like her daddy, I raised my forefinger in front of her face and said, "Be careful of her. You don't know what she's into."

Ariel said, "And what do you think she's into?"

"Maybe if you find out, you can tell me."

"Is this all a part of your job, or are you just as rude as your friend?"

"Yes to both," I said. She started to slide by me, and before I could catch myself, I reached out and grabbed her arm. She started to pull it away from me. "I'm sorry, Ms. Alves." She slowly smiled. "Maybe we could meet sometime and I could explain myself."

She smiled at me with that crooked smile of hers. "I don't think so," she said. She turned and walked away from me, but I hadn't given up.

"I occasionally make it to Lajitas," I said.

She stopped and faced me. The sun caught her golden hair, and her nose made a shadow on one side of her face. In this part of the country the brown, sun-dried natives were short, perhaps to stay low to the ground to avoid the sun. To them and me—a short half-Mexican who spent most of his time squatting behind cactus trying to catch other Mexicans—seeing her made us feel what the Aztecs must have felt when they first gazed upon Cortés's light-skinned soldiers. "Okay, look me up, Dolph," she said, and the smile filled her face.

She slowly turned away from me, and I watched the swivel of her hips. If she stayed here, she would become as short and brown as everybody else. The desert cooks everybody, even with hats, sunburn creams, and long sleeves. Red-haired and Irish, Sister Quinn and Pat Coomer stayed scalded.

When I got back to the truck, I asked Pat what he had said to her. He didn't answer. I asked him again. "I said she had nice looking *chi-chis,*" he answered.

"Jesus, Pat, she's not a whore."

"Yeah, sometimes around here you forget the difference."

"You're not married to a whore."

"Sometimes I forget."

"That you're not married to a whore or that you're married?"

Pat shrugged. "Both, I guess."

I shook my head. "She's got a nice car, too," Pat said.

BRONCOS

When we left Sister Quinn's *templo,* I pulled off the highway and up a ranch road, then drove cross-country as far as I could up a mesa. Pat held his wrist in front of my face to show me his watch. "Come on, it's near four—quitting time."

"I just want to high point awhile."

"What you need to do is relax. You know you could stress yourself out, a man your age. You could give yourself a heart attack."

I didn't answer Pat; I just stopped the truck and trudged uphill to the top of a mesa. Pat grumbled behind me. If your ground is just six feet higher than the elevation around you, you can get a good view of the desert. I ended each day high pointing.

We both squatted on the mesa, and Pat pulled off his baseball cap and wiped his sleeve against the sweat on his forehead. After fifteen minutes I spotted some dust raised on another ranch road. "Probably some lost snowbird," Pat said.

"He's headed toward the river." I shaded my eyes with my hand.

"Shit," Pat said. "We're working extended shifts and overtime already."

"You're right. He's harmless," I agreed, and we started trudging down the hill.

When we got back, the radio buzzed and a dispatcher reported that someone from the new Texas state park—Big Bend Ranch—had run into a Suburban cruising around the various camping places along the river. They had US license plates, but when park attendants asked them to buy a camping permit, no one in the cab could speak English. Dede had called in and reported that she had seen the Suburban on a back road. And now Roland Cardeñas, another agent, had called in to report that he had seen it parked near one of the picnic areas along the river. "Come on," I said.

"Shit," Pat said. "Don't you ever go home? Shit, we're goddamn government workers; we're supposed to be fucking off."

We met Dede and Roland and pulled off 170 onto a rutted dirt road that ran toward the river. We spotted a Suburban with Missouri license plates. Two men were pulling themselves across the river in a rowboat. Another man was fishing from the American bank. Across the river was a stack of wooden crates. We all got out of our trucks and met. "Snowbirds," Pat said.

"With a rowboat?"

"You really think there's something going on?" Cardeñas asked.

"Yeah," I said.

"He don't give up," Pat said, then added, "so what's the plan?" I told Dede and Roland to question them, and Pat and I would climb up a rise behind them. As Pat started up the hill, I pulled a rifle out of the truck and gave it to him. "You're a better shot." He looked at me, kind of puzzled.

"You think Mom and Pop got firepower?"

From the top of the rise, I watched through my binoculars as Roland walked up to the man fishing, a Mexican, not a snowbird, and Dede walked to the bank, raised her hands to her mouth, and yelled at the guys in the rowboat. The men in the boat starting rowing faster, and the man fishing dropped his pole and started shuffling his feet. "Get a bead on the guys in the boat," I said to Pat.

Dede yelled again, this time in Spanish. One man jumped out of the boat and, waist deep in the river, started pulling the boat to the far bank. The other jumped into the water, reached into the back of the boat, and pulled out a semiautomatic. Pat got off the first shot. It slashed through the water, two feet from the guy with the gun.

Roland pulled his pistol and then dove to the ground and kept his aim on the guy fishing. Gravel and rocks kicked up around Dede's feet, and then she dove to the ground. Her first shot was over the two men's heads.

The guy on the Mexican side spotted the direction of Pat's shot and started shooting blindly toward us. Pat hit him in the leg, and he limped off, deserting his friends. His buddy swiveled his head toward Dede, then toward us, and sloshed backward through the water, almost getting drug under by the current. Dede kept her head down, Roland kept his bead on the standing Mexican, and his captive hopped around, scared that *la migra* would shoot him if he dove to the ground. "Gimme your pistol," I said to Pat as he worked the lever on his piece.

"Your Glock," I said. Pat threw me his nine millimeter and I ran down the ravine, picking my way through the reeds and mesquite and firing Pat's Glock, knowing I wouldn't hit anything. Pat carried one of the newly allowed semiautomatics; it would get more attention than my .357.

The guy in the river saw me and tried to hit me. With his attention, aim, and shots toward me, Dede was able to put some bullets around him. I felt my shoulder and thigh muscles work smoothly and efficiently, as though I ran on all fours and could jump from rock to rock and yet stay hidden. And then too, with the zing of bullets, I anticipated the wasplike sting of nine-millimeter slugs in my body, but as I fired Pat's pistol and rationality took over from feeling, I knew that just as I couldn't hit him, he couldn't hit me, not with the silly semiautomatic and their field of fire. The man in the river (unable to hit me and getting shot at by Dede and Pat) made it to the bank and, like his buddy, ran off into Mexico.

I stopped, no longer feeling like a puma or a lizard, and became fully human, and thus scared and out of breath. I sucked up some air, put my hands on a boulder, and leaned over. Soon Pat came trotting up to me and, out of breath himself, said, "Goddamn, you asking to get shot?"

I wheezed before I could answer him. "Scared bad guys with

automatics don't take time to aim. Besides, I think I was out of range."

When I got some of my breath, we both started running and sliding down the rocks toward Dede and Roland. Roland's guy immediately started begging in Spanish for us not to shoot him.

Dede pushed herself up, holstered her .357, then brushed off her dusty thighs and chest with her scraped and bruised hands. She was trying to keep her bottom lip from quivering. "You all right?" I asked.

"God, I can't believe you did that," Dede said. Her left hand started to shake, and she tried to keep it behind her back.

Pat walked up to the bad guy and said, "Should we shoot him?"

Roland cuffed him. Pat opened the back of the Suburban and found some more wooden crates. I climbed in, found a tire tool, and tore the slats away from the top of one crate. They were smuggling automatic weapons across.

An American with a federal firearms license can buy guns here and then sell them for three times their price in Mexico. He can get even more in Central America. And he can always exchange them for dope for an even bigger profit. The only problem is getting the guns or dope across our side of the border. Mexicans don't check their side too much.

I turned back and looked at Dede. She smiled. "Your arrest." She smiled more broadly.

I walked away from her and to the fisherman. I stared at him long enough to make him nervous. Pat picked up on my clue. "Let's just shoot him," Coomer said, and touched the handle of his holstered pistol. Dede and Roland stepped up to us, but both Pat and I gave them quick glances that told them to hang back.

"Que mala suerte!" I said to the man. He'd had the bad luck to be left behind. His hand shook a little. I stared. Pat stared. I yelled, *"Donde está Vincent Fuentes?"*

"Aw, fuck him," Pat said.

The man bit at his bottom lip. *"No sé."*

He was pressured and confused, and he gave the standard answer, but in claiming he didn't know where Vincent Fuentes was, the gunrunner had admitted to knowing him. I smiled at Pat.

Pat and I watched as Dede and Roland loaded up the arrest and drove off. We sat by the edge of the river behind some salt cedars and watched the boat and the guns across the river. "Maybe we could swim across and row them back." I didn't answer but thought about taking the advice.

After a while R.C. joined us, and we all went out to the sand and sat, waited, and watched until some Ojinaga police came to the river, opened a crate, held up a gun for us to see, nodded, then packed and pulled the crates and the rowboat to their own cars.

"Well, nothing ever goes for naught. Now the Ojinaga PD's got some new weapons," Pat said.

The guy we captured mentioned Vincent Fuentes and then called the dead guy we found the day before his *compadre.* He wouldn't admit to killing him. We housed him in a locked room in the Presidio city hall, then sent him to the Presidio county jail in Marfa, which would be glad to house him and charge his upkeep to the federal government. From there he'd go to the big lockup in El Paso or Pecos, and someone from the ATF or FBI or DEA, not the Border Patrol, would question him and try to get some answers. And I hoped that they'd let us know whatever they found out. He probably wouldn't be prosecuted because he wasn't a big enough catch, just a foot soldier. And if nobody in the county wanted to prosecute him for concealing a weapon—and they wouldn't because nearly everyone in the county carried a gun—he'd probably be back across the border before too long.

He wasn't a real *bronco,* and the guys he worked for weren't real *broncos,* not yet. They were trying to break into the business. So their biggest problem was the real *broncos,* not us. His best hope was that I could bust Vincent Fuentes and Sister Quinn.

After we shipped him off, Pat and Dede and I drove to Cleburne's Hot Springs Resort for a couple of beers on Pepper. We watched the sky turn orange and purple, and when it was dark, we went into Pepper's bar and continued drinking beer. Ignacio answered the phone when it rang. "Your wife says to get home," he said to Pat.

"Shit," Pat said, and started to push himself from the table.

"Wait, wait." Pepper spit into his sliced beer can, got up, went behind the bar, and came back with a bottle without a label. "Some sotol."

"Hell, no," Pat said.

"Come on." Pepper grabbed shot glasses from his bar, lined one up in front of each of us, and poured the liquor into the glasses.

Ignacio pushed his out of the way. "I don't drink that shit."

Dede raised the kerosene-smelling stuff to her nose and sniffed it. She wrinkled her nose, then set the drink back down.

"I've been saving this for a special occasion. What's more special than my friends busting gunrunners? Bottoms up," Pepper said, and gulped his down. Pat swallowed his and started coughing. I downed mine and grimaced against the hot, bitter feel working its way down my throat and into my stomach, threatening to tear it up more than a nine-millimeter bullet. I chased the burn with a big gulp of beer.

We all turned to look at Dede, all except Ignacio, who had no interest in the silly games that gringos play. She swallowed the stuff and wrinkled her face to keep it down.

"Now, let's shuck down to our civvies and jump into a bath," Pepper said.

Pat laughed, and I looked at Dede. I smiled, and she shot a glance at Pepper. "I'm not about to get in some hot water with you testosterone cases," she said.

Pat was the first to laugh, and he slapped her on the back. "Come on, baby," he said.

Dede laughed too, but she said, "I better get going." She pushed herself up, weaving a little as she stood.

I walked her outside to her car and hunched my shoulders against the chill in the December desert night. "You do want to help me with this?" I asked.

"Why me?" she asked as she backed away from me to lean against her top-of-the-line Jeep Cherokee.

"'Cause I like you. 'Cause you have the best chance of getting out of here."

She nodded, but we both knew that I hadn't really explained anything. She turned away from me and opened her car door, and the interior light caught her face so that I could see just how young she was. "I was so scared," she said.

"Everything by the book. I wouldn't have blamed you for hitting the guy."

"I was trying to," she said.

I reached to put my arm around her but let my arm drop. "Ten or fifteen years, it gets real easy," I said.

She moved toward me, stopped, then got into her car. "Thanks, Dolph," she said. "I really don't know why you want me with you, but thanks." When Dede first spotted footprints in a drag, she stuttered and giggled over the radio. R.C. had thought twice about sending her cross-country, tracking the wets, so he called me and asked me to help her. I told him to let her have at it. Hours later, after Pat and I had picked up the wets she had chased to us, she came trudging down from a ridge, just barely moving her feet. Her pants were ripped, her lips swollen from the sun, and she had drunk all her water. She wasn't in good shape, but she had chased them to us and hadn't gotten lost. When she saw the wets, she giggled again and hugged me.

I once tracked some wets for two full days and spent the nights sleeping on rocks, hoping nothing would bite me. R.C. could remember horses and tracking for days.

I watched as Dede climbed into her Jeep and then drove off. I hunched my shoulders, shoved my hands into my pockets, and walked back to the steps at the bar. Pepper and Pat had come out. Each had a beer, and Pepper handed me one as I stepped up to them.

"Scary shit," Pat said.

"I almost shit a green Twinkie," I said.

Pepper sat on his steps and looked over at his empty pool. "Want me to call my whores?" he asked.

"I got to get home," Pat said.

"Pat," I said to stop him as he stumbled down the steps. When he looked up, I could see his glassy eyes reflecting a bit of the light from Pepper's single yellow lightbulb. "You ever think about quitting the Border Patrol?"

Pat shrugged. "Jobs are tough to get, especially a good one."

Pepper had heard the litany so often that he rattled it off for us. "Good benefits, great retirement after twenty years, lots of independence, good salary for the border."

"What's not to like," Pat said, and took uneasy steps toward his pickup.

I sat beside Pepper. "That goddamn pool," he said.

"Forget the goddamn pool." I rolled my shoulders uneasily.

"Forget the goddamn Border Patrol," he said. "What the hell you doing in it anyway, pretty boy? You ought to be a brain surgeon or something."

Pepper's grandfather, at the end of the nineteenth century, intended to drive a herd of cattle from central Texas to Arizona. But he got as far as Alpine and bought or stole a lot of the good high grazing land in the Davis Mountains. He owned a lot of the property in the area but had ten kids, starting in his late forties when he finally settled down. In turn those kids had lots of kids. So the most successful or promising relatives got the good ranch land or oil investments. The last stop before getting kicked out of the family was Cleburne Hot Springs.

My father's middle-class people ran away from the Mexican Revolution and settled in the Rio Grande Valley. While learning to speak English, they slid down the social scale but retained their educated atheism. My father, Miguel Martinez, was enough of a "pretty boy" to marry a pretty gringa wanting to piss off her Anglo father.

When I started school, my father's pretty boy good looks and my mother's Anglo lines had not yet molded my face. I had the fat cheeks and straight black hair of any *mestizo* boy. So for the first day of school, at the end of August in south Texas, my mother dressed me in a coat and tie from her father's store. She knew that the other kids would stare at me while I sweated and tugged at my tie, but she also knew they'd know that I was white or at least that I had her, a classy rich white woman, as a mother.

"Want to drive over to Ojinaga?" Pepper asked.

"I've got to work in the morning. I can't just sit on my ass all day."

"That goddamn pool," Pepper said.

I looked over at Pepper and said, "That goddamn pool."

Pepper sighed loudly.

"When I was in El Paso, I once caught the same guy three times in one day," I mumbled mostly to myself and took a drink of beer to wash down the way I was feeling.

Pepper stared down at the ground. "I've been here longer than you." He hesitated while I turned to look at him. "I wouldn't worry too much about this gun-smuggling business. People here don't care who's killing who over drugs."

"Somebody local is involved."

"Then nobody local will help." Pepper spit a stream of brown liquid into his sliced open beer can.

PRESIDIO

Old man Spencer, Reuben and Joe Alamendariz, Pepper Cleburne, Deputy Sheriff Raul Flores, Presidio policeman Al Sanchez (one of three policemen), Ben Abrams (the newly hired city administrator), and I were gathered around a cardboard table in the back room of the Presidio city hall, where the council usually met. We all looked at and listened to the DEA agent in the navy blue nylon windbreaker with the DEA initials on the back. With the FBI or DEA, you didn't get a choice; you listened to them.

Outside, Dave Devine, the editor of *The International,* the Presidio paper that Dave himself started, listened at the door. Dave had seen all of us go in, and when the DEA agent showed up, Dave knew that next to the actual shooting, he probably had the biggest story of the year. But Raul Flores closed the door on Dave to keep the meeting private.

Pepper, holding a Coke with its top sliced off instead of the usual beer can, had started the conversation by asking the DEA agent, *"Qué pasa?"* Then he spit into his can.

"Please, let's speak in English," the DEA agent had said. Pepper then looked around at the rest of us, and Reuben Alamendariz looked down at his pointy-toed boots and giggled. His brother Joe crossed his arms and hunkered down, as though this would be a long meeting. Raul Flores sat stiffly, trying to look officious and important, and Al Sanchez tried to copy him. Old man Spencer just let his head fall to one side and closed his eyes.

The Spencers and Alamendarizes generally ran things on this side of the river. Old man Spencer's father was the first Anglo to come off the range and into town to start making money with a bank and a grocery store. He and his son both learned to speak Spanish and made friends with and bought the produce of the Alamendarizes on both sides of the river. Reuben and Joe handled the onion and cantaloupe crops for the family on this side of the river and tried to make sure that the city didn't do anything to hurt the Alamendarizes' name or pocketbook. Pepper rented a post office box in town and then got himself elected to the city council, even though everybody knew that he lived out of town. The fact was that Pepper ran unopposed, with the approval of the Spencers and Alamendarizes. Most people had jobs and thus no time to serve on the city council; other residents had lots of time because they had no job and thus were not proper representatives. Pepper was a good compromise, and Pepper saw a seat on the city council as a chance to promote tourism and thus Cleburne Hot Springs Resort.

Ben Abrams was the only Jew in town and the only paid city official. Just a year before, he and his wife were looking for a quiet desert community, a good place to raise their kids, so they pulled up their stakes in Illinois and moved to the third world here in Presidio. In his spare time Abrams jogged with Father Guzmán, and he and his wife tried to learn Spanish by listening to Berlitz tapes and taking lessons from the locals.

Nobody liked shoot-outs close to town—bad for everybody's business. So Abrams had called the meeting and asked me to explain things. Then the DEA had called and wanted to be a part of everything. So we sipped coffee and Cokes and listened to this guy explain what the DEA knew and suspected. We were all getting bored.

I straightened in my folding chair when the DEA man said, "The FBI has looked at the guns and will trace where they come from."

"There's no need to call the goddamn Feebies in over this," I said. We had all had enough. It was time for the meeting to end.

Abrams stopped drumming his fingers and looked at me and

then over to the DEA man. "What Agent Martinez means is that we seem to have an idea and a plan."

Al Sanchez, basically a functional illiterate but a friend of Joe Alamendariz, looked to Raul Flores for guidance. Flores smiled at me. "We've already got federal people involved with the case," Raul said, and motioned toward me. I forced myself to smile back at him.

"This is not a case completely for the Border Patrol," the DEA agent said, and pulled his gold-rimmed glasses off and worked their arms. Used to be they all wore black plastic, horn-rimmed glasses; now they all wore the gold-rimmed, aviator-style frames. And typical of other Feebies or DEAs, he didn't raise his voice, not a hair rose on his head, not a bead of sweat ran down his face. At one time I sent in an application to the FBI, even got accepted, but I said to hell with it. "We look for drugs. The *FBI,*" he emphasized, and looked at me, "wants to investigate the guns."

"We have jurisdiction," I said.

"We are better equipped," he said.

"So we'll call you if we need you," I said.

Flores interrupted. "And we are assisting Agent Martinez in the investigation. Too many cooks spoil the soup."

Al Sanchez shifted his head from Flores to the DEA agent and then said, "Us too." What they meant was that we all wanted credit for a drug bust so our agencies would get more federal money. Together we were the "war on drugs."

Reuben looked at his pointy-toed boots, Joe seemed to scoff at us all, Ben Abrams nervously drummed his fingers, and old man Spencer's eyes fluttered as he hovered between consciousness and sleep. "This is our matter," the DEA agent said, and worked the arms of his glasses some more before he put them back on.

I scooted to the edge of my chair. "Look, you came in last night about nine p.m. You checked into the Three Palms Inn, had breakfast across the lot at the Three Palms Inn Coffee Shop. I think you had coffee and toast. You drove around town, then out El Camino del Rio before coming to this meeting."

The DEA agent blinked, then he breathed in and said, "What is your point?"

I looked around at the men. "You can't fart without everybody in town hearing it." Pepper smiled, and only Ben Abrams grimaced. "What good can you possibly do?"

"What about you? You wear a uniform. Everybody knows you."

"So people talk to me. And the bad guy is somebody local. Nothing is coming across until things calm down and the guns are sold. So we stretch our shifts, ask for some help from sector headquarters in Marfa, and look for any suspicious cars."

"Playing cowboy," the DEA agent said, and pulled his gold-rimmed glasses off to look at me. I had made him sweat just a little.

"Look, we are concerned about the dope," Joe Alamendariz said to rescue me. "We know that it comes across, but these shootings have to stop."

Reuben nodded, then looked away from his boots to Pepper. He made Pepper's speech. "This sort of crap hurts tourism. Decent, middle-America, Yankee tourists aren't going to come to town if they think it's still the wild West out here. We just want it to stop." Joe looked at his brother and rolled his eyes. Pepper jerked himself straight up, causing the sunlight to reflect off his diamond stud earring, and nodded to show the importance of what Reuben had said. When no one paid much attention to him, he pulled at the corners of his waxed mustache and settled back into his chair.

"That is precisely why I am here," the DEA agent said. "I just want your cooperation."

Abrams drummed his fingers. "Well, you certainly have it."

"And I think Raul and Agent Martinez can handle it," Joe Alamendariz said.

"With or without your help, my investigation will continue," the DEA agent said. "Thank you, gentlemen." He stuck his glasses back on, then carefully folded his papers and put them in his briefcase.

"We will cooperate," Ben Abrams said, and looked at me. The DEA agent nodded.

Old man Spencer shook his head to pull himself fully into consciousness, and then we all lined up to shake the DEA agent's hand.

Through with our hands, the agent opened the door, and Dave Devine, pencil and pad in his hands, tumbled into the room. The agent looked around for an explanation, but before any of us could introduce Dave, he was pumping the agent's hand and asking him about what he was after. The agent said nothing but walked past Dave, and Dave followed, trying to get an answer.

With the DEA agent gone, Joe Alamendariz grabbed me by the arm to stop me, then looked over at Raul Flores. "Now you *vatos* better get it done," he said.

Raul slapped me on the shoulder and nodded. "I will," I said.

Pepper walked in between us. "How you going to stop it?"

We all turned to look at Pepper. "How can you get your tourists with gunrunners shooting at them?" Reuben asked him.

"Look, all I'm saying is that we can't stop it. Hell, ask Dolph. I say in a month or two this shit stops, and everybody forgets about it."

Raul nodded, then added, "Just like I said. Let's just stall this guy until things get back to normal."

"We gotta do something," I said. And Joe and Reuben both nodded to line up on my side. Old man Spencer left the room and slammed the door.

"I'm just saying we're fucking around," Pepper said.

"Maybe it will just go away," Reuben repeated.

"Always does," Raul said. "The bad guys shoot somebody, and it will stop. Remember how bad it was when Pablo Acosta was running his *la plaza* out of Ojinaga? And once he got killed, everything quieted down?"

"Okay," I said. "But I'm going to find out about it."

"Look," Joe said. "It's not that we don't appreciate the Border Patrol; it's just—"

I interrupted him. "It's just that this is our job. Look, we get cats out of trees and sponsor barbecues. Our agents drop a lot of money in this town. Pay taxes. Just don't get in our way."

"That's not what we're saying," Pepper said.

"No," Reuben, then Raul agreed.

"We're not saying anything," Abrams said, and we all turned to look at him, sitting with his head in his hands. He slowly slid his head up from his hands. "Just everybody do what you're supposed to do."

"Thank you, Ben," I said. "That's what I'm saying. We've all got jobs." Ben ducked his head and picked up his briefcase while everyone else watched him get up. He raised his head to look at all of us. His lips seemed almost to quiver as he tried to force something out of his mouth, but he kept himself from saying anything. "Go on, Ben," I said. "You have something to say."

"Nothing." He shrugged. "See you later, gentlemen," he said, but looked at me. Raul slapped Al on the shoulder and laughed, and Pepper followed the Alamendarizes out and talked to them about tourism. I waited for everyone to leave, then looked at Ben.

"Everything is backward, convoluted here. It's like the third world," he said to me.

"The third world is simpler. This is the border," I replied. "There's a difference." He hung his head again. "Aw, hell, Ben," I said. "You and I will do something to put a stop to this." Ben nodded, then I left him and walked through the city hall building.

When I got outside city hall, Pepper opened the door to his orange-and-white '55 Chevy with the white leather upholstery and rested his arm on the top of the door. He had on an old-style cowboy hat, the kind you see in thirties movies, with a pinched crown that stuck up about a foot, then slid into a wide, curled brim. Before Pepper could say anything, Dave was at my side. "I don't suppose you have anything to say?"

"Didn't the DEA tell you anything?"

"You federal people," Dave said.

"Look," I said. "It's real simple. We're going to try to catch the bad guys."

"You want to elaborate any?"

"There's nothing to elaborate," Pepper said. "By the way, I liked that editorial about giving up our wild West ways."

"Shit," Dave said, and sat on the steps outside city hall. Dave was actually a good addition to the town. He was like the teachers, a regular American looking for some challenge, so he came to Presidio and started a newspaper. He bought a computer, hired a woman who knew how to use it, got some volunteer help from the local Ladies Auxiliary unit of the American Legion. For years Presidioans had been content to read the Alpine newspaper, but now we had Dave covering the county commissioner's meetings up in Marfa, advertising sales at Baeza's groceries and Spencer's Department Store, and writing literate editorials. Dave looked up at me. "I've had nothing but stories about road rights, water pipes, and petty thievery. Now this comes along, and nobody talks."

I shrugged. "Sorry, Dave. You'll get exclusive rights when I can talk."

"How about a hint?"

Pepper interrupted us. "Let's go over to Ojinaga and get ourselves a drink."

"I'm on duty," I said.

"So am I," Dave said.

"Then lunch, goddamn it."

"Too early for lunch, and I've got business to tend to," I said, and Dave simply asked me to let him know about anything and walked off.

Pepper slammed his door shut and walked back to me. Holding his can in front of him, he spit at the open end, then wiped at the end of his waxed mustache with the tip of his forefinger. "Why don't you get out of the Border Patrol and do something important?"

"Like what?"

"Dogcatcher, garbageman, brain surgeon."

The pretty boy did well in school, tested at the senior reading level when he was in the fifth grade, won the science fair, was cited for math, took calculus in high school. But with his mother raving about him at graduation, with an acceptance into Rice University, he said, "Fuck it," and joined the army. Spent three years in Germany and learned to drive a tank. Never saw a gun fired, never heard a shot—all during Vietnam.

When I came back, I let the government pay for my school and got two degrees in four years. Again my mother was excited when I got accepted at the University of Texas School of Law; again I was the pretty boy. But again I said, "Fuck it," and joined the Border Patrol.

Now Pepper, who had heard my confessions, was asking me to repeat the whole story. "I'm on the downside of twenty years; I've got twelve years in. Good retirement coming up."

"Just my point. You got no problem. Relax. Come on, let's get a beer and a taco."

I dipped my head. "Okay, lunch only, if we stay on this side of the border. I can't wear this uniform in Mexico. Somebody'd kill me."

"Like that Texas Ranger in Nuevo Laredo, at the Cadillac bar, back in the thirties."

"Not quite like that," I said.

I got into the passenger side of Pepper's restored Chevy and gently pressed my back and butt against its white leather interior. As Pepper drove, he spit at his split beer can. "You better be careful," I said. "You might miss and stain this interior."

"Hell, I don't miss," he said, and tugged at the end of his waxed mustache.

We drove to a Dairy Queen that went broke and was resurrected as a taco joint. As I sipped some iced tea and Pepper downed his second beer, he said, "Come on, have a cool one. It's not like you're breaking any rules; just a beer."

"Toast," I said, and pointed my large glass of iced tea at Pepper.

When his third beer came, Pepper got into a foul mood. "We ought to just legalize drugs," he said. "Just like Prohibition. People are going to buy the stuff."

I sipped my tea. "Then what would I do for a living, Pepper?"

"Hell, you wouldn't be getting shot at all the time. Legalize, and no more dead cops." That spark of insight ignited a familiar thought in Pepper's head. "Imagine if I could sell pot from Cleburne Hot Springs."

"Excuse me, Pepper," I said. "You're going off to never-never land again."

"No, I mean it," Pepper said. "Think about it." He was captured by his fantasy, so I scooted my chair back, got up, and took my iced tea with me to phone the *comandanté* at the army garrison and get a number for Colonel Henri Trujillo.

"No *mordida,*" I told the colonel when I reached him.

"Of course not. All I will offer is my gratitude," he said. He wanted to tour the Big Bend area, probably at the government's expense, so he wanted to meet me at Lajitas. He had a room and a golf game. "The state of Coahuila will buy you lunch and a couple of beers."

"Thanks," I said, and congratulated myself for my own *mordida:* a $3.95 lunch from Pepper today and a couple of fifty-cent tacos from the Mexican government in two days. The Border Patrol, the only uniformed federal police force in America, never gave *la mordida;* only the un-uniformed police, the FBI and DEA and customs, had all sorts of Mexican officers, ministers, informants, and pimps on their payroll.

MACHISMO

The only battle that Miguel Martinez ever won against my mother was naming me. While she was under anesthetic—back before natural childbirth recorded by husbands with VCRs—my father, with a delicate, looping script, right under my footprint, wrote *Adolph Miguel Martinez.* When he read that his grandchild would have the same name as Hitler, only with an anglicized spelling, my grandfather, Charles Beeson, the owner of the Beeson chain of clothiers, wanted to shoot ol' Miguel for the second time in his life.

But murdering in-laws was something that Mexicans did, not prominent Anglo Rio Grande Valley citizens. My grandfather helped bring the touring opera companies to the valley and always bought season tickets. He gave to fashionable charities and tried to start a minor league baseball team for the area. He was twice elected to the Brownsville City Council and had a Brownsville city street named after him.

The first time that my grandfather wanted to shoot Miguel was right after his daughter told him that she was pregnant by a "Mexican." The wonder to me was why Sandra Beeson ever let Miguel Martinez get close enough to her to get his hand into her panties and then to get her panties off. I also wondered why she married him. There were, of course, even in those days plenty of solutions.

Maybe she was fascinated by the jet-black hair of the "pretty boy" greaser who hung around the high school and tried to pick up the

Mexican girls. This *pachuco,* this hood, this aging Hispanic teen-ager, was probably bound to be stabbed or thrown in prison. So why did my mother, a member of the privileged Anglo aristocracy, a girl who could have chosen any boy she wanted, especially a prized Anglo boy, let this trashy Mexican in the leather jacket stick his dirty hand into her panties? Why did she conceive me in the backseat of his old car? Maybe she saw in this *güero*'s brown eyes and black hair and high cheeks face some trace of the Spanish aristocracy that Miguel's father was so proud of. Maybe she sensed the Mexican middle-class status that the Martinezes gave up when they came to south Texas from Mexico.

Probably, whatever the main reason, she took a secret delight in plunging into the backseat with the type of boy she was supposed to stay away from. She must have had a good time pissing off Chuck Beeson. And back then, sometime during my conception or shortly after their marriage, or maybe around my birth, she must have loved him somewhat or somehow.

The Martinezes, I understand, were happy to see Miguel married. A wife might calm down their troubled boy. And marriage to this rich gringa would lift Miguel and his children into the type of social position the Martinezes enjoyed in Mexico but could never have in the US. And Miguel must have strutted for a while after he "scored" with the popular gringa. He might have felt a little of the Hispanic machismo that comes with getting a woman pregnant. He might have been a whole lot scared at suddenly getting married and giving up loafing and speeding around the valley with his *vatos.* He too, at some point around my conception or maybe around the marriage, might have loved Sandra. But by the time I was born and became "Adolph" and then spared from that name by my mother nicknaming me "Dolph," they had started their war.

Charles Beeson tried to clean Miguel up. He bought him a suit, gave him some credit at his department store, and tried to teach him the correct way to pronounce English words. He gave Miguel a job as a suit salesman and had hopes to promote him first to the manager of the men's department in one of his stores and then to a manager of an entire store so that his wife and grandson could have the type of life they deserved as their birthright.

But Miguel didn't work on his accent, his manners, or his salesmanship; instead he drank more. The day my mother bundled me up and moved out, my grandfather fired my father. Even Miguel's own parents disowned him for blowing his chance to jump up some social rungs.

My mother insisted that she take some kind of job in order to support the baby that her father was more than willing to support. So Charles gave her Miguel's old job. And Sandra led the department in sales and then became the men's department manager, and then store manager, and then took over Charles's business. And just before the malls completely destroyed her family's heritage, she sold her small chain to a bigger chain of discount department stores. Someday the money that was left would be mine.

I met my father on one of my walks home from my first year in junior high. I walked along an irrigation ditch and was still young enough to be interested in the frogs that gathered in them. Sometimes I'd slide down the banks, soiling the clothes my mother still picked out for me (still slacks and dress shirts, though I had talked her out of a tie), and stick my hand into the tepid, stagnant water and try to come out with a pet frog. He'd only remain a pet until I got him home and lost interest in him or my mother threw him out. Other than looking for frogs, I liked to lean my head back to my shoulders while I walked and gaze up at the tops of the palm trees, which were planted in rows to serve as property markers. I'd imagine myself standing still and the palm fronds passing over me. I was doing this when my father saw me.

"Hey, kid," he said, and I brought my head down to see a scrawny man eating a bean burrito and drinking a Falstaff beer. He squatted next to his pick and shovel. His dirty, sweaty T-shirt clung to his chest and stomach, and sweat dripped down his forehead, off his nose, and onto his burrito. "What you doing?"

"Looking at the palms," I said.

"Looking at the 'palms,' not the 'trees.' " He laughed. "*Son los árboles de palmas.* You got it, *las palmas,*" he said. "You a smart boy. You know where they come from?"

I shook my head.

"From Spain and North Africa—I bet your mama don't tell you that. *"Hablas español?"* he asked. I just stared at him.

"You speak Spanish?" he said, and hung his head.

"No," I said.

"I guess your mama won't let you?"

As young and surprised and curious as I was, I didn't like him picking on my mother. "She says I should, for business. My grandfather says I shouldn't worry about it. Let them speak English."

Miguel put back his head and laughed, then he pointed the neck of the beer at me. "You learn to speak it. You speak it, you'll be an important man. *Mucho muy macho,* huh?" He nodded as if asking if I understood.

"I don't have to listen to you."

He got up and pushed out his hand with the burrito in it. "You want some?" I shook my head. He offered me a drink of his beer. I shook my head again. "Yeah, you too young to drink much now."

"I could drink."

He poked the bottle of beer at me again, and he laughed when I grabbed it, took a big sip, and grimaced to get that first taste of the lukewarm, bitter, metallic liquid down my throat.

"Maybe next time I give you a Coca-Cola," he said.

"What next time?" I said.

"You come by here after school. I'll be here."

"Who are you?" I asked.

"Yo soy tu padre, muchacho." Then he looked down as if to correct himself and said, *"Mijo."*

I cocked my head to look at his sweaty, sun-dried face. The sun had darkened him, but he could still be considered a *güero.* Then I looked down at my arm; he wasn't as light as me. He smiled with both his eyes and mouth, and I could see remnants of that pretty boy, the *pachuco* hood. And in his eyes and nose, though he seemed ancient at the time, I could see myself, what I had become, though he was aging faster than I was. Evidently his genes were a lot stronger than my mother's. "You mean you're my father?" I asked.

"Sí," he said.

We didn't talk much after that, and I grew nervous and started to move past him. He scared me when he reached out to take me by the shoulders and look me in the eye. "Maybe you won't come back," he said. "Maybe your mother won't let you see me. Maybe I won't be able to find you no more. But some things sometimes you got to do for yourself. You understand?" I nodded, though I had no idea what he was talking about. "No, you don't know. Sometimes you got to go against what your mother and your grandfather say. Okay? *Muy macho,* huh?" he said.

And I left him to his shovel and pick, to dig out the dirt, rocks, and trash blocking the irrigation ditch. I later learned that clearing out blocked irrigation ditches was one of the odd jobs he picked up when he was sober. Thus began my meetings with my father.

The time I was gut shot and barely conscious and Sister Quinn showed up to drag me down a trail and put the vial of silver-blue metallic liquid in my hand wasn't the first time I had seen a *curandera.* On one of my later visits with my father, he took me to a *curandera.* She scared the piss out of me at first. She had a lazy eye, so that you couldn't tell if she was looking at you or lost in some trance and staring off at God. She turned over tarot cards and told me that I was going to face great trials in love or some other vague shit that anybody could figure out. Then to protect me she sold me a charm: a special candle to burn at night.

Miguel waited for me outside her shack, and when I came out, he put his hand behind my back as though to help me walk across her dirt yard, but I really knew that he was trying to steady himself. As we walked down her barrio street, only kids in dirty diapers and their mothers out at this time of day, all of them staring at the drunk loafer and his son, Miguel moved his hand to the top of my shoulder so that I could better steer him. When he saw a scraggly mesquite, the only tree in this dusty, dirty, dried-out housing division of tar paper shacks and discarded lumber, he steered me to it, and we both sat while he mopped at the sweat on his face.

My mother would have been incensed had she known that I was in this neighborhood with the low clotheslines that made sheets and towels almost hit the dirt, the stray dogs that sniffed at everybody, and the open tin drums used to burn trash. She would have exploded if she had known that I had just been to see a *curandera.*

"What did you think?" he asked.

"Not much," I told him.

"Good, good," he said. He dug in his pocket and pulled out two cigarettes. One had already been lit and charred. He offered me the whole cigarette. I shook my head because my mother told me not to ever smoke. Besides, I didn't want to spend my spare change on cigarettes.

"What's the difference between that old witch woman and the Catholic Church?" I shrugged. "See, you got it right. None. Worst thing to ever happen to Mexico was the Catholic Church."

"Why?" I asked.

"Never mind, I tell you later. This ain't the point." He frowned as he looked at me as though to discover the point. "Oh, yeah, yeah. What's the difference between this old witch woman and whatever church your mama takes you to?"

"She takes me to Saint Luke's Episcopal Church."

"Don't matter which one. What's the difference?" I shrugged again. "See there. You are a smart boy. Ain't no difference. They're all the same. Some *penitentes* whip themselves. The *santerias* gut chickens and goats. What's the difference between them and drinking the blood of Christ?"

He pushed himself up along the skinny trunk of the mesquite and tried to stand even though some of the limbs were in his face. "Remember, religion is for weak people. A man don't need no religion. He looks at things the way they are. He don't need some old crazy woman, priest, or preacher. Religion takes away dignity. It don't give you none." He tapped his chest with the flat of his hand, then he put out his hand, extended his forefinger, and shook it once.

"What?" I asked.

He shook his hand again, and I gave him the candle that the old *curandera* had given me. He threw it on the ground and stomped it with his heel.

"She said that would be bad luck."

"Fuck her," he said.

"Okay, fuck her," I said. "But what about the things the church teaches? Like forgiveness and grace and mercy, compassion, sympathy." He had already taught me to cuss the Church and to shoot the finger, so he was no longer shy about cussing around me, nor I around him. He liked to hear me cuss. When I wrapped my lips around a *fuck* or *goddamn,* he probably had visions of his corruption of me, of my growing up to be some sort of successful and rebellious misogynist like him.

"Fuck them, too," he said.

"Naw, you still need those," I said.

He looked at me and wove a bit as he held on to the tree and moved a limb out from in front of his face. Then he smiled. "Okay, okay." He hesitated while I stood up, and he patted my shoulder. "Now you starting to think for yourself. Pretty soon you don't need no papa."

"Okay," I said, and started to back up. "I've got studying to do."

"Hey, wait," he said. "You think I give you these lessons for nothing? I even paid for that old witch to read your future."

I had begun saving my lunch money or giving him some of what I made from my own odd jobs or summer jobs—bagging groceries, cleaning up my grandfather's stores. I pulled out my billfold and unfolded my two crispest, newest dollar bills and handed them to him. "Get something to eat," I said.

"You a good boy," he said, then looked back at me to smile. "No, you a good man."

My catechism with my father also extended to women and beer. He bought me my first six-pack and helped me drink most of it. He gave me my first sip of tequila. And, of course, he was the first to take me to the boys town outside of Matamoros. He insisted that every boy, "No, every man" (he deemed me a man when I was seventeen, a year earlier than the army), needed to knock off his first piece at a whorehouse. "A whore knows what to do. She shows you good," he said.

I didn't like the smell or the impatience of my whore, whom my father picked out and I paid for. She was a young woman with a cesarean scar, and I didn't like the way she held my tool in her hand, washed it, then idly said, "Okay." Maybe it was a bad pick.

And afterward, with my father slumped in a chair in the cheap bar, a couple of strippers serving drinks, a few college boys clapping and hooting, and a little man with a dainty mustache announcing in English the arrival of "the monkey," my father gave me my lesson. "So what was it like?"

"Okay," was all I dared to say. I didn't know whether to fess up that I was a little scared and a whole lot embarrassed or whether to boast that I slammed it to her.

"That's all?" He slapped the table and tried to straighten up in his chair. "It should be . . ." His mind got cloudy, and he couldn't finish his sentence.

"It was. It was. It really was great," I said, and smiled.

"Good. Remember that." Then he put his elbow in the middle of the table and leaned toward me. His tequila breath hit me and nearly knocked me backward. "Don't ever confuse that with no love." I nodded. But he shook his head. "No, you not so smart, smart boy. You don't understand. What if some gringa you go to school with comes up to you and says to you—no, no comes to your mama and says—'Dolph made me pregnant'?"

While his finger waved in front of my face, I tried to second-guess what he wanted. I mostly wanted to be home in the safe, civilized world of my mother. By this time, he had stopped being amusing and was mostly annoying. I guess I went with him because I felt that I ought to. I gave my mother's response to his question. "I'd sit down with her and her family and with mine—my mother and grandfather—and decide what was best for all of us."

"No." He slammed the table with the flat of his hand. "You get out. You run away." Though he was drunk and impatient with me, he must have seen the shock or hurt in my face. After all, even though I had just had my first piece of ass, I was still mostly a child.

"Well, no, no, not really," he said. "What I mean is you can't let no woman control you." He squinted and exhaled as he thought, and a smelly but invisible cloud of his breath hung in the air. "What I mean is you decide." He pointed at me firmly with his gnarled finger. "What I most mean is a woman is fine for fucking, you know. And maybe that's all. But you don't let nobody have your life. A woman comes up pregnant, you run like shit."

His eyes came together. He said some more, but I couldn't understand his words. I helped him up, and we sloshed through the mud of the Matamoros boys town, refusing the drugs and sex toys of the street peddlers until I could flag down a taxi.

On the way back to Matamoros, my father passed out. I drug him out of the taxi and paid the driver. As I tried to drag him around the square, a couple of Matamoros policemen tried to question me about the drunk. The only Spanish I could think to say was, *"Mi padre."* They looked at me suspiciously but didn't take either one of us to jail. I couldn't carry him across the bridge into Brownsville, and even if I could, I had no idea where he lived. So I left my father on a park bench in the Matamoros square closest to the US border, and I walked home. I saw him again the next week, and he thanked me for taking care of him.

Soon after, my mother found out that I was meeting him. She had heard rumors of her "pretty boy" going to Mexico, walking some bad streets with an old drunk. She forbade me to see him. To make sure that he was out of my life, my grandfather put a peace bond out on poor ol' Miguel. So when I had my application and the scholarship to Rice University accepted, I turned it down, just like a stupid greaser would do, and joined the army.

I didn't see him again until his funeral. By that time I was out of the army, out of college, and in the Border Patrol, and I could finally speak Spanish. It was my hardest course in the Border Patrol school in Georgia. Miguel never saw me in a Border Patrol uniform; he probably never heard that I had joined. Had he known, my guess is that he would have laughed.

"MARÍA," "CONSUELO," "GUADALUPE," "EUGENIA"

Above the south rim in the Davis Mountains, around Alpine and Marfa, the weather gets cooler; the landscape becomes gentler; the cacti, rocks, and jagged peaks turn into clumps of cedar, grazing land, and higher rounded peaks. It has some decent shade. The area has a kinder disposition toward humans. Marfa, Alpine, and Fort Davis have hospitals, courthouses, paved streets, and city budgets.

After half a day of work, I was headed to kinder and gentler Marfa in order to bargain with the Presidio County sheriff about the fate of a criminal I had arrested. Tomás had snorted too much glue and destroyed his good sense.

For two years, he had survived by sneaking across the border to steal food or small tools. Citizens of Presidio and Redford and ranchers along the river had come home to find him sleeping in their cars or living rooms. Whoever would find him or whoever had been robbed called us. An agent would arrest him, me the last time, and then send him up to Marfa to sit in jail for a couple of days.

Since the county didn't have enough money to prosecute for petty thievery and since he was an illegal and probably certifiably crazy, he'd spend a couple of days in jail and then the Presidio County Sheriff's Department would return him to us, and we'd send him back across the border. He'd drool, cuss, or spit as he crossed back to Ojinaga, but he'd always come over again. Snorting the airplane glue, a kids' product, he had reverted to a child, and the biggest and best toys were across the river.

But on occasion, some adult envy or meanness would get into Tomás. For his last arrest, he had broken into Gerald Galván's farmhouse, and since Gerald and his family had taken a two-day vacation, he spent the night. When he woke, maybe looking at a fellow Hispanic's American toys and feeling jealous or mean, Tomás tore the hell out of the Galváns' living room and shit on the sofa where he had just slept. The Galváns had worked themselves up from being farmworkers in Colorado to being farm owners in Presidio. Gerald found good, cheap land in Presidio and thought that he could guard his family from the thieves and psychopaths in the rest of America. So the Galváns drove up the gravel road off 170 to their house and saw a drooling, cussing glue head charge out of their door. When Gerald saw what Tomás had done to his living room, he grabbed his rifle and, just for the general principle, fired at the man running down the gravel road. I caught Tomás when he got back to 170.

Usually R.C. made the trips to Marfa, but since he had taken the day off and I was training for the possibility of getting my own station, I went to deal with the county. I got along well with Abe Rincón. Better than his predecessor, Joey Latham. When the Feebies and DEA found the cocaine in Joey Latham's horse barn, Abe won the next election. Latham's arrest was the biggest news since the film crew for *Giant* came to town. The Vietnam-vet sheriff with two new pickups and oil-pipe fencing around his horse barn that had no horses was busted for the drugs he confiscated, and then a Mexican became sheriff. Abe wore slope-heeled cowboy boots, a wide-brimmed hat, and cheap suits and ties he bought from a discount store in Midland. His outfit comforted the Anglo ranchers who were used to running the county, but Abe didn't wear a gun. He figured the old ranchers weren't yet ready for a Mexican with power and a gun.

Fewer people clung to this high desert town than to Presidio. But though there wasn't much to it, Marfa resembled the civilization that I missed. And it was cold. As soon as I got out of my vehicle, I shook. The wind was stronger, colder, and even drier than in Presidio. And the shade from the cottonwoods on the courthouse square, a prize commodity farther south, made me even colder, so I found myself hunching my shoulders and shoving my hands in my pockets. I cussed the border because it had made me unsuited for anyplace farther north; a cushy Border Patrol job close to the Canadian border was now out of the question.

Inside the courthouse, I warmed up and met Abe Rincón and Gerald Galván. After handshakes and introductions, we walked across the street to the cinder block jailhouse. A female jailer led us to the cell block and then to Tomás's cell. The cinder blocks made the place cold.

Tomás sat on his bunk with his arms wrapped around his bent knees and his head buried between his knees.

Sheriff Abe Rincón turned to Gerald and asked in Spanish if this was the guy. Gerald just looked at Abe. I let my shoulders sink. "Gerald speaks English," I said.

Gerald said, "My parents never taught me Spanish." So Abe asked in English if we were looking at the right guy.

"This is the man I saw running from my house," Gerald said.

"I want you to get a real good look." Abe turned to the cell. "Tomás," he said. Tomás wouldn't look up. "Tomás," he said again.

Abe stuck a key in the cell door, opened it, and went in. Tomás started cussing all of us, his eyes rolling around in their sockets.

"It's him," Gerald said. "It's him."

Abe Rincón stepped closer to Tomás, and Tomás spit at him. The spittle hit the pointy toe of Abe's boot. Abe stopped, pulled his thick glasses off, squinted to see, and then pointed a finger at Tomás. "I don't give a damn if you are brain-dead. You spit on me, I'll whip your ass." Tomás went back to cussing us. No one knew if Tomás understood English. At times, he pretended not to understand Spanish. Abe stepped out of the cell and locked the cell door.

Abe looked back at Gerald. "Now, what a defense attorney is going to do is question your identification because you saw this man so briefly." Abe looked at me and rolled his eyes. "Let's step outside."

We all went to the foyer of the jail, the female jailer looking at us, and Abe started, "Mr. Galván, you see, there's really not a whole lot we can prosecute Tomás for, and it costs the county money to keep him locked up and then to try him."

Abe looked at Gerald, hoping he understood. "So? So what?" Gerald said. "He destroyed my property."

Abe reached up to straighten his tie. "I don't like this any better than you." Abe patted Gerald on the shoulder.

"So you just going to let him go?" Gerald said. "After he . . . he shit on my sofa?"

"You have a right to press charges," Abe said. I stared down at the toes of my own boots. My purpose here was to nod and then haul Tomás back to the border. "But the DA tells me we'll have a tough time getting a conviction."

Gerald interrupted again. "Wait a goddamn minute. I am a citizen, and this wetback thug shit on my furniture. And you're telling me I can't press charges."

"I'm telling you that we can't afford to prosecute. And if we do, it's your taxes that pay for it."

"Jesus," Gerald said, and swung his fist at the wall. When it thudded against it, the jailer sprang from her swivel chair, but Abe Rincón motioned to her to stay seated.

"Could I make a suggestion here?" I said, and the men's eyes swung toward me. Abe looked grateful. "My boss, R.C. Kobel, has called the Mexican consulate in Odessa on behalf of Tomás."

"Does everybody take his side?" Gerald asked.

"Just a minute; let's listen to Agent Martinez," Abe said.

I looked at Gerald. "Nobody likes this, Gerald, but it's just the way it is."

"Can't shoot him," Abe said.

I continued. "But the consulate can possibly have him declared insane. And if he can do this, then we drop him off to some people from an asylum, and he's not our problem anymore."

"He's a criminal," Gerald said.

"Look." Abe put his arm around Gerald's shoulders. "If the Border Patrol can do this, then he'll be out of the way. And . . . ultimately it would be cheaper for the county to buy a new sofa rather than prosecuting Tomás." Gerald listened.

"We can get it done," I said to Gerald.

"We have a furniture store here in town. Why don't you take a look, see what you like, and you'll have it delivered tomorrow, courtesy of Presidio County." I turned my head away from Gerald to wink at Abe.

"Jesus, what a fucking world," Gerald said.

"It's a bitch," Abe said.

Abe stuck out his hand, and Gerald shook it to seal the bargain. The female jailer went out with Gerald to help pick out a sofa, so Abe and I were alone.

"Makes you proud to work for law enforcement, doesn't it?" I said.

"We do what we can." Abe pushed his cowboy hat back on his head with his forefinger. "Raul tells me you've found some bodies and are getting into shoot-outs. What the hell's going on down there?"

"DEA wants to find out too."

"Why don't you give your *vatos* up here a call? Let us get a little action."

"Because at first Raul wanted nothing to do with the case."

Abe shrugged. "Raul isn't too bright. Me, I like drug busts. They get the Anglo votes."

"If it's my case, then I'll call."

Abe stuck out his hand, and I shook it. "Thanks for the help," Abe said. I nodded. "I got some more business for you," he said. "Pretty sad stuff."

Abe drove to a small clinic, and I followed in my truck. Inside, a nurse led us to a room and opened a door. The blinds were pulled closed, so the room was dark, and as we walked through it, Abe explained, "We found this wetback woman. She just wandered into town. We took her in. She was beat up, we thought. Anyway, we brought her here instead of to jail." Abe took off his cowboy hat when he stepped into the room, so I did likewise.

Abe hesitated, so the nurse took over. "She was beaten and raped."

Abe continued: "I imagine it was the coyote. She fought back, and either he left her or she ran. It was lucky she got here."

The squat Anglo nurse went to the venetian blinds and twisted a cord to let some light into the room. The woman was lying on a hospital bed with a sheet over her. She had the good side of her face turned away from us and the bad side with the bruises turned toward us. "Physically she's able to go," the nurse said.

"What else we gonna do?" Abe asked.

"Did you look for the guy?"

"He's a coyote. Who knows where he is?"

"Did you question her?"

"You try to get an answer out of her."

The woman rolled her head to look at me. I closed my eyes. "Consuelo," I said.

Her mouth twitched as she tried to smile. "Consuelo?" Abe asked. "Told me her name was Guadalupe. That's all I got out of her." I stepped toward her and reached toward her face. She stayed still while I rubbed the back of my fingers along the battered side of her face.

As I looked at her, she slid her hand out from under the sheet and touched my fingers. *"Yo no soy un pollita,"* she said. *"Estoy un politíca."*

"That's all I can get out of her," Abe said.

"I'll get her clothes and dress her." The nurse moved to the door of the room.

"I imagine her clothes are in pretty bad shape," I said, and the nurse stopped. I looked at Abe. "You think the county could afford some clothes for her?"

"Hell, not much, no evening gown or jewelry; we just bought a sofa for Gerald Galván."

The nurse nodded and left the room. The woman pulled her fingers away from mine. *"Yo no soy un pollita."* I nodded. *"No me llevas pá mexico."*

I turned to look at Abe. He said, "What else you gonna do?" and backed out of the room.

"Shh, shh," I said, and again brushed my fingers against the bruised side of her face. I leaned down until my head was in front of hers and smiled. She didn't smile, she just shook her head, but I heard the sheet rustle and then felt her fingers around mine. When I lifted my hand, her grip tightened and her arm, slipped out from under the sheet. She knew that I was all she had.

The clinic nurse dressed her in a surgeon's smock and pants, put someone's old sweater over her shoulders, and gave her her bloody, dirty, torn clothes in a paper bag. Nurses rolled her out of the clinic in a wheelchair, then stopped it so that she could walk to my truck. When she saw *la migra's* sign on the door, she started to back up. The nurse and I forced her into the passenger's seat.

As I came down and out of Marfa, Consuelo sat curled up like a bug and wouldn't look at me. I tried to make some kind of small talk, but she wouldn't say much.

By the time I got back to the station, it was dark and closed. I parked the vehicle, helped Consuelo out, unlocked the back door, switched on a light, then led her to a desk. She sat in front of the desk and crossed her arms. She wouldn't look at me; she stared at the back door that I had locked behind us. When she pulled her head back toward me, I put out my open left hand. She stared at my hand, then slowly she took it.

I had trouble writing without my left hand to hold the forms steady, but I processed her and got what answers I could from her. And she remained consistent. She said her name was Guadalupe. We sat for a while in the dark office, both of us knowing what would come next but maybe both hoping that I wouldn't do my duty. I led her back out to the truck.

As I drove to the port of entry, she calmly sat in the seat and stared out at Presidio. She must have resigned herself to the fact that she had again failed.

I parked next to the customs officers' cars at the port of entry and led her through the various checkpoints to the pedestrian walk on the bridge. The whole time I held her arm, and she strained against my grip, not breaking it, not challenging me, just showing what resistance she could. I walked her to the middle of the bridge and told her to walk on across. She walked toward the third world and looked once back over her shoulder at me, as though I would let her turn around. When I said nothing, she turned away.

"Guadalupe," I yelled, but she didn't stop. "Wait." She kept walking. I switched to Spanish. *"Espara!"* She still kept walking. *"Espara,"* I screamed. She stopped and slowly turned around. I ran up to her and into Mexico. I checked around me, then I pulled a pen out of my shirt pocket and one of my cards out of my wallet, and I wrote down Sister Quinn's name and drew a small map.

Consuelo turned the card around in her fingers when I handed it to her. *"Gracias,"* she said.

"Como te llamas?" I asked.

The small *mestiza* looked up at me as though trying to decide if, with all the men who were shoving her around, with all the stories that she had heard down in the interior, she could trust me, *la migra,* enough to give her real name. "Eugenia Suarez," she said.

"Gracias," I said.

She turned from me and walked away. The loose surgeon's uniform bagged around her butt, and the long legs bunched up around her ankles so that she stomped on the edges. She clutched at the sweater wrapped around her shoulders and shivered when a gust from off the river hit her.

I backed up toward my side of the river and wondered if she would try again, or if she would try the equally hard trip back to wherever she was from, or if she would just try to make do in Ojinaga. And I hoped no matter what she did that I would not see her again. And then a worse thought hit me, and I hoped too that she would never come over to Pepper's Hot Springs Resort with some of his whores.

LAJITAS

Eastward from Presidio, past Redford, El Camino del Rio curves along with the Rio Grande through broad patches of farmland. The rises in the road give a view of the cracked, gray desert beyond the green and gold fields of onions, corn, and cantaloupe. And from the rises in the road, you can look across the river and see glints of sunlight from the steel and aluminum in the *ejidos* that dot the Mexican side.

Then El Camino del Rio climbs toward Lajitas and follows the canyons' north walls. In stretches where you can see it ahead of you, the rising, twisting road looks like the engineers just hung it from the walls of the canyons. Cars with standard transmissions and trucks have to shift into low gears to pull up the inclines. Automatic transmissions crawl up the slopes.

Like Big Bend National Park, the area around Lajitas gains more colors than Presidio. From the road, you can look ahead or behind at the space of the desert and see sharp pointed mountains, which are actually broken domes. They are off in the distance, surrounded by desert space, and that space is mostly a burned-out white streaked with gray shadows, but at different times of the day, in different seasons, the burned-out desert space shines with combinations of pinks, blues, purples, or oranges.

The details are here too but hard to notice because the road encourages you look off at the "view." But if you pull off the road and get out of your car so that you don't have a windshield making a frame, you notice what is around you. Ocotillos reach up with their dusty, withered arms like they are begging the long, thin clouds for rain. The chollas swell up with heat. Like the mountains, the rocks are jagged. They are all oblong with one end planted in the tough ground and the other end sticking out to break your ankle if you don't watch your step. "Badlands" was the usual name, but I thought "mean" described the area better.

Lajitas is the last pass on the river before the huge canyons—Santa Elena, Mariscal, and Boquillás—make the river bend. The flagstone on the river bottom makes Lajitas an easy place to cross. The Comanches used it for raids into Mexico. Today it's kind of like Disneyland on the western edge of Big Bend National Park.

Since before World War I, Mexicans rowed across the river to trade candelilla or fur pelts for goods with Tommy Lawler's great-grandfather. During the Depression, you could get sotol or good Mexican tequila in Tommy's grandfather's store—despite the fact that the Mexican government prohibited the sell of sotol or candelilla to Americans. The local Mexicans, our Mexicans, to get more money for the goods their government wanted to tax, had to evade not only our lawmen but their own.

Now Tommy still gets some sotol and most of what candelilla comes across to this country, even though the Mexican government still forbids trading the waxy cactus product with gringos. And his customers go back across the river, stocked with farm tools, pack saddles, oil filters, and groceries. Pretty soon the cosmetics companies that use the candelilla will invent some artificial stuff to take its place, and Tommy will have to rely more on selling tampons, Ding Dongs, potato chips, and beer to snowbirds.

When Tommy's father was running the store, back when it and the family house were the only repaired, fully standing adobes at Lajitas, Walter Bean, a Houston businessman with money to waste, got the idea of Lajitas before Pepper got the idea for Cleburne Hot Springs Resort. Walter Bean bought all the land around the Lajitas Trading Post. Tommy's father got rich selling Bean the land but refused to sell his store or move away from it. First Bean put in a nine-hole golf course and an airstrip several hundred yards away from the store, then a motel across the road, then a bigger hotel, then shops, then condos to rent or sell.

In fact, Walter Bean's idea worked so well that an *ejido* developed across the river from "Wally World." The Pasa Lajitas entrepreneurs opened two restaurants, Dos Amigos and Garcia's, and stationed an English-speaking teenager on the American side to row gringo tourists across the river for a good plate of enchiladas.

Now, on the American side, between Walter Bean's clean, faux Western architecture and the river, is Tommy's authentic, crumbling, dirty store. And now Clay Henry, Tommy's beer-drinking goat and mayor of Lajitas, drinks as much soda water, given to him by tourists' kids, as beer.

Lajitas was where I was to meet Henri Trujillo. It was also where Ariel lived and worked.

Neither R.C. nor I knew if this meeting was official, if it was a con job, or if it was my delusion. So I drove my own car up El Camino del Rio and wore only civilian clothes. I pulled up to the Lajitas Hotel, which was in the middle of a row of wooden shops, each with its own false front. It looked like a duplication of Matt Dillon's Dodge City, but it didn't look like anything that ever existed in Big Bend. A teenage Mexican girl at the desk told me that Henri Trujillo had risen early to get in eighteen holes in the nine-hole course that hugged the Rio Grande.

The wind had died and the sun had warmed the air, so I sat on a bench outside the Lajitas Hotel with the sunshine slipping up under the awning. The gravel parking lot in front of me was busy. Winnebagos, Suburbans, and trucks stopped while daddies or moms or retired snowbirds went into the stores along the wooden sidewalk and under the wooden awning. Most were buying the present-day desert necessity: ice.

A string of horses, most mounted by kids, walked past me. Bobbing with the steps of his own mount, an Anglo, his skin burned to brown leather, a thick black mustache drooping over his mouth, led the horses. Unlike the kids and tourists following him, he had ridden before. His bent, twisted, and cracked straw hat was pressed down on his head. He had cut off the sleeves of his thick denim shirt to show tattoos on either arm, one of a screaming eagle and another of a parachute with 82nd Airborne scratched beneath it. His boots and his spurs were Mexican made. He stared at me as he rode past. And he didn't return my wave.

Some of the kids behind him stared and giggled at the fresh, hay-filled horse apples falling in front of them. I hated horses.

After an hour the traffic died down, and with the sun in my face and my head against the wall, I had nearly dozed off, but crunching woke me up. I opened my eyes to see Ariel, in shorts and a white sweater, a golf bag around her shoulder, punching the spikes of her golf shoes through the gravel. Behind her was a diminutive man, shorter than me, straining against his own overloaded golf bag and grinding his own golf spikes into the gravel.

Ariel put both feet on the first step leading to the wooden sidewalk and smiled at me. She let her golf bag strap slide from her shoulder, and as the bag thumped against the wooden sidewalk, she stuck out her hand and said, "Agent Martinez."

Her blond hair seemed to trap sunlight. It glowed behind her and made her long nose more prominent. "Ariel Alves," I said, standing to shake her hand, and as I did, a bead of sweat dripped off her nose and splattered on the light, white sweater she wore.

"We've been expecting you," she said, and turned to look behind her. Smiling like a used-car salesman, not much taller than her armpits, the man with a pencil-thin mustache stepped up to her side and stuck his hand toward me. "Agent Martinez, this is Colonel Henri Trujillo." When I reached, I got ahold of just his fingers and shook those rather than his hand. "We've just played two rounds," Ariel said. "And Henri mentioned a meeting with you."

Ariel pulled her leg to pry her spikes from the wooden sidewalk, stepped toward the hotel, opened the door, and held it. I motioned for Trujillo to step ahead of me, and he too pried his spikes loose to step in ahead of us.

Inside, Ariel set down her golf bag. The girl behind the desk snapped to and said something to a boy sitting behind her, who was also up and standing immediately. "I read about you, Dolph. You're kind of a hero."

"Other agents were there." I shrugged.

"But the paper mentioned you," Ariel said, and moved her arms in a smooth manner that matched her speech. The Associated Press got the story from Dave Devine and a few comments from R.C. Dave thought that I had referred the AP to him, so he had given me a lot of credit in his comments to the AP and a lot of space in his article for Presidio's *International.*

"Agent Martinez has something of a reputation as one of the best border guards," Henri Trujillo said from behind me.

"Border Patrol," I corrected him. "We don't really guard much."

He was about to say something when the boy from behind the counter was tugging on his golf bag. "Can I take this to your room?"

Trujillo pulled his keys and a dollar out of his pocket. He told the kid his room number in Spanish and patted the kid's shoulder as he hefted the golf bag.

Ariel raised her long, slender fingers up to her face, then ran them through her hair to pull it over her shoulders. "I was thinking that we ought to have lunch outside, across the river."

This was supposed to be a private meeting, but Trujillo said, "I would love some more of this beautiful lady's company." I thought he was going to bow or kiss her hand.

Ariel smiled and clasped her hands. "If you don't mind, Dolph, we'll get cleaned up and meet you here in say . . ." She looked at Trujillo. "Fifteen minutes?"

"Of course," he said, and nodded to her as he climbed the steps to his room.

When he passed from sight, Ariel's smile dropped somewhat, and she said, "It's good to see you again, Dolph." Then we both heard a thumping coming down the steps and turned to see the bellboy running down them. "Good job, Domingo," Ariel said, and the kid stopped and looked at her. "But take it easy coming down." She smiled at him, then turned the smile back to me. "I better hurry."

She hefted her golf bag and started for the door but stopped, turned, and walked to the desk, her shoes stabbing the wooden floor. The girl snapped to. "Trini, go to the store down the walk and get some fruit, candy, or some snacks, and make up a complimentary food basket for Colonel Trujillo." Trini nodded. Then as an afterthought Ariel said, "We want his business. Other Mexican officials might start coming by."

Ariel started to take a step forward but stopped, bent over, untied one shoe and then the other, slipped off one shoe then the other, put both on top of her bag, and then in her socks covered the entire length of the lobby in a couple of long strides. "In a second, Dolph," she said as she went out of the hotel to her own room, cabin, or condo. I felt like I had missed something.

Fifteen minutes later, showered, legs shaved, hair shampooed, makeup on, squeezed into jeans, Ariel again looked like the towering Viking goddess that Pat Coomer and I saw at Sister Quinn's. Colonel Henri Trujillo came down the steps of the hotel in pressed khaki slacks and a starched pale blue shirt. The sleeves of his shirt seemed too long, the shirt too baggy. And it occurred to me that he probably had just a little too much pride to shop for his clothes in the boys' department. He also had a small leather briefcase under his arm.

The top down on her red convertible Mustang, Ariel punched the sports car for the short ride down a few yards of asphalted El Camino del Rio as it curved and dropped out of Walter Bean's fantasy to the dirt road that led to the river. From the backseat, I watched the wind pick up her hair and spray it back over the headrest toward me.

She parked next to a pickup truck, and the kid who spoke perfect English rowed us across the river. Depending on the rain farther upriver and in the mountains in Mexico and then depending on how much water the Mexicans decided to let spill over the dam on the Rio Conchos, the rafters could float quickly by Lajitas or just barely scoot over the flagstone at the bottom. When the river was low, smugglers with wets or drugs could drive across.

Ariel was quick to tip the kid who rowed us across. Then she also insisted on paying the kids who picked out donkeys for us to ride up the hill and into dusty Pasa Lajitas.

As I rode my donkey and watched Ariel from behind, she glancing around to smile at me, I noticed that the boy's saddle couldn't quite contain this lady. Folds of her butt, wrapped in jeans, pushed over the edges of the saddle. Her long legs dangled past the stirrups and nearly reached the ground.

The Mexican boys who walked alongside the rangy, sick burros, like most Mexican boys, stared at her, poked elbows into each other's ribs, and jerked their heads toward her. Trujillo rode in front of Ariel. He nearly dropped his briefcase. Ariel swiveled around in her saddle to look back at me.

The dust swirled around in the wind once we got into Pasa Lajitas, and we dismounted our burros, and Trujillo and I tipped the boys who handled them. Kids were suddenly around Ariel. She dipped her head and let a few stroke the gold stuff they hardly ever saw. Like the defeated Aztecs or like trained monkeys, the dark children held their tiny palms open in front of us for any gringo coins. "That's enough," Trujillo finally said to the kids. *"Vete de aquí,"* and the more timid ones ran away while the braver ones trailed behind us.

As the official guide, Ariel took Trujillo and me to the El Tejano bar. Inside were *Playboy* centerfolds and a big sign that translated into something like, "You owe money, I own your ass." And under the sign was a list of names of people who needed to pay up. "*Qué 'onde,* Ariel," the bartender yelled. She nodded and waved to him.

"Quieres cheve," Ariel said as though she were just learning phrases and the reactions they brought and not the language. Trujillo immediately pulled money out of his pocket to buy the first round.

"You come here often?" I asked Ariel.

"Surprisingly, this place is good for our business. Come across the river and see Mexico."

Just like an American bar, the El Tejano had a men's and women's room, marked *caballeros* and *señoras,* but once the American tourists at Lajitas went through the doors, they found themselves outside in the bright sunshine. With another step, though, they were on the proper gender side of a crumbling adobe wall. If they walked out to the edge of the wall, three feet after it ended, they could see a cliff littered with beer cans, and below the cliff was a goatherd's shack. The habit was to piss off the edge of the cliff and then throw your beer can over the edge. So over the years, rusting in piss and baking in the sun, the beer cans made the cliff into a more gentle slope.

Trujillo, Ariel, and I stood on the edge of the cliff outside the El Tejano bar, sipped our beers, and looked down at the shack and the goats gathered around it. "The goatherd's name is Pepe," Ariel said. "He sells his goat kids to the restaurants for *cabrito.*" He was sitting out on his falling porch, and his wife was hanging up laundry. Pepe stared up at us.

"Pepe claims to have a good life," Ariel said. "Where else, he asks, could he watch Yankee tourists piss down a cliff and throw a beer can or watch the fancy Japanese cars pass him on the other side of the river?"

"He's got a sizable chunk in change with that aluminum," I said.

"On the Mexican side, the closest town is fifty miles over a dirt road," Trujillo said, and smiled at Ariel and then dropped his smile to look at me.

Trujillo was right: it was a good place to exchange guns for dope. We walked across the street, a few kids following us, reaching to touch Ariel. We came to the open-air restaurant, Dos Amigos. A few tourists sucked down beers and ate tacos, but we found an empty corner and sat down, and a waitress brought us three warm Tecates.

Ariel tried to pay for these beers, but Trujillo was quick. "Courtesy of the state of Coahuila."

He insisted on buying the lunch too. We gorged ourselves with freshly made corn tortillas filled with *picadillo,* chicken, beef, *cabrito,* and beans. As we ate, Ariel shifted her smile and her conversation between the two of us. Walter Bean had a valuable employee.

After another round of beers, the afternoon sun making us all sleepy, I looked at Trujillo. "Maybe we should talk."

"What have we been doing?" Ariel asked.

Trujillo laughed and pointed his beer can at her. He took a long sip, brought down his can from his lips, and said out loud, *"Tres cervezas."*

"Please, no more," I said. Then I leaned across the table toward Ariel. "Could you excuse us, please?"

The crooked smile flashed at me, and she gently reached across the table to touch the back of my hand. "Of course," she said.

Trujillo rose as she did. He looked up to say to her, "A pleasure."

"No, all mine," she said, and patted my shoulder as she left. Trujillo started to talk, but I watched Ariel lope out of the restaurant, then down the steep hill to the outhouse below it.

I tuned in Trujillo when he mentioned the shoot-out. "Mr. Martinez, I have talked to a DEA agent. I didn't like him. The people I talk to about you say you are my man."

"I'm nobody's man yet," I said, and glanced out of the restaurant down the long path to the outhouse to see Ariel walk up to the door. "And I can't make deals."

"We are willing to inform you as to when a few shipments of drugs will be coming in." Ariel pulled open the door to the outhouse, then pulled her head back as the smell rolled out at her. She smiled to herself and went in. "Do we have a deal, Mr. Martinez?"

"What about the state of Coahuila, the minister of defense? Does he like me?"

"I represent my state in this matter."

"Well, I represent the whole US Border Patrol."

"I was hoping that we could strike a gentlemen's agreement. The *'mordida'* that you are afraid of is simply professional advancement for the both of us." He raised his hands to emphasize his point.

"What do you really want?"

Trujillo let his wrist flop backward over his hand and said, "Vincent Fuentes."

"That guy again?" I asked.

Trujillo smiled and, with the middle and index fingers on his left hand, he stroked the mustaches on either side of his upper lip. "Vincent Fuentes was a priest, then a professor, then a writer, then a revolutionary." Amused with his tale, he looked at me. "We caught him smuggling guns to various urban rebels across Mexico. After a few months in prison, he decided to help us. I 'escorted' him as he gave lectures and seminars in the US and South America. He worked with us to destroy those who smuggled guns into Mexico." Trujillo smiled very broadly.

"How long is this story?" I asked.

Trujillo's smile dropped a bit; he breathed in. He forced his smile across his face and started again. "But now we find that he has been betraying us. He works with several Mexican criminals. He supplies the guns through his American connections, and they then buy the drugs that go to the US. He does this all now because what he most wants is to get into the USA. He wants to get away from me and his promises to my office."

"I suppose it's a real pleasure working for you."

Trujillo smiled, but this one was a vicious, teasing little smile, and I knew that he could be dangerous. "I'm not having too much fun working for you, Agent Martinez."

I smiled at him to match him. "Maybe we can do business." I looked over my shoulder and saw the door of the outhouse open and Ariel come out. She shook her head, sending her hair over one shoulder. "Tell me what you want and what I get."

Trujillo reached into the pocket of his shirt, pulled out a pack of cigarettes, and offered me one. After I shook my head, he reached into his other shirt pocket and pulled out a cigarette holder. After carefully placing the cigarette into the holder, he held the thing backhanded, like a European, lit the cigarette, and took a long drag from the holder. "It's good to have a smoke after a good lunch and a few beers," he said after exhaling smoke.

"What I want is the guy on our side."

"I can let you know when and maybe where Fuentes's people will ship something across. He is presently in Chihuahua City . . . as are the guns."

I looked at him. "We saw the Ojinaga police get the guns."

Trujillo shrugged. "A few corrupt people." He inhaled, held the smoke in his lungs, then exhaled it. What he meant was that the

Ojinaga police had bartered the guns back to the people who had smuggled them across. "But if you catch these people, you will probably catch the people on your side. Whatever the case, your career grows."

"What do you get?"

"Sometime, somewhere Fuentes will try to move across the river." Trujillo pulled his cigarette holder out of his mouth and then pounded the table with his left forefinger. "I want you to get me Fuentes. You either find out where he is or if you catch him across the river, you return him to me."

"I'll process him. If he has no criminal record in the United States, I'll take him to the bridge at Presidio. I have no control over who's waiting for him on the other side."

"Fine," Trujillo said, and exhaled some smoke.

"What about the dope? We going to stop that?"

Trujillo shrugged. "How do you stop it? My concern is Fuentes."

"No *mordida,* huh?"

"You want me to take my *mordida pequita* to customs, to the DEA, to the Feebies?" He shook his head regretfully.

"How do you know when he'll move across? How do you know where he is?"

"Informants." What he meant was that the army was involved with the people doing the smuggling or their competition.

"What about *la plaza?*"

"What's *la plaza?*"

"Maybe we can't work together." The Mexicans called the ring or organization that controlled the drug or smuggling traffic in a certain area of the border *la plaza.*

"Okay, okay," Trujillo said. "Fuentes is with some upstarts, people who haven't gone through the 'channels.' He also has a reputation, so he brings notoriety. *La plaza* wants to see him go."

I smiled. I understood. The government and *la plaza* wanted Fuentes dead. I stood and held out my hand. "You've got my number. Give me a call."

Trujillo raised his cigarette holder to his lips, took a puff on his cigarette, and grabbed my hand with both of his. "Just a small present." He lifted his small briefcase that he had kept on his lap all during lunch, reached into it, and brought out a book. "Research," he said, and handed me the book.

The title of the book was *The Snake and the Eagle,* by Vincent Fuentes. I grabbed the thick book and looked back at Trujillo. "Know your enemy," he said. I flipped over the book and looked at the dust jacket photo of a smiling author who wore round glasses that made him look like a scholar from the twenties or thirties. He had a cowlick on the front of his head so that a strand of hair dangled over his forehead. The thin, angular, youthful face made him handsome, full of promise, a good-looking, talented Hispanic man: a pretty boy, *un güero.* Now he smuggled dope and double-crossed some bad people on both sides of Mexican law.

I pulled the cover from around the book to keep the dust jacket photo and handed the book back to Trujillo. "All I need to know about him is that he's smuggling dope. The picture will do fine."

Trujillo nodded. "The book is shit."

Trujillo and I found Ariel sipping a straight-up bourbon at the El Tejano with a little girl standing beside her and staring up at *la güera.* The little girl followed us back to the burros, watched *la rubia* as she once again squeezed her butt into the same small saddle, and waved goodbye as *la rubia* rode back down the trail and twisted in her pinching saddle to wave back at her.

We drove back up the road to the hotel, and in the lobby Trujillo excused himself. He said that he had phone calls to make and wanted to take a nap, then he added, "You two should go enjoy yourselves." He smiled to emphasize what he might be suggesting.

Ariel and I walked down the gravel slope, past Walter Bean's buildings and condos, to Tommy Lawler's Lajitas Trading Post. We gave Clay Henry a beer and watched as he flapped his long lips over the rim of the can, then tilted his head back to drink the beer, then looked at us from the narrow slits that were goat eyes. Clay Henry had long before lost his appeal for both of us, so we didn't feed him another. We sat at the picnic table under the thatched porch in front of Tommy's store.

After a while, Tommy came out and sat across from us. Then a Border Patrol truck pulled up. Dede was just coming off patrol. She nodded to me and went into Tommy's store. When she came out with a Coke, Dede hesitated, then sat by Tommy and across from me. I introduced her to Ariel, and the two women reached across the table to shake hands. Tommy asked about Pepper and laughed when I told him Pepper wanted to buy Clay Henry. Then I explained to Ariel where I lived and invited her out.

Soon the string of wanna-be cowboys rode past us, and bringing up the rear was the tattooed cowboy who had led the boys into the desert. He reined his horse to a stop, swung down from the saddle, and tied the reins to one of Tommy's posts. As he ducked under the awning, he stared at Dede, then at me.

Tommy nodded. Then Ariel said, "Hello, Socorro." Socorro nodded toward the two of them, then ducked into the store.

Tommy looked at one of his crushed, thick, dirty thumbnails. He tilted the one he looked at toward Dede as if to show her, and she scooted toward the edge of the bench. With some effort, Tommy put both of his hands in his lap and smiled at Dede. "Socorro doesn't like anybody in uniform—has something to do with getting drafted and going to Vietnam."

Ariel sipped her beer. "You ought to try being his manager. That's probably some Church of Christ group of kids he's got there, and he's stopping in for a beer." Dede looked past Tommy at Ariel, then held her gaze at me.

Tommy said, shrugging, "You're having a beer."

Ariel smiled. "I'm the boss."

Socorro came out of Tommy's store, sipping a beer. He pulled off his hat, crushing it and bending the brim some more, and a braided ponytail fell down from his head. With his hat in his hand, he pressed the cool can of beer against his sweaty forehead.

"Have a seat," Tommy said. Socorro stepped toward us but looked at Dede and Ariel, a uniformed policewoman and a boss. "Soc, this is Dolph; you met him yet?" I stood up, and he shook my hand, nearly crushing my fingers.

"Dolph works for the Border Patrol, like Ms. Pate here," Ariel explained to Socorro. Socorro looked at Dede momentarily and then over at me again. He cocked his head as though studying me, figuring how he might get the drop on me if he had to.

"Glad to meet you," Soc said, and his large, drooping mustache seemed to move from his breath as he talked. "But I got to catch up to those kids and make sure they get the horses unsaddled." He looked at Ariel. "When you work for Wally Bean, you put in the hours." He didn't smile. Ariel did.

He turned his back to us, walked to his horse, and in one motion, like a good horseman—holding his beer, swinging into the saddle, jerking the reins—he was mounted and moving with the horse as it trotted off. "What a pain in the ass," Ariel said.

"He's not a bad sort," Tommy said.

Tommy stared at his thumbnail again, then at me. "What he really doesn't like is law enforcement people who don't wear uniforms—they're even sneakier, he figures. That's why he's here. Doesn't like any government." Tommy shifted his glance to Dede and smiled. "He once shot at one of you guys. The agent was cutting across the property he lives on. He doesn't own it but thinks he does. He's good to have around because he's real protective."

Dede said, "I've probably cut across the property he lives on," and smiled up at Tommy.

Ariel said that she had books to do, and I walked with her halfway toward the hotel in order to thank her for helping me and to apologize for chasing her away in Pasa Lajitas. "Maybe you should call me," Ariel said.

"Soon," I told her.

When I got back, Dede and Tommy both stared at me. "Hell of a boss," Tommy said.

"What is she doing out here?" Dede asked.

"Manages that whole goddamn place. Word has it that profits were down and employees lazy, so ol' Bean sent her down to kick ass and take names," Tommy said.

Dede ran her fingers through her short hair, cocked her head, and wrinkled her nose. "She's too old to keep her hair that long."

Tommy smiled at Dede. Then he pulled his buck knife out of the attachment on his belt and began intently whittling at his thick, tough thumbnails.

On the way back to Presidio, after I cleared the steep canyons around Lajitas and neared the gentler rises, I pulled off 170 and onto a rancher's road. I checked in my rearview mirror and saw Dede pull off behind me.

As I climbed out of my Toyota station wagon, Dede stuck her head out of her window and asked me what was wrong. "Thought I'd high point for a while," I said over my shoulder.

"You're off duty," Dede said.

"Just out of uniform. Go on," I yelled. "Call it a day."

But Dede got out of her car and followed me up a rise. It was a small, flat hill between two washes, so I couldn't see much, but I could see several fields on the other side of the river, and a rowboat going slowly across, and several cows watching the boat nearing them, and 170 twisting up toward the canyons.

Dede came up behind me and looked around. "You really do like doing this."

"It's just something I do at the end of the day," I said.

"How did the meeting with Trujillo go?"

"With them there's always some fucking *mordida.*"

"It's the way they do things," Dede said.

"Hell, it's the way we do things anymore. No, it's the way the fucking Feebies and the DEA do things. We don't . . . or can't."

Dede smiled at me. "Be careful of that woman."

VATOS

Pepper, Pat Coomer, Ben Abrams, and two peroxide blondes from Odessa were looking at Bubble Butt. The bar we most liked in Ojinaga, El Guacolote—not really sleazy, yet not one of those places that advertises itself as a "ladies' bar"—had a velvet picture of a mournful, black-haired woman looking over her shoulder. You could see one tit and her butt. The owner of El Guacolote bought the painting from the owner of a bar and whorehouse in *la zona.* Rumor had it that she was one of the best-looking *putas* who had ever worked in Ojinaga and had left with one of her clients from Chihuahua City. So all that was left of her was the painting. The artist who painted her had most of her anatomy right, but her butt poked out too far. It looked like you could set a mug of beer on the shelf that asymmetrical butt made.

The problem, Pepper pointed out, was that one cheek was bigger than the other. And he argued with the bartender that with a little black paint, he could make Bubble Butt look a whole lot better. The bartender-owner argued that it would be sacrilege to the painting and the artist's integrity to deface it. Pepper argued that it was sacrilege to the woman and her memory to leave her with an oversize butt. Pepper, who had studied philosophy and had become a practicing sophist, was winning this argument.

The Odessa blondes, with visions of Acapulco in their heads, had driven from that ugly oil patch where they lived to the closest

Mexican town—Ojinaga. They pronounced the *j* as an English *j*. Pepper of course invited them to his resort, and they thought that the owner of a resort, a city administrator, and three law officers for the federal government were pretty sophisticated company. And listening to Pepper explain the debate, they were convinced that the honor of the subject was more important than the product of the artist, so they urged the bartender to let Pepper trim Bubble Butt's cheek with some black paint.

When he saw them in a ladies' bar, Pepper pulled off his Stetson, stroked his mustache, and said, "Ladies, perhaps I could buy you some more of those drinks with the little umbrellas in them." The blondes, over forty, spreading and stretching their tight jeans, veterans no doubt of come-ons from other West Texas lotharios, thought Pepper charming enough to join us.

Maybe it was the contrast of his diamond stud earring, pointy-toed boots, waxed mustache, and lazy eyelids. Maybe something in his voice indicated some wild, good-time evil. Maybe he was just good at the mating practices of West Texas. Despite his looks, Pepper could get women; it was keeping them that was his problem. As was his style and his rightful place, once we got to the Guacolote bar, Pepper stood between the two women and wrapped an arm around each, and one blonde kept an arm around Ben and the other blonde kept an arm around Pat. Dede and I drifted off to a table in the back of the bar.

Dede had scooted closer to me when the women joined us. She didn't complain, she never did, but she wasn't interested in the two blondes or in the artistic debate. Ben Abrams had this shocked look on his face. Somehow Pepper had persuaded Ben that he ought to come with us across the border to see the quaint Hispanic customs. So now the good Jewish boy was standing next to two big-breasted, Texas-style shiksas with nasty thoughts on their minds and staring at a velvet painting of a nude Mexican woman.

Pat Coomer was almost slobbering at the thought of a blond gringa even rubbing up against him. To Pat, a woman like Ariel was so far beyond his grasp, beyond the stretch of imaginable possibility, that she was like the woman in the velvet painting. But having spent enough time in desolate places in the Southwest, Pat knew that these two dyed blondes were in the realm of possibility for him. I'd be hard-pressed to say whether the image of his young but expanding Mexican wife with her three kids, waiting patiently at home for him, held him back or pressed him further into the side of the blonde who had her arm around him.

Pepper squirmed against the side of one woman, then the other, and turned his smile from one to the other. The woman with her arm around Pat laughed as he pressed even closer into her. The woman with her arm around Ben looked over at sheepish Ben, who found it hard to smile, then turned her smile back to Pepper. She was to be Pepper's.

The bartender disappeared for a moment and came back with a small brush and some black paint, and Pepper jumped over the bar in one fluid motion, surprisingly graceful for a man with a beer belly, and grabbed the brush and dipped it in the paint. With the bartender looking over his shoulder, with the two blondes giggling, with Pat yelling encouragement, with his tongue hanging out one corner of his mouth, Pepper meticulously painted an inverse black moon next to Bubble Butt's creamy hip. The blondes clapped. Pat whooped. But the bartender pointed and argued that Pepper's stroke wasn't quite straight enough.

I watched this from our table away from the bar and tried to conduct a conversation with Dede. Dede twirled her drink in her hand and looked into the glass. She wrinkled her nose as though she smelled something in the glass. Her short hair frizzed. "It's just fun," I said.

"I know it's just fun. It's always fun for you guys. But what about me? When do I get to have some fun?"

I sipped my beer and took a look at Pepper's second swipe at Bubble Butt's cheek. When I turned around to face her, Dede frowned because I smiled. "It's the Border Patrol, Dede. We all know that."

"Shit," Dede said, and looked away. I waited until she turned around. "I want to do something, really bad, so bad, I could just scream."

"Do it, then," I said.

"I don't even know what 'it' is." Dede wrinkled her nose and went back to staring in her glass. "Go back and join them if you want. I can get a taxi back." I was tempted to join them, but I reached out and patted Dede's hand, and she swiveled to face me. "I'm just so restless."

"It's this place."

"Would it be different anywhere else?"

Dede was a working-class girl from Tucson. She wasn't dumb, wasn't smart, had few aspirations, just wanted some nice comfortable life and job. The old term "civil service" conjured images of offices full of Dedes. The perverse thing about her was that somewhere in her life, when most girls were thinking about steady, traditional marriages, families, or jobs, Dede started to imagine herself in law enforcement. She spent a year studying for the Border Patrol test. And now, with one more year to go in her probation, she was about to achieve her low-level dreams. Sitting next to me in jeans, a low-cut blouse, and a Mexican sweater, Dede looked like a midlevel bureaucrat. As for me, I had started wondering what I was doing in the Border Patrol when I got to Presidio. "If you want out of the Border Patrol, now's the time to get out," I said.

"I don't want out." Dede shook her head.

"High divorce rate in the Border Patrol," I said.

"I don't want to order my life around a marriage."

"What do you want from it?"

Dede dropped her head, then pulled it up with this serious look on her face. "What about you, Dolph? What about your life? Look what you gave up to be in the Border Patrol."

"It's a good job. What else could I be?"

"No, no," Dede said, and pounded the table with her fist. She tried again to make sense. "Do you really like this? Do you get used to it? Do you think that Ariel girl is really going to turn out to be anything?"

"Too soon to tell."

"Maybe so." Dede looked around. "I haven't gotten any since I've been in the Border Patrol." I couldn't help but laugh, and Dede smiled. "It's easier for you guys," she said.

"Like hell it is," I said. Dede dropped her head, then pulled it back up and laughed some more. "Let me buy you a drink there, cowgirl." I started to get up, but Dede reached out and grabbed my arm.

"Just one more thing," she said. She jerked her head toward the boys and the blondes. "What are you guys running away from? Everybody in this area seems to be hiding from something."

"Even me?" I smiled.

But Dede didn't smile. "Especially you."

"Maybe I'm running *for* something and got stalled here, just like everybody else around here."

"Just like the wets." Dede smiled at me.

"Only we get to play with guns." Dede wrinkled her brows. "I'll get your drink," I said, and left her at the table.

I brought back her beer, set it down in front of her, then jerked my head toward the boys. "Go on," she said. I left her to sip her beer by herself until we decided to go.

After an afternoon of drinking, Pepper invited all of us to his resort for a bath. Ben Abrams didn't show, and Dede asked me to take her home. I didn't go into Pepper's cabin and soak with the blondes; I called the hotel, conned the receptionist for Ariel's home phone, and got a date for Christmas Eve. I guessed that Pepper probably got lucky and that Pat probably committed adultery.

The answer to Dede's question about what I was running away from, as far as I knew, was a woman in El Paso. Maybe what I was running away from was the fact that the people you knew best and who knew you best were usually the ones you run away from. The last time I saw her, she was kissing a lawyer who knew both of us. It was in a bar right down from the house we rented. It was my bar, where I went with my agent friends. She knew I would be there, knew I was watching, so she planted this big wet one on the lawyer's lips. I could almost see her tongue working inside his mouth. Later I got a wedding announcement for her and this lawyer.

More than that kiss, I remember the start of our end. It was a Sunday morning; the coffee was perking and filling the house with its fresh smell. The morning sunbeams were filtering in through the eastern window of our bedroom and making the white sheets and pastel yellow walls bright. The empty bottle of wine lay beside the bed next to the plate of leftover cheese and crackers. The night before had been one of those calm, domestic Saturdays that make you feel good. We didn't go out, made a big dinner, ate too much, started drinking highballs then shifted to wine, climbed in bed to watch a late night movie, then ended the night by curling into each other and doing the little familiarities that excited each other.

I woke nursing a minor hangover and anticipating reading the morning paper. I clicked on the bedroom TV set with the remote control and flipped channels past the TV preachers and church services to a morning soft-news show. She rolled out of bed, and I watched her naked body as she left to fetch us both some coffee. She was younger than me, with tight muscles and firm breasts. She was Hispanic, black hair, green eyes, smart, a paralegal with relatives on both sides of the border, able to move through different levels of society in El Paso and in Juárez. She was the perfect woman for me.

She came back in with two mugs of coffee, her skin in the sunlight looking a little like the creamy coffee. "You're beautiful," I said as I took my mug and watched this guy talk about life on his Nebraska farm. Halfway through the report from Nebraska and my cup of coffee, she began nibbling at my ear, then ran her hand down my chest to my then scarless belly. I ignored her and my hangover until the end of the report from Nebraska; then I set my coffee on the nightstand, rolled into her, and kissed her. Our Sunday morning sex was an endearment that I had started and she had enjoyed.

As I worked at pleasing her and pushing back the throb in my head, she suddenly went limp beneath me, then rolled out from under me. "Where are you?" she asked. I thought that it was a stupid question and wrinkled my brows. "You seem so distant," she said. "What are you thinking about?"

In truth, I don't remember precisely what I was thinking about; I do remember that on Sunday mornings, I was usually planning something. Perhaps I was thinking about Monday morning at work, somebody I had caught, somebody I was looking for, some investigation. The required tactics of any love life differ from person to person. I didn't know her well enough yet. I said, "I'm thinking about you."

"Come on, Dolph," she said, and crossed her arms over her breasts as though she had suddenly grown embarrassed around me. "We're never together anymore. We just live with each other. You're just always so aloof, indifferent, distant, like there's always something other than me on your mind."

"I have other interests in my life than you. So should you."

That, of course, was the one thing I shouldn't have said because soon after, she found the lawyer. The lawyer must have convinced the ideal woman for me, the one whom I thought would finally be Mrs. Dolph Martinez or Mrs. Inez Camacho-Martinez if she wanted hyphenation, that he thought only of her. Maybe he did fess up and say that he was thinking about the research in his next tax case and then promised harder to make a compromise between his work and his woman. Maybe the fact that he took trips to the Caribbean, played golf at the country club, attended all the proper social and civic events, had five-hundred-dollar bar tabs, convinced her that he cared more for her than I did. Her word was *complement.* He complemented her more than I did. I suspect that my being more on the blue-collar end of the law and his being way up on the white-collar executive level had something to do with complementing.

And, of course, that Sunday morning wasn't the real end. We, especially I, had to go through several fights, bouts of crying, late night calls, cussing, her moving out, and finally her kissing the lawyer and marrying him. I ended up shaking a little too much on Sunday mornings because I drank too much on Saturday nights. I knew that I needed to put time and distance between her and me if I was to quit drinking. I decided that anyplace where I wouldn't be reminded of her and the lawyer was better than a haunted El Paso. I decided that I didn't need any love or sex life. So there was this job in Presidio that came open. And of course, the Border Patrol was very glad to have a senior agent volunteer to go to Presidio.

I told myself that with the glue heads, assorted junkies, and belligerent transvestites, El Paso was far more dangerous than Presidio with its rural wets. Then we all found out that some really bad *broncos* shipped their drugs through the Marfa sector because so much of it was isolated. Then I found out that nearly everybody in the Big Bend area owned a gun and thought he was a cowboy, that in Presidio you were either selling drugs, chasing drugs, working for the government, or bumming. Then I got gut shot.

Pepper's first wife lived in California with their eighteen-year-old son, who was trying to get into college. Pepper and Marilyn met in Dallas at a riding show. Pepper rode Western, and Marilyn rode English. And almost like in the movie *Giant,* Pepper brought this sophisticated Dallas urbanite home to a ranch in trans-Pecos Texas. But Pepper's Liz Taylor grew restless and bored on the ranch and began taking pills with her liquor. Pepper, meanwhile, further developed his taste in rough-looking West Texas waitresses. After Marilyn dried out in a facility in New Mexico, she started her life over as an accountant in Los Angeles.

When she came to pick up their child, I met Marilyn, a very good-looking woman, especially when you considered short, stocky, ruddy-complexioned Pepper. Despite the pills and the liquor, she had held up better than Pepper. I could see in the way she touched Pepper's hand and talked about their boy that she must have found something attractive and sexy in Pepper. And I could see in the way he looked at her that he would have liked to have made her a part of his dream at Cleburne Hot Springs Resort. But then she and wife number three, the one who ran off with the Alpine real estate developer (wife number two was a real mistake whom Pepper never missed), were the reasons Cleburne Hot Springs Resort bubbled up in Pepper's head in the first place.

LA GÜERA

Sister Quinn, for a fat lady, was light on her feet. She probably developed her skill at dancing from hiking up the narrow, rocky canyons where she would purposely set off some of our sensors. We'd race to a point on the trail, and when no one would come, an agent would walk or drive up or down the trail and find Sister Quinn waddling along. We stopped taking her in because we got tired of her accusing us of harassment and then having to let her go anyway.

But New Year's Eve, as I polkaed with her, to *norteño* played by a band from Alpine with accordion and steel-guitar players so it could be a country-western or *conjunto* band, she smiled like the East Coast Irish Catholic girl she must have once been. She didn't wear a tennis cap this night, had actually fixed her hair so that it made a tight, fluffy red circle around the top of her head. And her white blouse and blue Levi's had sharp pressed edges.

I scuffed the soles of my best black boots and Sister Quinn scratched her leather tennis shoes as we scooted across Tommy Lawler's Lajitas Trading Post gravel parking lot. As I crunched gravel, I looked over her shoulder to see Pat Coomer stiffly counting out his steps as he moved Ariel across the parking lot. His six-year-old stepson chased his seven-year-old stepdaughter through the dancers, and Pat jerked Ariel to a halt to yell at his kids to get their butts back over to their mother and big sister. Ariel laughed, and the light breeze from the north that made us all just a little cold lifted and lowered her golden hair.

And passing Ariel and Pat, Pepper, who liked to kick one leg up behind him, kind of like Henry Fonda in his old movies, guided the Odessa blonde who liked him best. And R.C. smiled and puffed a cigarette as he pulled Mrs. R.C. Kobel after him. Socorro, with one hand draped over her shoulder and the other around her waist, pulled one of his "old ladies" after him. His other "old lady" was under Tommy's thatched roof porch, along with Dede and Pat's wife and her oldest daughter and a crowd of people without partners. Screaming the loudest, dancing with everybody, were the teachers of Presidio ISD.

I got into the spirit of things and pulled Sister Quinn closer to me and pushed my head into her neck, then I spun her around under my arm, and she then took over the lead to spin me and started laughing loudly enough for Pat and Ariel to stop dancing and stare at us. I laughed too as I fought her to gain control of our steps. Once I was in control, I whispered into her ear, "Have you heard from Vincent Fuentes?"

She lost her step and looked up at me. She regained herself and said, "He's that writer, isn't he? I read some of his things. Really good."

"Come on. When you going to bring him across?"

She smiled and fought me for the lead in the polka. "Don't know the man."

"He's into some bad shit, and he's got some mean friends."

"Don't you ever take a night off?" Sister Quinn asked.

"Truce, then," I said, and led her to the edge of the porch just as the song ended and a chorus of trilling tongues and *"Ayyi, ayyi, ayyis"* spread across the parking lot dance floor.

Sister Quinn patted my chest. "You should listen to your blood, Dolph Martinez," she said.

"My blood's not very loud. I can't hear it," I said.

She slapped at my arm and said, "I mean your heritage. Your parents started out the same as the people you impound, only no one caught them. And you've been to Anglo schools and college."

"Don't you ever take a night off?" I asked.

"Just a question. I'm *not* investigating."

I put my arm around her back and was just barely able to reach all the way around her. "My heritage confuses me."

"You're still a Mexican."

"And I'm also half gringo, and a former soldier, and a Border Patrol agent, and a graduate of Jefferson High in Brownsville, Texas, and the University of Texas."

Sister Quinn squared off and stared at me, but before she could speak, Ariel was in front of me with her arms around me and kissing me. Pat stared at me with his mouth open, like I was the luckiest son of a bitch around to have this giant blonde sucking on my lips. Ariel had invited Sister Quinn to Tommy Lawler's traditional New Year's Eve bash. And I was hoping that Sister Quinn would drive back in Gilbert Mendoza's pickup truck and leave just me to spend the night in the condo that Ariel got rent free from Wally Bean.

Pepper came up to me, leading his blonde, who had her finger hooked through one of his belt loops. "Let's see if we can't steal that goddamn beer-drinking goat and take him to my resort."

Ariel pulled her face away from mine, let her hair fall back, and shook it. "Let's get Clay Henry another beer."

"He's not drinking no more," Pat said. "Tommy says he's too drunk."

Pat, Pepper, Dede, and I were almost as drunk as Tommy's goat. We started drinking beer with Clay Henry that afternoon. Pat's wife and Pepper's blonde drank rum and Cokes, and Pat's three stepkids liked to watch Clay Henry grab the beer can with his lips, throw back his head, chug the beer, then spit out the can. The slits that were his pupils seemed to roll back in his head as the afternoon wore on.

Then R.C. came down and introduced blue-haired Mrs. R.C. to all of us. Her name was Imogene. She looked and spoke like a society lady, and I wondered how she and R.C., the agent who almost shot a rancher for shooting his horse, stayed together. Then I wondered what Pat saw in his wife, who stumbled over English pronunciation, and what his life must be like in his crowded mobile home with some other man's three kids.

And then Ariel met us, and I forgot about everybody but her. She danced with everyone, made sure that everyone joined in the conversation, shook hands, introduced herself to new people, and, just by being there and enjoying herself, got the Mexicans from across the river talking about this beautiful, strange *güera,* this goddess whose fingers danced in front of her face when she talked. A good party, she told me, was good for Walter Bean's business.

It was now nearing midnight, and I had already been kissing Ariel. It had been a hot day, but a wind turned it chilly, a good excuse for snuggling with whatever woman you had brought or could find. With my arm around Ariel, I looked off into the crowd and saw the DEA agent. Eventually I caught his eye. "I'll be right back," I whispered to Ariel.

She just smiled, and as soon as I stepped away from her, Pepper put his arm around her and said, "I'll hold her for you." R.C. watched as I walked toward the DEA agent.

The DEA agent stuck out his hand as I neared, and I shook it. "Found anything?" he asked.

"No," I said. "You?"

He stopped shaking my hand, looked down at his hiking boots, and lied, "A little."

"So what you got?"

"What have you got?"

"You boys will be the first to know," I said. He nodded again, and I stepped up to him and tried to soothe him. "Look, I promise I'll let you know. But just back off for right now. I've gotten ahold of some people on the other side of the river, okay?"

"Who?"

"I can't tell you that," I said.

"Trujillo?" he asked. I didn't say anything, so the DEA agent continued. "He called me. He wanted some kind of deal. What's he told you?"

"What do you know about him?"

"You eat with the devil—"

"You better use a long spoon," I interrupted to finish the saying.

"Nobody really trusts him, but he has cooperated with us before. We're not exactly sure whom he represents or what his interests are."

The DEA agent waited for some reply from me, but I didn't want to give him one. "Loosen up a little." I backed away. "I will call you."

"That's the procedure," he said.

I turned my back to him to return to Ariel. R.C. met me before I got to her and asked, "What'd you find out?"

"He doesn't know anything," I said, and R.C. nodded, and I walked quickly back to Ariel. And when I put my arm around her and pulled her away from Pepper, I forgot about worrying over Trujillo and cooperating with the DEA.

"Shouldn't leave a pretty woman like her alone that long," Pepper said. But before I could answer, Tommy Lawler stepped onto the porch of his trading post, saw Dede, and put his right arm around her. In his right hand he had an old pistol, and Dede watched it as its hammer rubbed her cheek. Tommy turned his wrist over to look at his watch and started counting backward. Mrs. R.C. grabbed R.C.; Pat grabbed his wife; Pepper grabbed his peroxide Odessa blonde; I grabbed Ariel, who laughed out loud. Sister Quinn grabbed somebody's kid. Dede ducked out from under Tommy's arm, turned her back to us, and walked into the crowd of Mexicans, snowbirds, teachers, ranchers, and other local dropouts from the real world. I watched Dede make her way through the crowd. A sloppy-drunk fourth-grade PE teacher, who used to play football for Sul Ross State University, the tiny cow college in Alpine, wrapped his arm around Dede. I turned back to Ariel, so I didn't see if Dede ducked out from under his arm too.

Our first date was a week before, on Christmas Eve. We went to Sister Quinn's *templo* and sat through her sermon and Christmas Eve mass. Even though most of the people gathered spoke English only as a second language if at all, Sister Quinn preached in English. She didn't say much that sounded like a Christmas message. She spoke about duty: To see evil or injustice and not to oppose it is to side with evil or injustice. Pain could cleanse. It was pure. It could give a person some idea of the quiet universal suffering of the underclasses of the world. Suffering was far greater than pain. It was like sorrow. Only through understanding the pain of the poor and dispossessed could we come to an understanding of the universal suffering of the world. And through understanding this pain and sympathy with it, we should try in some way to relieve this pain. And so on. Exactly what I usually heard from her.

During the sermon Ariel squeezed my hand, and outside I commented that we didn't hear anything in Sister Quinn's Christmas message that sounded Christian.

"She's very secular," Ariel said.

I nodded. "Are you?"

"I am a Catholic," she said. "But not a very good one." She shifted her weight to one hip. "Or maybe I can't really claim to be a Catholic at all. I was just raised as one. And now I just sort of like the services." She chuckled. "Only my first marriage was annulled in good Catholic fashion; the second one ended a regular Protestant, run-of-the-mill divorce. What are you?"

"My mother drug me to an Episcopal Sunday school once."

Then we went to a party with the Presidio ISD at Cleburne Hot Springs Resort. We drank sotol with the ex-football player, who had just once again tried to grab Dede; Ben Abrams and his wife (both of whom coughed up the sotol); and even Father Jesse Guzmán. Late that night, or rather at the start of Christmas Day, a little drunk, I stood shaking in the cold night in front of my cabin, waiting for Ariel to go in. "A little presumptuous, aren't you?"

"It's seventy-five miles back to Lajitas," I said.

"You should have asked first," she said as she stepped into my cabin. Inside, we politely took off our clothes and lay down on my bed, and when I rolled toward her, she repeated herself, "You should have asked first."

A bit pissed off, expecting a hangover in the morning, disappointed, I said, "Hell, what did you think?"

"That I was going to a party with no further expectations."

"You are Catholic," I said, and worked through my haze to one clear thought: Maybe I had grown crude.

"No," she said. "I'm just egotistical," then she thought some more and smiled. "And particular." She rolled away from me and went to sleep. In the morning, as she rose and stepped out of bed, I saw that the mark across the arch of her left foot was a tattoo.

When Tommy, counting backward, reached "one," he fired his pistol straight at the wall of his adobe store to put another bullet hole in it. He liked to tell tourists that his bullet holes were from gunfights or from a raid that Pancho Villa made in 1916. A yell went up from the crowd, Clay Henry stomped around in his pen, and I threw back my head to look up into Ariel's face. She squeezed me harder, and as I kissed her, I felt her warmth spread into me. I would drink a few more beers so that I would have one of those pleasant drunks: the kind where you are just on the line, where you can still feel what is around you, the type where just a few more drinks would push you into numbness. I would not drink until I was numb, falling down, or puking. I would drink to heighten the feel of the night, which would end with Ariel in bed with me in Walter Bean's prefab condo right up the hill from the Lajitas Trading Post.

Ariel and I left the party holding hands and kissing. We walked past the fake Western town facade to her two-story condo. Before we even got to her door, I pulled her into me and gave her an open-mouth kiss, and she gently pushed me back and whispered, "Wait. Wait." She kissed me gently and squeezed my hand and raised the other hand to pat my face with her long fingers, all to reassure me that there was no deception going on here, that unlike at the Christmas Eve party, my expectations were to be met.

And when I led her up to her room and again pulled her to me, I could see her smile even though I could only see the outline of her face, and she whispered again, "Wait." She went into the bathroom. I listened to the wind shake the pane of glass that stretched up both floors of the loft-style apartment so that I could see the party and beyond it the salt cedars that lined the river. I heard the toilet flush, then I heard water running in the bathtub.

When Ariel came back out of the bathroom, she was naked, and her long blond hair just barely covered her breasts. She stuck the back of her fingers against her hair and flipped the palomino mane behind her shoulders to let me look at her tanned body glowing in the moonlight. We simultaneously reached for each other's hands, and she led me into the bathroom.

The bathtub was full of steaming hot water and bubbles, and it was lined with a dozen tiny candles. A bottle of Tommy's cheap complimentary champagne was chilling in a plastic motel bucket of ice that sat on the toilet. She helped me slip out of my jacket and shirt, lowered my jeans, but we both had to grab and tug to get my boots off. And then we both slowly stepped into the tub, facing each other but keeping our distance, touching only each other's fingers. We lowered ourselves into the warm water and bubbles. I guided my legs over her thighs to rest them around either side of her waist, and she did the same. Thus in the candlelight, I was finally able to see the tattoo on the arch of her left foot. It was a stylized, green-eyed panther, shaped with differing widths of intricate, curving black lines, one line a tail that rose partway up her ankle.

She giggled at me while I looked at the tattoo, then giggled as I traced it with my finger. She soaped a washcloth, and with a slight, crooked smile, began scrubbing my chest. After I just as slowly washed her, she reached to the top of the toilet and grabbed the bottle of champagne. I opened it and the cork shot to the top of the bathroom ceiling, then splashed into the water between us. We laughed and drank the champagne right out of the bottle. The cheap champagne would bubble up out of the mouth of the bottle and inside our mouths.

In the candlelight she saw my scar, felt it with her long forefinger, and when she looked at me, I shrugged and said, "Got shot." With the bar of soap, she gently rubbed the scar. And I braced my feet against the back of the tub and slowly raised my body out of the water. Ariel wiped the soap away from my scar with the damp washcloth. Then she kissed my wet scar, her hair dropping into the water, until she nearly submerged her head. And I pulled her left foot out of the water and kissed the tattoo of the panther on the arch.

I felt lucky just to be here with my legs wrapped around her, hers around me, feeling her body, seeing it softly lit, slightly out of focus and gold, by the candlelight. I expected no more. But she took my hand and pulled me up after her as she stood and dripped water on my face. When I stood, she dried me. Then I dried her. And she took my hand and led me up the stairs to the bedroom, then she lay down in front of me.

I looked at the shaped, shaved, trimmed, soft blond hair between her legs. I kissed her all over. I rubbed my face, now grown stubbly with whiskers, all over her clean, soap-scented body, down her chest and stomach, up her legs. And then finally, when I got up on her, she let out little gasps, and I felt like I was really with her. No distance, not aloof, not with my job. And afterward, both of us exhausted, she traced my scar with her finger, then kissed it, then licked the length of it.

I forced myself to stay awake when she rested her head in the soft part of my shoulder. I wanted to feel as much of her as possible as long as I could. I stayed awake until my arm went to sleep and fought the needles pricking it. And when she rolled away from me and started to sleep, her breasts slightly heaving as she lay on her back, I watched her, as though to memorize her in case this was not real, and I wished that she were back on my useless, tingling arm.

Then, to make sure that this was indeed real, perhaps to gloat on my luck, I rolled out of the bed, put on my clothes, pissed in the upstairs bathroom, felt my way down the dark stairs, and went out for one last beer with my friends.

AÑO NUEVO

From Ariel's long window that rose the entire height of the condo, I could see that the party was over, but I knew that at least Pepper, usually unable to sleep, would not leave until everyone else had left. I shut her front door behind me and walked past the Western town, then headed down the slope toward Tommy's parking lot. The band members were packing their instruments, and a few Mexicans drunkenly argued. The wind had grown colder and blew some trash across the parking lot. An Alpine newspaper page caught against my leg, and I kicked into the wind to get it loose, then watched it as it blew toward the river.

I stepped on rocks and gravel and made my way around the Lajitas Trading Post to Tommy's house, then went to his back porch with its view of the Rio Grande. The house protected us from the chilly wind, but the air had some of the coolness from the river in it. Tommy had one of those big Western dusters on and sat on his steps. Pepper had on a down vest and claimed the one folding chair, and Dede, with only a Levi's jacket on, hugged herself and sat on the porch railing. Socorro sat on the wooden floor of the porch under Dede and seemed to be lost in his stare out toward the river.

"Yo," Pepper screamed when he saw me coming. "Stud duck." He leaned his chair back on two legs and stuck his hand straight above himself. Tommy scooted to one side of the steps, and I stepped by Tommy and gave Pepper a medium-high high five. "Stewed and screwed; where's the tattoo?" Pepper asked.

"On the arch of her left foot," I said. "This cute little black panther with a green eye."

Dede perched uneasily on the porch rail, shifted her weight from one side of her butt to the other. Socorro pushed himself up, looked at me and at Dede, then creaked the slats of Tommy's porch as he stepped across it to stagger back toward the trading post and walked into darkness, on his way to wherever it was he stayed.

"Where's your date?" I asked Pepper.

"Piss, fuck, shit fire," Pepper said, let his chair down to all four legs, leaned to the railing, and spit tobacco juice out toward the slope to the Rio Grande. "She passed out on me. I got her up in my motel room. Hoping she'll sober up a little before I get back."

"Hell, should of told me," Tommy said. "I'll sneak up there and service her for you."

"Be like a dead cow."

"Yeah, you should know from cows," Tommy said.

"Anybody got a beer?" I asked.

Tommy reached down to a step below him and pulled a can out of the cardboard surrounding a six-pack and handed the can to me. "That's a buck-fifty you owe me," he said. I popped the top and looked for a place to light. Dede balanced her butt on the railing, leaned her back against a beam, raised her knees up to her chin, rested her heels on the rail, grabbed her knees with one hand, and lifted a beer to her mouth with the other. We were all impressed, and I plopped half of my butt on the rail next to her. With both of us trying to balance on Tommy's flimsy railing, me a little drunk, we shook and shifted to keep ourselves upright.

I heard a groan. Dede jerked her head toward the shadows close to Tommy's trading post, and I saw a lump of clothes. "That DEA fella," Pepper said.

"Is he okay? Hell, somebody didn't stab or shoot him, did they?"

"Almost as bad. Pepper and some of the Mexicans gave him some of their homegrown sotol," Tommy said. "Last time I drunk any of that shit, I ended up getting my stomach pumped in the Alpine hospital."

"You sell it," Pepper said.

"So I learned not to drink it."

"We can't just let him stay here," I said.

"We'll drag him to my car and throw him in the backseat." Pepper shrugged. "But first let's drink some more."

"Goddamn, Pepper, can't take you nowhere," I said.

"Hell, you didn't like the son of a bitch anyway."

I swung my legs over the railing, precariously balanced my back and butt on Tommy's railing, and looked out over the tops of the salt cedars and willows to see the Rio Grande. In the moonlight that made silver streaks in the river, I could clearly see several Mexicans pushing aluminum rowboats into it. They probably bought the rowboats on time from Tommy. On these dry, brittle desert nights, the glowing (not twinkling) stars and moon were lantern enough. You didn't need infrared to see. You could easily spot a white shirt from two hundred yards away.

One rowboat, full to the gunwales, was halfway across the river, and the Mexicans were trying to sing some song. The drunks trying to man another rowboat couldn't get their boat moving. They dipped one oar in and then the other but couldn't coordinate their rowing. Tommy said, "I told them all not to bring their own liquor. They got to buy mine. But just like that goddamn Pepper, they brought that goddamn sotol with them and fed some to that poor bastard," and Tommy jerked his head back toward the crumpled DEA agent.

As the drunk oarsmen gained control of the boat, leaving successive black-and-silver inverted *V*s behind them in the water, I thought that I had probably arrested some of them for crossing the Rio Grande in the other direction. But this was New Year's Eve, a kick-ass, bad drunk on both sides of the river, and Tommy's Lajitas Trading Post was the demilitarized zone, same as Big Bend National Park. We wouldn't dare arrest somebody on Tommy's property. Nor do I think, we, no, just I, would arrest anyone on Sister Quinn's property.

"Well, goddamn there, pretty boy," Pepper said, leaning back onto two legs of his chair and resting the heels of his pointy-toed boots on the rail. "How the hell was it? Had the best-looking woman ever to scoot a tennis shoe across ol' Tommy's gravel. Give us the report." Tommy pulled out his buck knife and went to work whittling on one of his tough, hard thumbnails but shifted his weight so he could look back at me. Even leaning back, Pepper was able to drool a stream of spit into his sliced-off beer can, and when he turned his head to look at me, his diamond stud earring reflected some of the silver moonlight. Dede shifted her weight and shook the railing that we both sat on.

I looked back at her and started: "We took a bath."

"Hell," Pepper interrupted, and shook his head, his earring sending darts of moonlight out around his head, "you can do that at my place."

"A bubble bath," I added. "In candlelight . . . drank champagne." Dede shifted to look at me, Pepper brought his chair down to all four legs, and Tommy looked up at me. "She kissed my scar."

"Goddamn, you lucky son of a bitch," Tommy said.

"Second-best piece of ass I ever had," I added.

Pepper pushed his chair back onto two legs and provided the straight line. "What's the first?"

"That whore you bring over."

Pepper and Tommy chuckled. "You guys are pigs," Dede said, and then laughed too and nearly fell off the railing so that I had to grab her.

"Well, shit," Pepper said, "if it wasn't for that furry spot between their legs, there'd be a bounty on 'em."

"God gave 'em vaginas," Tommy said, "so men would talk to 'em."

"I beg your brazen fucking pardon," Dede said.

"We'd talk to you more," Pepper said, "if you'd take more baths with us."

We drank until two six-packs were gone, then the four of us picked up the DEA agent as best we could and carried him to Pepper's orange-and-white fully restored '55 Chevy with the leather upholstery and threw him in the backseat. "Hope he don't puke," Pepper said. "Once had one of my Ojinaga whores puke back there. I almost got it reupholstered rather than clean it."

"Y'all go home," Tommy said, turned his back to us, and walked back toward his house. He must have given up on Dede.

Tommy had long legs that made him lope, he had a little ass that didn't quite fill the back end of his jeans, and though he was only thirty-four, the mass of wrinkles on his brow and chin made him look ten years older than me. He must have looked like his great-grandfather, a lost, poor, out-of-work cowboy who decided to become a peddler. Tommy had never married; he lived alone in the back of his store, and he never complained. Maybe, with his heredity and the years he spent here, sitting out on his porch, drinking beer, and staring at a river that shifted in the wide, sandy parts of its bed and the mountains that never moved was enough for Tommy. Maybe the desert space that reminded you of geologic time was enough for Tommy. Maybe Tommy was what we were all destined to be if we stayed here. If we couldn't find someone like Ariel.

Dede shivered in the wind, so Pepper and I both swung an arm around her and walked past the complex that gave Pepper economic wet dreams across El Camino del Rio to the Cavalry Post Motel. "Hey, Dolph," Pepper said when we stepped under the awning of the motel. "How about you and me exchange keys. When mine wakes up, she'll be ready for action. I figure you wore yours out, but I'd still rather just lay beside her than go home to my old bar hide."

"Why don't you do a forward roll and jump up your ass," I said.

"You know what Pat Coomer would tell you, don't you, son?" Pepper put his hand on top of his head to hold his hat in place against the wind. When I said no, to tell me, his words got caught in the wind, but I heard him say, "He'd say, don't get used to it. Somebody that good looking just ain't gonna have much to do with the likes of us."

Pepper staggered off when I told him to go to hell, and Dede turned away from me. I ran up to her and walked her to her room. "Why didn't you find a date?" I asked her when we got to her room.

Dede shrugged. "Who?"

"Tommy?" I said.

"Sure, stand around and watch him carve up his dirty fingernails."

'One of the teachers?" Dede just shrugged again. "That fourth-grade coach kinda likes you."

"Only when he's drunk."

"The DEA agent," I said.

We both laughed, and Dede said, "That was dirty what they did to him, daring him into drinking that sotol."

"Initiation," I said.

"Pigs," she said.

Dede opened up her door, turned around to face me, hugged herself, and shivered. "Good night, Dolph."

"Dede, I didn't mean what I said about her." I tried to look at Dede's eyes to see what her reaction was, but all I got was an inquisitive look. "I mean, do you ever think that certain things are just bound to happen? That suddenly your life, and what you are, and where you are make sense. That suddenly," I stuttered, "that things are turning out, in a weird sort of way, as they should, for the best."

Dede's mouth sort of hung open. "I don't know about things that are bound to happen. I don't expect anything. I'm working hard enough trying to stay happy with what I have."

"She's special," I said.

"Congratulations, Dolph," Dede said, and walked into her room. I stayed looking in after her as she turned around to stare a moment at me and then shut the door, and then I heard her lock it.

I walked back to Ariel's condo, carefully opened the door, quietly stepped in, climbed up the stairs, and took one quick look out the long picture window at the salt cedars and the tiny silver streak of the Rio Grande. In the bedroom, I started to hop on one foot while I tried to pull my boot off my other foot. "Where did you go?" I heard. I let down my foot and looked toward the bed but couldn't see her in it. Then the upstairs bathroom light came on, and I jerked my head to see her standing in the doorframe of the bathroom, the light from it touching her hair and making her body dark and her nightgown nearly invisible. She ran a hand across the side of her head to brush some of her hair over a shoulder.

I braced myself and smoothly pulled off one boot, but then when I put my foot down, I teetered between my booted foot and the other one. "I went for a beer with Pepper."

She turned out the light to the bathroom and crossed in the dark to the bed, and I watched her form and the silk negligee floating around her. "I thought you had left me," she said as she slid her legs under the bedspread and the sheet.

"Oh, no, no," I said. Stepping out of my jeans, I crawled under the covers with her and held her until she went to sleep.

When I felt her breath on my cheek, I pulled my pinpricked arm out from under her head and rolled away from her to get my own sleep. But before I could, I wondered if my mother or ol' Miguel ever felt like this.

I remembered that my mother had a few "dates" as I was growing up, but I never saw her hug or kiss a man as though she really cared for him. A "gentleman" would hold her hand or her elbow as he helped her up the stairs of our porch, and she might give him a respectful kiss, but I never saw a full, long, passionate, tongue-in-the-mouth kiss. My mother was a businesswoman, or Charles Beeson's daughter, not someone's lover.

When she retired and sold her stores to the discount store chain, after I had already made my move to Presidio, my mother might have tried falling in love. She decided to spend my inheritance and "did" New York and Europe. Somewhere in her travels, she met a man with a Winnebago and a tiny poodle that had been his dead wife's. He came to Brownsville in his Winnebago to see her during the winter when all the snowbirds hit. Maybe, as they walked along the beach at South Padre, maybe even hand in hand in moonlight, he told her about the desert. So when he left, she went with him, not for my desert, here in Presidio, but for the high desert around Santa Fe and then on to Prescott, Arizona.

I imagined Harry driving slowly down desolate southwestern two-lane blacktop with the rest of the retirees in their irritating tanklike mobile homes, pissing off the truckers and salesmen who want only speed, stopping and barely pulling off the road to empty a Porta Potti or to let that stupid poodle, who was probably bounding around and yapping during the whole trip, out to pee-pee. But I couldn't imagine my mother inside that hulking piece of metal with him.

After three months I got a postcard from Prescott, telling me to wire her a ticket for a bus ride home. I drove from Presidio to Prescott in a day to pick her up. Harry answered the door of his Winnebago. "How you do, sport," he said, and tipped his martini at me. He offered me one.

Harry's nervous poodle jumped from his miniature sofa to the sink to the driver's seat of the Winnebago. Finally Charlotte calmed down, growled, then slowly wagged her tail. "Pet her," he said. "That dog is fifteen years old. Has a little bladder problem, but she's a good dog." Charlotte's age showed in the rough patches of raw skin with clumps of hair. The hair that had fallen out was all over the Winnebago. As I held out my hand, she started to growl again. "Not used to young men," Harry said. "Sure you don't want a drink?"

Harry's bowed legs curved outward from his knee-length shorts. His bald head was pink from the desert sun, and his nose was red, I guessed, from the martinis. "Charlotte and I just hit the road after Mama died." I scooted back to the wall of the living-room–kitchen–den and asked about my mother.

My mother appeared from the bathroom, looking younger and even more dignified than I remembered. Her hair, cut short, was in place. She wore shorts that came to midthigh and showed off still shapely legs. Her designer T-shirt bulged a little at her belly, that place where women my age start to puff out. But she didn't look like someone old enough to be my mother.

She smiled when she saw me and said, "Dolph, maybe we better go."

She didn't hug me when she saw me but hugged Harry when she left. She carried her own suitcase out to my car, wouldn't let me take hold of it. As I pulled out of the snowbird trailer park, Harry came out of his Winnebago, spread out his bowed legs, held Charlotte in one hand, and flopped his wrist vigorously to wave goodbye. My mother didn't wave, didn't even look back.

At about Deming, New Mexico, I asked her what had happened. She turned her head to look at me and said, "Things just didn't work out. It was a mistake."

"Did you love him, Mom?" I asked.

"Don't be silly," she said.

During the trip she kept her mouth straight, neither a smile nor a grimace, talked to me about the money in various stock accounts and IRAs, told me the gossip about friends I had grown up with. Before she went to sleep in the motel we stayed at, she pulled neatly folded clothes out of her suitcase and set her outfit for the next day's ride on the motel armchair.

She hung around with Pepper and me for two days. At first I was worried, but she and Pepper got along. Pepper, from his experience with his past wives and his family, knew how to treat dignified, rich ladies. My mother, in turn, knew how to treat Pepper. She encouraged his entrepreneurial spirit when she heard his plans for his resort, went on shopping trips with him to Ojinaga, and asked for Pepper's recipe for his chili. She took a day to ride with me out on duty and met R.C. Then I drove her to Midland, Texas, to catch a flight back to the Rio Grande Valley.

Months later, she called me late one night, crying. She said that she couldn't stop crying. From a letter, very precisely written, she told me she stopped going to her civic meetings and social clubs. A few calls later, I found out that she was talking to a psychotherapist and taking some kind of antidepressant. "Oh, Dolph, have you ever felt bad?" she asked. "My doctor says these depression symptoms are all chemical. And he says they're hereditary." I told her that I was fine.

Ol' Miguel never had somebody like my mother's Harry. He told me about the *putas,* and about the nice legs of so-and-so, or about how he got lucky with so-and-so's cheating wife. But he never talked about a lover. Neither my mother nor father ever married after being married to each other, as though that first brief, intense relation just wore them out. I wondered if either of them after divorcing had the hope of a love (surely not Harry) like I had sleeping next to me, or if they just resigned themselves to what they had made themselves: a businesswoman and a drunk.

I pushed myself up on one elbow and looked at Ariel sleeping, and then I looked at the orange edging the borders of the closed curtain. The sun was coming up. It was a new year.

NIEVE

The day of our nighttime stakeout, we Border Patrol agents, all born and raised in the Southwest, watched the snow.

This snow had come in late afternoon in big, slow-floating flakes that stuck to the spines of the cacti. We stopped watching for wets, stopped tracking for signs, woke from our naps, and put on our heavy coats and went outside. We turned our faces up to the falling flakes and felt them on our lips and tongues. We held out our arms and watched the white designs disintegrate into a wet spot on our nylon coats. Then when the sun went down, the temperature continued to drop as the sky cleared so that the loose, dry flakes didn't melt.

As the group of us sat in the dark, under a clear, cold, star-filled sky, hugging ourselves, flipping the collars of slick coats over the back of our necks, getting used to the strange feel of cotton or leather gloves, we took turns looking into infrared binoculars. We didn't need the binoculars in the silver, white, blue, and black world, but we wanted to see the change the infrared made in the look of the snow.

When we first started the stakeout, at sundown, with the sun making orange and yellow patches in the snow, Pat Coomer had stuck out his tongue to taste the flakes. With the darkness and the oncoming hard freeze, R.C. Kobel just crossed his arms and cussed the cold. Roland Cardeñas tried to scrape enough of the thin layer of snow off some boulder for a snowball. Because it was so dry, it wouldn't make a decent snowball (of course most of us wouldn't know a decent snowball), and he tried to throw it at Dede. Dede shot him a drop-dead look, and R.C. said, "This ain't no goddamn junior high picnic."

Only the Yankee DEA agent, his gold-rimmed glasses fogged over, didn't get excited. He looked at us as though we were children. He acted like he didn't even want to look at a tiny layer of snow resting on the needle of a cholla or prickly pear.

We were planted on the first high rim and waiting for a string of mules to make it up the old Comanche trail to a clearing. We guessed that at this point, the only point where a truck could drive, they'd have somebody coming to pick them up, or if no one came, we'd get them easy.

I had sent Mark Bankston and Louis Parker behind the mules, tracking them from behind and radioing ahead to us when they could get clear of a dead zone. Bankston and Parker hit snow when they got into higher elevation, and the snow they saw, bright and spotted with footprints, made it easy for them. And somewhere, cruising overhead, was a helicopter from the Marfa headquarters. Even R.C. was out this coldest night in memory to be in on the kill.

We had followed a rutted road that the state was bulldozing so that tour buses and Winnebagos could make their way into this remotest part of Big Bend country. Not yet asphalted, the road was now even more rutted and slippery from our trucks. We would probably need four-wheel drive to get back out. Our trucks were parked in a clump of juniper. We had strung flares and sensors in this flat part of the trail. I had chosen the people I wanted to be in on the bust: Pat Comer, who was our best marksman and always good to have behind me; Roland Cardeñas, who liked teasing everybody but was quick to respond to any emergency; Dede Pate, who needed the experience to become a really good agent; and R.C. Kobel, who knew more than all of us and who knew when to shoot. And with Bankston and Parker behind the mules, the helicopter overhead somewhere and shining down a beam, and the rest of us waiting here, we were going to catch them—unless, of course, Colonel Henri Trujillo had lied.

I got my phone call from Trujillo late at night two nights before. I heard him say over the typical Mexican static that the crossing would take place on this night, at a place east and south of Redford but west and north of Lajitas. Like their other groups, they were on foot and would cross over rough country, where fewer people would be looking for them. He didn't know if Fuentes would be with them.

"Look," I had told Trujillo, "I need some more information if I'm going to do this for you."

"Just get Fuentes for me," he said.

"Where are you?"

"Saltillo," he said.

"How do you know they're coming across? Who's your source?"

"Someone trustworthy," he said.

"What is your connection? Who are you really working for? Why didn't you work with the DEA?"

"Trust me," he said.

"Look, meet me again."

"I'm in Saltillo," he said.

"Take another vacation to Big Bend," I said.

"My vacation time is over. Please, Agent Martinez. You remember our agreement? I've lived up to my end of the bargain."

I hated the static in the long-distance phone call. It kept me away from him. I couldn't see his eyes or his hands as he talked, so I couldn't judge him. Whatever the case, I decided to do my job and let whatever was to happen in Mexico simply happen.

I told R.C. "We got to go with it," he said. "And we got to stay legal." That morning we had picked up fresh tracks earlier in the day and guessed it was Trujillo's group. R.C. and I gambled. We didn't go after them right at first. We wanted to let them get farther in so that we could catch whoever was picking them up. So we checked the gates, the crossing, and sent Parker and Bankston up after them. Then it started to snow. Once we had everything set up, we called the DEA agent, and he now stomped the snow with us and stared up the trail.

As I rubbed my hands together and squinted in the silver-blue half-light that the snow created, my stomach tightened as though to anticipate bullets. To loosen the knots in my stomach, I stared into the snow and relaxed. But relaxing was worse than tightness. Somebody could get a drop on you when you were relaxed. So I thought of the wasplike stings of nine-millimeter bullets and suffered through the tightness of my scar. Then I watched the snow again.

Rare as it was, it wasn't the first snow I had seen this year. A few days before, Ariel and I camped out high up in the Chisos at Big Bend Park. We started in late morning from the Chisos Basin Lodge and climbed the trail up toward Emory Peak, got past the last cacti, got past the short pines to the sturdy ponderosa pines. We got nearly as high as you could get in the state of Texas and saw a line of purple-and-orange mountains, beneath us, with snow clouds passing over them. We watched the clouds' shadows move across the hazy desert floor.

Later we saw a cougar. Suddenly he was right beside us. His sides pulsed as he breathed, and his eyes moved to watch us, but his head stayed still. Then he sprang away quickly, but not so quickly that Ariel and I didn't see his muscles contract and then release. "He was just so . . . ," Ariel said.

"Smooth," I said.

"Yes," she said, "had you ever seen one?"

I gambled and said, "I once dreamed I was one." She cocked her head and frowned. My breath becoming vapor, I told her about getting gut shot, and Sister Quinn pulling me out of the canyon, and my clutching the vial. When I had finished, she kissed me. And then she held out her foot and pointed her toes to remind me of the black panther arched over the instep of her left foot.

She had gotten the tattoo in college, a dare, she said. It was fine for a college girl, she told me, but a businesswoman, especially one working for Walter Bean, shouldn't be marked by a tattoo even if an intricate, expensive one.

As the sun went down, we zipped up our parkas, set up the tent, ate dried fruit, and kissed. I borrowed a special set of sleeping bags from Pepper, the kind that could zip together. They were clumsy for hauling around on a hike but romantic for a night with a woman. And I made room in my pack for a bottle of wine. We broke the park rules and consumed the wine by the light of a Sterno and a candle, ate the heated freeze-dried dinner, then watched the snow fall into the pine trees around us.

With the tent flap open, snuggling in the large sleeping bag, I pulled her to me, then I pulled off her clothes. We both had the smell of sweat, we felt each other's greasy hair, and I had stubble on my face, she on her legs. With the cool air and snow blowing into the tent, we were warmed by the sleeping bag but chilled when we pushed a body part out from under it.

After our freeze-dried meal, sex by candlelight on a mountain, snow falling through pine trees, Ariel blew out the candle and closed the flap of the tent. And we both lay on our backs to stare up at the dark top of the tent and felt our bodies, tired and sore from the hike but exhilarated from our lovemaking. "What happened to your husbands?" I asked.

She turned toward me and smiled. "I guess while I was married to them I was more interested in myself than my marriage." We both watched our vaporized breath as we talked.

"Why do you hang out with Sister Quinn?" I asked her, and looked up at the tent and thought that I could hear a soft crackle and see the darkened spot in the nylon when a flake floated onto it.

I felt Ariel's breath and the tip of her nose on my neck when she rolled over to answer me. "Full of questions, aren't you? Is this for your investigation?"

"No, I just don't see why you'd be there. You know, you're from Houston, you're sane."

"I guess I like her." I rolled to her so that I was nose to nose with her, and I kissed her. Then she said, "She's consistent." She turned away from me and looked up as though thinking. "Sister Quinn is just as poor and lonely as anybody she helps."

"Sister Quinn doesn't have to be poor. And she's got plenty of people around her."

"I think she yearns to be around people who are at her own level."

"Level of what?"

Ariel pulled back from me. I could see the outline of her head as she raised one forearm from the elbow and rested her head on her palm. "Intelligence, interests, maybe just something unlike most of the people around here."

"She's dealing with some very bad people."

"Is she in trouble?"

"Yes," I said.

I leaned toward her head to kiss her. I didn't want to stumble into an argument, especially on this night. Ariel reached under the sleeping bag until her hand touched my belly, and she guided a finger down the length of my scar. "I'm sorry," she said. Then, maybe because it was a cold night and I had just talked about weirdness, I told her how my father died.

Ol' Miguel was drunker than usual on one of the coldest nights in the Rio Grande Valley in a decade. It had been years since I had seen him, but I heard that he just got old, his liver gone to hell. On this cold night that did years' worth of damage to the citrus, ol' Miguel tried to stagger home to the shack he then lived in. He must have known that home was somewhere along the irrigation canal in the little barrio where he took me to see the *curandera.* He had a bottle with him, so he sat on the irrigation ditch and took a long drink, or so the police guessed. When he got up and tried to stand in the loose dirt of the ditch, he slipped and rolled backward into the cold, stagnant water. He was lucky he didn't drown. He clawed his way halfway up the ditch and simply passed out. Wet, out in the open, in a place where nobody ever dies of cold, Ol' Miguel froze to death.

When I finished telling the story, Ariel kissed me and rolled her naked body into mine. And we huddled in the cold, kept warm by the sleeping bag, almost the way my fellow agents and I now squatted in the juniper, kept warm by heavy coats we almost never wore, watching the silver-blue darkness, which made the desert look stiff, crystalline almost, as if the cacti needles, the ocotillos, the mesquite branches would snap in the cold.

We heard from Mark Bankston that they were moving toward us. Then in the clear air, we heard the rumble of a car motor. "Oh, boy, more cowboy shit," Pat whispered to me. "Think we'll get to shoot somebody?" He giggled.

The DEA agent pulled off his fogged gold-rimmed glasses to look at Pat. I didn't want to wait with Pat and listen to more of his jokes and watch the DEA agent slowly get pissed off, so I sent Pat crunching through the snow and ice to circle around to our right. I sent Dede and Roland off to my left. I figured that I would most enjoy the wait with R.C.

As R.C. and I watched him slide through the snow, Pat kicked up a covey of quail, and R.C. immediately swung the infrared binoculars up to his face to spot the quail; then he whispered to me, "Boom. At least one of 'em was mine." After we relaxed and Pat moved farther into the stiff, cold darkness, R.C. whispered again, "More quail up here. Better eating than dove."

"More reason to stay?" I whispered back.

"You like quail?" R.C. whispered to the DEA agent.

"Shouldn't we be quiet?" he said.

"If we got nothing to talk about," R.C. said.

Then I saw the silhouette of men in cowboy hats move into our silver-blue, still, cold world. I raised the infrared binoculars to my eyes and counted eight of them, all dressed too lightly for this cold in light jackets and boots, hiking shoes, or tennis shoes. They all had backpacks. Three of them held blankets around themselves and their backpacks and thus looked like they had humps. They picked their way carefully through the frozen desert. No one straggled behind; no one stepped too quickly or hesitated too long to put his foot down. They knew how the lechuguilla could bite them, how a rock could twist their ankles, how dangerous wildlife, even in the snow, could hide behind bushes. Each knew that nothing good could come from being a crippled dope runner in the desert.

"Let's let them get closer," I whispered to R.C. I could almost feel him tense up. I knew he had slipped off his gloves and had raised his rifle up to use his scope to sight the mules. And I heard the slide of metal against leather as the DEA agent slipped his Glock out of his holster.

And then R.C. and I both looked behind us because the rumbling and groaning shocks of an old pickup truck had grown louder. I turned and brought the binoculars to my eyes and saw Gilbert Mendoza's truck bouncing along the state's newly bulldozed road. I had no idea how Sister Quinn planned to get this many mules into the truck. "Who is it?" the DEA agent whispered as though he were annoyed.

"Shh. Shh," R.C. scolded him.

"Damn, R.C.," I whispered to him. "We should have tried to follow her out of here."

"Shh," R.C. said.

"We need to catch the guys she's delivering to," I said, and R.C. just looked at me to tell me to be quiet.

With the snow covering the ground and the rutted road, driving without headlights, Sister Quinn must have had a hard time keeping the pickup on the road and out of a gully. It stopped. A beam of light from the mules came across the desert and lit the withered arms of the ocotillos in gray shades. The beam went out and left the ocotillo, creosote, lechuguilla, and guayacan as dark shapes against a darker sky. Sister Quinn flashed the headlights of Gilbert Mendoza's pickup truck. In her quick flash, I spotted Dede and Roland and hoped that no one else had seen the two of them.

The string of men moved farther on and tripped a flare, and suddenly the desert became a kaleidoscope of red, white, and blues. I slipped off my gloves and flipped on the beam from my large lantern, and the white desert around me lit up. Then crisscrossing beams from Pat's, Dede's, Roland's, R.C.'s, and the DEA's flashlights added more light to the desert. Now the stiff frozen cacti and mesquite seemed to move in the strobe light show.

When a light beam caught him, a mule would freeze, just like a deer. The lights made two eerie worlds: one light, one dark. The lit world was in white, bright enough to see the snow on the ocotillo arms, the dirty, sweat-stained jackets on the mules, their vaporized breath, and the holstered pistols on a few of them. My scar pulled my stomach tighter.

Sister Quinn opened the door of Gilbert Mendoza's truck and stepped out into the dark, the crisscrossing flashlight beams, and the cold. Her tennis hat pushed down on her head, only a light jacket on, she shook her shoulders against the cold, and as she ran, her large breasts and stomach jiggled. "Don't move," Dede yelled. Sister Quinn stood perfectly still as Dede and Roland advanced to her.

But then she ran, as best as a fat woman could, toward the mules, waving her hands as if she were a heavy owl trying to take off. Dede immediately caught up with her, grabbed one of her arms, and tried to pull Sister Quinn down. But the bigger woman drug Dede until Roland jumped on top of her and pulled her down.

"Para y arriba las manos," I yelled, and R.C. said the litany in Spanish and English as we moved out of our brush with our pistols drawn. The wets started to slowly raise their hands, straining against the backpacks, looking around at one another, trying to get a cue from somebody as to what to do, looking for a leader.

"Tira las pistolas," Pat yelled.

"Good work, good work," the DEA agent whispered. I wiggled my fingers around to keep them warm while I held my pistol and my flashlight. I found the guy who didn't seem nervous, who didn't look for orders. If he wasn't yet, he'd soon be the leader, and I kept my flashlight beam and my pistol on him. All of us started to circle the group caught by the light. Dede was soon beside me, and Roland was beside her and dragging Sister Quinn behind him.

Sister Quinn yelled, "These people have done nothing but been born on the wrong side of an artificial line."

"Shut up," I yelled at her. I wanted everyone to be able to hear my orders. The mules started babbling, and then we all barked orders at them. Throw down your guns, put up your hands. They got the idea. Very slowly, gingerly, the man I lighted, the leader, bent over and laid his rifle on the ground.

R.C., the DEA agent, Roland, and then Pat walked into the group and pushed them away from their guns. They made them take off the packs and then begin to frisk them. Dede led Sister Quinn toward me. "Good job," I told Dede.

"Let us go, Dolph," Sister Quinn yelled at me. "Or keep me, but let them go on."

Sister Quinn was putting everybody in danger. "Can't you see," I said. "See the goddamn guns that they're dropping."

As soon as I said the words, though, I swung my flashlight and my eyes back toward the group. The DEA agent went up to one of the mules, unzipped his jacket, and pulled out his shirttail. The mule looked like he was going to spit on the man pulling off his clothes. But when the DEA agent lifted up the shirttail and saw nothing taped to the man's belly, his smile dropped, and the mule's smile stretched his mouth.

Then the DEA agent turned to one of the backpacks and unbuckled a flap and reached in. He pulled out an Uzi. He reached in again and came out with a plastic Baggie, full of pills—not powder. Again he pulled out a Baggie full of capsulelike pills. He looked up like he was stumped. "They're pharmacists," Dede said.

"Take it easy," Sister Quinn yelled out to the group.

Then the DEA agent slowly started to smile as he figured out what he was finding. He went to another backpack and pulled out plastic-wrapped clumps of pills. His smile spread, and he held up two handfuls of pills so that we could all see what we had caught.

"Medical supplies," Sister Quinn said. And Dede giggled at her.

We had all let Sister Quinn and the DEA agent take our attention. Before we could frisk the rest, Roland started shouting, "A gun. One's got a gun."

Flashlights went out. The only light was from the few flares still burning and the moon and stars. R.C. dove to the ground, and the DEA agent and Roland also hit the ground. But I stayed where I was and shifted my beam from one mule to the next, hoping to catch sight of the man with the gun. "Get down, Dede," I yelled. I thought and then yelled again, "Get down, Barbara."

As I lighted one mule then the next, each holding his hands up in my beam, Pat was suddenly standing at my side, his rifle raised and his aim following my light. "Don't be stupid, Dolph," I heard R.C.

yell. But I stayed standing. Though I anticipated the wasp stings hitting me again and the final teeth-clenching shot and though I was sweating, the sweat turning cold as soon as it left my pores, I knew that I could do this and could take the wait.

My flashlight caught movement, and Pat yelled, "There." His rifle immediately leveled. The mule stepped out of my beam of light. *"Para, para,"* Pat and I yelled. I found him again with my beam and saw him jumping over low brush. "What else can I do?" I heard Pat whisper. "Give me an order."

"Go on," the DEA agent yelled.

We were to fire only when our, another agent's, or a wet's life was in danger. And even then we were to be sure that we had no other recourse. "Shoot," I said.

Just as Pat fired, Sister Quinn lunged for the barrel of his rifle. But I got my foot in between hers and my elbow in her chest and knocked her backward. Pat's rifle and Sister Quinn's fall thudded at the same time. I hoped that the snow softened her fall.

"I think I got a piece of him," Pat said.

The flashlight beams came back on and added to the light of the still burning flares. R.C. ran to the point where the mule bolted and shined his flashlight on the ground. "Got some blood," he yelled back. The rest of the mules put their hands behind them and waited to be cuffed.

I knelt beside Dede, who sat on Sister Quinn. "Are you all right?" I said to Dede. I didn't want to talk to Sister Quinn.

"Your uniforms make you like fascists all over the world," Sister Quinn said toward Dede and Pat.

Pat stepped up to her. He couldn't help himself. "And you a nun. Shame, shame, shame."

"These are the poor and the dispossessed. They are political prisoners. Anytime you see evil and do not oppose that evil, you aid evil."

"Jesus," Pat said. "When you going to stop that kind of preaching, *curandera?* What's next? *Santería?* Gonna start nailing goat skulls to your *templo?*"

"Because I minister to the people, because I give them faith and aid their faith, you call me a *curandera.* Faith cures, not the form the cure takes." She started to babble and scream: "Greasewood tea can cure constipation. Doctors and scientists now say what the locals and Indians have known for centuries: aloe vera could cure nearly anything. Lechuguilla has cortisone in it. Guayacan relieves rheumatism. Who knows when mind and matter meet. Faith, faith is the answer."

"What do you want to do?" Dede asked me while Sister Quinn preached.

I knelt beside Dede and grabbed the fleshy part of Sister Quinn's arm. "Shut up," I yelled, louder than her. She stopped the sermon. "I guess the first arrest didn't take," I said to her. "Get her up," I said to Dede. Pat came over to help.

"You, you . . . ," Sister Quinn stumbled, trying to call Pat something. "These are people, not some kind of big game."

"The son of a bitch shoulda known better," Pat said to her.

R.C., the DEA agent, and Roland begin leading the handcuffed mules in single file toward us. R.C. stopped by me. He looked down at Sister Quinn and then at Pat. "Good shot," he said. "He'll be easy enough to find in the morning, Dolph. My recommendation is that we don't go stumbling around in the dark. Somebody'd fall off a cliff, get stung or bit. And with any light, we'd make a good target for him. Better to wait until daylight."

I nodded. Sister Quinn, still lying prone, Dede still on top of her, said, "I'll look for him if you're too scared to. You owe it to him now that you shot him."

R.C. said, "Bring her to the car and read her her rights." He walked toward the parked trucks.

I again grabbed her bicep and, with Dede and Pat's help, tried to pull her up, but we got her only into a sitting position. "Goddamn it. Nun or not, get your ass moving," I said.

"We've got to go after him," Sister Quinn said.

"Don't make me use cuffs this time," I said. "That man ran—"

"Because he was scared," Sister Quinn interrupted.

"He ran because he was carrying dope," Coomer said. "Somebody on one side of the border or the other will eventually kill him."

Sister Quinn grunted and pulled her arm out of my grip. "He was a Salvadoran refugee. That is why he ran. That is why I am here to pick him up. You shot a political refugee."

Pat finally circled around her and grabbed her feet. With Dede and I each on an arm, we were able to hoist her. But she started to squirm, and Dede almost lost her grip. "Damn you. Damn you," Pat said. "I ought to just let you drop and let you break your fat ass." She twisted, and Pat Coomer did let go of her feet. Then I let go, and again she fell onto the sharp rocks of the desert floor, only slightly cushioned by the snow. She gasped when she hit the ground and lost most of her breath. As we bent over to drag her to her feet, she grunted as she tried to breathe.

"No more fucking around," I said. "Like us or not, we are the law, and we're not obliged to let ourselves be treated like this. And I'm tired of standing in the cold messing with you."

I started walking toward the parked trucks. Pat whispered to Dede, "Pretty cool, huh?" and followed me. Then Dede followed me. Then Sister Quinn walked up to us to let herself be handcuffed.

The man I guessed to be the leader looked up from the others and straight at me. At last, I thought, one who didn't duck his head, a real criminal. "*Cómo está* Vincent Fuentes?" I asked him.

"Qúe?"

"*'On' 'ta* Vincent Fuentes?" I shouted so that they could all hear me. Then, with the dust jacket picture in my mind, I looked at all of their faces but could spot no one with his black hair forming a cowlick in the front of his head, the pale skin, the bright eyes.

"We going to have quite a crowd here," R.C. said.

"Yeah," I said, and stared at the Mexicans, hoping to dare someone into telling me about Fuentes.

"*Dónde está* Vincent Fuentes?" I shouted again.

Together with R.C. Kobel, I broke more policy. We barely had enough room to transport all our prisoners. Sister Quinn wouldn't hear of leaving with a wounded man out in a freezing desert. So Pat

Coomer and I waited in our truck for the night to pass and to begin our search for the runaway. And since she did have some medical training back when, maybe even because she could perform some voodoo, Sister Quinn waited with us. We made her sign the release vouchers and made her promise to go peacefully to jail with us. The rules were bent, but we couldn't imagine any trouble.

I curled myself into a ball in the driver's seat and pulled the collar of my coat up around my neck. Pat huddled in the passenger side, and Sister Quinn lay across the backseat. Pat and I kept a thermos of hot coffee in between us and passed foam cups of our coffee back to Sister Quinn. We all tried to sleep, but we woke up because of the cramping, the coffee, the wind whistling outside, the cold that finally got to us, or the chattering of Sister Quinn's teeth. She wore only a light jacket and so tried to curl up in the dirty wool blanket we had stashed in the back. Asleep or awake, she couldn't control the muscles in her jaw.

A cramp at the base of my neck woke me up, and I glanced at Pat, who was also awake and staring blankly out into the black-and-white, snow-filled desert world. I turned to look at Sister Quinn. She was moving under the blanket. She reached up and rubbed a smear in the vapor on the window nearest to her and looked into the desert. Then as she peered out, she ran her rosary through her fingers and silently prayed. For all I knew, she might also have had some charm in her pocket, a white handkerchief, a vial of silver-blue liquid, or a picture of Pedrito Jarmillo. "Wish we had something to sweeten that coffee," Coomer mumbled.

"Against regulation," I said, "but on a night like this . . ." I twisted to see the dark shape of Pat's grinning face.

"Keep you warm, man," Coomer said.

"That's a myth. Alcohol hastens freezing," Sister Quinn said from the backseat.

"Yeah, well, it makes me feel better," Coomer said.

"I'd settle for a pillow," I said, and looked back at Sister Quinn. "How do you feel? Have you slept?"

"I sleep in spurts."

"Any pain from when we dropped you?"

"This is just discomfort, not pain. Pain can cleanse. It is pure. It can give a person some idea of the quiet universal suffering of the underclasses of the world. Suffering is far greater than pain. It is like sorrow."

Pat mumbled, "Shit," and I could tell that he rolled his eyes. "Let's shoot her," he said loud enough so that she could hear.

"I've heard your sermon," I said, and looked at Pat, whose teeth caught some of the sparse light. "I was there Christmas Eve."

"You should have listened harder." She lay back down and wiggled under the blanket, but she kept talking. "When you were shot and first felt the bullets, didn't you feel as though you experienced something of the pain of all mankind?"

"I felt like a wasp stung me," I said, and peered at the lump in the back of our truck.

"Okay, right," she said, and rose from the seat and pulled an arm out of her blanket to point a finger at me. "And that pain was a pure feeling, nothing else, either physically or emotionally. It took all your thought, all your concentration."

"I was shot in the gut," I said.

"Right," she said. "That wound only approximates the dismal suffering of two-thirds of the world's people. Because we are white in a white man's land and privileged, all that we can know of the suffering of being dark, disenfranchised, and poor is pain."

I looked over at Pat and saw him hold his nose, then stick his forefinger into his open mouth like he was gagging himself, so I interrupted. "So why don't you stick your fingers in candles instead of doing this? I've arrested you twice. A judge put you on probation. And I know that the bishop in El Paso has told you to stop."

"Because these people need someone to help them. It is not our right to judge them. Pain helps us identify, but we must not just suffer, we must help."

Pat couldn't control himself. He swiveled around to look back at her. "You're not helping them. They don't need you or want you.

Dolph and me have been here almost as long as you, and still we're outsiders, same as you."

"Come to my church and see for yourself if I am not accepted."

"I'm a goddamn Catholic too, you know," Pat said. "Your *'templo'* isn't a church. It's got nothing to do with any Catholic Church I ever knew about."

"It's the people's church."

"No, it's your church. The bishop himself would as soon it closed down," Pat said.

"I'd rather answer to God and that part of him that is in me than to the bishop."

"Maybe you are some witch doctor. Go to sleep," Coomer said, and slumped into his seat. "God in you. Shit," Coomer mumbled.

I looked back at Sister Quinn and then at Pat. When his anger left him, as it usually did, and I heard him snore, I whispered into the backseat, "These are drug dealers, Barbara. Not refugees."

I saw her vapor breath rise from her mouth just as she spoke. "Sometimes they are the same. Maybe they were forced into this."

I bounced my fist off the back of the seat. "Fuentes is going to get you excommunicated."

"He was excommunicated himself."

"You trust him?"

"Yes."

"Where is he?"

"With the poor."

"He's a criminal."

"To the real criminals, he is a criminal."

"You once helped me. Now let me help you."

"Then help the people whom you arrest."

I put my head back against the back of the seat.

"Ariel is a nice girl," Sister Quinn said. "And very pretty. She has talked about you." It was funny, I never thought of Ariel as a "girl." She couldn't have been much older than Dede.

I looked in the back, and because I was a Border Patrol agent and had forced my eyes to see in the dark and because the white snow reflected the night light, I saw Sister Quinn smile, but I didn't know if she was mocking me or was happy for me.

When the sun first came out, I woke and rubbed the vapor and frost off my side of the windshield. I squinted and looked at the melting snow that looked like the ice that freezes on the top of sitting water; it made the desert look like a sneeze could shatter the cacti, rocks, and cliffs. The normal tan of the desert reflected the sun strongly enough, but this inch-deep white layer made the sun blinding. Just like the desert, the snow in it was both harsh and as delicate. Like the tiny fish in the desert oasis, most of the desert's plants and animals, maybe even the rocks, tough as they are, mean as they look, as dangerous as they are, couldn't survive anywhere else.

I looked into the backseat and saw that Sister Quinn was also squinting into the white brightness, maybe thinking, the same as me, about the desert. Maybe she'd start flapping her arms and fly out of the truck and across the desert. "It's beautiful, isn't it?" she said to me.

"What it is is damn cold," Pat said to interrupt us. He too rubbed his window and gazed out into the white desert. "Fucking snow," he said, and then looked away from it to me. "Let's go get that *cabrón*."

I started the truck and moved slowly into the white desert.

"What I wouldn't give for some *huevos* and a cup of coffee," Pat said as he reached down to turn on the heat.

I drove as far as we could, the truck crunching the snow, spoiling it, bouncing over the rocks and screeching as cacti and creosote scratched the paint off its sides. The wet left tracks in the snow and tiny but visible dots of blood. Eventually he started going up. We would have to follow on foot.

As I stepped out of the truck, the reflected sun hit me, and I heard the crunch of my foot in snow, and I lifted my foot to look at how its impression had ruined the delicateness. Sister Quinn also started to climb out of the truck. "Whoa," Pat said. "Where do you think you're going?"

"With you," Sister Quinn said as she stared down at the snow, hugged herself, and stamped her feet, leaving a mushy blob of sand and snow underneath her.

"You're waiting in the truck," Pat said, and jerked his head back toward the truck.

"I can help," Sister Quinn said.

"How?"

"Let her go," I said, knowing that we'd have to handcuff her to get her to stay behind.

"It's against regulations." Pat smiled, and I just shook my head.

"Let up on her," I said.

Pat looked at me like I was a fool, and Sister Quinn walked to a small cholla. She got down on her hands and knees and squinted at the furry spines that covered the cholla. Pat and I walked up behind her. Pat said, "Are you praying? You praying to rocks now, *curandera?*"

She looked at me when she answered. "In a way, I am."

"Loco en la cabeza," Pat said.

"Let's go, Sister Quinn," I said. She slowly pushed herself up and wiped at the dirt on her knees with her flat palms.

"It's snow," Pat said. "You're a Yankee. You've seen it."

Pat and I walked ahead of Sister Quinn, leaving tracks in the snow, while she waddled behind us, putting her hands on her knees to brace herself as she climbed.

The bright spots of blood on snow got brighter and closer together. Though our feet slipped, Pat and I started to run. I looked behind me and saw fat Sister Quinn plodding behind us. "Plodding" was her style in everything.

The footprints and red dots led behind a large boulder with tiny, frosted prickly pear growing out of dirt-filled indentations.

Pat saw the frozen body first. "When the snow melts, the buzzards'll come out," he said.

The face and exposed hands were blue. Dried, nearly black, flaky blood with red speckles in it made a jagged hole on one thigh. The black blood ruined the seamless white snow under and around the body. Through the jeans, we saw that the wound itself, gushing blood until the end, was still pink; the skin around the hole had not yet frozen.

I watched as Sister Quinn bent closer, and both of us saw that the wrecked, dead mule was a woman. Her two arms twisted up, like an ocotillo's branches, as though her last thought was to reach for help.

I had almost died, but still I couldn't account for what you think, for the dreams dying gives you. Who knows, maybe this woman saw some kind of god. Maybe she had a *curandera's* vial like I had, maybe she gave in to the Indian genes in her *mestiza* blood and prayed to the rocks and cacti, or maybe she saw the Indians' trickster god become some animal and then dance in front of her. Maybe she thought she could become a puma or a lizard. Then, with no Sister Quinn to pull her to a radio, she just died. Sister Quinn crossed herself and wiped at her tears. "You've just added to the misery in the world," she said up toward us.

I bent over the body, unzipped the woman's jacket, and yanked her shirt up over her blue belly and stiff, naked breasts. She had no package taped to her belly. "Just thought I'd check," I said toward Sister Quinn.

"You have no compassion," Sister Quinn started again. "Have you forgotten what it's like to be poor? How do you forget that you're Mexican?"

"Compassion? Mexican? My father named me *Adolf.* My mother's half-German. Hell, I'm a Nazi. And I don't believe in all that shit and magic cures and evil spirits."

"How does it feel to be raped?" Pat asked her.

I started again. "Fuentes has just been using you. Now how do *you* feel? Why do you do it?"

Sister Quinn didn't answer me. She knelt by the woman's body and prayed. Who knows if she prayed to the Catholic God or her own weird demons?

We drug the stiff, rigid body through the snow. It slid easily and left a wide track of spoiled snow behind it.

Pat and I had trouble lifting the frozen body and positioning it into the back of the truck. Sister Quinn cried. As we drove back, Sister Quinn stared over her shoulder at the body. The truck warmed up. And we all heard the stiff arm thud against the floor when it thawed and fell.

OCOTILLO

Sister Quinn sat on the edge of her bunk in one of the drafty, cinder block Presidio County Jail cells while Chief Deputy Sheriff Raul Flores, the DEA agent, and Pat Coomer begged, then threatened her. She kept her chin poking firmly in front of her and either laughed at their comments or twisted them around.

"Maybe you don't read the papers," Pat said, "but six illegals died in a boxcar just outside of El Paso. That's the kind of people you're dealing with. They're scum."

We had taken the mules to the Border Patrol holding cells in Marfa, but because she was a citizen and because the US government needed the help of a DA to prosecute her, we drove Sister Quinn to the county jail. R.C. had called Raul Flores the night before and gotten him out of bed. Pissed as hell that we didn't invite him to the bust, he drove to Marfa to meet us and get some credit. Raul didn't call the Presidio County sheriff, Abe Rincón, and get him out of bed because he knew that Abe, who after all was the one who had to get elected, would also be pissed that he wasn't in on the bust.

The DEA agent took off his gold-rimmed glasses and said, "This is a federal case. You can do some serious time." When she didn't say anything to him, he looked at me as though her silence were my fault, like I was in on this with her. I shifted my weight from one foot to the other, then folded my arms, stepped away from the others, and leaned against the bars of Sister Quinn's cell.

Raul tried the "good cop" approach. He knelt in front of her and put his hands on her knees. "I understand; I'm a Chicano. I know what these people face." She shifted her eyes away from him in the middle of his sentence to look at me and smile. Unable to fight my own smile, I turned my head away from her.

When Raul was through, Pat asked her, "Do you really turn yourself into a *tecolote* and fly around at night?"

"And I perch on the tombstones of the recent dead to scare off evil spirits. I've heard the stories too," Sister Quinn said, and folded her arms across her large breasts.

Pat said, "You can go ahead and cook yourself." In that moment of silence, when no one could think of anything else to say, we all knew that Sister Quinn had won. Pat added, "You gonna end up in hell," and he held the cell door open as the others left.

I hadn't asked my questions, so I stepped into the cell before Pat could close the jail cell door. The others looked at me, and then, as if to say, "What the hell," they left the cell door open and walked out of the cell block, leaving me alone with Sister Quinn. Sister Quinn patted the bunk for me to sit. I sat beside her.

"Where is Vincent Fuentes?" I blurted right out. "You saw what his people were doing. They're professionals; they'll go back and smuggle more drugs. They are not poor." She hung down her head and then looked up at me. Sister Quinn's ringlets of red hair stuck out from under her tennis hat. She had lines of sweat in the folds of her body, some old salty stains, long dried, others newly wet. Sitting so close to her, I could smell her too. "Maybe he has lost his sense of right and wrong," I said.

"We have helped Nicaraguans and Salvadorans into the United States. We found people decent lives."

"But not this group."

"What does it matter to a *pelado* in Mexico if Americans have a taste for dope?"

"Be careful, Barbara. If you eat with the devil, you better use a long spoon."

She leaned away from me to look at me squarely. "Are you so sure that he's the devil?"

"You're an educated woman. You know religion. You know the law. You have so much. Why do you do it?"

"Why do you do it?" She looked at me and spread out her hands. "Why do you arrest people for doing what they have to, for merely trying to survive? If these were Russians, you would be welcoming them in."

I didn't want to hear another sermon, and I knew that she was about to slip into one. "Prove me wrong," I said. "Tell me who is receiving the drugs. Surely they're not as holy as Fuentes." She rolled her head away from me. "Okay, just tell where you planned to take these people."

Sister Quinn let out a slight groan as she leaned her back into the damp cinder blocks of the jail wall. "What would you do to prove me wrong, Dolph?"

"What do you want me to do?"

She put her hand on my knee. "Let yourself go, feel the suffering of these people. And if you can feel the suffering, as you felt when you were shot, and you can still believe that Fuentes is wrong, then I'll cooperate."

"Are you talking about sticking my hand in some candle?" I asked. Her smile didn't come back. She shifted her eyes like she was disgusted with me. I looked around and then confessed, "I wish I could get rid of these 'feelings' or dreams you gave me."

She cocked her head. "Perhaps they are grace," she said.

Before I could get her to explain, the door to the cell block creaked, and Raul Flores brought Father Jesse Guzmán into the cell block. I stood while the deputy sheriff walked the priest through the open door and into the cell.

Father Jesse Guzmán, from Saint Margaret Mary's, Presidio's modern, cinder block and tin church, nodded to me and shook my hand. Then he turned his attention to Sister Quinn. "I got a call from the bishop," he said, then looked over at me.

"I'd like to hear this," I said.

"Hell, I don't," Raul said, and walked back out of the cell and out of the cell block.

"Please, Agent Martinez," Father Guzmán said.

Sister Quinn darted her eyes between us, then let them settle on me. "I have nothing to hide from Dolph," she told Father Guzmán.

Father Guzmán tried to grow a beard to look older. But he had only a few scraggly hairs on his chin and a thin mustache. Further, his lean body from jogging made him look younger. In this part of the world a priest needed heft, like Sister Quinn's, to have authority; otherwise the winds we get might blow him away. He wore a down jacket over a sweatshirt, jeans, and boots. His flat nose was just two nostrils coming out of a face, like a black man's, except for the upturned point; it wouldn't support a pair of glasses, so his glasses fell and rested just above the point.

Once a month, early on Sunday morning, starting before the sun came up, he drove the Saint Margaret Mary's bus to Sister Quinn's chapel and took her and some of her people to mass at his church.

Father Guzmán hunched his shoulders, paced the cell, and said, "It's cold in here." He looked at the moisture stains in the cinder blocks. He put his hand out and pressed it against the wall to feel the cold stone.

"It's colder in my church, Father." Sister Quinn giggled. "You should come by some night and see how over three-fourths of the world shivers or sweats."

Father Guzmán looked around for a chair but saw none. Sister Quinn scooted across the rickety bunk, and I heard it groan from her weight. She patted the mattress next to her, but Father Guzmán sat on the toilet. "You haven't stopped these cures, this hocus-pocus, these half-pagan rites." I remained standing, backed away from them, and pressed my back against the bars of the cell and muttered just loud enough so that they both could hear me, *"Brujería."* They paused but neither looked at me.

"Well, not this time," Father Guzmán said, and pushed his glasses a little farther up his nose with his thumb. Sister Quinn looked up at me, and I had to bite down to stop my laugh. I wanted to tell her that I had told her so, and then I wondered if I could come up with the bail because she didn't deserve to spend a month or more in this jail waiting for a trial. "Even the archbishop told you to stop," Father Guzmán said, rested his elbows on his knees, and looked at the ground.

"Did he or the bishop ever stop to wonder if what I do helps these people? Isn't the Marianist order devoted to healing and teaching?"

Like me, Father Guzmán sensed the start of a long sermon. So he pushed his glasses farther up his flat nose and interrupted her without answering her question. "What you are doing is against all Church doctrine."

"You know these people. You know what they believe. And . . ." Sister Quinn paused and forced Father Guzmán to look up at her. She smiled. Loony as she was, she could con people with just her smile and her voice. "And you know what I believe."

Father Guzmán dropped his head to look back at the ground. "No, I used to know what you believed. Now I don't. My parishioners refer to your chapel as a *'templo.'* They talk about your *'oraciones.'* I've heard the word *curandera.* I can no longer defend you."

Sister Quinn put her hands on her knees and strained to get up from the bunk. She waved her hands as she spoke. "The people call my church a *templo.* So what? It is their church. And I teach about the same God that you do."

Father Guzmán rose off the toilet and slammed his right fist into his left palm, once then twice, then he shook his finger at Sister Quinn as though scolding her. "But it makes them and the bishop think that you practice *curandos.*"

Sister Quinn looked at the end of his finger and smiled. Father Guzmán curled his finger back into his fist. "What if I were practicing? What would it hurt?" Sister Quinn asked.

Father Guzmán shouted, "It is superstition and magic."

"Atheists think Christianity is superstition and magic," Sister Quinn said.

"Now you side with atheists," Father Guzmán said quietly, and hung his head. He bent over to whisper to Sister Quinn. I thought that his glasses would fall off onto her lap. "It is preying on these poor people's ignorance. You exploit them as much as the coyotes."

"I've never taught them about any miracles except our Lord's ascension. And I've never sold them any cures. Better they come to me than to the *curanderos* in Presidio or Ojinaga."

"But you do take donations to your *templo,*" I interrupted, "if someone wants to repay you, just like a *real curandera.*" Father Guzmán looked at me for a moment.

"Just like an *honest curandera,*" Sister Quinn said.

Father Guzmán straightened up, turned his back to Sister Quinn, snuck a glance at me, and this time tried to straighten out his glasses by tugging on the arms. "Okay, so you are not a *curandera.* You just don't discourage some unfortunate rumors. But now a second arrest for breaking the law." He turned to face Sister Quinn. "We are still Americans. The Church can no longer defend you."

You could see in her face that she was sure she could defeat him. "A rabbi once told me that in America, even Jews are Protestants. Father Guzmán, you are Mexican and Catholic at birth. Have you become another American Protestant?"

He turned to look at her, and his eyes showed his confusion. The poor bastard, with his jogging shoes, clumsy beard, and blend of Catholicism and self-help, was not at all suited to be Sister Quinn's inquisitor. I had been doing a better job. He cocked his head as though trying to understand her. "You're smiling at me." Sister Quinn nodded.

"Don't laugh, Sister Quinn," he said, then dropped his eyes so that he wouldn't have to look at her. "Excommunication proceedings have been started."

"By whom?" Sister Quinn asked, and smiled.

Father Guzmán tried to look her in the eye. He muttered, "The bishop, and he has written to the archbishop. And the archbishop agrees." Father Guzmán held his hands in front of him as if to beg her to give him the proper dignity and this affair the proper severity. Sister Quinn stared at her toes.

"Very well," Sister Quinn said.

Father Guzmán nodded. "Very well, then. You must first stop your practices and move into Presidio. We will then try to find a lawyer."

"No, no." Sister Quinn chuckled. "I will go on without the Church if need be."

Father Guzmán's shoulders dropped. He waited, then to his credit found some humor. "Sister Quinn, you should have been a Marxist rather than a Catholic." Sister Quinn giggled and patted him on the shoulder. He would have been a good priest in some quiet suburban parish.

Then the door to the cell block opened again and Raul walked in. "Okay, you got bail," he said.

"Who?" Father Guzmán and I asked at the same time.

But the deputy sheriff didn't answer. He walked to the cell, opened it, and then gently took Sister Quinn's elbow to lead her out from the cell. Father Guzmán and I followed them into the booking room of the jail, and I saw Ariel Alves waiting for the prisoner. Pat Coomer leered at her. The DEA agent cocked his head and squinted through his gold-framed glasses to look at her. And Father Guzmán took off his round glasses and cleaned the lenses with his sweatshirt.

I walked past Sister Quinn and up to Ariel and muttered, "Where did you get the money?"

"Walter Bean pays me well," Ariel said, and raised her chin so that she was taller than everybody.

"Why?" I asked.

"Who else would have?" Ariel said, and Sister Quinn smiled and walked up to her rescuer.

I didn't talk to Ariel when she led Sister Quinn out of the Presidio County jail. Sister Quinn jammed herself into the front seat of Ariel's red Mustang and looked out the window at the jail. So far, Ariel had been separate from this, but now Sister Quinn had contaminated her.

The DEA agent stepped out onto the porch of the jail and watched with me as Ariel pulled away in her Mustang. "Now why the hell would she put up that kind of money?" I didn't answer the DEA agent; instead I watched as the Mustang pulled through another wonder for this part of the world: muddy slush from melted snow. Then I watched as Father Guzmán jumped off the porch of the police station, walked briskly to the Saint Margaret Mary's van, and drove away.

During the sixty miles back to Presidio from the county seat in Marfa, I slumped forward in the seat of the truck. I tried to stay awake by humming to myself or listening to the static on the radio. The long shadows of afternoon made parts of the road dark and kept some of the snow from melting. What had melted covered the highway with a thin layer of water, and I hoped that layer wouldn't refreeze. The hard freeze had won for a while but was now gone, as though the needles of the cacti had finally punctured the thin skin of snow so that this storm's life just fizzled out.

In the warm truck, I slipped off my jacket and filled up the cab with my own rancid smell. Despite the cold, I had been sweating into my clothes for two days, so that now my uniform was stiff under my arms, across my chest and back, and in the crotch of my pants. Then the thought of a hot bath at Pepper's resort and a cold beer followed by a shot of tequila nearly put me to sleep again.

But tired as I was, as I pulled into Presidio, I drove through town, on past Redford, then down the steep farm road that ran through the Alamendarizes' fields, and finally to Sister Quinn's *templo.* As I neared the parking lot, I saw Ariel's red Mustang next to Gilbert Mendoza's pickup; we had called Gilbert to pick it up, and even after her arrest, he must have already returned it to her.

I turned off my headlights and pulled off the road. I got out of the truck and stepped into the damp gravel and sand that sucked at the bottom of my boots as I crept through the dark shapes of mesquite, ocotillo, and yucca toward the *templo.* A light was on in Sister Quinn's shack, but then it went off, and a dim light came on in the *templo.* Yes, I was sneaking up on Sister Quinn and Ariel. At first, when I pulled onto her road, I didn't know what I was going to do, but when I saw the red Mustang, I wanted to catch them unguarded because I knew Sister Quinn would give me no explanation, because I didn't want to confront Ariel, and because I was investigating a case.

Watching where I put my feet in the clear, starlit night, the mud sucking at my boots, I crept to one window of the *templo.* The shutters inside the window were closed, but I pressed my face against the screen and stared into the seam of light coming from the crack made by the poorly fitting shutter doors. The *templo* was filled with yellow light and black shadows, and as I adjusted my eyes, the shapes at the front of the *templo* by the altar became Sister Quinn, Ariel, and Azul. Azul cried.

I put my ear against the screen and tried to hear but could make out only a low rumble. I pressed my face harder into the screen until I bent the screen into the glass of the window. I heard no more, so I pulled back, pushed my nose into the screen, and saw Sister Quinn stroke Ariel's golden hair and look at her face. Ariel looked puzzled.

Sister Quinn shifted her gaze from Ariel to Azul and spoke softly to him, and he breathed hard to stop sniveling and walked through the door back to the shack. The two women whispered. Sister Quinn seemed to be pleading with Ariel and touched her shoulder and hair. Ariel stepped back from her, then Sister Quinn stepped up to her to plead some more. Then Ariel held her ground, raised her long fingers in front of her face, and wriggled them as she began her argument.

Azul came back into the room carrying a dried ocotillo branch. He had started crying again, and I could tell by the shape of his mouth that he said, "No." Sister Quinn smiled at him, patted his head, and took the ocotillo branch from him and pointed toward the door into the shack. Azul backed slowly toward it, then turned from the two women and hurried to the shack.

Sister Quinn handed the ocotillo branch to Ariel. Ariel's mouth made an *O,* and she dropped the ocotillo branch, raised her hands to her face, and screamed loud enough so that even I could hear, "No." Sister Quinn smiled, gently picked up the ocotillo branch, and handed it to Ariel. Then Sister Quinn undid the buttons of her white blouse and knelt by the altar so that half of her was out of my sight. But I did see her lower her blouse down below her shoulders, showing a back so white it gleamed. Ariel began to shake.

I cocked my head and twisted it at every angle to try to see Sister

Quinn. My mind conjured images from men's magazines or dirty movies or pictures across the border of lesbian couples. "They're queer?" I dumbly muttered to myself as though I had now answered the DEA agent's question. Then I felt ashamed of myself for having somehow betrayed Ariel, a woman I could now dream about at night instead of lizards crawling through the desert or pumas chasing prey.

Then Ariel pulled back the ocotillo branch and lightly swung it forward. She gasped. She shook her head, but Sister Quinn must have pleaded, so she pulled the ocotillo branch back again, and this time I caught sight of the long shadows on the wall of Ariel's batter's stance and Sister Quinn's bare back, and I saw the shadow of the ocotillo strike into the shadow of Sister Quinn's back. And I felt more embarrassed for even imagining the simplistic answer to the tough question about what these women were doing. And then I wished that some kind of subdued, feminine titty fondling were the answer.

I shifted my eyes to see Ariel rear back with the twisted bat and swing it. My eyes swung with the ocotillo and saw it slam into the white sliver that was Sister Quinn's back. Three pink welts rose on the part of Sister Quinn's back that I could see. Then I heard Sister Quinn's voice shout, "Harder, harder."

I shifted my eyes to see Ariel, and I could see by the way the light reflected off her cheeks and could hear by the tremor in her voice as she screamed, "No, no, no," that she was crying.

And then again, as I pressed my ear against the screen and it against the window, I heard Sister Quinn say in a loud voice that at once was commanding yet gentle, "You aren't swinging any harder than Azul."

"Please," Ariel screamed, and threw down the ocotillo branch.

"I want the pain," Sister Quinn yelled, and was quickly up and beside Ariel, and again she bent to the ocotillo branch, gently grabbed it, and simply held it front of Ariel. By the shape of her lips, by the slight hiss I heard, I knew that she whispered, "Please," to Ariel.

Ariel took the ocotillo branch. Tears streamed down her face now and splattered on her breast, and I could tell that she formed the words, "Goddamn you," and this time she showed that she had played softball sometime in her life because of her smooth, hard swing. Sister Quinn was knocked forward by the blow.

Kneeling by the altar, Sister Quinn must have looked at the tortured face of Christ in the crucifix and the picture of the Virgin. From my vantage point, I couldn't see Christ and the saint, but if I shifted my eyes toward the back of the *templo,* I could see the photo of Pedrito Jarmillo. His eyes smiled. And when I shifted my eyes back to the shadow of Ariel swinging the club into the shadow of Sister Quinn's back, I knew that after the hard whack, Sister Quinn smiled and imagined herself flying through the night to a tombstone. "Harder," I heard, and the shadow of Ariel took two quick, hard strikes, missing the ball but contacting with Sister Quinn's back. In a way, Sister Quinn was right: pain was pure; with pain, you dealt only with it, no right or wrong, duty or honor, just the pain and the dark dreams it gave you. But she was also crazy.

After another halfhearted whack, just a pat really, Ariel shouted, "No, no," threw down the ocotillo branch, put her hands over her face, turned her face to the wall, then pressed her whole body against the wall. Then Sister Quinn came up behind Ariel and whispered gently to her. Maybe she said, "Thank you." But Ariel kept her face to the wall so Sister Quinn's soothing manner wouldn't convince her to do more whipping, and I could see the bloody, already swelling welts across Sister Quinn's back.

I turned away from the crack in the shutters and its seam of light and walked across the desert toward my truck because I felt ashamed, scared, and guilty of some awful un-Christian sin. Then, as though I sensed the light, I turned back to look at the shack and *templo* to see the light come back on in the shack. I stopped. The door opened, and Ariel stepped out of the light coming from the shack and Azul waved to her as she walked to her car. I started to run cross-country past the parking lot, then away from the road but parallel to it. The gurgle of Ariel's sports car's engine carried through the still, clear, cold desert air as Ariel twisted the keys in the ignition.

Glancing over my shoulder, I saw the Mustang's headlights gaining on me, and I knew that I wouldn't make it to my truck, so I ran off the road and out into the chollas, ocotillos, yuccas, and creosote. My feet slipped in the gravel and stuck into the wet sand, and I got scared that I might plant one foot in a deep crevice and fall. So I tried to keep my feet away from the really dark lines. And then I stopped, put my hands on my knees, and breathed deeply. I was stupid. My truck was parked right off the road. I should have pulled it into the brush.

I saw the headlights of the Mustang coming up the road from Sister Quinn's and lighting the shapes of the cacti. Then the lights lit up my truck and stopped. A door slammed. Ariel appeared in the beam of light from the car. She turned circles in the mud, looked around, and raised her long fingers to her face to rest their tips on her cheeks. "Dolph," she screamed. "Dolph, Dolph, Dolph. Come out here. Where are you? Talk to me."

But I couldn't move. I sat in the wet sand and kicked at a rock. I didn't scream back. I didn't go to my truck. I kept still and let Ariel catch her breath to stop the sobs and the choking on tears and scream out my name so that anyone close by could hear, "Dolph, Dolph, where are you?"

Then I started to run, not just because I was ashamed but because if I listened to that scream, I'd end up in Sister Quinn's *templo,* getting whipped by Ariel or a child and imagining myself curled up deep down in a burrow, waiting for the cold to go away and the hot summer to warm my blood.

MALPUESTA

I had the next morning off, so after eggs and coffee with Pepper and Ignacio, I started calling every phone number at Wally's World trying to find Ariel. Pepper and Ignacio stared at me, and they dipped their heads when I called her condo number for the third time and pleaded through her message machine for her to pick up the phone. Their silence made me wish that I had paid to get a phone connection in my cabin.

When I stepped away from the phone, Pepper said, "Holy shit, when you gonna start shaking so bad your bourbon spills out your glass?"

Later in the morning, after Pepper and Ignacio left for whatever chores they could find, I called R.C. and found out that none of the detained mules would talk and that our lab test showed their pills were designer drugs, illegal cancer "cures," rhino horn or Spanish fly or other aphrodisiacs, amphetamines, quaaludes, and anything else that the FDA didn't approve but could be shipped through Mexico.

After I walked around Pepper's resort, tried to read, adjusted the antenna on my TV only to find some stupid game show, I found myself driving around Presidio, then through it, then somewhere past Redford. At Sister Quinn's turnoff, I pulled off the road. I wanted to square off with her, accuse her, beg her, but I didn't want to find myself again creeping up on Ariel (if she had come back), so I backed up and turned around.

On the east side of Presidio, I stopped at Saint Margaret Mary's Church, a prefab building of cinder block and tin, which looked more like a tractor dealership than a church. The real Catholic-looking church with a bell tower and an iron gate around it was on the main street next to Spencer's Store. An old, conservative priest, Father Calles, who learned to speak English as a teenager, ran San Fernando and the parishioners' thoughts, just as all the priests had done dating back to the Spaniards, who tried to give the Jimbres, the Indians who first settled near the juncture of the Rio Conchos and Rio Grande, hope against disease, Apaches, and crop failure. Inside Jesse Guzmán's church were pews and a stylized golden crucifix with an abstract Jesus—no Pedrito Jarmillo, no tortured faces or spurting blood.

I thought about talking to Father Guzmán, but then I realized that he couldn't tell me anything and that I might end up confessing something to him.

So I left Saint Margaret Mary's, and after a trip down the main street of Presidio, in front of city hall I spotted Raul Flores sitting outside in the sunshine that was burning through the remaining cold, and he spotted me. Clunking his thick-soled boots as he ran, his belly shaking, trying to catch me, he yelled for me to stop. I pulled over to the curb. He circled behind my car and came up to the driver's window. I rolled down my window, and he rested his forearms on my door and poked his head, cowboy hat and all, through my open window. "Big bust," he said. "What was it you found?"

"Stuff that makes you hard, soft, up, down, inside, outside. Anything you can swallow that ain't legal."

"Cool," he said.

"We should have waited and followed Sister Quinn," I said.

"Still, we got a lead on a crime wave. What do *we* do next?"

"*We* do just what *we* normally do."

"I thought this was *our* gig. No DEA."

"The DEA is always involved."

"What about us? *Cuñados, sí?*"

"We'll call you if we need you."

He let his head drop a bit, but his cowboy hat stayed on his head. "You federal guys," he said. "You get all the money and all the headlines. Look, Dolph, I need the publicity. Gimme some *pelón,* huh, let me do something, just to get in on it."

"I'll give credit where it's due."

"Come on, bro," he said.

"I'll call you."

His head drooped again, then he pulled it out of my station wagon and said, "Yeah, you bet." He gave me a lazy wave, and I left him kicking at the rocks in the road as he walked back to his sunning spot outside of city hall.

Before I could even pull away, as though the two of them had synchronized their movements, Dave Devine was sticking his head in through my open window. Dave was a buddy or I would have rolled the window up to his chin. Instead I told him, "Go away, Dave."

"Dolph, Dolph, Dolph," Dave said as though scolding me. "Come on. You owe it to the community. This is the biggest story ever, since the Spaniards founded this place."

"I've submitted my reports," I said, and stared straight ahead.

"Dolph, come on. You got to give me something. This is my chance. This is big."

"R.C. is the official spokesman for these matters."

Before Dave could respond, I started to ease out of my parking place, and he slowly pulled his head out of my car.

After another night of restless sleep and a day of light duty at the station, I tried to forget about Ariel and Sister Quinn by soaking in Pepper's bath with Pepper and his Ojinaga whores, Wilma Flintstone and Alice Kramden. The two had become his favorites. I insisted that he put candles along the side of the bath.

The steam was coming off the hot water and was coaxing me back to sleep. The tequila and beer also helped. Wilma put her head on the soft part of my shoulder so that I could feel her coarse black hair on my skin. Ariel's blond hair was silky and fine. Sometimes when her hair got wet, I could see her scalp in between strands of her hair.

I could call Ariel and immediately start to apologize. I could ask her to meet me somewhere and talk it over. I could act like nothing ever happened. "Hell, women are just like buses," Pepper said, and leaned across to kiss Alice. "Another one will come along in fifteen minutes."

"Not like her," I said.

"That's what I thought about every one of my wives," Pepper said. "Shake it off, boy. Leave her to it. Either she'll forgive or she won't."

"Pepper, you stay shit-faced for a couple of months after you lose a woman."

"I'm just telling you what you should do, not what I do." Pepper slid his hand down Alice's chest and giggled.

"Qúe quieres?" Wilma asked me, and rubbed my chest. I shook my head and took a sip of my beer.

Before I could pull the beer from my lips, the door to Pepper's cabin squeaked on its hinges, and some cold air blew into the room. I pushed Wilma away from me, then raised a foot, planted it in Wilma's stomach, and shoved her into the water. At the same time I twisted and shoved with my other foot so that I was outside of the tub, on cold cement and half sliding and half wriggling toward my gun. Then I heard Ariel say, "Dolph?"

I curled into a ball and knew that everyone was looking at me. "Goddamn it. I am a law officer. Knock first," I said as I uncurled and stood, completely naked. I looked first at Pepper and the two whores, who were clumped together and staring me, and then shifted my eyes to Ariel. She glanced at the tub, then kept her eyes on me.

I spotted my towel and pulled it and my bunched-up uniform and holstered gun off the bed. *"Qúe pasando?"* Wilma Flintstone asked.

"Shuck off your clothes and come on in for a dip," Pepper said to Ariel.

Ariel stared at me but talked to Pepper. "That man outside told me to come on in," she said, keeping her chin pointed down and jerking her head toward the open door.

"My pet Mexican's got a sick sense of humor," Pepper said. "To tell the truth, I think he's a little jealous, too."

"Dice que es católico," Alice Kramden added.

"Let's go to my cabin," I said as I wrapped a towel around me.

Ariel immediately turned to the open door and walked out of it. Bare chested, holding my towel around me, cradling my clothes and gun belt with my empty hand, I followed Ariel out the door. The cold made my skin tingle, and Ignacio stood to one side, showing no outward emotion but laughing, I was sure, at this silly gringo and gringa. I sorted through my mind for what to say, and at the same time I stared at her rear end in her tight jeans. Ariel opened my cabin door for me.

Once inside, I began to shake. Ariel stepped in and closed the door. Neither one of us turned on a light, and I dried as quickly as I could with my damp towel. Somewhat dry, in the dark I tried to stuff my legs into my pants legs.

"Who were those women?" I heard Ariel ask.

"Pepper brings in Ojinaga whores."

"There's two," Ariel said. I didn't answer, and she didn't say anything else. I worked my pants up to my waist, zipped, and then tried to get into my shirt. "I've tried to call you. I couldn't reach you, so I came over."

Dressed, I scooted across the floor to a bedside lamp and turned it on. My bed was unmade, and dirty clothes were spread across the floor.

Ariel dropped her head. "Ariel?" I asked. She raised her head, and I saw her swollen, puffy eyes. I stepped toward her, but her gaze held me back.

"I don't know what you saw the other night." Ariel wiped at one eye with the back of her hand. "But I assume that's killed it between us." She didn't wait for me to say no. "Whatever the case is, I'm not here to get you back."

"I never left you," I butted in.

And she butted back in, "I can see you were *lonely.* What's her name?"

"She's Pepper's whore," I said. "Tell me what's going on with you. That's why you're here, right? I'll understand."

She lifted her head to stare at me. "I don't know if I like what I see here."

"I tried to call," I muttered again.

But she wasn't listening to me. "I have nobody here. I just don't know anybody but you and Sister Quinn." I took a step toward her and put my hand on her shoulder, but she dipped her shoulder and brushed off my hand with hers.

"Please, let me explain," I said.

Ariel shook her head and raised her long fingers in front of her face and wiggled them as she stuttered through some prerehearsed speech. "Barbara Quinn needs help. I think she's lost her mind. Whatever you think about me, about us, and I don't think that you're right, you still maybe can help her. I need to know what to do." She looked at me, then shifted her speech to what she needed to say. "She seemed so convincing. Somehow, for a while, she made sense. And then I found myself doing *it.* And then I saw your car. . . . I've had nightmares these past nights."

"Sister Quinn is good at giving people nightmares," I said.

Ariel rubbed at her eyes with the tips of her fingers, then flung her long blond hair over her shoulders with the backs of her hands. When I didn't say anything, Ariel asked, "Please, Dolph, help me with Sister Quinn?"

She looked at me for some kind of answer, and I said, as much to myself as to her: "I'm in love with you."

It was simply a statement of a suddenly clear fact in the midst of all our confusion. I didn't need a response, but Ariel tried. Her lips and mouth moved, but she made no words, and she took a step backward away from me. "What about the other night?"

"When a person gets around Sister Quinn, the weird doesn't seem weird anymore."

"So what about Sister Quinn?"

"You can help me catch the guys she works for."

Ariel just wrinkled her brow. I reached, took her hand away from her face, and pulled her behind me to my bed. We both sat, and I put my palm against her cheek. "Talk to your people. Let it be known that you'd like some drugs—quaaludes, amphetamines, ecstasy, acid, any prescription medications. Better yet, ask for some large quantities. Just get me some names."

"Dolph," she said. "I could get fired."

"People know me. I won't get any answers, but they'll trust you. With all the kids, dropouts, and ranch hands that work for you, somebody has to like a little dope."

"I can't pull that off," she said.

I rubbed her cheek with the back of my fingers. "I'll be behind you."

Ariel looked down at her lap, then up at me. "So I betray her."

"You help her. You get her away from the people who are hurting her." I put my hand on the back of her head. "That's how I can help."

Her eyes caught on mine for a moment. "You're in love with me?"

I slowly nodded, then moved my face close to hers, and she moved close to my body, and I slid my hand from the back of her head to her neck, then down her back. Kissing, we slowly stretched out on the bed. And because we had both missed a lot of sleep and were each suddenly relieved and relaxed, we went straight to sleep. In the middle of the night, I woke when she suddenly jerked up and stifled a scream. "A dream." She shook her head.

"They'll go away," I said, not knowing if I was lying.

And in the morning, with the sun coming in through my window, I checked beside me to see if she had left during the night. Ariel had rolled to one edge of my bed, her hair trailing behind her, and I got up, put on my sweats, and went outside to lift my weights and then to go work.

With my scar pulling my stomach tight, the sun reflecting off the Chinatis as I lowered my bench press onto the arms of the weight bench, I saw Ariel come out of my cabin.

She raised her fingertips to touch her face, then wiggled them. "I think maybe I am in . . ." But she trailed off, pulled her long fingers away from her face and looked at the sun on the mountains, then said, "It's so rich."

When we went in for breakfast with Pepper, Ariel was gracious even to Pepper's whores, but Ignacio would hardly speak to her, and Pepper was sullen. He growled at me and his whores, and I wondered if he had lost another woman.

"IGNACIO"

When Ariel told the UT kid who worked in the pro shop that an elderly couple had asked for some "medications," he told her to check with Socorro. You could always count on a little something from Socorro, he said. I told her to leave Socorro alone, but she asked him.

"Lady, you're in a place you shouldn't be," he told her.

"I hear that you're the man to see."

Socorro checked over his shoulder, as if looking for me, Ariel told me, then said, "Don't you think I know who you're fucking?"

"Who I am fucking has nothing to do with your job, with Walter Bean, even."

"And it's none of your business what I do or don't do when I ain't working for him or you." And Ariel told me that his hard stare shifted down toward her chest, then to her stomach, as though he could see through her clothes, but she didn't look away from him. "Look, boss lady, whatever you're looking for, I ain't hiding it." He smiled too broadly and turned away from her, but then turned back to face her. "You don't belong here," he said, then added, "you're too pretty. You stay here, you get ugly." Then he walked out, and she heard his heavy boots pound against the board slats of the lobby of the hotel and his Mexican spurs with blunt rowels jingle like a set of keys.

Over the phone at the Border Patrol station, I told her, "You should have sprayed him with your Mace, then stabbed him and punched him. Hell, I wish I'd given you a gun; then you could have shot him." Through the receiver, with R.C. now looking over my shoulder, I heard her giggle. "Stay away from him," I said.

I hung up, and R.C. nodded to me. I followed him to his office and sat in front of his desk.

R.C. didn't look at me but stared down at his boots. "I'm not going to ask what you're doing, Dolph. But you better keep it unofficial." He first signed on when *la migra* would take a troublesome wet out to a pasture and let him wander around for a day or two without food before they'd ship him back across the border. He'd lasted long enough to attend sensitivity training sessions in El Paso.

A couple of nights later, I put on a coat and tie and went with Ariel and the elderly couple who wanted medications to La Kiva for a plate of La Kiva's barbecue. The couple were friends of Walter Bean, and he wanted them treated cordially and formally, so Ariel pulled back her hair and put her own diamonds in her earlobes. Earlier she had told the couple to talk to Socorro.

Half underground, with a door that you had to pull up toward you to get in, built with rock along the dry banks of Terlingua Creek, La Kiva stayed cool in summer and warm in winter. An RV park grew up around it, so La Kiva complex had a steady business.

When we walked in, Socorro, dusty from a day on the trail, was bellied up to the bar and drinking a beer. He darted his eyes toward us, then back to his beer. We sat at a table behind him. From my seat by Ariel, across from the elderly couple, I could see Socorro keeping his gaze on his beer. He was older than me, but bigger. His back looked powerful, and his faded tattoos seemed to bulge because over the years, his biceps must have grown.

After drinks, barbecue, and small talk, the elderly lady began to compliment Ariel for the facilities at Lajitas. She told Ariel that the nice cowboy at the bar even helped get some medication for her husband; even better, it was half the price of what they normally paid in Houston.

So when Socorro sucked down his last beer, grabbed his Levi's jacket, and walked out of La Kiva, I excused myself and followed him out into the dark parking lot. He was reaching for the door of a faded red van when I spotted him. I lowered my shoulder, ran, and rammed my shoulder into the small of his back. His face hit the side of his van. "Come on, motherfucker," he said even as his face smashed into the van, and quickly spun around with his fists up and blood dribbling from his nose.

I stepped back and shoved my badge out and up in front of his face. "You know who I am. I can bust you without a warrant. But I can't prosecute for drugs."

"Go fuck yourself, or pull your pistol."

I eased back from him. "What I'm saying is that if I was customs or DEA or the deputy sheriff, I'd be searching your house and van and trying to arrest you. As it is, alls I can do right now is arrest you and turn you over to somebody else."

"Fuck you, buddy," he said, and, "Fuck all you son-of-bitching police motherfuckers." He stepped toward me, his fists still up, but I ducked under him and punched him in the stomach. He bent over, his hat dropped, and his ponytail fell over the back of his head.

"Now listen. Nobody really gives a shit about you right now."

Socorro curled over his knees, leaned against his van, and tried to suck up some air. "Go ahead, kick my ass," he wheezed.

"All we're doing is having a discussion." The tension in my shoulders eased, and the scar on my stomach loosened. I waited for him to gain some breath. "We're both too old and too smart to risk fucking ourselves up real bad in a fistfight."

Grunting, he reached down to pick up his hat, grabbed it, pushed it down on his head, and tried to straighten up. Upright, he pulled a pack of cigarettes out of his pocket. "So either I fuck somebody over or you gonna fuck with me."

"You got it." He shook the pack and offered me a smoke, trying, maybe, to get me to drop my guard.

"Somebody's got to get blamed for the shit going on, right?" He raised the pack, shook it so that one cigarette stuck out, and pulled the cigarette out of the pack with his lips.

"And you can't afford an investigation into your past. You talk to me, you're an unnamed source."

"Well, I been doing my own investigation. I know some things about you."

"You heard of a Vincent Fuentes?"

He laughed, turned out his palms, and carefully reached into his jeans to bring out a book of matches. I waited while he lit the match, cupped it between his palms, then lit his cigarette. "I don't like you in particular, or any of you cocksucking federal bullshit people. Why don't you just leave this place as it is? Fucking back off, let us live like we want."

"You gonna talk, or do I start filling out my bullshit federal forms?"

He raised his hand to his mouth, pulled the cigarette from his lips, and pointed his fingers, the cigarette between them, at me, so that I breathed in the curl of cigarette smoke. I coughed as I asked again, "Where is Vincent Fuentes?"

"And I don't like that prick-teasing bitch that runs my outfit." I almost grabbed at the orange spark of the lit cigarette and threw it into the gravel.

"You mean Walter Bean's outfit."

"Tell her and him to fuck off. I bet you ain't even getting none of that."

"I get my sermons from Sister Quinn."

He giggled. "I don't like her either, and 'cause I don't like any of y'all, I'm giving you a name. I don't know this Fuentes guy you got a hard-on for, but you gonna laugh. This ain't nothing big, little bitty amounts, so no decent judge would bust my ass too bad." He looked at me, then smiled. "Ask Ignacio."

I almost swung another fist into his stomach. "If you're lying . . ."

He smiled, took a deep drag, and without taking the cigarette from his mouth, blew more smoke at me. "I can't afford to lie."

"That smoking is gonna kill you. Get out of here," I said.

"You sure you don't want to take just a little ol' swing at me or something?" He blew more smoke in my general direction. "You don't seem that old or that smart."

"I'm just gonna be around when you fuck up real big."

"I don't plan on fucking up."

"Then maybe I'll bust you for smoking in a nonsmoking area."

Socorro laughed. "Same as I told your girlfriend. You people shouldn't be here. This isn't your country."

"What makes it yours?"

He chuckled and opened the door to his van and pulled himself into it. He spewed out gravel as he backed out, put his head out of his open window, and yelled, "Does she give good head?" Then he pulled out of the parking lot, and I noticed that I had ripped the shoulder of my sport coat.

I had seen the big picture, but I had missed those tiny, telling details that make up that big picture. I would see to it that the Border Patrol, not the DEA or the Presidio County Sheriff's Department, got the credit for busting Pepper.

The next day, as the sun was setting and shadows from the Chinatis were creeping toward the Rio Grande, I found Ignacio out in the old pickup, trying to mend a hinge on a gate. When I pulled up in the Border Patrol truck, he kept right on working. When I walked up to him, he nodded. I grabbed the gate and held it steady as he pounded some nails into the new hinge. The hanging skin on the dried-up little man's biceps swung with his arm and would tighten into a bulge when he pulled back his hammer.

"Ignacio, a man said he gets drugs from you." He kept pounding at the nail, and I grunted from holding up the gate.

He finished pounding. "You can let go, too," he said.

"Then it was a mistake?" I asked, but Ignacio said nothing, just walked back to the bed of his pickup and sat on the bumper. He held on to the hammer and let it dangle from his arm. He pulled his dirty forearm across his sweaty forehead.

I squatted down beside him. He started to get up, but I grabbed his arm that held the hammer. "Dammit, you're going to have to talk to somebody. There's going to be people coming here to talk to you."

"I don't know nothing about no dope." He tried to stand, but I tightened my grip on his arm. He tried to pull away but couldn't.

"Raul Flores, the Border Patrol up in Marfa, or probably the DEA or all of them are going to be tracking you down and are going to ask you more questions than I am."

Ignacio relaxed his arm and dropped the hammer. "You going to arrest me?"

"Not yet. I don't have a warrant. But I can get one."

"Then I got no problems yet."

I let him rise, and when I too stood, he started walking around the truck toward the cab. "Wait," I yelled after him. He stopped, turned, and stared at me.

"Do you know what this means?"

"I go to jail?"

"Are you a citizen? Did Pepper ever get you to take a citizenship test?"

"I went in a while ago with Pepper, and we reported I been in this country for a long time."

"Okay, okay," I said. "Do you have any kind of lawyer?" He shrugged; I asked again, *"Abagado?"*

"No," he said. He turned away from me and walked toward the driver's side of his truck.

As Ignacio reached for the handle, I ran up to him and grabbed his hand and pulled it away. "Goddamn, I know that you're not in on this alone. You're not behind it. Tell me right now that Pepper is doing this."

Ignacio stared up at me. His lips started to move, but he couldn't say anything. He cocked his head as though to think. "I don't know nothing."

"Come on, dammit."

"No hablo inglés," he said in a lilting, mocking manner. *"No sabe. No sé."*

He reached for the door again, got it, and opened it, but I slammed my palm against the car door to shut it. "You do know, and they're going to be tougher than me. You're going to have to tell them something."

Ignacio tried to explain whatever was going on in his head, but neither English nor Spanish worked. Then he, like R.C. and Ariel, patted my shoulder. "I won't say nothing about Pepper." He smiled.

"No, no, no." I grabbed him by the shoulders. "You've got to. Tell them about Pepper. Tell them that Pepper is doing this. Tell them who got him to, if you know. Tell everything."

"What happens to Pepper?"

"Nothing as bad as what could happen to you."

"I'm old."

"You won't survive prison."

Ignacio shrugged and said, *"Viejo,"* and tapped himself on the chest with his thumb. *"Dios decide la muerte."*

"No, no," I said, "you can beat this." I hesitated. "Pepper can't."

His lips twisted as he tried to find words once again, but age, inability with two languages, and weariness kept the words away from him. I thought for a moment that he might suffer a stroke, some blood vessel in his brain rupturing, as he tried to turn a thought into words. "Pepper always took care of me. But I always took care of him too. I got no wife, no kids." He hesitated as he tried to account for the way his life had turned out. "Pepper loses every wife and kid. So we tied, we even, we okay. But I'm a lot old. More than Pepper. Whatever kind of times I got, I can do. Pepper can't."

My mind twisted up like Ignacio's. I tasted the dust hanging in the air. I felt the coolness in what shadows there were and anticipated the sharp drop in temperature that would come in the next thirty minutes as soon as the sun went down. I zipped up my jacket with one hand but kept my other hand pressed against Ignacio's pickup door. He looked at me like he had grown impatient with me. "Trujillo told you when the drugs was coming. Who you think told him?" Ignacio tapped his chest with his thumb. "Maybe, I think, if Sister Quinn gets caught, Pepper quits. He's with some bad people."

I waited to absorb what he said. With my hand quivering, I gave him advice. "I'm not coming home tonight. You tell Pepper you saw me. You tell him to get the both of you out of the country tonight." Ignacio looked at me and shook his head, either because he was ashamed of me or because he wouldn't run away. So I let him get into his truck and drive off.

I got into the Border Patrol's truck, drove to the station, then drove my station wagon to Ariel's condo. I curled up with her and a bottle of bourbon. She laid her head on my shoulder, kissed me on the neck, and rested her long fingers against my face. Looking in my eyes, she said that what she was trying to tell me that morning while I was lifting weights out behind my cabin was that she thought she was falling in love, too.

CONTRABANDISTA

At 6 a.m., R.C. put in one phone call to the Border Patrol section headquarters in Marfa and asked for a helicopter; then he made another phone call to a federal magistrate in Alpine, at her home before her morning coffee, and asked her for a search warrant for Cleburne Hot Springs Resort. By 7 a.m., Raul Flores and the DEA agent were in R.C.'s office asking for time to get their manpower ready for the possible assault on Cleburne Hot Springs Resort.

I left R.C. in his office arguing with the DEA agent and Raul Flores, but R.C. followed me out with his eyes, pleading with me to help him with this. I left him to his job.

Out by the other desks Pat, Roland, then Dede asked to back me up, but I told them just to get the search warrant and get to Pepper's cabins before the goddamn U.S. Attorney General herself busted in on Pepper. Dede followed me as I walked toward the door, and I felt her staring at my back. I turned around to face her. "What is it?" I asked.

"I thought that I was going to help you with this case." I dropped my eyes. "Did you really need her, Dolph? Was it something I couldn't have done?"

"Dede, don't make me start asking 'what if' now. Save it." Dede turned away from me. "Dede," I said after her, and she turned to face me. "I'll make it up to you. Only right now, just watch out for Pepper." Dede smiled and gave me a thumbs-up.

I went to our garage, kick-started one of our trail bikes, and drove it toward Pepper's resort. I got on one of Pepper's graded roads, knocked a rusted lock off a gate, and drove on old, crumbling ranch roads that hadn't been used since Pepper's grandfather tried ranching in this area. I drove as high as I could or walked as high as I could and stared off into the faded desert through my binoculars.

The dust devils, the wispy winter morning clouds, the hawks circling and looking for plump doves all fit the view; the Border Patrol helicopter didn't. Somebody on board spotted me, and the agents in the helicopter and I exchanged waves. But the goddamn helicopter, when it dipped low, kicked up dust that I could have mistaken for something else.

After I made one slow pan of a wash from a slope above it, my hands almost automatically stopped leading my revolving head, as though the binoculars had caught the sight for me. My eyes stuck on an old line shack, left over from a time when cattle were scrounging for food and making Pepper's family a living.

I had left my motorcycle at the opposite base of the slope, so I eased myself down the incline, holding anything that didn't have thorns until I got into the wash. A truck could come off the old ranch road and make it up this chalky wash to the cabin. I saw car tires, not truck tires. The DEA could get a cast of the treads. Then I saw powdery tracks of pointy-toed boots. When I crossed the wash and got to the slope and the cabin, the sun reflected off a shiny, new padlock on the door; the tin roof was bent and curled and rusted.

I pushed on the door, but the lock held. So I went to the side, and after a few kicks with the heel of my boot, my foot went through the old lumber. I pried a few boards loose and followed the sunshine through the hole I had made.

When my eyes adjusted to the dark cabin, I first saw swirls of dust in the beam of sunlight. Then I saw Westinghouse printed on the side of a cardboard crate, then on another one. Three Westinghouses stared at me. Someone had pried the staples out of one side of the cardboard crate so that it opened like a door. I pulled back the cardboard. Inside was a new almond-colored refrigerator. And in the others, both with the cardboard doors, were your choice of white- or olive-colored Westinghouse refrigerators. I pulled open a door, and in the dark refrigerator, on the top shelf, I saw an Uzi and a couple of Glocks. I opened the others and saw automatics or ammo. In the vegetable bin of one, I saw several packages wrapped in green plastic trash bags. I punctured the plastic with my buck knife and watched as loose pills rolled out. The other refrigerators also had the pills or capsules collected in pillboxes or wrapped in plastic, all in the vegetable bins or in the freezers.

I bent and stepped through the opening I had made in the shack and ran down the wash to the ranch road, then down the road to my motorcycle. I spit gravel then dust all the way down the road, then down the wash back to the cabin, and set off three flares. Then, not waiting for the helicopter to land (they'd know what to do), I raced back toward Cleburne Hot Springs Resort, hoping to beat the federal, state, and county police to Pepper.

I didn't beat anybody. Raul Flores and his deputy, Freddy Guerra, wore surgeons' gloves and dug in the trash cans outside Pepper's cabin. The parking lot was filled with our trucks, unmarked vehicles, and Presidio County trucks. Shaking pillowcases and sheets, the DEA agents in their navy blue windbreakers came out of the cabins. I saw an agent come out of my cabin and empty a drawer full of my underwear on top of the clothes, TV, ironing board, radio, and microwave he'd already brought outside. Dede came out after him with my spare gun, towels, and books. She stopped when she saw me. I forced myself to smile and wink. She smiled and shook her head, then she gently set the gun on top of the pile of my stuff.

Suddenly Pat Coomer was by my side, and I thought for a moment that he'd raise a rifle and start picking off the rummaging feds. Pat's face was red not only from the sun but from the work. "I tried to stop this," he said. "So did R.C." I nodded and walked around the pool with its growing crack and walked into Pepper's bar, dining, and game room.

When I walked into Pepper's bar, a DEA agent looked up at me from the pool table, which had a slice in its faded, warped green felt. Another agent was prying behind the bent and folded almond linings on Pepper's bar with a screwdriver. The sleeve of his nylon jacket had a long, frizzing tear; he'd caught it on the poorly beat copper. The discounted lamps from the Holiday Inn were on the floor, and I could see the dust caked to their topsides and their lightbulbs.

In the middle of the room, R.C. Kobel was talking to our DEA agent and waving his hands. And his right hand trailed a wisp of smoke. R.C. probably figured that Pepper wouldn't mind his smoking, especially given the circumstances. "Goddamn, you're making this a circus," R.C. said. "Why don't you call the fucking National Guard for an air strike? Pepper Cleburne is not some crazy, drug-dealing gangster," he said.

"This is our game," the DEA agent said.

"The hell it is," I said from the door, walked up to them, and pushed in between them. "I, we, us, the Border Patrol found what you're looking for, and we're handling it."

"Where?" the DEA agent said, and took off his gold-rimmed glasses; R.C. quickly inhaled on his cigarette.

"You don't worry about where. You just make sure you put everything back just like you found it, including my goddamn clothes and shit." And suddenly on either side of me were the DEA agents who were disemboweling Pepper's pool table and curling up the copper lining on his bar.

"You're not cleared of this yet." The DEA agent pointed the arm of his glasses at me. "I want you to stick around until we have a chance to talk to you."

"You got it, but right now I live here, so you take a hike."

The DEA agent put on his glasses and started toward me, and I stepped forward so that my forehead was nearly against his nose, but R.C. was in between us, saying, "Okay, we got our answers. We're cooperating in this, remember?" I looked around me at the DEA agents and smiled.

"Okay, fellas, I'm cool," I said.

"Okay, okay," the DEA agent said. "Where's the owner?"

I turned to look at him and was about to threaten him when R.C. broke in. "He's ours. We deserve it. You'll be around for everything."

The DEA agent took off his glasses, chewed on the end of the glasses' arm, and said, "Okay, okay, okay."

I grabbed R.C. by the arm, pushed passed the DEA agents, and pulled him across to the bar. "Where's Pepper?" I whispered.

"He's in the kitchen." R.C. spotted an ashtray, and his hand darted out toward it to crush the lit end of his cigarette. "They came busting in here pointing guns, and there wasn't even any TV news camera. Pepper was sitting waiting for them. Before they could handcuff him or shoot him, I told him to go wait for us in the kitchen."

"Thanks, R.C.," I said. "Anybody arrested him?"

"Naw, not yet."

"Look, you arrest him," I said, swallowed, then continued. "I can't do it. But let me go talk to him first."

"What you gonna talk about, Dolph? . . . You know I got to ask."

"I want some information from him, but I want it private, to me, not official." R.C. ducked his head. "We owe him that."

R.C. slowly shook his head like his neck was hurting. He slapped me on the back. And before I stepped away from the bar, the DEA agent who had been assigned the bar had picked up his screwdriver and poked it into the copper. "Hey," I said to him, "what the hell are you looking for? Didn't you hear me? I've got it." He and I both looked at our DEA agent, who rolled his eyes.

As I walked toward the swinging doors that led to the kitchen, the DEA agents started to follow me, but R.C. said from behind me, "Be patient, boys." And the DEA agents stopped at the door.

I pushed the swinging door to go into the kitchen, and the smell of Pepper's chili hit me, and I saw his big steaming kettle on the stove. Pepper sat at a table with a cut-up beer can, spitting his snuff juice out from under his handlebar mustache. His tall boots with the legs that went up over his calves stood beside him. And he crossed his socked feet under the table. He looked up at me and smiled in a way that looked as though it was the first smile in his whole life. "Why you cooking the chili?" I asked.

"Thought these boys might need some lunch," he said, and let a stream of brown juice leak out of the corner of his mouth and spill into the jagged beer can. "Probably the best chili they'll ever get. You want a beer?"

"I'm on duty, but I'm talking to you off duty."

"I forgot." He reached up with both hands toward the lobe of his ear and pulled the clasp from his diamond stud earring, pulled the earring out of his ear, then hooked the clasp back on. He handed his earring to me. "Here, hold on to this for me."

I took the earring and put it in my pocket. "Where's Ignacio?"

"He's out watching those morons tear the shit out of this place. I told him to take off, just run away. But he's gonna wait it out." Then Pepper got up, went to the refrigerator, pulled out a beer, pulled the tab, and drank. "I figure this may be my last one for a while."

"Maybe it's holding snuff, chili, and beer in the mouth all at the same time that made you fuck up so bad," I said. "I found your drugs. Hell, Pepper, not even real dope, this pharmaceutical shit."

"Figured you would," he said, and took a slow sip and concentrated on the taste of that first, morning beer. "Hell, probably if you would of asked, I would of told you where it was."

"Look, Pepper, R.C. is going to come in here in a minute and arrest you, but before he does, I need some answers. You talk to me first, then you call a lawyer, and I swear I'll talk only to him."

"I don't know if I can really tell what happened."

"Pepper, people were killed."

Pepper nodded and looked down at his beer. "Those guys you and Dede found, they were going to be dead no matter what."

"So what about you?"

"I like guns. You know I do, so I got this federal firearms license. A guy I know knows a guy this Fuentes character knows. So I get this strange call from Sister Quinn to meet Fuentes. What can it hurt, huh? She's nuts anyway. But Fuentes makes me a deal. I just get the guns. His people pick them up on this side and take them back. He promises to get me triple price for semiautomatics in Mexico. I agree. No hassle, no mess. A lot easier than carrying refrigerators across, and the price is better."

"So that's where the refrigerators come from."

"All us drug smugglers start out small. Jesus, I know why people turn to dope; it's harder than hell to swim a river carrying a refrigerator, but you can get double the price on them in Mexico."

"Jesus, Pepper. This is federal shit."

Pepper waved his hand at me and looked into his beer, then at me. "I don't need you to scold me, Dolph. Don't bring this down to simplistic shoulds and shouldn'ts." I nodded, and Pepper went on. "So I get guns, store them out at that old line shack; then one day they're gone, and in a day or two I get a phone call, and I drive to Fort Stockton, meet some fancy-ass *pachucos* in a motel room, and I get bags of pills—blue ones, pink ones, capsules. That's my payment."

"Aw, shit, Pepper," I said.

Pepper stopped to take another drink of beer. "I get ahold of Sister Quinn. She sets up a meeting with Fuentes in Ojinaga. He doesn't show, but some guys from Ojinaga tell me I'm in for another deal. Suddenly I'm in the pharmacy business, not even regular drugs, like you say, but shit I've never heard about. Who the hell do you see about peddling black market diet pills? I got fucking ground-up rhino horn to give newly immigrated Asians hard-ons. So I meet with this Alemán guy in Fort Stockton; he's some local drug peddler, so I got a partner, only he doesn't want the drugs I've got, not yet, wants me to hold them awhile. So I start doing a little business on the side. I run into Socorro. And this nurse who runs a hospice in Alpine starts buying painkillers from me. Jesus, I'm a humanitarian, helping dying people." Pepper tried to laugh.

"What about the shipment of guns that I caught?"

"You screwed my partners up, but the guns still got there. Whatever Mexican lawmen got ahold of them got them to the rightful owner."

"What about the group that we caught?"

"That was to go to Alemán, Sister Quinn was gonna drive them to Fort Stockton, but I think maybe he was gonna fuck me around and just take the delivery. Which would have been fine. I just want out now. And Sister Quinn, Dolph, that simple, dumb bitch; she don't know shit. Thinks these are a bunch of *mojados*." Pepper raised his beer and sucked it all down, then he crushed his can in his fist and threw it against his large, restaurant-size refrigerator. "I tell you,

Dolph, I was gonna burn that goddamn shack—guns, shit, refrigerators, and all—but I just couldn't bring myself to do it."

"Pepper, where's Fuentes?"

"Jesus, Dolph, Fuentes isn't the problem. He's not running anything. He's some poor, dumb son-of-a-bitch like me. That's why two guys are dead. The really bad guys who are behind this got into some kind of feud. So they kill each other on this side."

"Pepper, you're not in the big-money drug business," I said. "It's not *la plaza*. So your partners are desperate and thus dangerous."

Pepper thought for a moment, then added, "So what's it matter to them if me or Fuentes turns up dead?" Pepper made himself smile. "In a way, it was almost fun. For a while, I thought I could do it."

"You know anything about Fuentes?"

Pepper shrugged. "I wouldn't be surprised if he was already dead."

I stood and walked to the wall so I could turn my back to him and not look at him. "I gotta know why," I asked over my shoulder.

Pepper giggled. "That pool."

Pepper's laugh made it okay for me to turn back around to face him. "Jesus, Pepper, nobody has vacationed at a hot springs since the early part of the twentieth century."

"That's why I need to fix the pool," Pepper said. "Hell, up until this morning, I had all the money I needed to get me an Olympic-size pool and renovate all the cabins, but I couldn't spend it without making you suspicious."

I choked off a laugh, and Pepper put his hand over his mouth to gag his laugh. "Pepper, my report is going to say that Ignacio turned state's evidence. I'm going to say he agreed to talk."

Pepper nodded and said, "Just like a goddamn 'Meskin.' Can't trust 'em."

I smiled and nodded too. "I'm gonna yell for R.C. to come in here."

"Let me put on my boots," Pepper said, and he pointed his toes to slide one foot then the other into his hand-crafted Mexican boots. Then he turned off the burner under the simmering kettle of chili.

As soon as I yelled, the DEA agent, R.C. Kobel, Pat Coomer, and

Dede Pate came in to arrest Pepper. R.C. stuttered as he read Pepper's rights to him. Pepper held his hands out in front of him and asked, "Can we do this front ways?" Pat whispered, "Sorry," when he handcuffed Pepper. And Dede kept looking at me like I'd give her some kind of clue as to how to act. Pepper, with his hands bound in front of him, looked around him at the DEA agents, the Border Patrol agents, the Presidio County deputy sheriffs, smiled, and said, "You fellas help yourself to that chili. I made it for y'all."

When we all led him out of the kitchen, then through his demolished bar, he looked around, and his mouth twisted so that one end of his handlebar mustache rose. Outside, he squinted at the hot, high sun and looked around at the piled contents of his resort. Then he looked at the DEA agents and at Dede, Pat, R.C., and me as if to ask how we could do this. His gaze settled on his dry pool with the sand caked up on its bottom curves, the widening crack down its middle, and Ignacio's rocks. "Take care of that goddamn pool for me, will you, Dolph?" Pepper said to me.

"Fuck that pool," I said. Pepper smiled, and then we all looked to see Deputy Raul Flores, Freddy Guerra, and another DEA agent leading a handcuffed Ignacio to join Pepper.

When I joined the army rather than going to Rice University, my mother asked if I was crazy. I said that I knew exactly what I was doing. She tried pleading, begging, and then threatening. It took me ten years to realize how much I had hurt her and how little she had really asked. I was not soldier material and clearly had no business in the army. But with Miguel's preaching buzzing around in my head, I thought the army would make me taller than five-foot six. And as much because of Miguel's inarticulate explanations of manhood as because of my mother's pleading, I agreed to see my grandfather and get his judgment on me. My mother secretly hoped that my grandfather might be able to scare me or convince me into not joining the army.

I drove our car to Charlie Beeson's big house, and the maid, who lived in the barrio where my father worked, led me through the house, where I had one time lived when my parents first split, to the screened-in back porch, where Charles Beeson sat stroking his cat. When I walked up to him, he smiled and pushed the growling cat out of his lap. He motioned to a lawn chair beside him, and I sat. We both stared out into the twilight and listened to the mosquitos and gnats buzzing on the other side of the screen. "Your mother tells me you don't want to go to Rice University."

"No sir," I said. "I mean, she is correct, sir."

He nodded and said, "You don't call me Grandpa anymore?"

"Yes sir, *abuelo,*" I said, and darted my eyes to see his reaction but lost my nerve and shifted them just as quickly away from him.

His eyes shifted just enough to see me. He spared me the stern, Mount Rushmore stare that might have made me, even at eighteen, cry and back down. "You know that you are giving up something that most residents in this area could never even dream about."

"Maybe that's why I don't want to go."

"Can you be more specific?" he asked, and the maid brought in a tray with two bottles of beer on it and set it down between us.

I stared at the beers, then looked up to see him glaring at me. I braced myself. "Rice is my mother's decision; the army is mine." I clenched my teeth and glared back at him.

Charles Beeson nodded and asked, "And when did you make this decision?" I started to answer, but he held up his hand and wrinkled his brow. "No, I mean how long have you been considering this option?"

"Since Christmas of last year. Since I stopped seeing my father." I prepared to get slapped.

My grandfather closed his eyes, and I could tell from his tightened jaw that he clenched his teeth, and I immediately wished that I had given him some other answer. He opened his eyes and looked at me. "Do you think that there might be some other choice than the army? Maybe another college? Maybe a few years off? Young people are sometimes hasty."

"I've considered everything," I said, and sat rigidly in my chair. "I was not hasty."

"So this is not a whim; it is a carefully thought-out decision?" A vein in his neck bulged.

"Yes, sir," I said.

Charles Beeson nodded, said, "So be it," and motioned toward the beers. "Have a beer, soldier."

Neither he nor my mother had ever offered me a beer before, so I reached hesitantly for it. "Go on," he said, and grabbed the other beer. He pushed his bottle toward me as though in a toast and then took a drink. "Your mother will forgive you," he said, then added, "after a while."

He sipped his beer and looked out at the twilight. "It is hard for a parent to just suddenly change what he thinks of his children or what he had planned for them. On the other hand, Dolph, you be very careful with this and all your decisions; some you won't be able to change. And be very careful in the army; don't get hurt," and then he said the tough part, "Don't get killed—stay away from the war if you can." He shook his head. "Oh, I'm just rambling." He turned to me, and looking at me, not staring, he didn't ask or command but made a simple statement of fact. "I wish you wouldn't go."

I had no response for him, but we finished the beers, and he said, "I'll explain to your mother." We shook hands, and I showed myself out of that old, airy house.

That meeting, so long ago it was beyond years, was in my mind as I left the Border Patrol station and drove to Ariel's condo. It was the most like my conversation with Pepper. And I wanted to tell Sister Quinn. I guess because she was the only person around who might understand what I felt and what my grandfather and Pepper had felt. But I couldn't talk to her because I also hated her for forcing me to do what I had just done to Pepper.

When I opened the door to Ariel's condo, she greeted me wearing a negligee. I heard the bath running. She took me by the hand and led me to the dark bathroom, lit only by candles spread around the tub. As she unbuttoned my shirt, I felt something tiny in my shirt pocket. I unbuttoned the flap on the pocket, stuck my hand into it, and pulled out Pepper's diamond ear stud.

"What is that?" Ariel asked.

I pushed it toward her and said, "It's Pepper's. He wants me to take care of this as well as everything else he goddamn owns."

Ariel took the earring and turned it over in her fingers. "You don't have to let this bother you."

I kissed her. "Let's just sleep tonight," I said, and held on to her as tightly as I could, as smelly as I was from a full day's work. I took my clothes off and bathed with her in the upstairs bathtub.

CURANDERAS

Our DEA agent called the FBI and came up with a file on Alemán, and immediately our DEA agent and some Feebies put together some sting operation to trap the nurse at the Alpine hospice and Alemán. Then, because my stuff was scattered across the front of Pepper's property, even though I had turned him in, several Feebies showed up and asked me questions. When I passed a lie detector test—me wired, the Feebies looking on, our DEA agent pulling off his glasses and staring down at his feet to keep from looking at me—they all said they were sorry. They didn't ask me about Socorro, and I said nothing about him.

When I showed up for work, R.C. told me to take a few days off. "Go home," he said. But I wasn't sure where home was. It had become Ariel's condo, so during the days, while Ariel worked, I'd sit on her warm balcony and stare out past the river to the mountains in Mexico or drive to Marfa to see Pepper in jail.

"Why did you come out here?" I asked Ariel one night. "Did you have a choice?"

"My second husband had left me. I figured I was no good with husbands but good for Bean's business. So I came here because he needed help here. I figured I'd have no men but lots of scenery. It's beautiful, right?"

"It's mean. It's beautiful if you can discount humans," I told her.

"Exactly," she said, and kissed me. She pulled away from me and said, "Where are you, Dolph? You seem a thousand miles away."

So I went back to where I thought I was (only eighty miles away) and tried to clean up what I could at Pepper's resort. And then I called the *comandanté* of the Ojinaga garrison and asked for Trujillo to call me.

When he called me, he said, "Congratulations, I'm sure you have helped your career."

"But I haven't completed our deal."

"I was going to ask about that." His voice crackled along with the Mexican static.

"You've taken your time."

"Fuentes is moving from city to city—Juarez, Chihuahua City, Ojinaga. He is running. He will cross soon."

"When?"

"I was hoping you would find out."

"Okay, here is *la mordida.* I want to catch him. This side or that, I want to be the one to find him."

"Just tell me where he is."

"That's not the deal."

"Okay, you find him and call me," he said, and then after I listened to the Mexican static on the telephone, he added, "He's prosecuted in Mexico by me."

"It's getting a little personal," I said to Trujillo.

"And your case hasn't become personal?" Trujillo said, and I hesitated then hung up on him.

I put on civilian clothes but got my gun and my badge and drove my station wagon back down El Camino del Rio toward Lajitas, vowing that I would get my ass out of this place as soon as I had Vincent Fuentes. As I drove, I cussed the sunset that turned the undersides of the thin low winter clouds into bright streamers. I cussed the sun that was always there, drying up all rain even before it fell, and then I cussed those days when the sky blackened and the winds blew and just enough rain fell to tease you. And then I cussed the warped mentalities resulting from living in a place without rain, without shade, without green. I cussed the mix of Catholicism and Indian religion that made the *cholos* see God in everything and the gringos' tough, posturing, pragmatism that kept them from seeing any god.

Ariel cocked her head to look at me when she answered her door. "Let's go," I said. "I need your help."

"It's late, Dolph," she said.

"Let's go."

She didn't say anything until we were in the car and going back down the high canyons toward Redford and Presidio. "Are you on duty or off?"

"What's the difference?" I said.

"I'm beginning to wonder about that," she said. And since I made no comment, she said nothing else. When we approached Redford, I spoke to her. "I'm going to get Sister Quinn to tell me where Fuentes is."

"I don't want to see her," Ariel said, and folded her hands across her chest. "Maybe you should just drop me off."

"You've got to help me," I said.

"What makes you think I can help?"

"I don't know that you can, but I'm playing every angle with that crazy bitch."

"Drop it, Dolph," Ariel said, and reached across the seat to touch the back of my hand. I kept my hand on the wheel but looked first at Ariel's hand and then at her face. And she pulled her hand away from my arm, hugged herself, curled up in her seat, scooted to the very edge of it, and looked out the side window at the dark shapes passing by.

At Sister Quinn's *templo,* Ariel watched as I buckled on my holster and gun. "You're not going to shoot her, are you?"

"Suppose Fuentes is here?"

When I knocked on the door of Sister Quinn's shack, Ariel turned her back to me and the door. Sister Quinn answered the door and shined a flashlight beam into my face. "Dolph, Dolph," she said, "I heard about Pepper. I can't believe that." She turned off the flashlight. "Another example of the totalitarian designs of law enforcement in this country. Now do you see?"

I shoved open the door, pushing Sister Quinn against her wall.

Ariel waited outside and folded her arms. I looked back out at her and shouted, "Come in."

Sister Quinn looked at me like I had slapped her. I pointed at Sister Quinn. "You're in more shit than Pepper. You've got a trial coming, and I'll see that you're prosecuted for running those drugs with him."

"It's not me. Look in your own heart if you want to see the cause."

Sister Quinn tried to walk past me, but I shoved my palm into her shoulder. "That shipment is going to get him some prison time, and you caused that, so things aren't even yet."

"Can't you see who is responsible, Dolph?" she asked.

And this time I shoved both my flat palms into her shoulders and knocked her back against her wall, and when she hit the wall, her weight shook the whole shack so that some dust drifted down from the ceiling and the bare lightbulb swung lightly and made our shadows grow and contract along the walls. And I noticed Ariel's shadow scooting away from my thin shadow and Sister Quinn's bulky shadow. I turned, and Ariel stopped. She raised her long fingers to her cheeks and said, "Dolph, stop this."

Then I heard Sister Quinn. "The people whom I help—"

I swiveled my head back toward Sister Quinn and interrupted her. "If you say one goddamn word about poor people or refugees or the misery of the world or any of your other horseshit, I swear I'll slug you." I stared at Sister Quinn. She showed no emotion. Then she shifted her head to look at Ariel. "Look at me," I yelled. "Now you tell me where the hell Fuentes is. He's the goddamn prince of darkness. He's the enemy."

Sister Quinn jerked her head away from Ariel and back to me. "You might as well start hitting me," she said, and smiled at me.

Then behind me I heard, "Barbara, tell him what he wants to know." I turned my head and saw Ariel slowly stepping toward me, her hands in front of her face, saying, "Tell him, Barbara. You're misguided. You've been fooled. You have to admit it. You've got to tell him." Ariel's words sounded soothing, and Sister Quinn's smile dropped.

"Ariel, stay out of this." Sister Quinn turned her head toward me. "Why did you bring her here? Do you have to hurt everybody?"

"Me? You're the professed Christian, the *sympático,* and you've put Pepper in jail, ruined Azul, and given Ariel the same types of nightmares you've given me." Her mouth started to move, but I put my finger into her chest and pounded. "And don't give me anything about 'grace' or 'insight' or 'compassion.' I've heard everything you have to say. So don't blame me for the misery you've caused."

And then I felt Ariel's hand on my arm, gently pushing me away from Sister Quinn, so I stepped back, and Ariel took my place in front of Sister Quinn, and her tall shadow towered over Sister Quinn's shadow and mine, and then her hands were on Sister Quinn's shoulders. "Barbara, in this case, to help people, not the abstract poor you talk about, but people right here in the community, in this room, me, for God's sake, you need tell Dolph what he needs to know."

Sister Quinn's eyes darted between me and Ariel and then settled on Ariel. "What has he told you? He's gotten to you."

Ariel bent over Sister Quinn and said, "No, no, tell him. Please, Barbara, out of love, out of love for me."

Sister Quinn slid quickly along the wall so that her face was out from under Ariel's nose. "No, no, I can't; not now."

"Where is he?" I yelled.

Ariel shot a glance at me, then looked back at Sister Quinn. "Please call him."

Sister Quinn hung her head. "No."

I whispered, "Goddamn," to myself and turned away from the two of them, and I spotted the long ocotillo branch on the wall opposite me. I turned back around to them. "Come on," I said to Ariel, and reached to grab Sister Quinn's arm. But Sister Quinn pulled her arm away from me, and when I made another try and snagged her arm, she twisted it to break free of my grip and backed up. She squared off like she could duke it out with me if need be.

I crossed the room and grabbed the ocotillo branch, "You want purity? Pain? Okay, let's see who can take it. Or you want to burn some fingers in a candle?"

Sister Quinn smiled. "Be careful. You don't know what you'll see."

"So you'll fly around and perch on tombstones, and I'll prowl around looking for game. Let's see." I held the ocotillo branch in both hands out in front of me like a baseball bat. "But if I can do this, you can tell me where Fuentes is."

"My God, Dolph, don't," Ariel said.

Sister Quinn walked to the door to her *templo,* inserted a key into the padlock, and smiled to me as she pushed open the door. Ariel started backing away from both of us. Sister Quinn paid no attention to her and went into the *templo.* "No, Dolph, no. This is sick," Ariel said. "Take me back."

"Come on," I said.

"I'm not getting involved in this. No fucking way."

I reached toward her and grabbed her forearm, and she twisted it but couldn't break my grip. She twisted her arm the other way and pulled back, but I still held on and finally jerked hard to pull her into me. I circled the ocotillo branch around her, clasped both hands around it, and looked up at her face. Her hair caught and reflected bits of light. A strand of her hair tickled my forehead and nose. Her nose divided that attractive face into uneven halves; the smile was crooked; her eyes were frantic. I stood on my tiptoes and lifted my chin up to kiss her. Just as our lips were about to touch, she turned her head away from me. "No," she said. "This won't work."

"This is the way it's got to be."

"Dolph, no, no." She wriggled in my arms.

"Maybe I just want to do it."

She dug the heels of her hands into my shoulders and tried to push herself away, but I tightened my grip, pulled the ocotillo into the small of her back, and drug her across the floor. "Goddamn you, Dolph," she said as I pulled her into the *templo.*

Looking like a squat lump of clothes, Sister Quinn was already kneeling at the altar and staring up at the pained face of Christ and the suffering Virgin. She had lit candles all around so that our long shadows danced on the walls, and old Pedrito Jarmillo stared at us from the other side of the wall. Probably he smiled and nodded.

"Barbara," Ariel yelled as I tried to pull her to the altar, and Sister Quinn turned her head around and lifted her face up to see, and she stood, though she looked no taller than when she was kneeling. I saw Ariel's long shadow struggling against my shorter shadow. Her shadow arms stretched all the way to the ceiling then halfway across it and shook above the shadow of us joined.

"Let her go," Sister Quinn yelled to me.

"This is what you want, isn't it?"

"Let her go."

"Where's Vincent Fuentes?"

"Let her go. That's not the way."

"You heard her, goddamn it. You son-of-a-bitch, Dolph."

I let Ariel go. She crouched over, raised her hands in front of her face, and backed up from me. "You son-of-a-bitch. You heartless bastards. How could you even think that I'd do such a thing?" And as she talked, Sister Quinn walked up beside me and took the branch from my hand, then walked to Ariel and held it out to her.

"You too?" Ariel asked.

"Please, you don't understand this. It has to be. We will both see what we need to. I am doing this for him and for the poor." Ariel backed up, and Sister Quinn, speaking like Ariel's mother, said, "You are not a part of this. But from what visions it can give me, you can see too. Dare, Ariel. Dare. Cross a line with me once more. It is worth it."

Ariel threw the ocotillo branch down on the ground, but Sister Quinn bent over, picked it up, and offered it to her again. "Please," she said. Ariel turned to look at me, and I saw sparks of light on her cheeks where the candlelight reflected in her tears.

"I'm sorry I got you involved in this," I said. "But my friend's going to prison, and now like it or not, you're involved."

Her mouth formed a crooked frown that begin to quiver as tears glassed over her eyes. She raised her hands to her eyes and rubbed. "I will not cry," she said, and looked at Sister Quinn, then at me.

"You two—you're the same." She slowly bent over and picked up the ocotillo branch. Sister Quinn patted her shoulder, and the short, squat shadow and the long shadow moved along the wall and across the dark floor toward me.

I turned my back to them, knelt, and looked up at Mary and Christ. My mother's straitlaced Episcopal training that had made me into an Anglo had nothing to do with this dark, Hispanic-Indian voodoo, which had nothing to do with good or evil, sin or salvation. I wanted to cuss it, like my father cussed the Church, but I knew that his insistent atheism was no different from Sister Quinn's fanatic Catholicism, and when he cussed the Church and God and made me cuss like him, even though I had no idea what I was saying other than nasty words, he showed me the dark anger or fear or humiliation or whatever it was that could lead you to such extremes. The cussing and the whipping are just the results. Let it happen. Then a wasp stung my back.

I turned just my head around and saw Ariel begging me with her eyes to ease the pain in her. She held the ocotillo in her hands, the end hitting the ground as though it were too heavy to lift. "Harder," I said, turned my head around, and waited.

I heard, "Damn you both," and the blow didn't sting but clenched my teeth. I turned my head to see kneeling Sister Quinn with her elbows locked and her hands against her knees. She turned her head to look at me, smiled, then grimaced when Ariel's blow caught her.

I waited for the next blow, but instead I heard, "Fuck it, no," and turned to see Ariel fling the ocotillo branch down. "You two can whip yourselves. I'm through. Do your own perversions."

Then another shadow stretched up the wall, and Sister Quinn and I both turned to see a woman enter the room. She had on baggy green pants and pulled a ragged, frayed sweater around her shoulders. I reached down for my gun. "Go back," Sister Quinn yelled to her, but the woman kept walking toward us. Ariel backed up to the wall, leaned her back against it, then slid down the wall until her butt was on the floor.

Eugenia stepped closer to us and picked up the ocotillo branch, and I turned to look at Sister Quinn. "She's real, Dolph," Sister

Quinn said. "She's been here two days. She ran out and hid when she saw your headlights." But I knew she was real. I could smell her. She must not have bathed in those two days. Eugenia walked toward me and rested the ocotillo branch on her shoulder, like she was walking toward home plate.

I turned my back to her, and my teeth clenched three times, and my head started to hurt, and I heard a whack but didn't feel it but did feel tears in my eyes and turned to look at Sister Quinn. Her shoulders curled forward, her head drooped. She seemed to struggle to keep her eyes closed. She didn't look at me. She was already flying over the desert and looking for a perch. Then I looked at Eugenia. Her eyes were vacant, but then, as she raised the stick to strike Sister Quinn, her eyes filled with tears. I looked at Ariel, who had raised her head to watch. "Damn you," her mouth formed as Eugenia's blow hit Sister Quinn. I turned my head around and knew that my next blow would be harder.

I closed my eyes and kept them closed to take the blow, and I thought about my father curled up in an irrigation ditch, the water getting colder, his fingertips and toes getting numb, and then the numbness going up into his arms and then into his chest. I heard my mother shouting at me to quit all this silliness. This was stupid, useless; it did no good, I heard her voice saying to me. But Sister Quinn was right, the physical pain was pure. It was easier than the pain you build up over the years. Once the physical wound heals, it is gone and will stay gone, replaced only by other, different physical wounds that in turn heal. And like some of the Indians say, maybe if we can take that pain inside and turn it into the pure physical pain, then the pain inside will go when the wound heals. But Sister Quinn was wrong, too. I didn't feel any closer to any poor people or anybody else for that matter; pain was pure but private.

And on the next blow, I felt myself dragging my pulsating belly across cooling rocks with my short legs and then felt my legs grow longer and sinewy and smooth, and I moved effortlessly as I chased a rabbit that I previously could not have even seen without infrared binoculars. I was suddenly thankful to Sister Quinn—and Gilbert

Mendoza and R.C. Kobel and Pepper Cleburne and Tommy Lawler and the Alamendariz brothers and the 110-degree-plus summer weather that cooked you and the dust storms and the terrible isolation. This place and fellow inmates and expatriates were like the pain. In a civilized, real, American world, exchanging whacks with a crazy nun would be *just* crazy, nothing more, maybe just a story in one of those newspapers on the grocery store rack.

Then I heard Ariel scream: "No more, no more." I turned to look and saw Eugenia whirl around and raise the ocotillo branch as if to attack Ariel. Ariel took a careful step toward Eugenia, but Eugenia threw down the branch, stared for a moment at Ariel, who would not back down, then ran out of the *templo.*

I slumped forward because the pain, now that I noticed it, seemed heavy. I tried to stand, but my legs wobbled, and my back didn't seem capable of keeping me straight. As I tried to straighten, Ariel was suddenly beside me and whispered, "Damn you. Damn you. Are you okay?" And she reached around me to hug me, and when her hand touched my shoulder, a shiver shot from between my shoulders and into my neck. "Look, look," she said. And I turned to see Sister Quinn sprawled out on the floor, her eyelids open but her eyes rolled back in their sockets.

I crawled to her and put my hand on her chest and under her nose to feel her breathe. "CPR," Ariel said.

"It's like she's awake but not conscious," I said. Ariel crouched beside me.

Sister Quinn's eyelids fluttered, her breathing became labored, and then she opened her eyes and smiled at me and then at Ariel. She frowned. "One time, just once, I turned into an owl and flew out into the night and perched on Lupe Rodriguez's tombstone." She looked at me as her bottom lip quivered. "It is what they want. It would help them; it helped me. For a while, when I did, I was indeed a person who could help, more than just being a nun, a nurse, or a Catholic." She turned from me to look at Ariel and reached to lay her palm over Ariel's. "I've never been able to do it again."

"Forget that," I said. "Where's Fuentes?" Ariel looked at me like I was stupid.

"They had drugs," she mumbled. "They did have drugs. He told me that. He told me to follow my conscience, but I didn't know what it was." She swung her head between me and Ariel, and we both nodded, then she groaned as I pulled her up and she felt the lumps and bruises on her back bite her. She almost whimpered. "Now I know what to do." She turned to look at me. "He's in the goatherd's shack at Pasa Lajitas. He's coming across."

"Let's go," I said.

"No, no, honey," Ariel said. "Wait, rest." She gently touched my shoulder, then leaned to me and kissed me. I circled my arm around her, and the motion made my back ache, but I pulled her as close to me as I could. I didn't want to let her go. For a moment, I wanted to forget all about Pepper and Fuentes and just press my head against this tall girl's breasts.

Ariel gently circled her arm around my waist and helped me toward the door. "Tomorrow, in the morning," she said.

As we stepped into the doorway, I halted and looked back over my shoulder. Sister Quinn knelt under Christ and the Virgin, cried, and prayed. "Are you all right?" I asked, and interrupted her prayer.

"Was I wrong?" she asked, not as a question to me but as though it were a liturgy or a chant. Then she turned to look at us. "Sleep in my bed." And Ariel, her arm gingerly around me, led us toward Sister Quinn's bed.

We both turned toward the door to Sister Quinn's shack and saw Eugenia's form. "Shoo," Ariel said. Eugenia ran again, out the front door this time, and then Ariel helped me through the door to the bedroom and into the bed. Afraid of lying down, I sat on the edge of the bed.

"That woman, Eugenia," I said. "Don't chase her off."

"Shhh," Ariel said as she sat beside me and gently unbuttoned my shirt and kissed my shoulders. As I rolled onto my stomach, she kissed the bruises on my back, and I could feel tears drip onto my back. It hurt when I rolled over, but to have her on top of me this night seemed worth the renewed pain. But she sensed my pain, sat me up, and then ran her tongue from my chin to my throat, then slowly down my chest, to my stomach, over my scar, then even lower. And despite the pain, with her kneeling in front of me and with my arousal, pain, and pleasure, I felt that I had crossed some line and knew as much and had as much as I had ever had or known before.

LA MORDIDA

In the morning my back had bruised lumps, some cut and bleeding. The only muscles that seemed to move freely were in my legs. Everything above my waist hurt. I was back in the real, American world. I was again my mother's pretty Episcopal boy. Whipping myself was again stupid. Even old Miguel would have thought I was stupid. Facts became clearer. Sister Quinn was guilty. Pepper was a criminal. Trujillo was slippery. A wet had beaten me senseless. I had no reason to give a shit about Fuentes. I should just do my job. I could get out of here and get transferred to Nogales. And most real of all, Ariel was lying beside me.

She had her head toward me, and I could feel her breath on my cheek. Part of the reason my body hurt was that we were cramped together on Sister Quinn's rough single bed. We had fought and pushed against each other during the night, and with each roll, each shove, a dull ache replaced the initial spark in my back. I kissed her cheek, then lightly kissed her lips. Her eyes fluttered, and she was awake. She smiled when she saw me, then quickly frowned. "Are you all right? How do you feel?"

"Sore," I said.

"That was so stupid," she said.

"Yeah, you're right," I said. "I feel like I been eaten by a wolf and shit off a cliff." She didn't smile or giggle, so I reached and put my hands on either side of her face. "I'm sorry," I said.

Ariel sat up in the bed. "Every time I see you, you're sorry," she said, smiled, then asked, "How is Sister Quinn?"

"I just woke up."

Ariel stood up. She had only her panties on. And I watched the sunbeams spotlight patches of her smooth, tan body and golden hair. She crossed her arms over her breasts. "Stop staring," she said, and backed up to her pile of clothes. I tried to get up, but some parts of my body wouldn't move. Ariel put her hands behind her back and went into those female contortions to hook her bra; then she came over to me and slowly helped me up and over to my pile of clothes. I watched her button her shirt, then slide her legs into her jeans as I struggled to stick my arm through the sleeve of my shirt.

When I tried to raise my arms to button my shirt, Ariel saw me and stood in front of me to do it for me. Our eyes held onto each other, and we both wished the other had the right thing to say. When we got my shirt buttoned and neither of us said a thing, Ariel swung open the bedroom door and looked into the rest of the shack. "Where is she?"

My gun belt seemed to weigh a hundred pounds as I pulled it up and tried to get it around my waist. I was moving before I got it wrapped around me and in the main room of Sister Quinn's shack before I got it buckled. I followed Ariel into the *templo* and could see nobody. We both stepped outside and yelled for Sister Quinn. Gilbert Mendoza's pickup truck was gone. "She's gone to warn Fuentes," I said, and looked at Ariel.

Ariel dropped her head and her shoulders like she was tired. "So let her." But I was back, no longer in Sister Quinn's unreal world but in my own world.

I struggled against my stiff, aching shoulders to slip my jacket on while I ran as fast as I could to my car. I pushed myself up under the steering wheel and pressed my lumps and bruises against the padded seat. I slammed the door as Ariel plopped into the passenger side. As I turned the keys, Ariel crossed her arms and looked at me and then pulled her head away from me to look stiffly out the window. I pulled out of the parking lot, and as I drove up the

Almendarizes' road toward 170, a figure in a tattered surgical uniform darted in front of me. I stopped the car and watched as Eugenia ran through the brush. "You can't catch her and Sister Quinn at the same time," Ariel said without looking at me. I checked in the rearview mirror and saw Eugenia circling behind me and running back down the road toward Sister Quinn's *templo.* I hit the gas.

I drove fifteen miles above the speed limit, looking when I could at Ariel, who opened her window so that her hair whipped around her and across the front seat. She would look at me when I shifted my eyes to the road.

When we got to Lajitas, I pulled up first to her condo. "Stay here—don't come across," I said.

"Like hell," she said.

"I'm sorry, but I'm in a hurry, Ariel."

"Then you don't have time to argue. I'm going," she said. "You owe me."

The teenage kid who spoke good English was already ferrying people across the river. I parked my station wagon next to his beat-up truck, but I didn't see Gilbert Mendoza's pickup. As I pulled myself out of the car, I took off my gun belt but stuck my revolver in the back of my pants, the back of my jacket covering its butt, and put a few bullets and my handcuffs in my jacket pocket.

As Ariel sat beside me in the back of the rowboat and watched the kid row, I said to her, "Mexican *federales* shot it out with Pablo Acosta at Santa Elena, right down the river from here."

Ariel looked down at her feet, then back up at me. One strand of blond hair dangled in front of her eyes, then came to rest on the side of her nose. She brushed it back into the mess that was her tangled, windblown, slept-on hair. "You're not going to scare me."

We didn't ride the donkeys but walked up the hill toward the town, and the kids gathered around Ariel to touch her hair. This time she jerked her head away from them, and I yelled at them to go away.

We walked to the El Tejano bar, and I asked Ariel to please stay there. She agreed. "Now look," I added, "give me a while to get back. If I don't show, I want you to call the Border Patrol station in Presidio. Talk to Dede Pate, Pat Coomer, or R.C. Kobel. Hell, talk to anybody. Just tell them where I'm at. Okay?"

"Okay," she said, and hung her head to look down at me, reached out to grab either side of my face between her palms, then kissed me, and I kissed back a little too long so that it was clumsy when we pulled apart. Martin, the bartender, stared and shook his head, like this was pretty hot stuff going on in his bar.

I walked out the front door and down the street and around the pissed-on beer cans that lined the slope from El Tejano to the goatherd's shack. When I got to the adobe shack and made my way through the goats standing in front of it and around the blowing laundry, I looked up the slope and saw Ariel standing on the edge of the cliff, above the pissed-on beer cans, looking down at me.

I stopped at the goatherd's door and kicked at a goat that was in the way. I had no authority, so I couldn't yell "police." I pulled out my gun, and just holding it up caused my back to knot, and I stood to one side of the door as I knocked and listened to see if I'd have to try to bust in. I heard whispering.

"Quién es?"

"Un amigo de la hermana," I answered, and heard more whispering.

After a few moments I heard the lock click, and the door slowly opened, and I saw Sister Quinn in the open doorway. I let my hand holding my gun ease down just a bit and stepped close to her. "Step aside," I whispered. Sister Quinn moved her body but not her feet, and I looked into the room, my gun ready. A college student with a backpack of dope once got the drop on me; Vincent Fuentes would not.

Sister Quinn smiled and moved to one side so that I could step into the room. As I stepped in, she closed and locked the door behind me.

The heels of my boots tapped against the plyboards that the goatherd had clumsily trimmed to make himself a floor. Still, in spots, where the plyboards didn't quite fit, the goatherd had a dirt floor. And like most adobes in winter, the mud walls absorbed any moisture, so the place smelled musty. And like most adobes, the house let in beams of sunlight from unrepaired cracks in the walls and splits in the tin roof.

A plump man, wearing khaki pants and a white T-shirt, sat in a wooden folding chair at a small table. Behind the table was a window that framed a view of the Lajitas crossing and, a little farther on and above, the start of El Camino del Rio. On the table was a half-empty bottle of tequila, a small white mound of powder, binoculars, and a cordless phone. The phone and binoculars made sense. Fuentes's gang had bought the goatherd the phone and the binoculars so he could sit by his window, stare at the crossing through the binoculars at the road, and call the smugglers or coyotes on the cordless to let them know when to cross. The cocaine didn't belong there.

"I've been expecting you," the man said, and Sister Quinn giggled. "There's no reason for the gun." The man slowly rose and stepped toward me, and I squeezed the butt of my gun but let it dangle at my side. He took a tentative step toward me and held out his hand. I pointed my gun at him. Sister Quinn tsked and the man said, "I'm Vincent Fuentes. You can put the gun away. I'm not dangerous."

Holding up the gun kept my back knotted and thus aching, so I lowered it but didn't shake his hand. "It's okay, Dolph, really," Sister Quinn said.

"Really," Fuentes said, and stepped toward me.

"Sit down." I turned to Sister Quinn. "I didn't see Gilbert Mendoza's truck. How did you get here?"

"I flew," she said, but didn't giggle. "How's your back?" she asked.

"Hurts like hell. How's yours?"

"I'm used to it. The pain is pure. It is only a part of what—"

Fuentes disrupted her by holding up his hand. "Please, Sister Quinn. Please. I'm sure that we have both heard."

My shoulders slumped forward, and the ache eased as I became less scared of this man. I shifted my eyes between him and Sister

Quinn. "Sister Quinn, Ariel is in the El Tejano bar. Go join her and tell her that I'm okay. Tell her we'll both be there in a minute."

She didn't budge. "I'll stay with Father Fuentes. I'm as guilty as he is. We both are just trying to—"

Fuentes shook his head. "I'm no longer a priest. Sister Quinn, do as Mr. Martinez says."

She looked at both of us, then got up and walked in back of me. Just as she opened the door, letting a gush of sunlight into the room, she turned to look at me and said, "Listen to him, Dolph. You'll see." Sister Quinn exited through the door and closed it.

When she left, I turned to Fuentes. "What am I supposed to see?"

"I have no idea, but really, Mr. Martinez. You can put the gun aside." He talked politely and used his hands to emphasize his points. His peppered hair had a cowlick in front that caused a strand of hair to dangle over his forehead. Though most of his facial muscles seemed to sag and his bloodshot eyes seemed held in place by the bags under them, his eyes shone. The softening form, the deep eye sockets of Fuentes's face, reminded me of Miguel Martinez's alcohol-soaked, aging European face. I'd seen that light-skinned, faded aristocratic look in photos of my grandparents, *un güeros*. When my grandparents fled Mexico, Fuentes's family must have stayed to become a part of the Mexican elite.

"How do you know my name?" I squeezed the butt of my gun.

Fuentes jerked his head toward the door. "Sister Quinn has told me about you. I knew you would come." He chuckled. "Whether she flew or not, she's still crazy." Then I chuckled.

"Sit down, Mr. Martinez."

"No," I said, and holstered the gun. "I'm not going to cuff you either." Fuentes almost fell into his chair and let his head fall back. He brought his head back up straight to look at me.

"I know that your back must hurt."

I looked at him, then pulled a metal folding chair up to the table but sat backward in it, my elbows resting on its back. Fuentes smiled, leaned across the table, and said, "You may have either or both." He gestured at the cocaine and the tequila bottle. His face was too pale. Tequila was on his breath.

"You're kidding," I said.

"You're not on duty here."

"You aren't going to have any either."

"I've developed a few habits." He reached across the table but didn't grab the liquor or the dope but instead brought back a pair of round-eyed glasses. He put them on and looked like a professor. He squinted at me; his head seemed to circle. "I want you to take me in."

"It's early yet. How long you been drinking?" I asked.

"For years," he said. "Want a drink?" I shook my head. "What if I have just a little drink?"

"Sit tight. We both should be sober."

Fuentes smiled, then repeated himself, "I turn myself in. Take me to the US."

"I'm going to turn you in to Colonel Henri Trujillo," I said. "I have no authority on this side of the river."

"I'll pay you more than him." Fuentes poked his forefinger into the top of the table, then his whole hand started to shake, so he pulled it off the table. "I have money."

"He's not paying me anything."

"Then I'll go across myself and meet you wherever you would like." He leaned across the table toward me and spread out his hands.

I stood up. "No more *mordida.* Not from anybody."

He hung his head like his back hurt as much as mine. "I won't live if I go to a Mexican prison."

"And you'll be extradited in America."

He got excited and almost jumped up. "No, no, my crimes are in America. I'll be prosecuted for those." He leaned across the table, and I could smell the liquor on his breath. "We could just walk across. Please," he said, and his head wobbled.

"You're a goddamn dope dealer. And Mexican taxpayers ought to pay to prosecute their own dope dealers."

He tsked and waved his hand, then looked at me with his unsteady eyes. "I'm a political prisoner."

"I heard that before. Most recently from a *mojada* at Sister Quinn's place."

He put his elbows on the table, then dropped his head into his hands. He used his hands to shake his head. "Is it nice, pleasant, comfortable to see things in such easy ways?"

"My friend is going to prison because he smuggled dope for you. I turned him in."

Fuentes lifted his head out of his hands. He smiled, but his eyes seemed ready to cry. "Like you, I tried to believe things. First God and the Church, then political reform, then literature."

"Sister Quinn says I don't believe in anything."

"Good, then you know what I mean." He leaned forward, and I tensed, causing a spasm in my back.

"What is this act you've got?"

He waved his hand in front of his face. "Your back hurts, huh?" He shook his head like he really was sorry. "I've got cigarette burns on the bottoms of my feet. My jaw doesn't work so well because I got hit too many times by the Saltillo telephone book. Your friend Trujillo did that." He smiled as if to say that of course he knew Trujillo had contacted me.

He continued: "So I made the best *mordida* ever. The PRI *kept* me. The best hotels, the best meals. I was a prisoner without a cell. Everywhere I went, saying what I wanted, usually to give the illusion that I was opposed to the PRI, there with me was Colonel Henri Trujillo." He smiled at me. *"Maricón, joto.* You've heard the words." He waited, then went on. "And on these trips I got guns for people, first radical groups, then drug dealers. I'd pay for them, then Henri Trujillo would arrest the people who bought them. The criminals lost money and went to prison." Fuentes shrugged. "I should have been a hero. I should have had statues of me in Mexico City and Monterrey."

"And now you want out."

"I met many people."

"The dope runners were going to get you out?"

"They didn't pay the *mordida* to Henri Trujillo, the PRI, the army, the police, or *la plaza.* I chose the wrong dope people."

"You chose wrong when you got involved," I said.

He exhaled. "Mr. Martinez, none of us have a choice. You think

Sister Quinn could choose not to be crazy? Could you really choose not to be in *la migra* in a little shitty place like Presidio? There is no real choice; this little thing happens, then this one, and you put them together and suddenly you feel like you are some desert animal." He rested his elbows on the table and looked across at me, and I felt like shooting him because Sister Quinn wasn't around to shoot. "Nobody is explained by some little choice." He gently tapped the table. "So take me across." He looked at me, but I wasn't yet ready to answer.

"Why did we find two bodies?"

Fuentes nodded. "The people I work with had a misunderstanding." He shrugged. "One side now cooperates with Henri Trujillo and *la plaza*. Both sides would like to see me dead."

"Why don't they like you?"

"We had some small disagreements." He looked at me but didn't smile, as though he didn't want to go through all of this again.

"You didn't deliver all the guns or all the money or all the dope, so they wouldn't get you across until you made good. Am I getting warm?"

"I'll be the next to get the bullet in the head. Inside or outside of prison, I am dead in Mexico. In a jail in the US, I'm a wealth of information. I can help fight 'the war on drugs.' "

"If you eat with the devil, you better use a long spoon."

He smiled at me and then frowned and pushed up the cowlick in front of his head. "We all have short spoons."

I tried running through the choices in my mind, tried to think whether to go with reality and America or the world of the border along El Camino del Rio. A little desperate, and a whole lot selfish, wanting only to go back to the real world and to take Ariel with me, I said to myself that Vincent Fuentes didn't mean a damn thing to me. "Why should I take you across?"

And Fuentes said words that sounded funny coming from his mouth. "Compassion, mercy, sympathy," like some kind of idle, meaningless litany that he remembered from the time when he was a priest.

"When did you have compassion, mercy, or sympathy?"

"Sister Quinn beats herself to find these qualities, and I got beaten and lost them. Now I believe in selfishness. Sometimes I think that I can even feel my blood gushing through my veins. I want to preserve that."

"As you said, she also lost her mind."

"What about you, now that you have been beaten? Are you like me or Sister Quinn? Saint or sinner?"

"I'm going to call Trujillo," I said.

"Wait," he said, and I hesitated. His fingers danced in front of his face like Ariel's, his eyes shone, and with some reserve energy he became a priest or a professor: "Dolph Martinez, little Dolph, the pretty boy, the boy full of promise, and now do you, pretty boy, wonder what became of your promise?"

I moved toward the phone, and he jumped up and waved his hands. "My family was destroyed in the Depression, so my Creole father, with his pure European lineage, no dark *mestizos*—in a long line of Mexican tradition—became a gangster. And I was his light-skinned European son with all the promise and opportunities. So to make up for him, I became a priest, then a professor, then a revolutionary, then a dope smuggler, then a drunk. Dolph Martinez, pretty boy." He hesitated to make sure that he had my attention. When he was sure he had it, he grimaced. "You, you became *just* a border guard, and now you are on the wrong side of the border and have beaten a nun. You know what it is like to feel your selfish blood beating in your veins."

The speech drained the blood out of his face and eyes. And the ache in my back became blood throbbing in my head, and I cussed Sister Quinn to myself for what she told Fuentes. And I cussed him for using her to bring me to him. I picked up the cordless phone and punched in the number for the *comandanté* of the army garrison in Ojinaga. Fuentes listened and stared. And I heard the Ojinaga soldier answer the phone and ask repeatedly what I wanted. Then the *comandanté* was on the phone, and I told him to have Trujillo meet me at Pasa Lajitas. "You sentence me, then, as well as arrest me."

"And I suppose you didn't sentence anybody?"

"Simple, too simple," he said, and looked away from me like he was ashamed of me. I waited for a response, but he was through arguing with me. Now he was trying to accept his sentence.

"I have to go to the bathroom," he suddenly said, and started for the door.

"Wait a minute." I stood.

"I have to pee," he said.

"I'm going with you." I walked to the door and held it open for him. He walked out of the adobe, me behind him, and turned the corner and headed down a slope toward the goatherd's outhouse. I pushed a goat out of my way and looked up above and saw Ariel and Sister Quinn standing at the bathroom of the El Tejano and staring down. Ariel waved. "Go in a bush," I yelled at him, but he kept on toward the outhouse.

He started to hurry, and goats gathered around both of us and got in between my legs. Just as he grabbed the door to the outhouse, I put my palm against the door, and said, "Wait, I don't want you coming out with a gun." He shook his head. The door was on spring hinges, and as it swung shut behind me, Fuentes must have leaped into it so that the door caught me in the back just as I stepped into the outhouse. A flame shot up my back, and I stuck out one hand to catch my fall. When I caught myself, the flame went up my back again. But I was able to right myself, draw my gun, and shove myself through the door.

I saw Fuentes sliding more than running down the slope toward the river. I pointed my gun and yelled instinctively, *"Para y arriba las manos."* He didn't stop, and I didn't shoot.

I ran down the slope and started to gain on him, but he made it to a salt cedar, then bent over in the tall grass that grew close to the river. He thrashed around in the grass. I held up about ten yards from him and pointed my gun at him.

Fuentes rose up from the grass with his hands wrapped around a dirty plastic bag.

"What the hell is that?" I asked.

"Don't panic," he said, and held out his opposite hand as though to calm me. I heard Sister Quinn scream from the top of the cliff. Ariel screamed my name.

"Drop it."

"Please." He raised the plastic bag. And as his hand wrapped around it, I saw that he had a small-caliber pistol inside the plastic bag.

"Holy shit, don't do it."

"Please, please," he said. "Take me in, to America." His hand started to tremble as he raised the pistol but held the barrel away from me. "Please," he said. Same as the backpacker who gut-shot me, Fuentes was a man who looked to be no threat: dressed well, polite, calm. So, just as they taught me in the training school for the Border Patrol, I should have suspected both. If I pulled the trigger to my own gun, I could splatter his brains over the top of the tall grass, but I was also trained to give him every chance.

He raised the gun until it was even with his own head. His eyes filled with tears. "I don't mean to hurt you." I fought the tremor in my hand caused by my expectations of the wasp stings from his bullets. "Take me in," he said. And then a look of chagrin and disappointment came into his face as he stared at my face. "Don't you understand what I'm doing?"

I found myself wanting to promise to get him across the border and to think later about which of my many promises to keep, and then, second, to think about what was legal. "Drop the fucking gun," was what I did say.

Then a gun went off, and my teeth clenched because of the echo, not because a bullet struck me, and I steadied my finger on my own trigger to keep from putting one of my bullets into Fuentes's falling body. When his body curled in the tall grass, it twitched and then was still. The bullet made a small hole in his right temple and a larger exit wound near the top of his left ear and sent a spray of blood beneath him. Dead, Fuentes still stared at me as blood ran down the side of his face and gushed out of the exit wound to stain the grass.

I turned away and looked up at Sister Quinn, who screamed something I couldn't understand. And I saw Ariel running along the edge of the cliff. Then she lowered herself over the edge and stepped on, then slipped and slid on the piss-soaked, sun-bleached beer cans, risking a cut and a tetanus shot, to make her way to me. Then the goatherd, several of his goats following him, appeared from the river. Martin, the bartender at the El Tejano, stepped beside Sister Quinn. Then the kids who led the donkeys appeared around me, and a boy poked at Fuentes's body with a stick.

Though my training told me to squat by the body and try to revive him, I turned in circles to look at the whole scene, to memorize it for myself and for my report—because Fuentes was surely dead. I even looked up, then down to see if the sky or ground had changed. And only Ariel's hand on my shoulder broke the communion I had with the incident.

As the soldiers bagged the body and packed it with ice, Colonel Henri Trujillo shook my hand and thanked me. He wore a suit that was too big for him and a paisley tie. He wiped at the dust on his lapels with the backs of his fingers. "You will be repaid," he told me. "In an appropriate manner."

"The deal is done. There he is. I got him. You don't owe me anything."

"Very much appreciated," he said. He pulled his cigarette holder out of his coat pocket, stuffed a cigarette into the holder, and idly glanced at the two soldiers who hoisted the bagged body.

"I didn't kill him," I said. "I want your people to know that I didn't kill him. I want that in the reports. There are witnesses."

Trujillo nodded to me, then held up his hand, which automatically flipped back over his wrist, to the soldiers who were half carrying, half dragging Fuentes to the helicopter that they came in. It was a big day for the kids at Pasa Lajitas, first a killing and then a helicopter. The soldiers stopped and grunted as Trujillo stepped up to their load. He slowly unzipped the bag and cocked his head to look at Fuentes's bloodstained face. I stepped up beside him. Fuentes looked like the two executed mules that Dede and I had found. His face had lost even more color; the holes in his head were clogged with dried blood. The teenager who manned the rowboat had bought several bags of ice at Lajitas and rowed them across so that we could bag Fuentes's body in ice to keep it fresh for the autopsy. "Getting sentimental," I said to Trujillo.

Trujillo smiled. "I beat him, you know. Hit him with a telephone book. But I spent three years with him." He shrugged. "I liked him. Better than most. But I had to do my duty." Then he turned to look at me. "I killed him." Then he smiled. "And you turned your friend in so that he goes to prison. You learn to live with things. You'll get your *mordida.*"

"I don't want it. It's not like that."

"It's always like that." Trujillo reached down and zipped up the bag over his friend's face. He looked at his fingers as though they were dirty, then pulled a handkerchief out of his jacket and wiped his hands.

He and I both followed the soldiers down the goat trail to the helicopter. One of the soldiers told a joke about whores, but nobody paid him any attention. "He wasn't a criminal," I said.

As the soldiers hoisted the body into the helicopter, Trujillo shrugged again. "He committed a crime." The little rooster stepped to the helicopter and jumped in behind the two soldiers. "Step back," he said. I stepped into the small crowd, and the rotors to the helicopter started and blew dust on all of us.

As the helicopter rose, I worked my way through the small crowd to Sister Quinn and Ariel. Sister Quinn let go of Ariel's hand, looked at me, and shaded her eyes. "You could have saved him. You had what he needed, and you wouldn't give it to him."

"No," Ariel said, and tugged at Sister Quinn's arm. "Dolph couldn't do anything illegal."

Sister Quinn shot a glance at Ariel. "I'm not talking about legal." Then she turned to me and started her preaching. "He was among the dispossessed and the poor. All he needed was some compassion."

I wanted to stay away from her and her world, so I interrupted the sermon by stepping up to Ariel, taking her hand, and pulling her after me down the goat path and back to the river. "Maybe I could have saved him. But he wasn't among the poor and the dispossessed," I said to Ariel. "He just fucked up somewhere. And

Sister Quinn is just some Irish Catholic girl from the East who fucked up too."

"Dolph," Ariel scolded me.

"And you fucked up too," I told her. "And so did I."

"Mercy, compassion, grace," Sister Quinn shouted either to me, to the ascending helicopter, or to the boys soaking white handkerchiefs or rags into Fuentes's blood so they could have souvenirs to sell. Then with the helicopter's flapping sound, like a tire losing air, making her shout dim, I heard Sister Quinn scream, "Grace, Dolph." But I just kept walking away from her with Ariel beside me.

All I wanted to do was go back to Pepper's big cabin and spend a couple of days with Ariel and ask her to marry me.

EL CAMINO DEL RIO

At the end of my shift I drove up a mesa as far as I could, got out of my truck, and walked the rest of the way to the top, dodging the lechuguilla that could almost jump out to grab an ankle. Out of habit, because I sometimes just suspected something, because I was good at it, because it was just something I did, I took a few extra minutes to high point.

I looked out over the desert at the yucca and the ocotillo, whose twisting arms reached toward the sky like they were begging or praying, like the very definition of suffering and hard times. In the cracked flat spots between the jagged mountains, which were once giant domes that just caved in to leave the bottom rows of sharp teeth, were dust devils that twirled until they lost energy, one burst of an intensity that had built up over a long time and then just had to wear itself out. It felt good to know the difference between the dust devils and dust clouds churned up from the back of tires. At times, based on the way the dust moved, I could calculate the speed of the car, the care and ability of the driver, and I could then know if it was some local man, familiar with the back roads, or somebody with a trunk full of drugs and afraid of getting caught.

I could account for all the movements in the desert. I could track the signs with the best of them. I knew how to position the sun in front of me, how to calculate when a track was made based on its depth. How to use the rain, what few times it did rain. These skills were good, though, only in this little corner of nowhere. I would have to learn new skills in other places along the border.

I reached up to my eyes and felt the lines that had been etched into my pretty boy face by years of squinting across this desert and memorizing it. I looked up at the blue sky, made bluer by the dry winter, and followed the buzzards circling some roadkill. This time of year, cool air would blow down from the south rim of the Davis Mountains and mix with the hot air coming off the Rio Grande to make the climate that brought the tourists and made the long but slim clouds that turned purple and orange at sunset. The air, especially up on a mesa, didn't feel like the soft air that blew into Brownsville from the Gulf. It felt brittle, like the way the alkali rocks looked, fooling you into thinking that if you squeezed one hard enough it would disintegrate, but the alkali rocks wouldn't crush; they only left your hands a little powdered.

The air didn't caress you like a Gulf breeze, like the Brownsville breezes of my mother and father. You could even see this place as delicate, if you could figure it out, adapt to it—like a hawk, an owl, a cougar, or a lizard. Along with the heat, those animals keep this place clean without water. Ranchers don't belong in the desert. Cows are too stupid and too pampered for the desert.

As I returned to my truck, my feet rolling on the small gravel of the mesa, I tried to imagine myself back in El Paso, arresting hordes of wets as they came across the river to become absorbed in the barrios; or as a lawyer sitting on the top floor of a Houston office building and looking out over the haze that surrounded the Houston freeways; or as a political science teacher at some high school, say one in the valley in Brownsville with a bunch of Mexican students who didn't really know that they were in the United States but wanted desperately to stay here; or managing the clothing store that my mother sold to a statewide chain, measuring the gut and legs of some newly well-off Chicano, say a plumber buying a suit for Easter Sunday mass.

I got in my truck and drove back to the station in Presidio and walked into it without saying anything to anybody. Carmen was busy trying to position blanks on forms with the keys of the typewriter. Dede sat at a desk beside Carmen, filing a report. She noticed me but tried not to notice me. Pat came up to me and slapped me on the back. "How about a drink? A little *cerveza,* huh?"

"No, no, I'm going to go home," I said, and thought that I had made an error. How could I call Cleburne Hot Springs Resort my home? An uncle bailed Pepper out, and Pepper went back to the main ranch near Fort Davis and hunkered down to wait for a trial. I sent my rent to the uncle, and once a week or so Pepper called and asked about the crack in his pool.

I turned to leave, and R.C. Kobel appeared in his doorframe. "Dolph," he said. "Could you stop by for a second?" Dede looked up and watched me as I stepped into R.C.'s office. I could feel her eyes on my back.

R.C. walked behind his desk and sat. "Dolph, what's not to like about this place? Great hunting? The people here like us, especially you. You've even become some kind of a hero." I read the report that he had made of my "cracking" the case. He had made me sound like a hero. He also left out several facts about whom I got involved with and how I went about capturing those two dangerous criminals, those threats to society on both sides of the river: Pepper Cleburne and Vincent Fuentes. Maybe the "spirit" of the law excused my procedures.

Dave Devine interviewed me after Vincent Fuentes shot himself and scooped AP and UPI and the El Paso and Odessa newspapers. He too made me out to be a hero in his stories and in his follow-up editorials, in which he said that Big Bend citizens need to stress community and cohesion instead of wild-assed, unchecked frontier individualism. Rumor had it that his story and editorials had been nominated for Texas Press Association awards, and Dave whispered "Pulitzer" to Raul Flores.

I sat across from R.C. I didn't like dove hunting. Loneliness, isolation, and weirdness were what was not to like about this place. Ariel showed me that. Smoke, dust raised from speed, footprints on soft sand, the human details get easy to pick out in the desert. The details that blend into the space are always inhuman. And to become a part of it, to see any naturalness in it, you had to become, at least for a while, inhuman. But to understand it and you in it, you needed your humanity. This situation put Sister Quinn, Pepper, even Pat Coomer where they were. "You heard from Nogales?"

R.C. pulled opened his desk drawer, reached in for a cigarette, then said, "Goddamn it," and shut the drawer. "Because you are now a hero, they think you'd be good sitting behind a desk." I smiled and nodded. He cocked his head and leaned back in his chair. "You remember my offer?"

"Nobody could take your place, R.C. You're like a father to the rest of us."

R.C. stuck his tongue in his cheek and said, "At least you're getting your sarcastic sense of humor back. It's one of the most important qualifications for this job. Why don't you take it?"

I didn't answer because I didn't feel like sparring with R.C. "Come on, Dolph. Shake her off your back, out of your mind. And make a good decision."

"Like staying here," I said.

"Whatever you decide." R.C. held open his arms and leaned back in his chair until it squeaked. "Nice winter climate. Some of the best dove hunting in the world. 'Truly unique Hispanic influence,' to quote the new brochures those numb nuts at city council are circulating."

"Yeah," I said. "Ben Abrams came up with that slogan. Pepper will love it."

R.C. shook his head. "Pepper fucked up, Dolph. He just plain fucked up."

"Who hasn't?" I asked.

R.C. leaned forward and pounded his forefinger into the table. "Not that goddamn bad. Shit, Dolph, let's not talk about old morose shit that pisses us all off. What are you going to do?"

"Could you give me a couple of days?"

"Sure," R.C. said. I straightened up, stood, and turned my back to him. "Dolph," I heard when I got to the door. I turned around to see that R.C. had walked around to the side of his desk and was holding out his hand. "Good luck on deciding what to do with yourself." I shook his hand.

When I came out of the office, I caught both Dede and Carmen staring at the door. I smiled and tipped my hat to them. "Ladies." Carmen tsked, and Dede smiled.

As I let the screen door bounce behind me and headed for my station wagon, Pat happened to be climbing into his truck. Just as I put a foot into my Toyota, Pat noticed me and quickly shut his driver's side door and ran over to me. "Hey, let's say we go to El Guacolote and down a few."

"I just want to get home."

"Well, why don't you come over for dinner? Enchiladas tonight, man."

"No, no," I said. "I've got food at home."

Pat let his chin drop to his chest, then he raised his head to say, "Come on, Dolph, a woman's just like a bus—another one will come along in another thirty minutes."

"You really believe that, Pat?" I asked.

"Oh, hell, you're in the Border Patrol. You knew women were going to be scarce when you joined."

"Well, it's not just the women," I said, and got into my station wagon and closed the door.

Pat held on to the top of my rolled down window. Veins on his forehead seemed to pulse with blood, and his face grew redder than normal, almost like a blush. Even his hair seemed to blaze. The muscles in his jaws tensed. It was as though he were trying to think of something to say, to come to some wise conclusion or think of some funny anecdote. But Pat, as he so often was, was stumped. All he could do was step back from the car and move his hand from side to side. "See you tomorrow, partner," I said, then rolled up my window, turned on the air, and saw Pat smile and jerk up his thumb. It was always good to have Pat backing you up. It was his specialty.

I looked down into Pepper's pool and saw tufts of brown weeds poking through the crack at the bottom. Dust had settled on the cement and gathered at the curves from the bottom and the sides. The deep end had a mound of dirt that the winter north wind had left.

I stared until, from the angle that it hit my back, I could tell that the sun was setting. I walked up the steps, still expecting to see Ignacio around somewhere, and went into the bar and then the kitchen. Without Ignacio or Pepper around, everything was dusty. The stove had dirty grease in the pans underneath the burners. The cabinets and drain board had a layer of grime.

I tried cleaning once, and behind the cereal in the kitchen cabinet, I found a Baggie of marijuana with a couple of rolled joints in it. Feeling that I wanted to cross some last line, I soaked in Pepper's hot tub and puffed on one of the joints. But the next night, I drove out into the desert and emptied the Baggie into the wind. Maybe later that night some night owl, maybe Sister Quinn, was flying around stoned. Since the time I found the Baggie, I didn't clean; figured I'd hire a maid later, in the spring.

Remembering as I did every night but also anticipating this night, contemplating running away from this, figuring on telling the whole El Camino del Rio area just to go to hell, I went to the refrigerator and pulled out one of my six-packs of beer. And I also grabbed my bottle of bourbon that I had left on the drain board along with the empty cans of chili, tuna fish, and fruit. The canned chili would have shamed Pepper.

I took the bottle of bourbon and the cold six-pack to the main cabin with the large bath, Pepper's cabin, now my cabin. I didn't turn on a light; I didn't open up the blinds. I wanted it as dark as possible so that the candles that I had lined up around the tub would light the place. When I turned the rusted valve, the hot water and steam poured into the tub, and when I started slowly lighting the candles, one after the other, the sparks of light stood out in the steam and made streaks of color in the dark water that filled the tub. I had made some humidity, some soft air, mixed with soft light. Humidity would hug me.

When the tub filled and I had finished a beer and taken a long swallow of whiskey, I peeled off my clothes and stepped into the water. As I drank another beer, I looked at the shoe box and the letter on the lamp stand beside Pepper's king-size bed, where I now slept. The engraved letter was an invitation from Ben Abrams and his wife to attend a dinner at their house. "Invite that nice blond woman," Mrs. Abrams had written on the invitation. She hadn't heard. I kept the letter out to remind myself to send my regrets.

Inside the box was three thousand dollars. Two days after Vincent Fuentes shot himself, a UPS truck rolled up to Pepper's place just as I was getting off work. Since he wasn't the regular driver, the driver had no idea where in the hell he was, and I had to give him directions back after I signed for the package from Henri Trujillo. Since then, the box had been sitting by my bed. In a way the mere three-thousand-dollar *mordida* was an insult, not even proper gratitude compared to the amount of money changing hands or saved or made down in Mexico.

But tonight, like most nights, what I thought about most was what Ariel had said to me. She had called me and asked if she could come over; she had some important news. With Pepper gone, I had filled the bath in his cottage and had lined candles all along the edge of the tub. I had chilled a bottle of wine and set it in an ice chest next to the tub. And I had waited for her to arrive.

Ariel came in that night wearing a denim skirt that rose just above her knees and a denim jacket. She had put her diamonds in her ears and pulled back her hair. She looked around at the scene that I had created, and rather than smiling, she almost frowned. "Please, sit down," I said, "relax." She slipped off the denim jacket and revealed a low-cut, ruffled Mexican blouse. Her bare chest reflected the moonlight that came in with her through the still open door. Her tightly bound hair, like her arms and chest, had dancing shades of light and color streaked within it. She had put on makeup. She was the most beautiful that I had ever seen her, and I stepped toward her to kiss her. But she stepped back and said, "I have to talk."

"Later," I said. And she looked at the steam rising from the hot bath and the flickering candles.

"Dolph, you haven't done this for me," she said, and raised her long fingers to her face to touch her cheeks.

"Of course I have. I love you. Let's get in." I smiled, but she wouldn't.

"You don't love me. You love some ideal that you've made for me."

"You're perfect. We're perfect."

"There is not a 'we,' " she said, and hung her head. I stepped up to her and looked up at her face to try to see her eyes, but she turned her head away from me. I reached up and pulled her chin toward me. She tried to make that crooked smile of hers, but the corners of her mouth just wouldn't rise, as though they were weighted down with the job she had to do. "I'm leaving."

"What?" I said, and my trembling hand made her chin shake.

"I'm going back to Houston; I've spoken to Walter Bean."

"Why?"

She pulled my hand away from her chin and backed toward the door. She raised her hands to her face, and then her long slender fingers wiggled in front of her face as she tried to explain. "I can just barely take the environment, the isolation, the loneliness, the climate, the landscape. But the people are just too weird."

"They're the same, the land and the people, I mean. You don't have one without the other."

"You're a part of it all, Dolph." I knew that I shook my head, but I wanted to tell her that I was the "pretty boy" that my mother had made me. I wasn't to be a part of this. I could get out, too. "Just too much has happened here. I don't think that I like myself here," Ariel went on.

"What are you running away from? Us or yourself?"

"I don't know what's right here; I don't know what's real here."

"I'm real," I said.

"But what you want from me isn't real. It isn't me."

"Please," I said. "Just spend the night. Take a bath. Decide in the morning."

"I'm leaving in the morning."

I tried to think of something to say. I wanted to tell her that this was just too unfair. I wanted to beg her to stay; I wanted to hit her to make her understand what I couldn't explain. "What about me?" I asked.

"I just don't love you."

"Why not?"

She dropped her eyes to look down at me. "We're too different," she said, and I knew that she had rehearsed this speech and was now coolly going over the memorized lines.

"How?"

"We just are."

"Why?"

"This place, this land, these people have made you into something I don't want to be. It's like you once said, it's 'mean.' And it makes people mean."

"What about caring for poor, lonely people? Like Sister Quinn? Like me?"

"I can care for you; I can't love you."

"So you're going?"

"Yes."

"I'll go, too. I'll get transferred. I'll quit."

She smiled. "You can't quit."

And Ariel started to back out of my life and Pepper's cabin. I wanted to stop her, but instead I tried to memorize the way she looked so I could keep that vision in my mind. "You're all that I have here now," I found myself saying very low, not knowing whether I was talking to her or myself. "Don't go. Don't do it—give me a chance."

I grabbed at her and caught her arm, "Oh, Dolph. I can't take you. You have some strange, half-concocted ideal of your life. Some story only you know. And you want everything to fit, and it makes you as crazy as the rest of them." I dropped her arm, and she stared straight at me as she backed toward my door. Before she walked out, she reached into her purse, dug around, pulled out Pepper's diamond stud earring, and handed it to me. "Here," she said. "You left this at my place." I wished that she would have taken off her left shoe so that I could have seen the tattoo of the delicate, green-eyed, curved panther on her arch one more time.

After Ariel left the Big Bend area and I called Walter Bean's office in Houston and then her parents in Maryland and I finally got ahold of her in her Houston apartment, she told me not to call her anymore. I begged her to explain everything again. I got drunk in Pepper's hot tub. I got drunk a lot, mostly by myself. I called in sick a couple of days because I didn't feel like getting out of bed, even though I couldn't sleep when I was in bed.

And when I could sleep, I had these horrible dreams. In one, I stuck my snout into the steaming guts of a pronghorn antelope and gorged on its liver. In another, I was getting shot again and again, but this time none of the shots were wasp stings, all were teeth clenchers, and like in the movies, each shot knocked me farther and farther back and ripped open my chest. In the worst, though, I was trying to make love to Ariel. I could feel her bare thighs against mine. And as we kissed and I felt me in her, she started to scream and pushed me away, and I apologized and tried to get off of her, but the more I tried, the more I grabbed her and squeezed her, and she cussed me. Finally she would pull her eyes down to look at me and then twist her mouth under the large nose, as though not to smile at me but to laugh at me.

When I got drunk with Pat, I told him about my dreams, and that must have been how and why Dede and R.C. got wary and unsteady around me, like two dogs who didn't know whether to fight me or fuck me. It was R.C. who called me in and suggested I go see the counselor in Alpine. She suggested I see a doctor, and I got two types of prescriptions from him: "mood alterers," he called the pink pills, and the blue-and-white ones were antidepressants. Had I not caught Pepper, I probably could have gotten the pills from him for free. Father Jesse Guzmán heard that I was having problems and came out to Pepper's to see if he could help. He suggested that I come out to Saint Margaret Mary's.

I certainly did not want to go to Saint Margaret Mary's, but with my mood now altered, I thought about going to see Sister Quinn, but she scared the hell out of me now. Besides, Sister Quinn had her own problems. She was waiting for a judge and grand jury to decide whether or not to prosecute her. But hell, neither a judge nor grand jury in this area of the country would dare prosecute an ex-nun. Her excommunication was worse than her legal problems.

She still ministered and preached to a few of the faithful, but the majority of her flock deserted her for Father Guzmán's cinder block Saint Margaret Mary's. I was wrong about them. They weren't that faithful to her. It was as though the local faithful needed the endorsement of the Catholic Church, the Indian trickster gods, and Pedrito Jarmillo, plenty of insurance or assurance. Ol' Pedrito and her own dreams were all that Sister Quinn could offer now. Maybe if the gringos actually prosecuted, she would become saintlike and more people would come to her *templo.*

Several farmhands around Redford reported that a phantom dressed in green pajamas was stealing food and small tools. Gerald Galván saw Eugenia running down his dirt road with one of his kid's toys. Then she just disappeared. Maybe the locals, maybe Sister Quinn, would conjure her back up. Maybe I should have tracked this phantom. Tomás went to an insane asylum in Chihuahua City. They found him hanged in his dormitory after he had been there a week.

I saw Socorro at La Kiva. He was sitting at a table with a sun-dried, Big Bend woman on either side of him. "How about that—she's gone, and I'm still here," he said.

"And you didn't even thank me."

"I owe you one." And as I tipped my hat, he added, "For slamming me into my goddamn van."

I pulled my hand down from my hat. "Don't turn your back."

"I won't."

"Me either," I said.

I even called my mother and told her that my problems were hereditary. She invited me to spend some time with her, and she said she still had friends who might be able to get me into another line of business. Then she reminded me of what I didn't need to be reminded of: the time she ran off to Prescott, Arizona, with a guy named Harry and his poodle.

I remembered everything as I pulled open my second beer and sank deeper into Pepper's hot water, and I wished for the time when I would not need the hot tub, or booze, or pills. Then I heard the hinges of the door squeak. A long shadow stretched into the room, and I thought about jumping out of the tub and running to my gun. I imagined the headline, Border Patrol Agent Found Dead, Naked. Then I heard Dede's voice. "Dolph, Dolph, are you here?" Dede knew better than Ariel about not sneaking up on a person employed to carry a gun.

"Come in, Dede," I said. And she hesitantly stepped into the room and stared at the ideal bath that I had made in Pepper's cabin. Still in her uniform, Dede stood straight up in front of me and looked just a little embarrassed by me and for me. "What can I do for you?"

"I came by to see what I could do for you, Dolph."

"Want to go to the Abrams's dinner party?" I asked. "The social event of the year for Presidio. The Alamendarizes, the Spencers, Father Jesse Guzmán, the social elite will all be there."

Dede's nose wrinkled as she smiled. "I got an invitation too."

Dede dropped her smile. "Dolph, I'm your friend," she said, and hung her head so that I couldn't see her face.

"Want to join me?" I asked.

Dede raised her head and her smile spread back across her face, and then slowly she took off her gun belt, then her jacket, then her boots, her shirt, her pants. She stopped undressing and stood in front of me in her panties and bra. From her tight, defined muscles, I could tell that Dede had started lifting weights—probably bought her own junior Olympian set, like I had done, and then had started adding on. That was a nice surprise.

She put her hands behind her back and unclasped her bra, and her small breasts didn't fall out but poked out. She slid out of her panties, hung her head, and stepped into the hot water. And I circled my arm around her shoulders when she scooted next to me and said, "Dolph, what is wrong?"

I knew—as I told her what I thought was wrong, as she patted my chest and traced my scar with her finger, as she leaned her head on my shoulder and looked up into my face—that later in the night, she and I would dry each other off and then go into Pepper's king-size bed, and each of us would pretend that the other was somebody else, and we'd make confessions while we had our sex.

Maybe she'd even spend the night. And thus I would break some more rules.

I knew that her nakedness, her body, her head against my shoulder, and her sex were all a gift. She wasn't a lover but a friend, giving me what she could but not enough. It was something like compassion, salvation, or forgiveness. Maybe it was grace.

And once I became the agent in charge, after I turned down the job in Nogales, I would see to it that Dede, once she finished her last probationary year, got transferred out. It was something like loyalty, gratefulness, or admiration. I held my palm against Dede's cheek and gently patted it.

I would take the three thousand dollars and drop one thousand in Sister Quinn's collection plate on the next Sunday. I would send another thousand to Pepper to help with his defense, and I would get Pat and maybe R.C., if I could convince him, to go to Juarez and spend another thousand as foolishly as possible. It is something like acceptance of what you have become. I leaned toward Dede, and her arm came up out of the water to circle my neck.

I was far too old to be a pretty boy. I was no longer my mother nor my father's boy. I, this place, and *la patrulla* had now done more to make me than ol' Miguel Martinez or Sandra Beeson. But in getting free from my parents, I had become like them. It was time now for me, like them, to stay where I was, content with what I was. It was time to grow old with Pat Coomer, Sister Quinn, Pepper Cleburne, the Alamendariz brothers, and the few new agents who would come and not be able to get away.

There would be stories told about me. To the Border Patrol agents, I'd be like R.C., the tough, hard agent, a model for others: survived a gut shot, turned in his friend, took the case away from the Feebies and the DEA. To the different sets of locals—Presidio, Ojinaga, Lajitas—I'd be the outsider who didn't understand the nature of the area: got himself gut shot, betrayed a friend, sold out to the feds. The Mexicans, on both sides of the border, would sing about me in their *corridos*. I'd probably be the villain.

And I knew that I would live in Pepper Cleburne's Hot Springs Resort. In the summer evenings, after work, I'd sit in his shade, drink a beer, and stare out at the desert. And one winter morning, maybe sometime after Sister Quinn had finally learned to fly, a car horn would honk in the clear, brittle air. And I would go out to see a line of Winnebagos full of mamas, daddies, grandparents, and grandkids. I would rent cabins to them all. And the next day, once the heat built up, I would watch as they splashed water on each other and dove into and swam around Pepper's heated pool. Maybe I could use my mother's money to repair the pool.

I looked at Dede's eyes as we pulled ourselves closer, and we both closed our eyes as we kissed so we could both see who or what we wanted.

1. 45
85

2. 85
89

123

Curandera

IN ARM'S WAY

Turning, Longarm saw the one-armed ex–Confederate soldier moving toward the stage with a look on his face that could only signal murder and mayhem.

Longarm shoved his way forward, reaching the stage just as the one-armed man arrived at the same time. Longarm threw himself between the secretary of the interior and the man, just as the man drew his gun and screamed a terrible curse at Colonel Maxwell.

There was no time to draw his own gun, so Longarm lunged at the one-armed man in a desperate attempt to knock him down. But the assassin's gun was already coming up and when it exploded, Longarm felt a searing pain flash across his upraised arm. Then, he crashed into the hate-filled Reb and they both tumbled into the screaming crowd.

TABOR EVANS

JOVE BOOKS, NEW YORK

THE BERKLEY PUBLISHING GROUP
Published by the Penguin Group
Penguin Group (USA) Inc.
375 Hudson Street, New York, New York 10014, USA
Penguin Group (Canada), 90 Eglinton Avenue East, Suite 700, Toronto, Ontario M4P 2Y3, Canada
(a division of Pearson Penguin Canada Inc.)
Penguin Books Ltd., 80 Strand, London WC2R 0RL, England
Penguin Group Ireland, 25 St. Stephen's Green, Dublin 2, Ireland (a division of Penguin Books Ltd.)
Penguin Group (Australia), 250 Camberwell Road, Camberwell, Victoria 3124, Australia
(a division of Pearson Australia Group Pty. Ltd.)
Penguin Books India Pvt. Ltd., 11 Community Centre, Panchsheel Park, New Delhi—110 017, India
Penguin Group (NZ), Cnr. Airborne and Rosedale Roads, Albany, Auckland 1310, New Zealand
(a division of Pearson New Zealand Ltd.)
Penguin Books (South Africa) (Pty.) Ltd., 24 Sturdee Avenue, Rosebank, Johannesburg 2196,
South Africa

Penguin Books Ltd., Registered Offices: 80 Strand, London WC2R 0RL, England

LONGARM AND KILGORE'S REVENGE

A Jove Book / published by arrangement with the author

PRINTING HISTORY
Jove edition / November 2005

For information, address: The Berkley Publishing Group,
a division of Penguin Group (USA) Inc.,
375 Hudson Street, New York, New York 10014.

ISBN: 0-515-14030-9

JOVE®
Jove Books are published by The Berkley Publishing Group,
a division of Penguin Group (USA) Inc.,
375 Hudson Street, New York, New York 10014.
JOVE is a registered trademark of Penguin Group (USA) Inc.
The "J" design is a trademark belonging to Penguin Group (USA) Inc.

PRINTED IN THE UNITED STATES OF AMERICA

10 9 8 7 6 5 4 3 2 1

Chapter 1

Longarm stood beside the window of his upstairs office in the Denver Federal Building and studied the crowd that was gathering just down the street at the mint. It was a crisp and windy March and when he pulled out his pocket watch, he saw that it was getting close to noon.

"Big crowd gathering," he said to himself. "Could be trouble."

United States Deputy Marshal Custis Long was a tall man, somewhat angular, with wide shoulders and a Colt .44 on his left hip whose gun butt faced forward. His hair and handlebar mustache were brown and his eyes were blue-gray, with crow's-feet just beginning to appear at their corners. As he watched the crowd gathering for the dedication speech honoring somebody he did not know, Longarm absently pulled a five-cent cheroot from his brown coat pocket and stuffed it into the corner of his mouth. He didn't light the cigar, but instead absently turned it around and around because his attention was focused on the activity down in the street.

"Custis, what do you think?" a voice asked from behind.

Longarm didn't need to turn around to know that his boss and friend, Billy Vail, had entered his small, cluttered office.

"I think there's a good chance we're going to have some trouble down there."

Billy Vail was a much shorter man and about ten years older than Longarm. His forty years were already starting to show on him, as were the long hours he spent every day behind a desk pushing paperwork. Billy had a receding hairline and a paunch, but Longarm knew that his boss had once been one of the best federal lawmen in the country. And now, as they both studied the large and restive crowd gathering for the noon dedication, they agreed there could be some serious trouble.

"Why did Secretary of the Interior Gordon Maxwell have to come here and stir up bad memories?" Longarm asked. "There are still a lot of Southern sympathizers in Denver and this dedication is sure to make 'em madder than a nest of hornets."

"You know the answer to that." Billy folded his arms and frowned at the scene below. "Secretary Maxwell has every intention of becoming our next president. And if he doesn't get nominated this time around, he'll settle for vice president."

Longarm glanced sideways. "Do you think he has a chance at the presidency?"

"I sure do," Billy replied. "When I was in Washington, D.C., last summer I heard Gordon Maxwell address Congress. He's a powerful orator and has the pedigree to go about as high as he wants in the government."

"And," Longarm reminded Billy, "Colonel Maxwell is

one of the most decorated Union officers to survive the war."

"That too," Billy admitted. "So the secretary of the interior is a war hero, he's rich, and is a great orator. Put it all together, Custis, and I think what we might be seeing down there is the next president of the United States."

Longarm couldn't argue that possibility. He'd fought in the War Between the States, and once he'd seen Colonel Gordon Maxwell in the heat of battle. And while there was no doubt that the man was every bit as brave and flamboyant as General George Custer, like Custer, there seemed to be a flaw in the famous man's character. And the flaw most likely was Maxwell's burning ambition.

"What are you thinking?" Billy asked.

"That it wouldn't hurt to be down there to help our local law-enforcement people if there is a riot."

"They told me that they have it all covered," Billy said. "The secretary even has his own personal bodyguard."

Longarm was not a man to interfere when uninvited. However, he could see several men in the crowd waving Confederate flags and shouting in anger at the supporters of Secretary Maxwell. To his way of thinking, there was just bound to be trouble.

"Billy, this is our town. I don't care if the secretary does have his own bodyguard; this could still get out of control in a helluva hurry. Then what we'd have is a riot and people getting hurt, maybe even shot. It makes no sense for this damned dedication. I don't know why we have to put up with it."

"Gordon Maxwell is intent on creating as much publicity as he can," Billy explained. "Denver is only the first stop on his tour of the West. He's going to dedicate a dozen statues and create federal parks, which will gain him a huge amount of publicity. Lots of photographs and quotes. Maxwell, you see, knows that President Arthur is only in office because his boss was assassinated. The colonel sees a chance to grab the presidency, and I wouldn't be a bit surprised if he succeeds."

Longarm snorted. "I guess that's so . . . if some Southern sympathizer doesn't shoot him first."

"Well," Billy said, "if they do, they'll create one of the richest and most beautiful widows in America. Gordon Maxwell's wife is quite a looker."

"Is that a fact?"

"Oh, yes," Billy said. "Regina Maxwell is stunning and she comes from a family every bit as wealthy and powerful as that of her husband. I've heard it said in the Washington circles that she is his equal in every respect save her husband's runaway ambition."

"Is she in Denver today?"

"Yes. She always stands behind her husband when he gives his speeches."

"That settles it," Longarm said, turning away from the window. "I'm going down there to see what is going happen."

Billy didn't hesitate. "I'll go with you and maybe ask a few of our people to join us . . . just in case."

"Good idea," Longarm agreed. "We'd better hurry, though. It's almost noon and that's when the dedication is set to begin, isn't it?"

"Yes, but the secretary has a habit of always being about ten minutes late."

"Perfect," Longarm replied. "That will give us just about enough time to move into the crowd and be ready to step in if there are troublemakers planning to create some publicity of their own."

Longarm had always been a leader rather than a follower, and with his long legs he could walk faster than anyone he'd ever known. Because of that, he was ten feet ahead of Billy and the three other federal marshals who left the Federal Building and hurried up Colfax Avenue. The U.S. Mint was just up the street, and beyond it was the Colorado State Capitol Building with its impressive gold dome. Pigeons were flying around, and Longarm could feel an air of excitement and underlying danger. When he had been upstairs with a good view of the city, he'd estimated that the crowd was pushing five hundred. Even now, as he hurried toward the gathering, Longarm could see store owners and shopkeepers closing their businesses in order to attend this highly publicized dedication.

"Everyone wants to see Gordon Maxwell, but they want to see Regina Maxwell even more," Billy had observed as he'd left the Federal Building.

Longarm reached the edge of the waiting crowd. He was a man who was drawn to danger, and so he naturally moved toward a small group of ex–Confederate soldiers who were waving their fallen flag. Longarm was from West Virginia, and he had great sympathy for the brave men who had proudly worn the gray, but he wished that they would put the past behind them and move on with their bitter and often shattered lives. Waving their flag and even wearing their old uniforms was their way of telling people that they might have lost the Civil War, but they had never been defeated.

"Hey, boys," Longarm said. "You really don't want to cause any trouble today, so why don't you just put down the flag and go have a beer someplace?"

There were six of them and they were a rough-looking bunch. One was missing an arm, while another carried the scar of a terrible saber wound across the side of his haggard face.

The largest of the ex–Confederate soldiers, the one with the missing arm, whirled around to glare at Longarm eyeball to eyeball. "You tellin' us that, in this great Gawdamn Union, we haven't even got the *right* to gather and show our true colors."

"Johnny Reb, I'm telling you that the war is long done and gone. That we all suffered and we need to put the past behind us." Longarm had no desire whatsoever to fight these angry former soldiers. In a few respects he was even sympathetic to their lost cause. "You boys didn't come here to listen to what the secretary of the interior has to say. You came to heckle and maybe cause a fight."

The big one-armed man grinned, but it wasn't friendly. "You got that right. And who the hell are you?"

"Like yourself, I'm an ex-soldier, and it doesn't matter what side I fought for. I'm also a federal law officer, and I'd like you boys to take your flag and move along."

"What's your damned name?"

"United States Deputy Marshal Custis Long." Longarm showed the one-armed man his badge. "Now don't be causing any trouble here, boys, or innocent people could get hurt."

"I've seen innocent people get hurt before," the man spat. "My wife and sister were raped and murdered by Union soldiers. Maybe you were one of 'em."

"Never," Longarm replied, his anger starting to build.

"Marshal Long, you have a Southern accent, but I suspect you are a traitor at heart. Federal officer or not, you'd better get out of my sight."

Longarm realized that the other ex-Confederates had circled him, and that caused the hair on the back of his neck to stand up. These men were killers, and one of them might just stick a knife quietly between his ribs and lay him to an eternal rest. Just as he was about to say something, a bull-shouldered man wearing a buckskin shirt pushed through the crowd, drew his pistol, and placed it against the one-armed man's head. "Tell your men to drop that damned Confederate rag!"

"I'd sooner rot in hell!"

"I can take care of that too," the bull-shouldered man said, cocking back the hammer of his gun.

Longarm said, "We don't need to do this, so put your gun away. These Southern boys have had a little too much to drink and they mean to make no trouble."

"Is that right?" the man holding the gun said quietly. "And here I thought that they were itching for a fight. You see, I know Confederate trash when I see and smell it."

The one-armed man's cheeks burned red and he shook with emotion. Finally, he turned to his friends. "Boys, haul in the flag and let's go have another round. We'll meet up with this fella sooner or later and that's when he'll sing a different tune."

"If I ever see you again, Reb," the man in the buckskin shirt warned, "I'll shoot you down like the worthless dog that you are."

"We'll see about that," the one-armed man said as he turned and pushed his way through the crowd.

When they were gone, Longarm exhaled a deep breath. "I suppose I should thank you, but I won't."

"They'd *circled* you, mister. You were theirs for the havin'. But I don't want your thanks. I get paid by the colonel to take care of little problems before they become big problems. And that's what I just did."

"You're his bodyguard." Longarm studied the man. He looked to be about six feet tall and his eyes were gray, as merciless as those of a hawk. He had a square chin and a long crooked nose over a set of thin lips. "Isn't that right?"

"My name is J. D. Kilgore and I prefer to call myself the colonel's paid protector." Kilgore leaned in closer to Longarm. Too close. "And I take it that you are some kind of federal officer of the law."

"That's right. And Kilgore, if you'd have shot that one-armed man, it would have caused this crowd to stampede," Longarm said, his anger just barely under control. "There are women and children here today and they'd most likely have been trampled."

"I was just doin' my job," the man said. "And for what it's worth, I think those Confederate boys had you by the balls and were just about ready to cut 'em off."

Longarm bristled. "I can handle myself and I would have been fine."

"Bullshit!" Kilgore spit. "That's why the colonel keeps me at hand. If he depended on the likes of you for his protection, he wouldn't be long for this world."

Custis was about to say something when the crowd began to applaud. He turned and saw a face that he had not seen since the Battle of Shiloh.

"Ladies and gentlemen," the secretary of the interior said, his handsome face creased in a wide smile, "I am honored to be here today to dedicate this United States Mint in the honor of General James P. Montgomery, a great war hero and my personal friend. However, before I begin to tell you why this important federal United States Mint henceforth will be called the Montgomery Mint, I would like to present to you my beloved wife, Mrs. Regina Wilson Maxwell."

For a moment, Longarm and everyone else in the huge crowd forgot about whatever else their thoughts had been on as the secretary's wife stepped forward on the small speaker's platform that had been erected only a day earlier. She had auburn-colored hair, green eyes, and flawless skin, skin so white that it reminded Longarm of the purest Rocky Mountain snow. She was probably about five feet five, and was full-figured, with the face of an angel. Mrs. Maxwell raised her gloved hand to the crowd and smiled, and it made everyone smile with her.

Billy Vail was right, Longarm thought. *She is the most beautiful creature I think I've ever laid eyes upon.*

Without saying a word, the woman gracefully relinquished the stage to her husband and floated into the background. When Longarm glanced sideways, J.D. Kilgore was gone.

"Ladies and gentlemen," Secretary of the Interior Gordon Maxwell began, "let me first say that I am here at the request of our outstanding president, Chester A. Arthur, a man who stepped forward after the tragic assassination of his predecessor, President Garfield. And today, I want to tell you about another great man, General James P. Montgomery, to whom this mint is being dedicated today."

Billy Vail appeared by Longarm's side. "I saw the trouble you were in, but we were clear on the other side of the street and couldn't get here fast enough. What happened?"

"I'll tell you later." Longarm was about to whisper more, but he caught a movement out of the corner of his eye. Turning, he saw the one-armed man moving purposefully toward the stage with a look on his face that could only signal murder and mayhem. "Billy, follow me!"

Longarm shoved his way forward, but it was slow going. He finally managed to reach the stage and jump up on it just as the one-armed man arrived at the same time. Longarm threw himself between the secretary of the interior and the big ex–Confederate soldier just as the man drew his gun and screamed a terrible curse at Colonel Maxwell.

There was no time to draw his own gun, so Longarm lunged at the one-armed man in a desperate attempt to knock him down. But the assassin's gun was already coming up and when it exploded, Longarm felt a searing pain flash across his upraised arm. Then, he crashed into the hate-filled Reb and they both tumbled into the screaming crowd.

Longarm was fortunate to land on top of the big man, and heard the Reb's skull hit the sidewalk with a sickening crunch. The one-armed man went limp as Longarm tore the pistol from his hand. He looked into the man's eyes and saw them roll upward into his head. Blood began to pour from Reb's ears, nose, and even from the corners of his eyes.

Longarm placed his hand on the one-armed man's throat. There was no pulse. The hate-filled ex-soldier of the South had broken his skull against the sidewalk and died instantly. Women and children were screaming, but Longarm hardly noticed as he checked the body for more weapons. He found a derringer and a knife.

By then, J.D. Kilgore was at his side, his gun once more trained on the one-armed man's skull. Longarm pushed the gun aside and hissed, "Put that away, dammit, this man is already dead."

Kilgore actually looked disappointed. "Are you sure?"

"Hell, yes, I'm sure! Put the gun away and go to Colonel Maxwell and his wife just in case some of this man's friends decide to get even right now."

Kilgore disappeared while Billy Vail and several of Longarm's fellow lawmen began to calm the crowd, which had already diminished by half.

Over all the shouting and commotion, Longarm could hear the secretary of the interior telling everyone that the danger was passed and that the dedication would go on as soon as the body was removed.

"There is no need for panic," Gordon Maxwell said repeatedly, raising his arms overhead. "The danger is passed and everyone is safe. Calm yourselves! This dedication will not be stopped by radical Southern sympathizers."

The colonel kept talking, but Longarm didn't bother to listen. He was studying the face of the one-armed man, wondering if he had any family left that ought to be notified. Longarm recalled that this man had said that his wife and sister had been raped and murdered by Union soldiers. One of the sad horrors committed by both sides. Given that personal tragedy, small wonder this man had been permanently and irreparably crazed. Crazed enough to want to kill that rich and egotistical fool on the stage who was insisting that this dedication proceed as soon as a broken Confederate's body was dragged out of sight and out of mind.

"Custis, you've been shot!"

"It's just a scratch." Longarm wiggled his fingers and then he frowned. "But I'm out a good coat."

"You saved the secretary's life. He wants to see you right away."

"Tell him I'm busy."

"Custis, you need to see him," Billy insisted. "He is the secretary of the interior. Just . . . just for a minute."

Longarm didn't give a damn about meeting the man, but he didn't want to see Billy get into hot water, so he reluctantly nodded his head. "All right."

"Let's get this body to the undertaker," Billy said, ordering several men to take hold of the corpse. "The secretary is very upset by this delay. He's angry that most of the crowd ran off and he's giving our local marshal hell, threatening to have him removed from office."

Longarm shook his head. "A man just died here. Why doesn't Secretary Maxwell put this off for a day . . . or better yet . . . for good?"

"Because he came here to make the dedication and that's what he's going to do. Also, his schedule doesn't permit a delay. Now we'll take care of this. Go up and meet the secretary before he really loses his patience."

For just the briefest of moments, Longarm actually considered telling his friend and boss, and especially Secretary Gordon Maxwell, that they could all go straight to hell.

Chapter 2

Secretary Gordon Maxwell was six feet four, which was the same height as Longarm. However, the ex–Union colonel and war hero was heavier by a good fifty pounds. His face was beefy and flushed either by the longtime consumption of too much good whiskey or the current excitement caused by a near assassination.

"Secretary Maxwell," Billy Vail said by way of introduction, "this is United States Deputy Marshal Custis Long. He's the one that—"

Maxwell cut Billy off in mid-sentence. "I know what this brave officer of the law just did! I saw it with my own eyes, just like everyone else up here with me."

He studied Longarm with a smile radiant enough to win over a reptile. "Marshal, simply and humbly put, I owe you my life."

Longarm felt his cheeks blush. "I just did what I'm paid to do. I'm sorry about this, and I believe the war left a terrible mark on the man who just a few moments ago tried to take your life."

"The war left its mark on us all," Maxwell said. "Were you a participant in that great conflict to preserve the Union?"

"I was."

Maxwell nodded his head sagely. "Yes, I was sure of that. And I'll bet you were a fine soldier and received many commendations and battlefield promotions."

Longarm wasn't the kind of a man who wanted to go back into that nightmarish past or to admit that he had received many commendations, so he remained silent.

"I see that you were wounded," Secretary Maxwell observed, glancing down at Longarm's bloodstained sleeve.

"It's just a scratch."

Regina Maxwell stepped up to the men. "I've had some nursing training. I'd like to take a look at that wound. Please remove your coat, Marshal Long."

Longarm started to protest and say that he would go back to the office and bandage it himself, but the secretary of the interior's wife had such a powerful effect on him that he took off his coat and started rolling up his sleeve.

"You must see a doctor," Regina Maxwell told him as she studied the furrow across his lower forearm. "This is deep and it could get infected without proper medical attention."

She then used her own handkerchief to bind the wound and slow the bleeding.

No longer the center of his wife's attention, Maxwell turned his thoughts back to his own ambitions. "I need to get his damned speech over with," he muttered under his breath. "Is there some way to get the crowd all back?"

"Not that I can think of," Billy Vail said, noting that

where there had been five hundred or more, there were now less than half that number standing in front of the U.S. Mint.

At that moment, J.D. Kilgore hurried up and said, "Secretary Maxwell, I could go into the nearby saloons and offer the men a free beer if they come back to listen to you. We could probably rustle up fifty or sixty real quick. Make this a respectable crowd again."

"Go ahead and do that," Gordon Maxwell said. "Just make sure there are no drunken ex-Rebs in the bunch this time." He looked around. "Where is the damned local press?"

"They're around," Kilgore assured his boss. "I've been giving them statements about how you were not the least bit intimidated by those Johnny Rebs and that this dedication will go on despite any personal danger to you and Mrs. Maxwell."

"Good! I'd like the story of my scrape with death sent back to the East Coast at once."

J.D. Kilgore's head bobbed up and down with agreement. "Consider it done. What's the headline you'd like used, sir?"

Gordon Maxwell frowned in concentration for a moment, and then raised a forefinger to the sky. "Yes, I have it clearly. The headline should cry out: 'Assassination Attempt!' And the main text sent back to the East Coast newspapers should read that I narrowly survived . . . and *undaunted* . . . could not be silenced despite mortal danger."

"I'll make sure that it goes out," Kilgore promised, a pad in his hand and a pencil scratching out the message. "Also, I'll get photographers up here right away and we can send pictures. They'll make the front pages, I'll promise you that."

"They'd better," Maxwell said, looking exhilarated by this sudden turn of fortune. "The publicity will be sensational!"

Longarm was appalled by this man's unbridled egotism and need for publicity. He started to leave, but Gordon Maxwell grabbed his good arm. "Hold on, Marshal Long. We're not yet done with you. I want you in at least one of the photographs. This kind of thing can't help but help promote your career. Maybe we can even come up with some kind of certificate or award with my signature on it. How would you like that?"

"Thanks," Longarm said, firmly removing the secretary's hand from his sleeve, "but that won't be necessary. I've got some things to do now and . . ."

The secretary's voice changed. "Marshal, you'll stay until I tell you it's all right to leave."

Longarm was about to tell the secretary of the interior that he could go to hell, but the man's wife again interceded. "Marshal Long, please stay a few minutes. The speech will be short. Won't it, Gordon?"

"I suppose."

"That's right," Regina Maxwell said, looking straight into Longarm's eyes. "And I do want to see that you get credit for saving my husband's life and possibly my own as well."

Longarm realized that protest was futile, even though his flesh wound burned and he loathed being in front of a crowd. But Billy Vail was telling the secretary's wife that his best deputy marshal would be happy to remain for photographs and would greatly appreciate some official recognition for his act of bravery.

Longarm eased into the background and found a chair. He sat and lowered his head, wondering if it might have been better in the long run if the one-armed man had killed this arrogant, rabidly ambitious politician. He could hear the secretary giving orders for the photographers to come on up on the stage and how they should take the pictures to maximize the drama. Longarm's name was not even mentioned.

"I'm getting out of here," Longarm growled, starting to rise from his seat.

"Please," Billy Vail said, restraining him. In a low voice, he leaned close to Longarm and whispered, "Look, I know that the secretary is acting like a complete ass, but this will do wonders for your career."

"I don't give a damn about that, Billy! That one-armed man was probably insane and needed help, not getting his skull cracked open."

"That one-armed man was trying to shoot the secretary of the interior, but thanks to your bravery, that didn't happen. Now for once in your life, just go along with this, get your picture taken, and take the award."

"Will doing this earn me an immediate and substantial raise?"

"Yes, dammit," Billy agreed. "I'll put in the paperwork at once. I'll ask that you get a fifty-dollar-a-month raise starting today."

"All right then," Longarm said, always needing the extra money. "I'll do it, but this circus better be over soon or I'm leaving."

So Longarm sat in the background while the local drunks were shamelessly bribed to attend the dedication.

When the crowd was again large enough for the secretary, a short speech was given with photographers taking pictures and reporters writing about his coolness and bravery under fire.

After the speech, Longarm was pushed up to the podium, where he and the secretary were photographed. Longarm was asked a few questions by the reporters about the near assassination, but his answers were drowned out by the secretary's self-aggrandizing version of the event.

In the end, Longarm was shunted to the side and quickly overlooked and then forgotten. Secretary Gordon Maxwell was the hero of the hour.

"Marshal Long?"

He turned to see Regina Maxwell. "Yes, ma'am?"

"I'm sorry."

"For what?"

"For how you were just used by my husband for his political gain. And for the death of that man you said was probably insane."

Longarm instinctively knew that she was genuine and sincere. That not only was she beautiful, but also sensitive and kind. "Thank you, ma'am."

Regina looked over at her husband, who was surrounded by adoring reporters and photographers. "I think I'll leave now and escort you to a doctor."

He shook his head dismissively. "I don't need a doctor."

"Somehow, Marshal Long, I knew you were going to say that, which is why I'm making very sure that you do see a doctor right away whether you like it or not."

"What about your wifely duties?" Longarm asked, glancing toward the secretary. "Won't you be missed?"

Regina Maxwell looked over at her husband, who was

obviously enjoying himself. "No," she said, turning back to Longarm. "I won't be missed at all."

Longarm didn't know what to say about that, so he slipped around behind the stage and left the crowd and confusion with Regina staying close at his side.

All in all, he thought, the past hour or so had been rather strange and deeply troubling.

Chapter 3

"There you go," the doctor said as he finished wrapping the bullet wound. "It's going to hurt far worse during the next few days than it does now. Keep it bandaged and clean. I still think that I should have taken some stitches; it would have left a far smaller scar."

Longarm shook his head. "I don't care about the size of the scar, Doc. And stitches are worse than the wound itself."

"Another inch lower and the bullet would have damaged the ulna bone, and then we'd have had a major problem. And by the way, I heard about what happened out there in front of the U.S. Mint." The doctor looked at Regina Maxwell. "Your husband is quite a man."

"Yes," she said quietly, "he is. But so is your marshal."

"That's right," the doctor said. "Marshal Long is well known for his dedication to duty and his bravery. How many times have I patched you up, Custis?"

"More than I care to remember, Doc."

"Well," the doctor said, "keep the wound clean. If you have any sign of infection, hurry back and we'll clean it out and patch you up again. But my guess is that you got off very lucky, thanks to Secretary Maxwell."

Longarm wasn't going to correct the man, but surprisingly, Regina did. "Doctor, it was the *marshal* who was the hero today, not my husband. And I will pay his bill."

Longarm's didn't strenuously object. He figured that Mrs. Regina Maxwell was probably the richest as well as the most beautiful woman he'd ever met. When they left the doctor's office, Regina said, "I should get back to my husband. He might finally realize that I'm not at his side."

"I'll walk you back to the hotel," Longarm said. "You're a famous woman and you should be escorted."

"Thank you." Regina seemed pleased. "I noticed a city park across the street and a little ways down from the mint. I saw children playing around a water fountain. Could we visit there for a moment?"

Longarm got the distinct impression that the secretary's wife was in no hurry to return to her husband. This was very surprising, although he did not dwell on her reasons, which he took to be private. When they entered the city park, the trees were in bloom and their leaves were twisting in the breeze. Longarm watched children playing with a puppy and laughing as the puppy barked and chased them around and around the fountain.

"Do you and the colonel have any children?" Longarm asked when Regina sat down on a park bench.

A fleeting sadness crossed her face. "No. But I love

children. I'd like to have at least four. Unfortunately, my husband feels that they would be a liability."

Longarm didn't understand if he'd heard her correctly. "Did you say a liability?"

"Yes," she said quietly. "You see, Marshal, my husband is convinced that children would get in the way of campaigning and travel."

"Maybe he'll change his mind if he becomes our next president."

"I'm afraid that isn't likely." She looked at him and forced a smile. "And what about you, Marshal Long? Have you ever wanted children?"

He shrugged his broad shoulders. He had thrown his coat away at the doctor's office, and now wore a white shirt and brown vest, making him seem a bit undressed and too informal to be in the company of such a lady. "I've never given children any thought. Oh, sometimes I see kids like these and think it would be nice. But first it's a good idea to get married."

"Of course," she answered. "However, a lot of women have children out of wedlock and I know it's hard both on the children and the mother. There is a terrible stigma to illegitimacy. But to be frank, those unfortunate children that our society labels 'bastards' often turn out to be unusually strong and resilient adults. They have had to be strong and determined in order to survive their difficult childhoods."

"Makes sense," he said.

"Did you have a healthy and happy childhood?" she asked.

"Yes." Longarm had no regrets about his childhood although he'd grown up poor. "I grew up in the hill country of West Virginia. I had a lot of freedom and plenty of animals to play with. My parents were fine, hardworking people and they never fought because they were very much in love."

"That sounds nice. My parents were very rich and sophisticated. I grew up in private schools in Europe," she said, staring out into the distance. "I was never home. Never around my parents, except during the holidays."

"Oh." Longarm stirred uncomfortably on the park bench. He didn't know where this conversation was leading, and felt that he was hearing things that he shouldn't. "Well, we'd better get you back to your husband."

But Regina Maxwell did not move. She continued to stare into the distance, and he knew she was lost in unhappy thoughts of a lonely, unloved childhood. "What's it like to be a Western marshal?" she finally asked, turning to face him so that the sun shone in her hair and made her face even lovelier. "Do you enjoy the danger?"

"I suppose that I do," he admitted. "And I especially like travel. I'm rarely in Denver more than a couple of weeks at a time. I go a bit crazy when I am in the office for more than a few days. My boss, Marshal Vail, he knows that I'm no good in a building and he keeps me on the move."

"Do you live out of a suitcase?"

"No," he explained, "I have a set of rooms and a tomcat, but the cat likes to move around as much as I do, so I leave a crack in my window and he sneaks in and out. I have neighbors that leave him food, so he thinks that my rooms are his alone."

Regina finally brightened. "I love cats and dogs. Someday I'll have all three . . . cats, dogs, and children. At least, that is my dream."

"I would think," Longarm said carefully, "that a woman like you could have whatever you wanted."

"Yes, I imagine you would think that. But what you don't understand is that a woman like me is expected to behave and act in a very strict and confined manner. A manner that leaves little room for deviation and is always under scrutiny. I am the daughter of rich and famous people, and now the wife of a man in the national eye. What that means is that I must be very careful about where I go and what I do. Even being here now like this, with a strange man, is . . . is rather exhilarating because it isn't my normal behavior."

"All the more reason for us to get you back to where you belong."

"We're staying at the Broadmore Hotel."

"Nothing but the finest," Longarm said.

"Yes, it's very luxurious. But let's not hurry back to the hotel. It's good for me to feel free for an hour with a brave and handsome gentleman who risked his life to save my husband expecting no personal reward."

Longarm glanced away for a moment as he tried to find words for his feelings. "Mrs. Maxwell, I don't expect we will ever see each other alone again like this and it isn't proper that we do. However, I want to say that I hope that your dreams come true about the pets and kids. And I also hope you find the happiness that you seem to be lacking."

She jumped up and kissed his cheek. "Thank you, Marshal. You are someone I will not soon forget."

"Same here," he said, knowing how lame that sounded. "Now we'd better go to the Broadmore Hotel."

That evening, Longarm was sitting in his rooms near Cherry Creek still thinking about Regina Maxwell and their conversation. He had a glass of good whiskey in his hand and was sipping it thoughtfully, his mind very much on Regina Maxwell. For the past hour he'd been trying to plumb his feelings, and realized he felt a deep and inexplicable sense of loss and sadness knowing that he and that beautiful woman would never cross paths again. Funny thing how a man could be in the company of some women for years and they never left the least of an impression, while others like Regina got under your skin in a matter of moments. And it wasn't like he had really had any designs on the secretary's wife, in fact just the opposite. Regina lived in a far more rarified and genteel world. She moved among the rich and powerful, while he moved among the lawless maggots of society.

A knock on his door interrupted his unhappy thoughts. Since Longarm had sent a lot of men to prison and left more than a few vengeful widows in mourning, he always kept his door double-locked. "Who is it?"

"It's Gilda!" the voice on the other side of the door proclaimed. "Hey, Custis, the newspaper hit the streets just a while ago and you're on the second page. Congratulations!"

"Thanks," he said, going to the door and unlocking it. "How you doin', Gilda?"

"I'm fine." And she did look fine. Gilda was a pretty

woman, Swedish to the core and almost always in high spirits. She'd kicked her drunken husband out of their rooms last winter and now she was looking happier than ever.

Her wide smile died as she noticed the bandage on his arm. "The newspaper article didn't say you'd been *shot*."

He absently touched the bandage. "It's just a scratch."

"You look down in the dumps," the woman said, studying his face. "Are you feeling all right?"

"Really, I'm just fine," he told her, ready to close the door and get back to plumbing his complex and perplexing thoughts about Regina Maxwell. "And I appreciate you asking."

Her wide smile returned. "Listen, Custis, I have some cold chicken in the icebox. Do you want to come up and eat something? I think I can even rummage up some apple pie or some oatmeal cookies. Baked them all myself."

"Thanks but no, thanks, Gilda." Longarm went over to his liquor cabinet and selected a bottle of aged Kentucky whiskey. "I've been sitting here by the window sipping whiskey and waiting to see if my cat is hungry enough to make his rare appearance."

Gilda's eyes went past him to the open window. "If you ask me, a man shouldn't drink alone. Besides, that mangy old tomcat of yours sure isn't fitting company for a man who looks like he has a case of the lonesome blues."

"The cat and I get along fine," Longarm said. "Say, Gilda, do you want to share a drink?"

"Why not?" she asked, coming over while he filled a second glass and topped off his own. "Custis, you've never asked me to share a drink with you before, and tonight I'm certainly not going to pass up the opportunity to drink with the town hero."

"I'm sure that the newspaper said that Secretary Maxwell was today's hero. After all, he bravely went on and gave his dedication speech despite having just dodged a bullet."

Gilda's blond eyebrows raised in question. "Looks like you're the one that should have dodged the bullet."

"Yeah." Longarm lifted his glass. "Cheers, Gilda. To better days for both of us."

She drank deep and straight. "You really do look lower than a snake's belly, Custis. What's wrong?"

"Nothing."

"Sure there is. You need to talk to someone. Where's that young woman that comes around to keep you company?"

"You mean Lucy?"

"Yeah. The short woman with dimples and big . . ." Gilda pushed out her own large breasts in an exaggerated fashion and winked. "You know what I'm talkin' about."

Longarm chuckled. "Lucy wanted to get married and I didn't cotton to the idea, so she struck out for greener pastures. I saw her just yesterday with a very prosperous-looking businessman. It's clear that she wasted no time in mooning over our faded love."

Gilda nodded with understanding. "I could see that coming, Custis. The trouble you have is that you always pick the real young, beautiful ones. By now you should have better taste and better sense about women."

"You think I have poor taste in women?"

"No doubt about it," Gilda said flatly. "You need a woman who maybe won't turn every man's head, but will stick with you even in the bad times. A woman who doesn't have to be constantly wined, dined, and fussed over. A woman who will never want to try and fit you into a pair of lace hobbles . . . if you know what I mean."

Longarm found her frankness refreshing, and he had to admit that Gilda's words carried more than a touch of the truth. "Oh, really?"

"Yes, really," Gilda said, smacking her lips on the rim of her glass with pleasure. "This is very good whiskey."

"Thank you. Have all you want."

"I will," she replied. "But Custis, I'm serious when I say that you need to reassess how you pick your women."

"I do all right," he said. "And it's been my experience that women just naturally want to tie the knot and have a family. Leastways, all the ones I've been with do. And I can't do that."

"Of course you can't!" Gilda exclaimed. "What kind of a husband and father would you make being gone all the time and half the time coming back to Denver shot up and half-dead?"

"That's right," he agreed. "And a woman ought to see that. Glad that at least you are wise enough see it, Gilda."

"Oh," she said, laying a hand on his shoulder, "I see a lot of things when I see you, Custis. Trouble is, you just don't see anything in me."

He knew he ought to deny that fact, but couldn't. Gilda wasn't all that young . . . maybe thirty-five or even forty . . . and she wasn't the kind of looker that strongly attracted Longarm. She had a few wrinkles, a stray gray hair among the blond that she would probably deny, and a little bit of sag to her obviously full breasts. But on the other hand, her hips were still narrow, her ankles shapely, and

Gilda had a lusty laugh and a bold directness that he found very refreshing.

"Well," Gilda pressed, "you really don't see me, do you?"

"I see you, Gilda."

"Is that right. Well, see *these,* Mr. Long and tell me what you honest to God think."

Longarm had had a few drinks, but that didn't keep his jaw from dropping nearly to his knees when Gilda unsnapped her bodice and bared her mountainous breasts.

"Well?" she asked with a vixen's smile. "What's the matter, Marshal? Has the cat got your tongue?"

"What are you doing!"

"I'm showing you the best pair of boom-booms in Denver. Boom-booms that you haven't even noticed after all this time we've been neighbors. Finally, I decided that I had to do something drastic so you'd finally notice."

Longarm drained his glass. "Damn, Gilda, those are *really* fine. But how have you kept 'em from sagging down to your waist?"

She grinned. "I've got good skin and I keep 'em supported." She jiggled them enough to make his mouth suddenly go dry with desire. "Not bad, huh, Marshal?"

"That's an understatement." He refilled both their glasses, but Gilda made no attempt to cover herself. No attempt at all. He finally found his voice and said, "Are you just going to leave those beauties hanging out?"

"Why not? I like to let 'em be free. Besides, I'm enjoying the expression on your face. Your eyes are buggin' a bit."

He looked away quickly. "Oh, Gilda, the hell you say."

"I *do* say."

"I'll have to admit you have kinda caught me by surprise. I knew you were a spirited woman, but I didn't expect this kind of thing right here in my rooms without a hint of warning."

"You're a big boy and I'm a full-grown woman who has tasted about all there is to taste of life. And I like being unconventional and a little wanton. I read about that uppity Mrs. Gordon Maxwell and how fancy and refined she is . . . and how beautiful. So I got to thinking that I'm glad that I'm not that kind of woman. I'm glad that I am just everyday Gilda without any airs that I have to put on."

Longarm couldn't quite tear his eyes off her bosom, which was *really* big and luscious-looking. It made him wonder if what he couldn't see was just as attractive and inviting.

"Is Mrs. Maxwell really all that beautiful, Custis? To read what the newspaper reporters say about her, you'd think she was the goddess Athena or something."

Longarm took another sip of whiskey. He felt Gilda's eyes boring into him demanding an answer to her question. And he knew she really didn't want to know the truth, that Regina Maxwell was beyond beautiful.

"Tell you the truth, Gilda," he said, choosing his words with great consideration, "she is an eyeful, but I'd bet my bottom dollar that what she's got upstairs doesn't begin to compare to what I'm seeing right now."

His answer was perfect. Gilda grinned from ear to ear, and then she giggled like a little girl. "Custis," she said, "you are a gentleman and a flatterer. Furthermore, you're like me in that you don't want any strings or complications. Nothing to tie you down. Now, having said all that, why don't we go to bed and have some fun?"

"Damned if that isn't the best idea I've heard all day," he said, raising his glass in a toast that was more than enthusiastically returned.

Gilda tore off her dress and underclothing and threw herself on the bed saying, "Come on, Custis, I've been fantasizing about this for months."

He was flattered. "You have?"

"Yep." She licked her lips. "If we're playing show-and-tell, I've already shown you what I have. Now let's see what *you* have."

Longarm knew he was "well hung" and when he undressed, he guessed that Gilda was plenty pleased with his plumbing. Hell, he was already hard and sticking out like a big cob of ripe corn.

"Get over here and let's stop wasting time," Gilda urged, her breath already coming fast.

Longarm flopped down on the bed, but before he could even roll over to kiss his neighbor, she was kneeling over him, grasping his throbbing manhood in her hands, and then burying it in her mouth.

"Oh, my, oh, my," he groaned. "That *does* feel fine!"

She laved this big root with her tongue for a few minutes and when he was slick and wet, she scooted up and slowly eased down on him as if settling into a hot bath. Sighing, she willingly impaled herself with his full measure. "Damn, Custis, *this* is what a man and a woman ought to think about more often."

"Amen!"

Gilda obviously loved to make love, and after several minutes of moving slowly up and down, her desire became so strong that she began to get serious about their lovemaking. Her shapely bottom began to work vigorously over his big tool, and she obligingly bent far over so that Longarm could suck on her breasts until her nipples turned as hard as rock candy and stood out like licorice drops.

"Oh, this is good," she moaned, moving faster and faster over him until Longarm rolled her over and began to work her into a fever pitch. He kissed and sucked and pumped until Gilda was nearly out of her mind. Feeling that she had reached the point where she was ready to explode, Longarm began his deepest thrusting until Gilda screamed with intense pleasure.

"Here it comes!" he grated, slamming his rod in as far as it would go and then pumping her full of his seed until she bucked like a grain-fed filly.

At last, Longarm squirted the last of his seed into her honey pot and rolled over on his side panting for air.

"Was it worthy of your fantasies?" he asked.

"Every bit worthy," she said, large breasts heaving. "When can we go at it again?"

"We have all night," he told her. "And if my cat comes through the window, he'll enjoy watching us put on a show."

"That's an alley tomcat for you," Gilda said. "He'd know what we were doing and appreciate our talents."

Longarm laughed. "Gilda," he said, "You were right. I was feeling lower than a snake's belly until you walked in my door. I'm glad I finally got to know you."

She studied his handsome face. "I knew you'd like what I have to offer and the fact that there are no strings attached."

"No lace hobbles," he said, remembering her amusing analogy.

"That's right, and there never will be. I like to live for today and let tomorrow take care of itself."

That was Longarm's philosophy, and he couldn't have been more pleased with Gilda. "Well," he said, kissing her lips, "tomorrow may take care of itself, but tonight we take care of ourselves."

"My sentiments exactly."

Longarm cradled her head in the crook of his arm. And to think that he had said hello to Gilda a hundred times and never once realized what pleasures and insights this woman had to offer. He was glad that he had found out the real woman in Gilda, but he hoped his tomcat stayed the hell away from his place tonight.

He didn't want a mangy, grinning tomcat watching what he and Gilda planned to do to each other's bodies, and that was for damned sure.

"Custis?"

"Yes, Gilda?"

"I'm hungry for chicken and apple pie. Are you?"

"I haven't eaten since early this morning," he admitted.

Gilda climbed out of his bed. "You're going to need all the strength you can muster with me tonight. And that means you need to be well fed. So I'm going to get dressed and come right back down with that chicken and pie and some cookies."

"Good idea," he said. "And if my cat shows up, he'll want a piece of your cold chicken."

"It's a deal," Gilda said as she hurriedly dressed.

After she was gone, Longarm corked the whiskey bottle

and drank nearly a quart of cool water. Because of his exertions he was going to be sweating a lot tonight and couldn't afford to go dry on himself.

Not with a lusty and busty Swedish woman like Gilda.

Chapter 4

The next morning Longarm awoke to see his tomcat sitting on the sill looking as lean and hungry as ever. Gilda was cooking ham and eggs and the coffee was ready. The cat was sniffing and probably hoping for a piece of the ham.

"Good morning, Custis," she said brightly. "How are you feeling?"

"I'm sorta wrung out," he admitted, quickly adding, "But I'm not complaining."

"I'm going off to work in a few minutes, but I wanted to cook you a good breakfast." She brought him a steaming cup of hot coffee and sat down on his bed. "This is going to be a hard day for me. Did you know that I work at the Denver Boys' Home?"

He was still half-asleep. "Yes. I think so."

"I might have told you about it. But maybe not." Gilda went over to the kitchen and turned off the stove, then poured herself a cup of coffee. She came back to sit beside Longarm. "It's a wonderful orphanage. We care for twenty-four boys ages five to fifteen and we not only feed, clothe, and house them, we also make sure that they go to school every day and do their homework. Almost all of our boys have gone on to be honest and successful citizens. I don't make a lot of money working there, but I love the work and it's important."

"I'm sure that it is." Longarm drained his coffee and Gilda went to refill his cup. "So why is this going to be such a hard day?" he asked.

She came back to his bed. "There's another small orphanage in town that has only about fifteen boys. We've learned that they were being mistreated and their orphanage is shutting down. We were hoping to take those boys under our wing, but we just don't have the beds or enough money."

"What will happen to them?"

Gilda sighed. "That's a very good question. We've appealed to the citizens of Denver to take them in and give them homes, but some of the boys are older and that isn't going to happen. I'm afraid that at least half of those boys will return to the street. They'll have to take up petty crime again. Some will be exploited and others will never reach adulthood. You know what living on the streets can do to a man, let alone a boy."

"Yes, I do," Longarm said. "The kids get wilder and wilder until they become strong enough to assault and rob. Some become so violent from their hard existence that they even murder."

Gilda nodded. "The Denver Boys' Home needs three thousand dollars. Three thousand dollars to buy beds, clothes, books, and food for those extra fifteen orphans.

The money also goes to pay my salary and the salaries of our small, overworked, and dedicated staff. And for the general upkeep of our home. If we could have raised that much money, we would have been able to take on all of the extra boys."

"How much have you been able to raise so far?" Longarm asked.

"Only about half the money."

"So you need another fifteen hundred to take on these extra homeless boys?"

"Yes."

Longarm sat up in bed and scowled. "There must be some way to raise the money."

"Well," Gilda said, "we've leaned heavily on everyone that has any money in Denver. Some were already contributing a lot of money each year. We need to find new sources."

"Or a new source." Longarm brightened. "Have you hit the secretary of the interior up for money?"

"We tried to get through to him, but without success. His personal assistant, a man named Mr. J. D. Kilgore, told us that the secretary never donates to local charities. He put us off and not in a very nice way."

Longarm set his coffee cup down, got up, and started to dress. "Tell you what, Gilda. As you know, I had a part in saving Secretary Maxwell's life yesterday. I also got to know his wife, Regina. Maybe I can get them to help make up those fifteen hundred dollars by giving it my personal touch."

Gilda's eyes widened. "Would you try?"

"Of course," Longarm said. "I visited the Denver Boys'

Home several years ago and I know what a great job you do for those kids. If the Secretary and his wife haven't left town yet, I'll see if I can speak to them about this desperate need to take on those extra fifteen orphan boys."

"That would be a godsend!"

"Don't say a word to your boss or the kids," Longarm cautioned. "Promise me that you won't because I may be turned down."

"I won't say anything."

Longarm finished dressing. He went to the stove and watched while Gilda filled his plate; then he wolfed down the food and prepared to leave. He had never liked asking for money, but this was something special and it wasn't for himself. It was for some boys who needed a break in life.

"Custis," she said, helping him on with his coat, "if you can do this, you will be doing a very, very fine thing."

"No, the secretary and his wife will be doing the fine thing," Longarm corrected. "But again, don't say a word or get your hopes up. I'll just give it a try and see what happens."

"If the secretary and his wife could only see our boys, how good and upstanding they are and how much they just want a chance at life, I'm sure that he would be sympathetic and generous. I'm also sure that he and his wife could afford to give us fifteen hundred dollars. They're both rich, aren't they? What is that small amount of money to wealthy people like that?"

"People like the Maxwells are rich because they cling to their money," Longarm explained. "I'm not saying that all of the rich are stingy. But many of them are tighter than a virgin's . . . well, they're tighter than a blacksmith's clenched first."

Gilda giggled. "A virgin's what?"

"Never mind," Longarm said, buckling on his gun belt and reaching for his snuff-brown Stetson with its flat brim.

Gilda gave him a profusion of kisses at the door. "I'm so excited about this that I can hardly stand still."

"Don't be too hopeful," he again cautioned. "The secretary and his wife may have already left town. They were staying at the Broadmore Hotel and that's the first place I'm heading this morning. But even if they are still there, they might not consent to see me. They are very busy people."

"You saved Secretary Gordon Maxwell's life yesterday and took a bullet in the arm to do it," Gilda reminded him. "And who's to say that the assassin might not also have killed Mrs. Maxwell if you hadn't risked your life?"

Longarm nodded. "I'll let you know tonight if I have any success."

"I'll be waiting. And keeping my fingers crossed."

"That's good," he said. "Just don't think about keeping your legs crossed tonight and I'll remain a happy man."

Gilda was laughing and his tomcat was licking his chops expecting some breakfast of his own when Longarm closed his door and hurried off on his mission of charity.

The Broadmore Hotel was right downtown, not two blocks from the Federal Building, and Longarm was there in ten minutes. The hotel was four stories and had an impressive façade of granite and marble. The lobby was always filled with Denver's most distinguished and wealthy visitors. The Broadmore had hosted United States presidents, foreign kings, and politicians for more than ten years, and had no competition in Denver when it came to opulence or the caliber of its clientele.

Longarm went right up to the long registration desk

without bothering to admire the lustrous marble-floored lobby and supporting pillars. He stifled the urge to whistle a tune. He felt a tingle of anticipation about seeing Regina again as he rang a small brass bell at the desk. Almost at once a clerk wearing an immaculate suit and tie hurried over.

"Yes, sir?"

"I'm a federal marshal and I need to know if Secretary of the Interior Gordon Maxwell and his wife are still here or if they've already left."

"They are in the process of leaving," the clerk said. "But is there something that I can do to assist you, officer?"

It was clear to Longarm that the clerk was neither pleased nor impressed to have a lawman inquiring about two of the hotel's most celebrated guests. "Actually, there isn't," Longarm said. "I need to speak to Secretary Maxwell. It's quite important. Could you tell me what room he and his wife are staying in?"

The clerk suddenly looked quite uncomfortable. "Just a moment, officer."

Before Longarm could say another word, the man fled into a back room. A few minutes later that he reappeared with an older gentleman who Longarm immediately sized up to be the top dog at the hotel desk.

"What is it exactly that you wish to speak to the Secretary about?" the supervisor asked without preamble.

"That is my business and none of yours," Longarm said.

"It is very much our business," the older man said. "We have an obligation to protect the privacy of our guests. Is Secretary Maxwell expecting you?"

"No."

"Then I'm afraid—"

"Do I have to make a scene?" Longarm interrupted.

The desk supervisor blinked. "What kind of a 'scene' are you talking about, officer?"

Longarm slapped both of his hands down on the desk loud enough to turn heads across the lobby. "How about I arrest you for obstructing the law?"

The supervisor's voice turned quite nasty. "Bertrand," he said to the first clerk, "please escort this *person* up to the secretary's room and knock on the door. If the secretary refuses to see this *person,* then excuse yourself and escort this *person* back down to me at once."

"Yes, sir!" Bertrand exclaimed. Longarm almost expected the clerk to snap off a salute. The young desk clerk turned to Longarm. "Follow me."

"By all means," Longarm said, giving the supervisor a winning smile.

Secretary Maxwell and his wife were staying on the second floor. Longarm and the clerk hurried across the lobby, up the wide winding staircase, and down the immense corridor to the first room on the right. The clerk knocked timidly on the door twice, and when there was no response Longarm pushed the young man aside and gave it a manly hammering.

The door was opened by J.D. Kilgore, and he was not pleased. "You," he grated. "What do you want, Marshal Long?"

"I need to see the secretary and his wife."

"Yes, I suppose you are after that commendation. We'll see about sending it in the mail."

"Don't bother," Longarm replied, looking past the man and into the immense hotel suite mostly done in soft blue colors. "I've come for another reason. A far more important one."

"Tell me what it is and then I'll relay your request to the Secretary later. He and his wife are in the bedroom packing. Our train leaves within the hour."

"What I have to say will only take a couple of minutes and I'd prefer to talk to them in person," Longarm said. "I'll wait."

"Then wait here in the hallway," Kilgore snapped, starting to slam the door in Longarm's face. The bodyguard might have succeeded if Longarm hadn't managed to shove his boot into the doorway.

"What are you doing!" Kilgore demanded, his face turning hard.

"I'm coming inside to wait," Longarm told the man. "I'm no paid lackey. Step aside."

Kilgore had no intention of stepping aside. He threw his considerable weight against the door, but Longarm shot a right hand straight into Kilgore's enraged face. It staggered the bodyguard for a moment, and that gave Longarm enough time to push Kilgore even farther off balance and make a forced entry.

"You sonofabitch!" Kilgore hissed, blood dripping from his injured nose.

"You asked for that," Longarm said, raising his fists. "Now exactly how far do you want to go with this?"

Kilgore would have gone as far as he could have taken it if the secretary and Regina hadn't appeared in the doorway of their bedroom.

"What is going on here!" Gordon Maxwell demanded. "What—"

"I tried to tell this officer that you were busy," Kilgore

raged, grabbing a silk handkerchief and putting it to his dripping nose. "And I'm going to put him outside right this—"

"No!" Regina cried. "You fool, this man saved my husband's life! J.D., leave this room at once!"

"But . . ."

"I said leave us now," Regina insisted with a stomp of her foot.

Gordon Maxwell started to say something, but apparently changed his mind. "Kilgore, do as my wife says. Go attend to your injured nose and tell the hotel staff that we are ready for them to come up and remove our luggage."

If looks could kill, the bodyguard's would have put Longarm in the grave. His eyes held a hatred that was as pure as a ray of sunlight lancing out of storm clouds. Longarm gave the man a look to match his own and then let him pass outside.

Regina looked as stunning as he'd remembered, but she also appeared to be under considerable strain. "Officer Long," she said, coming over with her hand outstretched. "What a pleasure it is to see you again. And please forgive whatever it was that awful Mr. Kilgore did to cause you to punch him in the nose."

"Sorry about having to use force," Longarm said. "But the man is overzealous."

"Yes," she agreed. "I was just talking to my husband about Mr. Kilgore last night. He has a very quick and hot temper. He needs to be fired before he hurts someone and causes problems."

"That's right," the secretary agreed. "I was planning to tell Kilgore that he was fired when we got to the train station. J.D. Kilgore has only worked for me about two months, but he's managed to get into several ugly altercations that I didn't think were necessary."

"Sometimes a man can let authority go to his head."

"Well, yes, I suppose. Mr. Kilgore served in the cavalry under me and he is very brave and fierce fighter. He is a marksman and remarkable with a knife. But like my wife said, he is much too hotheaded. Also, unlike you, he failed to protect me yesterday. So he has to go."

"But we're a little afraid that he will react to his dismissal badly," Regina said, clearly trying to hide her deep concern. "In fact, we're *sure* that he will create an ugly scene that we very much would like to avoid."

"You need to be careful when you dismiss him," Longarm advised. "Because he is on a hair trigger."

"Would *you* like to replace him?" the secretary suddenly asked. He snapped his fingers. "By golly, that would be great! You saved our lives yesterday and we have complete confidence that you could do it again."

"I'm a federal officer of the law," Longarm reminded them. "And I like my job."

"I'll pay you double what you are now making."

"Please," Regina said, her eyes looking right into Longarm's soul. "It would mean so much to us."

"I just can't," Longarm told them.

"Marshal Long, I'll *triple* what you're paid! Just try it for the duration of my Western tour. If it doesn't work out, I'm sure that I can get your job back with a promotion." The secretary filled his chest and smiled at his wife. "As Mrs. Maxwell will tell you, I am not without considerable influence."

"I know. And thank you for the generous and flattering offer," Longarm said. "But—"

"Marshal Long," the secretary interrupted. "I don't believe that I properly expressed my gratitude for your heroics yesterday. And rest assured that I haven't forgotten that commendation. We'll take it up when we get back to Washington. That's my personal promise. And the offer of tripling your wage is also a promise."

Gordon Maxwell reached for his wallet completely confident no lowly paid U.S. marshal could resist the prospect of a windfall. "And Marshal, I want you to know that this money doesn't come from the taxpayers. Oh, no! Your wage is coming out of my *own* pocket. How about I start by giving you three hundred good old American dollars?"

Longarm shook his head and held up his heads. "Mr. Secretary, that is extremely generous, but I've come on another matter."

"What matter?" the secretary asked, his hands clutching a wad of greenbacks.

"It's about a small Denver orphanage that is closing down. Sir, some good boys are going to be without a roof over their heads tomorrow if we don't come up with fifteen hundred dollars. The Denver Boys' Home will take them in if they can raise enough money to—"

The secretary asked, "How much?"

Longarm managed a hopeful smile. Regina was staring at him intently as he gulped, "We need fifteen hundred dollars."

"Can't do it," the secretary told Longarm without a moment's hesitation. "I am not allowed to be spending money on local charities. Sorry."

Longarm's spirits plummeted. Gilda was going to take this hard, and what would become of those boys?

"I have a solution," Regina said, moving between them. "A compromise that will satisfy everyone concerned."

The secretary turned to his wife, and he didn't look pleased. "What are you talking about?"

"You want this man to protect you during our Western campaign and dedication tour. Right?"

"Yes," he answered hesitantly. "But fifteen hundred dollars is—"

"Is easy enough," Regina said. "I'll pay the money to the orphanage and you triple the marshal's salary for our tour. How is that for a solution beneficial to everyone?"

"Darling," the secretary said, caught off guard, "I don't think—"

"It's *my* money and I'll donate it to whomever I choose, Gordon." She turned to Longarm. "How about it? You get a windfall, the orphanage gets the money it so desperately needs and deserves, and my husband and I can travel feeling much safer than we've been feeling with J.D. Kilgore."

Longarm was really taken aback. "I . . . I've never been a personal bodyguard before. I've no experience at that sort of thing."

"Experience or not," Regina reminded him, "you were the one that saved my husband's life yesterday and we both feel sure that you could do it again, if necessary."

Longarm raised his eyebrows. "But I'm not sure I could get away from my office."

"I'll take care of that in the next half hour," the secretary assured him. "And you will receive a promotion after your service to me and my wife. Plus the sizable bonus you'll earn."

Longarm took a deep breath. "The orphanage needs the fifteen hundred dollars today. Not next week or even tomorrow."

"I'll write a check right now," Regina said, going to her purse. "It won't be a problem and I'll want to visit that orphanage as soon as I can." She found her checkbook. "Now what was the name of that orphanage again?"

"Denver Boys' Home."

"It's my pleasure," Regina said, writing out the check.

Longarm looked to the secretary. "Sir, are you sure about this?"

"I am very sure," the powerful politician replied. "However, I'm afraid that your first duty will be quite unpleasant and perhaps even a little dangerous."

Longarm understood. "That would be telling Mr. Kilgore that he is relieved of his duties."

"Yes."

"I can and will do that," Longarm said as the man pressed three hundred dollars in cash into his fist.

"We are leaving on *today's* train," Secretary Maxwell told him. "We need you on it with us."

"I'll be there," Longarm said. "I'm always ready to go at a moment's notice."

"Excellent!"

Longarm and the secretary of the interior shook hands on their deal.

Regina Maxwell gave Longarm the check made out to the boys' orphanage. "We are so relieved that you will be traveling with and protecting us," she said, her hand falling on his good forearm causing his heart to beat faster. "I know this is the right thing to do for everyone concerned."

"Thank you," Longarm said, wondering if he could

keep his mind off anything but this incredibly beautiful woman during the next few weeks of the campaign and dedication tour.

And then Longarm thought of J.D. Kilgore, and realized he'd better keep his mind on business or he might get his throat cut even before he climbed on the train about to leave the Denver station.

Chapter 5

Longarm didn't have time to go by his office, so he dashed off a note to Billy Vail and paid a boy to deliver it to the Federal Building. He knew that Billy would understand that a lowly federal marshal couldn't really turn down an offer from the secretary of the interior. He ended the note by writing: *I'll telegraph you when we get to our first stop. Custis.*

He then hurried back to his rooms. Gilda was away at work, so Longarm slipped Regina Maxwell's fifteen-hundred-dollar check made out to the Denver Boys' Home under her door. He also added a note saying that he had to leave town in a hurry and would be protecting Secretary Maxwell and his wife for the next few weeks and not to worry about him, but to feed his tomcat. Longarm was feeling very good about the check helping those fifteen orphans find a new home to grow up in, and ended his note by writing, *I'm pleased that I was able to do this for those kids. Gilda, don't worry about me, I can take care of myself. See you when I get back. Custis.*

He checked his Ingersoll pocket watch and saw that he had precious little time left before the train was set to depart. Longarm carried a Colt .44-40 on his left hip, butt turned forward, and he was very good with the side arm. But the weapon that had saved his bacon on more than one occasion was a deadly little twin-barreled .44-caliber derringer, which was soldered to his gold watch chain. Now, Longarm checked the derringer just to make certain that it was in good working order. He slipped the derringer back into his vest pocket where the watch fob would normally rest.

Taking a final glance around his rooms, Longarm thought of Gilda, and was sorry that he would not be enjoying the pleasure of her company this evening. Oh, well, he took a good amount of satisfaction knowing how thrilled she would be when she discovered that check that Regina Maxwell had so generously written.

Longarm arrived at the station just as the train was blasting its steam whistle announcing it was leaving Denver for Cheyenne. This was the Denver Pacific, which made a 106-mile run up to Cheyenne, where it connected with the Union Pacific Railroad, which would take a man all the way to California.

"All aboard!" the conductor shouted as the train lurched forward and Longarm swung onto the platform.

"Marshal, even for you this is cutting things close this time," the conductor said as Longarm caught his breath.

"Yeah. This trip was decided at the last minute."

"Where are you going?"

"I have no idea."

The conductor was a gentleman in his sixties with silver hair and a handlebar mustache. His name was Abner and he had worked this run for quite a few years. Longarm had no idea what Abner's last name was, and it didn't seem important.

"Got your ticket for me to punch, Marshal?"

"Sorry, Abner. No ticket."

The conductor frowned. "Well, I'm sure not going to put you off this train, but even you need a ticket."

Longarm quickly explained how he was going to be traveling as a guest and bodyguard for the secretary of the interior. "You can talk to the secretary about my fare. The man hired me less than an hour ago to replace a hothead that was supposed to be looking out for him and his wife."

"You'd be speaking of J.D. Kilgore," Abner said. "I know the man. He's rude and reminds me of a powder keg with a very short fuse."

"Well," Longarm said, "J.D. Kilgore is history."

"Is that a fact?"

"It is," Longarm said.

"Funny," Abner mused, "because J.D. Kilgore boarded the train with Secretary Maxwell and his lovely wife just ten minutes ago. And I'll tell you what, Kilgore was sticking to them both like glue."

Longarm had no idea why that would be, but Abner was not someone to make a mistake about his passengers. "I don't understand that," Longarm said with annoyance. "But I mean to get to the bottom of this misunderstanding right away."

"Be careful with Kilgore," Abner warned. "There's craziness in his eyes that you don't often see and want to steer clear of."

"I saw the same thing," Longarm replied. "Where can I find the secretary and his wife?"

"They're in the last first-class compartment on your right. It's extra large and the one this train saves for its own railroad officers and bigwigs. Has its own bar and is as nice as any hotel suite."

"And what about Kilgore?"

"He's also in first class, but he's ahead one compartment."

Longarm frowned. "Well, I'd better talk to the secretary before I go off half-cocked with Kilgore. But I sure don't understand why the man was rehired."

"Maybe he insisted that he be rehired," Abner said. "You think about that?"

"Yeah," Longarm replied. "Anything is possible, but I didn't think that the secretary would allow himself to be intimidated by a man like J.D. Kilgore."

"Go easy and be careful," Abner advised. "I'll be around to help if you need me."

"Thanks."

Longarm went through the train to the first-class coach and banged on the door of the luxury compartment. "It's Marshal Long! Mr. Secretary, we need to talk."

A moment later, the secretary opened the door to the compartment and motioned Longarm inside with his finger to his lips. Closing the door, he said, "We *do* need to talk."

Longarm glanced over toward Regina, but her face was fixed and gave no hint of what was about to be said. "All right, Mr. Secretary, but I'll tell you right here and now that I'm not going to work for you if Kilgore is still on your payroll."

"We had no choice about that," Gordon Maxwell replied. "Sit down and let me explain."

"I'll stand."

"Sure," Maxwell said. "I realize that you're probably confused about what is going on here . . . and with good reason."

"The conductor told me that Kilgore was with you when you boarded the train," Longarm said bluntly. "But you told me that you were firing him before you left Denver."

"Yes," Maxwell said, "I did tell you I was going to fire him. But it wasn't that easy."

"Firing a man never is," Longarm shot back. "But Mr. Kilgore is a loose cannon. He needed to be fired and I won't work around such a man. So the choice is clear, either you fire him . . . or I quit."

"We made a deal," the secretary said, anger rising in his voice. "And you were paid a hefty bonus as well as given a sizable check for the boys' orphanage."

"You can have your bonus money back," Longarm said, starting to reach into his wallet. "As for the fifteen-hundred-dollar donation, that was a gift from your wife. If she wants to stop payment, she'll have to do that herself."

Regina had turned away to face the window, but now she swiveled around and said, "Marshal Long, please sit down and let's discuss this rationally. There are some things that you need to understand."

"Such as?"

"Such as J.D. Kilgore is my brother."

Longarm sat down. "Excuse me?"

"Actually, he's my stepbrother. We were never close, but I was the one who pushed my husband to give him the job. That and the fact that J.D. went to war with Gordon and they bravely fought together on many battlefields."

"The Civil War is over, Mrs. Maxwell," Longarm said.

"And while I'm sympathetic to you helping your stepbrother by giving the man employment, he is still not someone that I'm willing to associate with in any capacity. I know his kind and they are unpredictable and dangerous."

"I'll fire J.D. in Cheyenne," Maxwell promised. "He's on the train now and there's nothing that can change that. When we get to Cheyenne this evening, we'll stay at a nice hotel and I'll tell him in private that I've hired you and that his services won't be needed."

Longarm frowned. "And how will Kilgore react to that bit of news?"

"Not well," Maxwell conceded. "But there is nothing to do for it. I agree that the man is dangerous and unreliable. It's just that I don't want to have a big scene on this train. It would cause a terrible scandal."

Longarm expelled a deep breath. "Is that what this is all about? You're worried about a scandal?"

"Listen, Marshal. If I discharge Kilgore in Cheyenne and give him a nice bonus, he can take that with him when he goes back to Washington, D.C. But if I discharge him on this train, he might go crazy and innocent people could get hurt."

Longarm wasn't buying into this. "Mr. Secretary, if you wait, then you and your wife could get hurt in Cheyenne. Let me tell J.D. the facts myself. If he goes crazy, then I'll handle him."

Regina got up and came over to stand between Longarm and her husband. "Marshal Long, Gordon and I talked about this until late last night. We decided that it would be in the best interests of all concerned to break the news to J.D. when we reach Cheyenne. I would be very grateful if you would accept that decision, if for no other reason than the check that I gave you for that boys' school."

Longarm looked down at her and found himself nodding his head. "All right," he reluctantly agreed. "But only on the condition that I'm present when you dismiss Kilgore in Cheyenne. Otherwise, I think something very bad could happen."

"You mean to us?"

"That's right," Longarm replied.

The couple exchanged glances, and then the secretary nodded his head. "Very well. We will tell J.D. that he is discharged when you are present."

"Good," Longarm said. "And now there is the matter of my train ticket."

"Pay it out of the bonus money I gave you," Maxwell said dismissively. "When we leave Cheyenne, you'll have a first-class ticket."

"And where should I stay for now?" Longarm asked.

"It would be best to stay out of my stepbrother's sight," Regina said.

"I'm not hiding from any man."

"You don't have to hide," she said. "Just . . . just please go back to coach class and help my husband and me avoid a potentially disastrous confrontation between you and J.D."

"Fair enough," Longarm said. "By the way, where are we going?"

"To the town of Rock Springs, then on to Elko, Reno, and Carson City, where I have scheduled public events and speaking engagements. After that our tour will go on to Sacramento, and have a grand finale in San Francisco."

"Long trip," Longarm said, not sure that he wanted to stay with this publicity and promotion tour that many miles.

"You'll be well compensated," Maxwell assured him.

"Yes," Regina added, giving Longarm a curious smile. "Very well compensated."

Longarm swore that this beautiful woman was sending him two messages. And that made him decide that he would take this as far as Regina Maxwell wanted it to go.

Chapter 6

Longarm wasn't pleased about hiking all the way back to the rear of the train and having to pay for his own ticket for the run up to Cheyenne. And he was even less pleased about learning that the hold that J.D. Kilgore had on the Secretary Maxwell and his stunning young wife was that he was a part of the family. But Longarm decided that the couple were probably right that it was best to allow the secretary to tell Kilgore that he was being fired after they reached Cheyenne.

"He'll probably pay him a bunch of money to go away quietly," Longarm said aloud to himself. "And that makes no difference to me."

Longarm laid his bags on a hard wooden bench and looked around at the other second-class citizens who were going north on the cheap. His eyes first fell on a cute but chubby dance-hall girl trying to avoid attention by reading a newspaper. There were also several farm couples, two Indians and two cowboys playing low-stakes poker, a man so drunk that he was snoring and drooling on himself, and a couple of town boys laughing, wrestling around on their bench, and having a little boyish fun.

The coach was half-empty, so Longarm chose a bench near the woman reading the newspaper and smoking a thin cigar. She looked over her paper at Longarm and gave him a brief smile, then went back to reading.

The poker game was for coins, but the players were all very serious. From what Longarm could hear, the cowboys were losing their change to the two Indians and they weren't a bit happy.

"Damn, you redskins sure do know how to play cards," one of the cowboys complained. "Is this deck of yours marked?"

One of the Indians said that it was not.

"Well, it must be or you wouldn't be winnin' all the time," the cowboy swore. "How much money have we lost, Clemson?"

"About three dollars and we're still only halfway up to Cheyenne. Don't worry, we'll get it all back before we get off this train."

"Three dollars is three dollars. It's time we started winnin' some money here instead of just losin' it."

The Indians did not say a word that Longarm could understand. Maybe they didn't speak English, but that was rather unlikely.

The foursome played on as Longarm stared out the window. The last time he'd gone up to Cheyenne he'd seen a lot of antelope grazing out on the open range, but not today. Longarm wondered if they'd all died, because it had been a hard winter with deep snow drifts covering these long, rolling hills. Now, the hills were covered with cattle and he saw cowboys off in the distance. Longarm knew that country had once been inhabited by vast herds of buffalo hunted by Cheyenne, Sioux, and other northern plains tribes. He was reminded of this because the green hills and valleys were still dotted with buffalo wallows.

Longarm closed his eyes to the rocking of the train and tried to imagine what a buffalo hunt must have been like from the back of a racing pony. The hunters would only have been armed with a bow and arrow and it would have been extremely dangerous. Buffalo were shortsighted and stupid, but they were also immense and plenty ready to fight. No doubt some of the Indian ponies had been knocked down and trampled along with their riders, or had stepped into badger holes and somersaulted into the stampeding buffalo.

There were also buffalo jumps in this country where the Indians had stampeded the herds over cliffs to kill and cripple them by the hundreds. Longarm could almost imagine the Indian families swarming over the broken bodies of the great beasts with stone skinning knives, cutting their throats and butchering them while they were still alive. Men who rode this country said that the buffalo remains were so numerous at these jumps that they formed hillocks of bone.

"You Injun sonofabitch!" one of the cowboys shouted from a seat four or five rows behind where Longarm was seated. "How'd you draw that third damned ace! By Gawd, you musta pulled it outa that buckskin shirt you're wearing. Roll up your filthy sleeve or I'll shoot you in the head and toss you off this train!"

Longarm's imagined picture of ancient and exciting buffalo hunts was shattered, and he turned around in his seat to see the two cowboys standing over the seated Indians. One of the cowboys had his gun out and was pointing it at the Indians.

"Roll your sleeve up, I said!" the cowboy demanded.

Longarm didn't want to interfere, but he wasn't going to allow the Indians to be killed. "Hold up there, cowboy," he said, taking in the pair and judging that they were somewhat drunk. "No need to pull that gun."

The cowboy sneered at Longarm and turned back to his friend. "Clemson, did I ask for someone to tell me what I can or cannot do here?"

"No, Dave, you didn't."

"Well, then, why in hell is that big man who has nothing to do with our card game telling me what to do?"

"I dunno," Clemson said with a shrug. "Maybe he's an Injun lover."

Dave nodded in agreement. "Sadly, you could be right because there are a few around these days."

He turned his gun in Longarm's general direction and his eyes narrowed to slits. "Mister, you need to shut up and sit back down. But most of all, you need to mind your own business."

"I'm a United States deputy marshal," Longarm said. "So when someone draws a gun, it becomes my business."

"You're a lawman?" Clemson asked.

"That's right."

"Dave, you better put away that gun."

But Dave shook his head, his gun and his eyes still focused on Longarm. "Prove it."

Longarm was careful to keep his hands away from his gun as he removed his badge and showed it to the cowboy.

"Well, if that don't hang it," Dave swore softly. "An

Injun'-lovin' lawman. I do declare that I've seen everything now." He suddenly began to giggle.

"Holster your gun," Longarm said. "The poker game is over."

"Oh, no," Dave said, shaking his head in an exaggerated fashion. "You see, it ain't over until me and Clemson win back our money."

Longarm had a decision to make. He could push this drunken cowboy harder and maybe get himself killed, or he could back down for a few moments and then take action. He decided on the second option.

"Okay," he said, putting his badge back into his pocket. "Go ahead and play cards."

Dave blinked. "And what about this gun in my hand that you were so concerned about?"

"Watch out or you'll accidentally shoot yourself," Longarm told the cowboy as he sat back down and turned to look out the window.

Clemson started laughing. "You got that right, lawman. Dave can't hit the side of a barn."

Dave grinned and turned back toward the Indians, who had not moved a muscle. He pointed his gun at the older Indian, but he didn't cock the hammer or squeeze his trigger. The Indian stared at Dave without a change in his expression even though the man's heart must have been pounding.

Dave said, "I told you to roll up your sleeve so I can see how many more hideout cards you got hidden."

The Indian rolled up one sleeve, then the other. No cards. Just terrible scars.

"Hmmm," Dave mused, clearly disappointed as he turned his gun on the younger Indian. "Maybe your friend is the one that's been passin' out the aces. Your turn to roll up your sleeves."

The second Indian was only in his twenties, and although he tried to remain as impassive as his companion, Longarm could see hatred welling up in his dark eyes. The younger Indian made no attempt to roll up his sleeves. In fact, he didn't do anything.

"What's the matter with him?" Dave shouted, his amusement turning back to rage at being ignored. "Don't he savvy English?"

"Take it easy," Clemson urged his hotheaded friend. "I don't think this one has been cheating."

"You don't think . . . period!" Dave swore.

"Now wait a minute, partner," Clemson told him. "I don't appreciate being insulted in front of a young lady."

Clemson smiled at the lady, and even tipped his hat to her, but she acted as if the cowboys didn't exist. Longarm admired that and said, "The lady doesn't want anyone to get hurt, do you, miss?"

"No," she said. "I wish everyone would just settle down and shut up. There's no need to be scaring those Indians and the boys."

The two town boys *did* look scared. Where a few moments earlier they'd been giggling, now they were quiet and pale.

Longarm nodded in agreement. "There you go, Dave. You heard the lady. Just put the gun away and enjoy the trip up to Cheyenne. It's too fine a day for someone to get killed over some pocket change."

Dave looked around at the other passengers and then back to the young woman. He gave her a bold and wicked grin. "Say, miss, I judge you to be a whore. How about that?"

"I work at a dance hall. I'm a dancer and a singer." She lifted her newspaper and tried to appear to start reading again, although Longarm knew that would be impossible.

Dave had momentarily forgotten about the Indians. "The only dance you do is on a mattress. So how much do you charge?"

She bit her lower lip and struggled to keep her composure, but Longarm could see that the young woman was on the verge of tears.

Dave was playing to an audience. "Dancer, the hell you say! I pegged you for a whore from the minute you climbed on board in that fancy yeller dress."

He holstered his gun, uncorked his bottle, and marched over to stand over the humiliated young woman. "How about a drink from my bottle and then we get acquainted right here on this train?"

Longarm had seen more than enough. He came out of his seat and reached the cowboy in two long strides. His fist was like a rock as it smashed into the side of Dave's jaw. The jawbone cracked and Dave screamed as he went to his knees.

Even with his jaw broken, the cowboy still had the urge to fight. He stood up and took a swing at Longarm, who blocked the punch and whipped a vicious uppercut into Dave's gut. The cowboy went down again gagging and fighting for air.

Longarm drew his own gun and turned it on Clemson, who had not moved a muscle. "Cowboy, so far you are in the clear. But that can change right now."

Clemson either wasn't as drunk as Dave, or he had a lot more sense, because he raised his hands and took a backward step. "Marshal, don't shoot me! I don't want any trouble with the law or anybody else."

"You should be more choosy about the company you gamble with," Longarm said. "And I'm not talking about your cowboy friend, who needs a serious lesson in manners. I just gave him lesson number one. The lessons get harder as they go along."

Clemson stared down at Dave, who was writhing in agony. "He's hurt real bad, Marshal."

"He'll live."

Longarm turned to the young woman. "I'm sorry about what that man said. I'd force him to apologize right now, but I don't think he can do that with his jaw broken and unhinged."

She looked down at Dave, who was still struggling to draw in breath and whose face was as pale as a marble headstone. "Marshal," she said, "the other cowboy is right, he's in a lot of pain."

"He's lucky that he didn't get himself killed," Longarm replied. "A man foolish enough to wave his gun at an officer of the law often doesn't get a second chance."

"He'll need a doctor as soon as we reach Cheyenne," the young woman said. "And he's going to have a long road to recovery."

Longarm wasn't a bit sorry for Dave. He turned to the other cowboy and said, "Pick your friend up and put him in his seat. And when he's sober, tell him that the next time we cross paths he had better improve his manners or he'll get worse than a broken jaw."

"Yes, sir!"

Longarm went up the aisle to the Indians. "Game is over," he said, looking at the older one and tapping his loose buckskin shirt. "And the next time I catch you cheating with hideout cards in your shirt, I'll make sure that you go to jail. Understand?"

The Indian nodded and gathered up the cards and money.

Longarm turned to go back to his seat. He gave the scared boys a wink, and then he said to everyone in the coach, "It's all right for folks to gamble, which is legal. And it's all right for folks to drink liquor. But it *isn't* all right to do both to excess. And it's *never* all right to insult a lady."

"Marshal, what is your name?" the woman asked Longarm in a voice so low that it was meant for him alone.

He told her.

"My name is Kathryn Hollis. Will you be staying overnight in Cheyenne?"

"I don't know. But it's possible."

"I dance at the Red Pony Saloon. I'll be dancing and singing there tonight. If you come by, I'll buy you a drink."

"If I'm in town tonight, I'll take you up on that."

She turned back to her newspaper. "I hope you do, Marshal. It has been a long time since any gentleman stood up for me."

Longarm studied her for a moment. "I'm sorry to hear that," he said. "It seems like men in the West don't respect ladies like they are respected in the South."

Her eyes lifted to his and she smiled. "As I live and breathe, you are a true Southern gentleman. Maybe I'll sing a special song for you and we can share a little time together later in the evening."

Longarm smiled. "You seem very interested in that newspaper."

"I like people to know that I am intelligent and educated," she told him. "And also I like to be left alone . . . except for an exception such as yourself."

"May I sit down with you?"

"By all means."

Longarm sat down beside the young woman. She smelled good and she looked just fine.

"Are you a married man, Marshal Long?"

"Nope."

"That is good," Kathryn said laying her hand gently on his upper thigh. "A man like you should *never* marry."

Longarm nodded his head and fervently hoped that Secretary Maxwell and his wife would be staying at least one night in Cheyenne, maybe two. They would send J.D. Kilgore packing and then everyone could relax and have a real good time.

Chapter 7

When the train pulled into Cheyenne, Longarm stayed in his seat. He watched Secretary Maxwell and Regina exit the train and go across the depot to ask someone to handle their luggage. Everything seemed fine until J.D. Kilgore suddenly rushed off the train and overtook the couple.

"Is there going to be trouble?"

Longarm turned to see Kathryn Hollis looking over his shoulder toward the Maxwells and J.D. Kilgore, who were already engaged in a fierce argument. "I think so," Longarm told her.

"Isn't that the secretary of the interior and his wife?"

"Yes. And that big man who is arguing with them was their bodyguard for this trip."

"Some bodyguard," Kathryn said. "He looks as if he wants to punch the secretary in the mouth . . . or worse."

"He's dangerous," Longarm told her. "And even though the Maxwells asked me to stay out of sight until they fired that man, it looks like that's not going to be possible."

Longarm saw J.D. Kilgore shove Gordon Maxwell hard up against a wall. Regina was shouting at him.

"I have to move fast," Longarm said, grabbing his bag and heading up the aisle.

"Marshal, I'll be looking for you tonight at the Red Pony Saloon," Kathryn called to him.

But Longarm didn't hear her. He was already jumping off the train and then striding across the platform. No one else was moving, and everyone was watching Kilgore and Maxwell as their argument quickly escalated into a shoving match with Regina trying to get in between.

"Kilgore!" Longarm shouted when he was still some distance away and afraid that the man might suddenly draw a pistol and actually gun down the secretary of the interior. "Kilgore!"

Kilgore turned, and when he saw and recognized Longarm, he froze for a moment, then swore an oath.

Longarm dropped his bag and unbuttoned his coat so that the butt of his six-gun could be seen by the man. "Step back from Secretary Maxwell and his wife and do it right now."

Kilgore shook his head. "You," he hissed. "You're the one that is trying to take *my job*."

"We can talk," Longarm said, hoping to cool the man down. "There's no need for trouble."

"Talk?" Kilgore challenged. "What's to talk about? Gordon says that you're replacing me. I mean to see that that doesn't happen."

Longarm was quick with a gun, but he wasn't the fastest or even the most accurate man around. A professional gunman who practiced the draw would be able to get the drop on him, and that was something that Longarm had never allowed to happen. So without waiting for Kilgore to yank out his six-shooter, Longarm drew his .44 Colt and leveled it at the enraged man.

"Raise your hands," Longarm ordered.

"Or what? Are you going to shoot me down in cold blood?"

Longarm realized this man wasn't going to raise his hands. He had decided that a federal marshal would not shoot him down just for disobeying an order. Instead of raising his hands, he balled them into fists and charged Longarm with a full head of steam.

Longarm had seen drunks do something this stupid, but he doubted that Kilgore was drunk. Rather, the man was so consumed with a sense of betrayal and hatred that he had completely lost his senses. Longarm decided that he would try to pistol-whip Kilgore and render him unconscious. Afterward, he could see that the man went to jail for years.

But as Longarm was taking his stance, he tripped over someone's dropped luggage and lost his balance. Kilgore seized that opportunity and launched himself into a diving tackle. He caught Longarm around the waist and knocked him over backward. Longarm's head struck the platform and he momentarily lost consciousness. His pistol skidded across the heavy planks out of reach.

Longarm was probably not unconscious for more than two or three seconds, but that was enough time for Kilgore to climb on top of him and draw back his fist. Longarm bucked and rolled. Kilgore was thrown aside, but his head was clear and he was on Longarm again in a flash. His fists were hard and fast, and Longarm took three thundering punches to the face before Gordon Maxwell ran over and scooped up Longarm's gun.

"Stop it or I'll shoot!" Maxwell shouted, cocking the six-gun. "You know I will, J.D.!"

Kilgore reared back his fist, aimed it at Longarm's nose, and struck downward with every intention of rearranging Longarm's face. But Longarm was able to swing his head aside, and Kilgore's fist missed and struck the platform.

Kilgore bellowed, and Longarm knew that the man had smashed his knuckles against the planks. In desperation, Longarm reached up and grabbed Kilgore by the throat just as his own gun went off in Gordon Maxwell's hand.

Longarm saw red as the bloody mass of Kilgore's ear sprayed across his face. He felt Kilgore's weight lift from his body, and then the man was rolling sideways screaming. Longarm pushed himself to his knees, and saw Gordon Maxwell holding the gun and Kilgore clasping the side of his head.

"Give me that!" Longarm ordered, wiping Kilgore's blood from his vision and trying to come to his feet.

Regina helped him to stand, and Longarm was given back his Colt. People were staring with shocked expressions at the blood and violence that had suddenly erupted in their midst.

Longarm wiped his face again, knowing that he must look hideous. "I'll take charge now," he said to the Maxwells. "This man is going to jail. Secretary, you and your wife collect your luggage and leave right now."

"We're staying at the Cattleman's House," Regina said, her face pale. "We'll be waiting for you."

Longarm didn't say anything else. Kilgore was coming

out of a daze and when he turned his bloody head around, Longarm saw him glare at Regina and her husband, then fix his hatred upon Longarm.

"You would have been better off to kill me," Kilgore choked. "Because sooner or later, I'm going to kill you!"

"I'll be sure and tell that to the judge here in Cheyenne," Longarm promised, picking up his bag with his free hand and keeping his gun trained on his prisoner. "It's sure to earn you extra time behind bars."

"I need a damn doctor! That sonofabitch Gordon blew off my ear and part of my scalp!"

"I regret that he didn't aim an inch to the left," Longarm said. "Then he'd have blown away what few brains you own."

"There will come a day of reckoning," Kilgore vowed, blood still streaming down the side of his head. "If you or Gordon think that I'm just going to disappear and let this pass, then you're dead wrong."

Longarm was sure that the man was not making an idle threat. He wished that Secretary Maxwell had shot Kilgore dead, but that would have probably cost the politician his career. Now, with Kilgore alive and vowing revenge, it very well might cost them their lives. A lot of men had sworn to kill Longarm, but they were all either dead on in prison for twenty years to life. Even the sternest judge, however, could not keep J.D. Kilgore locked up for too many years on the basis of an assault and a death threat.

"Move," Longarm said, prodding Kilgore with his gun. "We're taking you to jail."

Longarm knew the town marshal, whose name was Bill Ralston, and he took Kilgore directly to the man.

"Holy cow, Custis! What happened!" Ralston exclaimed, almost spilling backward out of his office chair. "Have you been in a knife fight?"

"Not exactly," Longarm said, pushing Kilgore into the marshal's office. "This man is under arrest for assaulting a federal officer as well as the secretary of the interior down at your train station."

"What did you do to him?" Ralston asked. "And even more important, what did he do to *you*?"

"Let's get him in jail," Longarm suggested, "and then I'll tell you the story."

"I need a damned doctor!" Kilgore bellowed. "I'm bleeding to death!"

"Shut up and get in that cell," Longarm ordered, his gun still trained on Kilgore's back, "or I'll shoot off your other ear."

After they got Kilgore into the cell and made sure that he had no hidden weapons in his possession, Longarm sank wearily into a chair. "Bill," he said, "you probably ought to go get a doctor for your prisoner."

"He's out of town on a call," Ralston said. "Some homesteader woman having trouble delivering her baby. If the doc gets back, it won't be until tomorrow. The woman he went to help lives clear up by Chugwater."

Longarm went over to a mirror. He shook his head, looking at his battered and bloody face. "Bill, which one of us looks the worst? Me or that fella in your jail?"

"I'd say that you do." The marshal of Cheyenne poured water into a basin. He found a towel and said, "Clean yourself up, Custis. You look like you've been in a hell of a fight."

Kilgore overheard that and shouted, "He's gonna look a lot worse the next time I run into him!"

"Shut up!" Ralston yelled at his new prisoner.

"I need a doctor right now! I'm bleeding."

Both lawmen ignored the prisoner. When Longarm had cleaned his face up the best he could, he shook his head with disgust. One of his eyes was already closing shut. If Gordon Maxwell hadn't grabbed his gun and blown off Kilgore's ear, Longarm might have gotten beaten to a pulp. J.D. Kilgore was animal-strong; so filled with rage that he seemed to have had inhuman strength.

Longarm walked over to the cell with the wet and blood-soaked towel he'd used on his own face. "Here," he said, pitching it through the cell bars, "use this to stop your bleeding."

"What!"

"You heard me," Longarm said. "Press that towel to the side of your head and settle down. The doctor is out helping a woman have a baby and he won't be back for hours."

"Then get another doctor!"

"He's the only one we have right now," Bill Ralston said. "But we got some tooth-pullers that would love to practice their stitches on your head . . . if that's what you'd prefer."

"Shit!" Kilgore cursed, gently easing the wet and bloody towel to the side of his head.

Longarm went back to the chair and sat down heavily. "Worst trip up from Denver I ever had," he offered. "Had to nearly kill a drunken cowboy. Then this thing happened in front of everyone down at the depot."

"Custis, maybe you should back up and tell me the whole story."

Longarm nodded. "You got a bottle in here so I could pour myself a drink? My face feels as if I've been kicked by a Missouri mule."

"It looks like two mules kicked you in the face," Ralston replied. "Sure I got some whiskey. I use it regularly. Help yourself."

He opened his desk drawer and pulled out a bottle with two glasses. Evidently, he was going to join Longarm in the libations.

"All right," Ralston said, lacing his hands behind his head. "Tell me the whole messed-up story."

For the next half hour, Longarm explained how he'd met the secretary of the interior and his wife in Denver and how he'd saved the politician from a bullet and then been offered a job that could not be refused.

"The trouble was, I'd be replacing that maniac we have locked up in your cell," Longarm said, with a sad shake of his head. "And now, the man has sworn to kill not only the secretary for letting me replace him, but also me."

"And I take it he almost succeeded down at the train a little while ago."

"That's right," Longarm admitted. "Gordon Maxwell was going to fire him this evening at the hotel, but I guess he decided to do it right away . . . or Kilgore guessed what was in store. Either way, it was a close call."

Ralston looked over at Kilgore, who was sitting hunched up on a bed with the towel pressed to the side of his injured head. "So the secretary of the interior actually shot his ear off?"

"Yeah," Longarm said. "And that isn't the whole of it. That maniac and the secretary were friends on the battlefield during the war."

"What about Mrs. Maxwell? How is she holding up to all this?"

"She's all right," Longarm said.

Marshal Ralston allowed himself a smile. "Is she as beautiful as everyone says?"

"Every bit as beautiful."

"Good. I'm going to have to talk to her and her husband about this. I'll need to testify in your behalf when this goes before our judge, assuming you won't be here."

"I won't be here," Longarm vowed. "And neither will the secretary and his wife. We're on our way west to Rock Springs."

"Tomorrow?"

Longarm nodded. "Probably."

"What a fine mess you're leaving behind."

"Sorry," Longarm said. "Do you think your judge will send Kilgore off to the state prison?"

"I'd expect so. I mean, from the looks of your face our prisoner was trying to beat your head in . . . and he almost succeeded."

"I tripped and hit my damned head on the platform. It knocked me out for a second and that was all that Kilgore needed to get me down and hurt."

"Our judge is named Henry Hawkins and he's tough. I expect that when he learns what happened today, he'll send your crazy man to prison for at least a year, maybe even more."

"That would put my mind and that of the secretary's at rest for a while," Longarm said. "For as you heard, he is vowing to kill us both."

"Well," Ralston said, "we'll see if we can't get that one-eared sonofabitch at least five years in prison. That ought to take the piss and vinegar out of him."

Longarm glanced over at J.D. Kilgore. "I wouldn't

count on it. He's still filled with hatred over the Civil War and that's been a lot longer than five years ago. He's a man that seems fixed on destruction and revenge."

"I've seen his kind," Ralston said. "If we're lucky, your man will get in a fight and get killed in prison. That's the way it often happens."

Longarm nodded in agreement. He never wanted to see Kilgore again, and he was sure that Gordon and Regina Maxwell felt the same.

"You could probably use a doctor yourself," Ralston offered.

"Naw. I just need to have a few more pulls on this bottle of yours and then to go find a hotel room and get a good night's sleep."

"Will you be staying at the Cattleman's House?"

"I expect that's a little rich for my budget," Longarm said.

"Keep me informed," the marshal advised. "I'm going to want to talk to a few witnesses and the Maxwells before they board that train tomorrow. And I'll probably think of a few more questions to ask you."

"You won't have much trouble finding me," Longarm said. "I might even stop by the Red Pony Saloon to have a drink or two before I turn in this evening."

"You don't look like a man that ought to do anything but take to bed," Ralston told him.

"I might take your advice," Longarm replied. He tried to wink and instead winced with pain. "After I meet a certain young lady I met coming up from Denver."

"Are you serious?" Ralston asked in amazement. "You look like death warmed over and you're still thinking of getting laid?"

"It would ease my pain just like your bad whiskey."

Marshal Bill Ralston laughed out loud. "Custis," he said, "you are some piece of work."

"Thank you, and don't let our prisoner get your goat today."

Ralston's smile died. "He won't. Because he's so crazy, I think I'll sleep on that cot over there in the corner tonight."

Longarm thought that was probably a very good idea. He glanced over at J.D. Kilgore and saw that the man had stretched out on his own jail bed. Kilgore must have been in a lot of pain and pretty damned unhappy about losing his ear.

To hell with him, Longarm thought. A crazy, hate-consumed bastard like that deserved the very worst that life can offer.

Chapter 8

"Marshal, you'd better wake up. It's nine-thirty and your train leaves at eleven-ten," Kathryn Hollis said, gently rubbing his bare chest and legs. "I'm not letting you get away from me this morning without us doing it one more time."

Longarm opened his eyes, or at least the one that wasn't swollen shut, and felt as if his head had been cracked open by a giant sledgehammer. It wasn't that he and Kathryn had drunk too much liquor the night before . . . although they had had their share. It was the thunderous punches that he'd taken fighting J.D. Kilgore on the train platform.

Kathryn's hands were soft and insistent. One of them now clenched Longarm's flaccid manhood as if it were the head of a bull snake. "Come on, honey, rise and shine."

He blinked and tried to shake away the night's cobwebs. He remembered how he'd gone to see the Maxwells after leaving the jail and how relieved the Easterners been that J.D. Kilgore was going to prison. Longarm also recalled how he'd had gone to the Red Pony Saloon and found Kathryn when he should have just gone to bed and gotten good night's sleep. But Kathryn had been delighted to see him, and after singing and dancing before her admirers until well past midnight, she'd led him upstairs to this small but nicely decorated bedroom. They'd made love through the wee hours of the morning, and now . . . if he was understanding her correctly . . . she was insisting on doing it together one last time.

"Kathryn," he groaned, "my head feels like a cracked walnut. Why don't we take a rain check on what you have in mind? I'll stop and see you on the way back and we'll take up where we left off at four o'clock this morning."

"Oh, no," she said, her hand sliding up and down on his tool until it started to stiffen without his conscious consent. "I've been lying here awake for an hour thinking about how good we were together last night. And the more I thought about it, the more I got excited. I'm *real* excited right now, Custis. And you've got to finish up with a bang."

Kathryn began to kiss his chest, then his nipples, and then on down his stomach until . . .

"Uh," he grunted when she reached his most sensitive piece of anatomy. "You are an insatiable woman, you know that?"

"I know," Kathryn agreed, her mouth and tongue doing wonders even for the aching in Longarm's poor head. "And you're a very skillful lover."

Longarm smiled, and this caused him to wince because his face was tender. "Kathryn, where did you learn how to do this so well?"

"The same places that you learned to pleasure your women," she said, looking up at him with a wink. "Marshal, you're standing at attention and I think you're ready for our grand finale."

"Have your way with me," Longarm said, loving it.

Kathryn climbed up on his stiff, wet pole and eased herself down until she was fully impaled on his impressive rod. Closing her eyes and throwing back her hair, she whispered, "Here we go."

The dance-hall girl began to raise and lower her bottom ever so slowly. Kathryn's eyes were shut and the sun was steaming through their window putting a soft, golden glow on her cheeks and hair. "This is so nice," she whispered, moving up and down and putting his rod just at the right spot for her maximum pleasure. "I could spend the whole morning just doing this with you."

Longarm laced his hands behind his head on the pillow and realized that he was a lucky man. How many other men were starting their day with a good-looking woman squatting on top of them and doing all the work? Probably none in Cheyenne and probably none in the whole territory. Hell, maybe there wasn't a man west of the Mississippi River that was having a beautiful woman like Kathryn make him feel so good and so special.

"It's starting," Kathryn moaned. "It's starting to feel so fine that I can't go slowly anymore. I'm going faster and faster."

"Go as fast as you want," Longarm said, his own breath speeding up. "Just don't stop."

"I couldn't if I wanted to," Kathryn panted, her bottom pistoning up and down and bonding them together with a burning, furious friction. She threw both hands up toward the ceiling and gasped, "Oh, Custis, this is so good!"

Longarm's hands were no longer laced behind his head.

He'd brought them up and was now gripping her hips, slamming her up and down. His lips were pulled back from his teeth, and when Kathryn began to quiver and shake, he let out a roar and shot his seed into her straining body until she pitched forward onto his chest nearly overcome with spent passion.

They lay tight together with his manhood still deep into her honey pot and both of them slowly regaining their composure. Finally, Kathryn raised her head, kissed Longarm's battered face, and whispered, "Thank you."

Longarm rolled over on top of the woman. "This is one hell of a fine way for a man to begin his day. I'm a pretty lucky fella to have met you and had you in bed all night."

"The feeling is mutual." She kissed his black eye. "And promise me that you'll take care of yourself on this trip. Don't take any unnecessary chances. Secretary Gordon Maxwell may be rich and famous, but I'll bet neither he nor his wife are half as sweet and valuable to the world."

Longarm reluctantly climbed off the dance-hall woman. "If I can hold over a night on my return trip, I'll look you up."

"Is that a promise?"

He started to dress. "It is."

"I've learned never to hold a man to a promise. I take them for the time I share with them and let the rest go without regret or expectations. It works out for me far better that way."

Longarm checked his pocket watch and saw that it was a little after ten o'clock. He had wanted to check on Marshal Ralston and perhaps speak to Judge Hawkins for a moment before boarding the westbound Union Pacific.

"I'll buy you breakfast," Longarm offered, "but it will have to be a quick one."

"Next time maybe," Kathryn said, pulling the bedcovers over herself. "I'm still all wet and tingling between the thighs. I'm probably flush in the cheeks too. People would see me and know that you'd just fed me every bit of your big hot sausage."

Longarm burst out laughing. "I never had a woman call it *that*."

"I'm a very descriptive person," she said looking quite pleased with herself. "But go do your business and I'll see you when I see you again. I've learned never to wait for any man. Some women have gotten old and bitter waiting for a man. Life is too short for that, so I'll just say good-bye and come again if and when you can."

Longarm placed his hat on his head and buckled his gun belt around his waist. He paused after opening her door and said, "I'll come around as soon as I can, Kathryn. I feel privileged to have spent this time together."

Her eyes misted and she blinked away tears. "Bye."

Longarm closed the door behind him. He was feeling better than he should, and even though he knew his face was swollen and discolored, he still felt right with the world. J.D. Kilgore was in jail and would soon go to prison, and Longarm had helped feed and put a roof over the heads of some good Denver boys.

All in all, Longarm decided that things were going to be just fine. With any luck at all, he'd have extra money when this tour ended and he returned to Denver. Maybe, with all the extra money he'd earned from protecting Secretary Maxwell, he'd buy his own little house in a good part of Denver.

Naw, why would he want to do that? A house tied a man down. A house always needed tending to, and it attracted women who wanted to be tended to and have children that needed even more tending to.

"I'll stick with Gilda and the tomcat," he muttered as he headed down the hallway.

Longarm stepped out into street thinking it was far better to be footloose and fancy free. To remain a man constantly on the move. An unfettered fellow who enjoyed meeting and bedding women like Kathryn while on the move. A man who might take a few licks, but gave back even better than he received.

He heard the train whistle down at the depot. Time was running short. He needed to hurry on over to Marshal Ralston's office, try to have a quick talk with the judge, then hotfoot it to the train.

After all, he'd almost missed it pulling out of the station back in Denver.

Chapter 9

Having precious little time to spare, Longarm made his way quickly over to Marshal Ralston's office and jail. He was aware that several people on the street stopped and gawked at him, and he assumed it was because of his black eye and swollen face. Longarm didn't care. His only regret was that he hadn't just shot or pistol-whipped J.D. Kilgore from the start, thus avoiding a brawl that had left him slightly worse for wear.

When he reached Ralston's office, Longarm didn't knock, but barged inside. "Bill?"

Not seeing the town marshal at his desk or lying on his cot, Longarm glanced toward the jail cell expecting to see J.D. Kilgore. Instead, he saw a motionless figure lying on the jail bed covered with a gray woolen blanket. Longarm started to look around, but then something clicked in his mind and he pivoted back toward the jail cell.

The figure draped with the blanket was too small and slight to be Kilgore, who was a very thick and powerful man. Longarm gulped, and dread flooded through his veins. He hurried to the cell and saw that it was locked.

"Bill!"

The figure moaned and quivered under the covers. It was then that Longarm noticed the spreading pool of blood beneath the bed. Bright, fresh blood.

"Bill!"

Longarm grabbed the heavy bars of the door and shook them with all his might, but it was a wasted effort.

"Bill!"

He pivoted around and ran over to the marshal's desk, panic rising in his throat. The town marshal's jail keys were not on his desk, and Longarm couldn't see them hanging from any of the many nails in the walls.

Longarm tore out Ralston's desk drawers until he found a set of keys hidden deep in the lower drawer. He grabbed the keys and ran back over to the jail door. He jammed three different keys into the hole until he found the right key and was able to turn the stiff lock.

"Bill!"

Longarm tore off the woolen blanket to see his friend and fellow lawman lying facedown on the bloody mattress. Marshal Bill Ralston had been severely beaten over the head with a blunt object. His hair was matted with blood, and when Longarm gently turned the man over, Bill's eyes were open but glazed and uncomprehending. Even worse, when Longarm put his fingers to Bill's throat to catch a pulse, it was so faint and feeble as to be almost nonexistent.

"Dammit, Bill!" Longarm cried, scooping the semiconscious lawman up in his arms, kicking the door fully open, and then staggering out of the office and into the street to yell, "I need a doctor! Someone find a doctor!"

A woman rushed over. "The doc was helping a woman having a hard time delivering out at Chugwater yesterday. I don't think he's back yet." She looked down at the man that Longarm held as limp as a rag doll. Her hands flew to her mouth and she screamed, "Oh, my God, it's Marshal Ralston!"

Longarm was filled with hopelessness, and he looked around trying to think of something he could do to save his friend. "Where's the doctor's office?"

The woman couldn't seem to tear her eyes off the town marshal, or what was left of him.

"Dammit, lady, where is the doctor's office!"

She was in her forties, heavyset, but with an intelligent face. Instead of answering, however, she just pointed up the street.

Longarm took off running with Ralston flopping in his arms. He shouted at anyone and everyone he saw until he found people who led him to the doctor's office. When he arrived there, he told them to open the door. When it was found to be locked, Longarm leaned back and kicked it free.

He rushed into the doctor's office and found the examination table. Longarm placed Marshal Ralston on the table and looked around for something that would save his friend.

There were jars and jars of medicines. Some were powders, some were liquids, and others were leaves to be soaked for poultices. But what, Longarm wondered, could he do to help Ralston stay alive?

Longarm found scissors, a razor, and some antiseptic. He got a pan of water and carefully clipped and shaved away Ralston's thick hair until the wounds were visible.

"Do you need some help?"

Longarm turned and it was Kathryn. "Yes. Your marshal is still bleeding. I'll try and stitch up these scalp wounds."

"Did that crazy man you arrested off the train and then took to the jail do this to Marshal Ralston?"

"I'm sure that he did."

Kathryn studied the marshal's bloodless face and listened to his rapid, shallow breathing. "This is bad, Custis. I'm not sure that Bill is going to make it through the next hour or so."

"All we can do is stop the bleeding and hope he lasts until the doctor arrives. Let's get these deep wounds sewn up. He's already lost a lot of blood and he can't stand to lose any more."

Kathryn was a strong and capable woman. She helped Longarm wash the scalp wounds with cotton balls, wipe them with disinfectant, and then she threaded suture through a surgical needle with steady hands.

"Here goes," Longarm said, choosing the worst of the lacerations and using forceps to pick up the needle and suture. "This won't be pretty, and I'm almost glad that he's unconscious for the next few minutes."

"Have you done this before?"

Longarm nodded. "I've had to sew myself up a time or two when no one else was around. It's not that hard, unless you're the one that is getting sewn up."

He began to make his stitches. Longarm's fingers were long and supple, and he kept stitching while Kathryn used gauze to keep the area as free of the welling blood as possible.

"You're pretty good at this," Kathryn said. "Maybe you missed your calling and should have been a surgeon."

"Not a chance," Longarm told her as he finished closing

the wound and then started on the next ugly laceration. "I don't like doing this one bit, but it has to be done. Check Bill's pulse."

"It has to be beating because he's still bleeding," she said, taking the pulse and glancing out the front door to where an anxious crowd was forming. "I'm afraid that it's very weak."

"I know." Longarm sighed with exasperation. "Dammit, I can't imagine how Kilgore managed to get the drop on your marshal."

"Maybe he overpowered Bill when he came in with supper or breakfast."

"I hope Bill lives to tell us what happened," Longarm said, hearing the train whistle blasting. "It looks like I'm going to miss my train."

"What about J.D. Kilgore?" she asked. "Do you think that he's on that westbound planning to get back at the secretary and his wife?"

"I sure as hell hope not," Longarm said. "The very last—"

Suddenly, a short, balding man in his late thirties appeared at their side. His hair was mussed, his suit caked with dust, and the man appeared to be totally exhausted and out of sorts. But when he saw Bill Ralston lying on his examination table with his head half bashed in, he said, "I'm Dr. Evans. What in God's name happened to our marshal?"

"We don't know," Longarm said as the doctor began to vigorously wash his dirty hands in a soapy solution. "We suspect that Bill was overpowered in his own jail and beaten nearly to death."

"Did you take his pulse?" the doctor asked, drying off his hands.

"Yes, but it's weak."

Longarm stepped aside as the doctor took charge of their patient. He examined Bill Ralston's eyes. "Pupils are dilated." Took his pulse. "He's lost a lot of blood." And then used his stethoscope to listen carefully. "His lungs are still clear and his heart is steady, but racing."

"What are his chances?" Longarm asked.

"At best fifty-fifty."

"Anything else that I can do to help?"

"No," the doctor said. "You've done all that you could do and I'm not sure that I can do much more. This man may regain consciousness or he may not. Sometimes patients with severe head injuries lapse in and out of consciousness. Nothing is more unpredictable than an injury to the brain, and this man could have suffered permanent damage. If that is the case, I regret to say that Marshal Ralston would be far better off dead."

Longarm's heart sank. "I understand."

"Whoever did this attack was savage," the doctor said bitterly. "One blow would have rendered our marshal unconscious, but he's obviously been beaten repeatedly. It seems obvious that whoever did this went into a rage."

Longarm quickly told the doctor about J.D. Kilgore. When he was finished, Dr. Evans said, "The man deserves to hang. I just hope that he's not after you or the secretary of the interior."

Longarm heard the final blast of the train whistle and knew that the Union Pacific train was leaving the depot. And he could only begin to imagine how upset Gordon Maxwell and his wife would be because of his absence. Longarm shook his head knowing that he had to stay with his friend Bill Ralston until the man's fate was clear.

"Look!" Kathryn cried. "His eyelids are quivering!"

Dr. Evans ran over to his counter of medicines and brought over smelling salts. "Sometimes these will clear the injured mind."

Ralston's head rolled back and forth. A deep groan escaped his lips, and then his eyes popped open and they were filled with pain and confusion. The doctor waved his hand in front of the eyes, but they didn't track. He snapped his fingers and the eyes did not blink. Longarm could see that they were unfocused.

"Bill!" the doctor cried, squeezing the marshal's arm hard. "Can you hear me?"

The marshal's voice was slow and almost impossible to understand. He attempted to sit up, but was held down. "I . . . I can't see anything."

"I'm Dr. Evans and the federal marshal from Denver is here beside me. Don't struggle, Bill. Close your eyes and try to remain calm."

"But Doc," he choked, again trying to sit up, "I'm blind!"

"Listen to me!" Dr. Evans shouted. "It isn't uncommon to have some temporary blindness with severe head injuries. Your brain has swelled and it is pressing down on optical nerves. If you get excited, your blood pressure will rise and you'll cause yourself even more pain and brain injury."

Ralston's face was as white as salt. He began to shake and throw his arms around. "I couldn't live being blind, Doc! Let go of me!"

"Bill, did your prisoner do this?" Longarm asked, knowing the answer but wanting it said out loud in front of witnesses.

"Yes. When I came in to feed Kilgore, he caught me by

surprise and slammed the door in my face. Knocked me down, and then I don't remember anything except him screaming that he was going to kill both you and Secretary Maxwell!"

"How?" Longarm asked. "When?"

"I . . . oh, God, my head is exploding!"

"Breathe deep and relax!" Dr. Evans shouted. "Calm yourself and . . ."

But the doctor's advice was too late. The marshal let out a terrible shriek and his hands broke free to grab his ears. His body stiffened and convulsed so powerfully that, for an instant, only his head and heels were in contact with the table. Then, he emitted a terrible death rattle and died.

The doctor stood helplessly over his patient. Kathryn fell back and began to weep. Longarm felt a fury that threatened to sear his very soul.

"There's nothing more that any of us could have done to save him," the doctor finally intoned. "A brain injury like that, swelling in the cranium . . . it can cause the central nervous system to overload and then suddenly shut down. That's what happened to our friend and marshal."

Longarm had seen it before, and walked over to the sink to wash the blood from his hands.

"Marshal," the doctor said, "at least you learned that your life and that of the secretary is in great danger. If this escaped prisoner is capable of this kind of physical atrocity, he will stop at nothing."

"I know that," Longarm replied.

Kathryn said, "Custis, you don't think that—"

"That J.D. Kilgore got on the westbound train?"

She nodded.

"I sure hope not," Longarm said. "Because if he did, the

secretary and his wife won't last long. J.D. Kilgore is fearless and so filled with hatred, that he'll kill them before they even get to Laramie."

"Can't you telegraph ahead to Laramie and find out?" the doctor asked, draping Ralston's body with a sheet.

Longarm nodded in agreement. "I can telegraph ahead and see if the marshal in Laramie will deputize some men and search the train before letting it go any farther west. I'll tell him that Kilgore is extremely desperate and not likely to be willing to surrender."

"Yes," Dr. Evans said, "that seems to be about all that you can do now."

"I disagree," Longarm said. "You see, Doc, Kilgore was hurt pretty badly. He'd just had his ear and some of his scalp shot away. He'd lost a lot of blood and he'd have found it very difficult hide his injuries and sneak about a train because of the bandages on his head."

"What are you suggesting?" the doctor asked.

"I'm not sure," Longarm admitted. "But Kilgore might have left the jail and immediately gone into hiding. He might also have stolen a horse and ridden out of town to find a place to lay low until he recovers. The point I'm making is that, given the amount of blood he'd lost, I'm not sure he would have been physically able to sneak aboard the train."

"But how can you know what he's done?" Kathryn asked. "The man obviously had enough strength to bash poor Marshal Ralston's head in. And for all you know, Kilgore might be hiding on a rooftop with a rifle planning to ambush you the minute you step out into the street."

"If he were going to do that," Longarm replied, "he would have done it when I was holding your marshal in my arms and yelling for someone to find a doctor. That would have been his easiest shot."

"Then we may very well have a vicious killer in Cheyenne," the doctor said.

"If he stayed, it's because he intends to kill me before he kills Secretary Maxwell," Longarm told the physician as he dried his hands and tried to decide what action needed to be taken right now. "But there isn't any way of knowing. Not until I wire Laramie and have them search the train."

Longarm placed his hand on the draped body. "Bill Ralston was a fine town marshal and a longtime friend. If anything, he was too trusting, too nice. And in the end, he was also too careless."

"We'll take care of him," the doctor said. "Ralston was well appreciated by the people of Cheyenne."

"Does he leave a wife and kids?" Longarm asked.

"No. He was a lifelong bachelor."

Longarm shuffled out onto the boardwalk, where the townspeople were gathering. He was careful to keep under a low roof so a marksman like Kilgore couldn't shoot him from the top of a building. There must have been over a hundred townspeople waiting, and they all began shouting questions at the same time.

Longarm raised his hands for silence. He noticed that he had missed wiping off all the blood and that his cuffs were bloodstained. "I have some bad news," he began when they quieted. "Marshal Bill Ralston has just died from head injuries suffered in a jail break."

At these words, men cursed and women cried.

Longarm knew he had to say more. "I had known and

considered your marshal my friend for more than ten years. Bill Ralston was a kind man and a fine marshal."

"Who killed him!" a heavyset man in a good suit of clothing shouted. "Who did it and why?"

Longarm studied all the angry and shocked faces. "The man's name was J.D. Kilgore. I brought him to the jail, and it's partly my fault that he killed your marshal. And for that, I shall always bear a deep regret. The important thing you need to know is what this man looks like and that he might still be in Cheyenne."

"What does he look like! If I see him, I'll shoot him on sight!" the heavyset man vowed. His intentions were echoed by most of the grown men in the crowd.

"J.D. Kilgore is a big man who stands about six feet tall. He has a square jaw, gray eyes, and a large, crooked nose. But the main way that you would recognize him immediately is that his ear has just been shot off."

The townspeople looked from one to another. Finally, a woman said, "Maybe we should start a door-to-door search right now."

"That's a good idea," Longarm said. "I'll be in the lead. But I need to warn everyone that this murderer is as dangerous as a cornered wild animal. If he needs to, he'll kill anyone who gets between himself and his freedom without hesitation, and that includes women and children."

Some of the anger that he saw on their faces was replaced with apprehension. Several mothers instinctively gathered their small children close to their skirts.

"For that reason," Longarm said, "I'd prefer to deputize a posse of men who know how to hunt and shoot before we begin this search. While we're doing that, those of you women and children who feel afraid can gather in a church or schoolhouse where we'll post armed guards for your safety."

"Where do we start?" a man from the back of the crowd yelled.

Longarm had been through this before, and he wanted to make sure that the rules were set down and understood before anyone moved.

"First, everyone who can hunt, stalk, and shoot—and is willing to risk their life—go arm yourselves. Shotguns will be the best weapon because, if we find this man, it will be close-in fighting. Second, no liquor. If any one of you has already been drinking, then I don't want you involved. Liquor has no place on a manhunt. And finally, is there anyone among you that has been a lawman before?"

"I have," a man of average height but broad shoulders and steely eyes said, separating from the crowd. "I was a town marshal in Kansas for ten years. I have shot and arrested several outlaws."

"Your name?" Longarm asked.

"Orvis White."

"All right, Orvis. When everyone is ready, you'll take one side of the tracks and I'll take the other. You'll keep your posse close together and you'll visit every house, building, stable, outhouse, and structure. You'll look in all the wagons and stacks of hay. You'll search everything so thoroughly that even a cat couldn't escape your eyes. Is that understood."

"Yes, sir!"

Longarm had a feeling that Orvis White could handle his side of the tracks. "Very well. Those of you who meet the qualifications I've stated will meet back here in five minutes."

The men dispersed and hurried off to arm themselves with shotguns, pistols, and rifles. Kathryn came up beside Longarm and asked, "Do you think he's still here?"

"I don't know," Longarm answered. "Sometimes I can feel a man's presence when I'm hunting him. But I don't feel Kilgore's presence right now. My guess is that he's gone."

"But, if you're wrong . . ."

"If I'm wrong," Longarm said, "then we'll find and kill him like the mad dog that he is."

"No arrest?"

Longarm understood the gravity of the question. As a lawman, he was supposed to uphold the law, and that meant bringing fugitives and murderers like Kilgore to trial. But he'd tried that once and it had gotten a good man killed.

"No arrest," Longarm vowed. "This time, we'll be giving J.D. Kilgore a one-way ticket straight to hell."

Chapter 10

Longarm counted twenty-three Cheyenne men who showed up to be deputized, and most of them were armed with shotguns. He deputized the entire bunch without hesitation, and then divided them into two groups.

"Remember," he said, looking directly at Orvis White, "this man is desperate and will kill without a moment's hesitation. Also, look for the wound on the side of his head where his ear was shot off. He'll be weak from loss of blood and probably not able to move very fast. But don't underestimate him for even an instant. Shoot to kill unless he's unconscious. Then fire a gun into the sky and we'll all come running."

Longarm looked around, then repeated his description of J.D. Kilgore. "Are there any last questions?"

No one had any questions.

"All right then," Longarm said. "I'll take this side of the railroad tracks. White, you and your men will take the other side. We should be done in less than two hours. If he's still in Cheyenne, we have to find him dead or alive."

Orvis White nodded, his face set with determination. Longarm headed up the street pointing his men to various buildings.

The manhunt had begun, and Longarm just hoped they found Kilgore before the killer somehow carried out his threat of revenge.

Kilgore lay hidden in a haystack behind Art Wipple's rambling old horse stable and wagon repair shop. It was a huge haystack, and he'd burrowed his way in carefully, then turned around and burrowed back to the outside just so he could rearrange the hay leaving no sign of his entrance. The only real problem he had was that the hay was crawling with mice. He could hear them around and above him. He could hear them eating and digging and they were making sharp little squeaks; maybe they were fornicating.

The thought of joyful mice fornicating all around him almost made Kilgore smile. He just hoped there were no rats among the mice. If there were, they might sneak up a man's pants leg and bite him on the butt, or even worse, slash and bite his privates. The idea of a rat crawling up his pants made Kilgore squirm with revulsion. He'd seen more than his share of rats in his lifetime and he hated the ugly bastards.

There were also lots of bugs and insects in the haystack. He could feel them beginning to explore his flesh. In his pants, up the back of his shirt, in his hair. Kilgore tried to scratch and dig them apart, but he wasn't having much success.

Be calm. No bug is going to kill you. No mouse or even rat will kill you in this haystack. The only thing that will kill you in here is the men that will be hunting you . . . or a rattlesnake.

Jesus! Kilgore hadn't thought of a rattlesnake. He didn't even know if there were rattlesnakes in Wyoming, but he guessed there probably were. And wouldn't a rattlesnake be where there were mice to eat? Hell, yes! If he were a rattler, he'd be in a haystack where there were dozens of fat and lazy rodents.

The idea of being buried in a pile of hay with rattlesnakes really was quite unnerving to Kilgore, who certainly was no coward or weakling. But damn! He just *hated* snakes. Especially poisonous ones. Once as a child, he'd been chased across the surface of a pond by a deadly water moccasin. It had almost overtaken and bitten him on his legs, which were churning faster than a paddle wheel. He'd barely made it to the bank, and the damned snake had stopped at the edge, just a few feet away. It had opened its terrible, gaping jaws to show its deadly fangs.

Kilgore had had nightmares about that water moccasin all through his childhood and even into adulthood. He'd killed every snake he ever saw since, whether or not they were poisonous.

What if there was a rattler in this pile? What if there were a *family* of rattlers? God Lord, he should have found a different hideaway, but it was way too late for that now.

In his holster he carried a six-gun, and he also had a good repeating rifle that he'd taken from the marshal's rifle rack. He had a large bowie knife in his boot, extra ammunition, two canteens that he'd snatched off saddled horses standing in front of a saloon, and enough bread that he'd stolen from the jail to last several days.

Kilgore knew with certainty that he would be the object of an intensive manhunt. He figured that Longarm would have discovered the marshal by now, and wondered if Ralston had died before or after being found. It had been a serious mistake not to finish the marshal off, and Kilgore wished he could have stolen a horse and gotten the hell out of Cheyenne. But when he'd exited the marshal's office shortly after daybreak, there had been several cowboys sitting slouched on their horses in front of a saloon. They had been drinking all night and were drunk and harmless, but they would have seen him and raised a ruckus if he'd tried to steal a cow pony.

Kilgore had gone to ground, so to speak, and he was pretty sure that no one would bother burrowing ten or twelve feet into the haystack only to get his head blown away.

The men hunting him would be furious and eager to get even for the death of their foolish marshal, but Kilgore was really far more worried about rattlers and rats.

I'll wait a day or two and mend. Eat, sleep, and rest. Then I'll find out if Marshal Long is still in Cheyenne. If he is, I'll kill him, and then track down the Maxwells even if it takes a year.

Kilgore knew that finding the secretary of the interior and his wife would be easy. They were a well-known couple. Gordon Maxwell had his sights set on the presidency, and he never missed an opportunity to get his name in the newspaper or his face in the eye of a photographer's camera. The rich and prominent politician's self-importance knew no bounds.

Kilgore could not believe how they had betrayed him. Had Gordon really forgotten that his life had been saved by none other than Sergeant J.D. Kilgore at the Battle of Bull Run? Or had Regina, high-and-mighty Regina, forgotten that he was her brother? Okay. Stepbrother, but still brother. And that he'd often beaten up her many lovesick suitors when she was still a blushing virgin and wealthy young men of high social standing had drooled at the very sight of her face and perfect figure?

The more Kilgore thought about it as he lay deep in the stack of grass hay and waited listening for the sound of the hunters, the more enraged he became at having been fired and replaced by the Maxwells. Having been discarded like yesterday's newspaper despite his years of service and devotion to that handsome but despicable pair of back-stabbers.

Kilgore scratched furiously at something that was biting him on the back. He was weak from loss of blood and in considerable pain. He needed a damned doctor, but he wasn't about to get one. No matter. He'd seen men who'd lost far more than an ear and some skull bone on the battlefield and had survived without any medical attention.

Sometime later, Kilgore awoke with a start and realized that he'd dozed off. He could hear men talking low and hushed, and that told him that they were hunting. Hunting him.

"Look up in the loft," someone hissed. "Be careful. If I was on the run, I'd go to a high place like that."

"Why do *I* have to go up there?"

"Just do it!"

Kilgore was glad that he had not chosen to hide up in the livery's hayloft. There had a goodly amount of hay stacked up there, but not nearly as much as this huge pile on the ground.

He heard the crunch of cautious footsteps passing his stack of hay, and held his breath.

"Get me a pitchfork," someone ordered. "We're going to make sure Kilgore ain't dug into this stack. Get as many pitchforks as you can find in a hurry."

Kilgore heard the crunch of boots moving around the stable and haystack.

"Ain't no sign of anyone in that haystack," another hunter said. "If a man had crawled into that stack, you'd see a hole."

"He might have covered it up," came another voice. "Give me one of those pitchforks and let's set to gettin' busy. Stab as far into the hay as you can."

Kilgore was sweating although it wasn't cold. Was he really deep enough into the stack that they couldn't reach him with the tines of a long-handled pitchfork? He wasn't sure, and he knew it was too late to try to burrow back any farther. Besides, before he'd started burrowing, he'd calculated the stack was about forty feet across, and so he'd crawled in about three of his body lengths. The stack was damned heavy. His air was fouled by mold and in short supply. And there were those rats and snakes to think about.

Kilgore heard the men as they grunted and sent the tines of their pitchforks piercing his sanctuary. He felt them coming closer and closer. The insects and the mice fell silent as the tines probed deeper and deeper.

"Climb into the hay a ways and keep stabbing," whoever was in charge shouted. "I want you to go right to the center of this stack before we move on so there's no doubt he ain't hiding here."

Right to the center? Kilgore drew himself up into as small a figure as he possibly could, not sure if he should expose his back or his belly to the flashing steel. If he were stabbed in the back, the tines might puncture his kidney or his spine and paralyze him. He could die in this stack and the rattlers, mice, and rats would feast on his body for months.

Get a grip on yourself! Kilgore knew that, even if he were stabbed in several places, to cry out would be to be caught and hanged. So he filled his mouth with hay, biting down on the thickest stems hard; he was determined not to make a sound even if he were pierced repeatedly.

And then, he *was* pierced by a tine. It came from the backside of the stack and caught him in the back of his left thigh. The pain was incredible! He bit down even harder on the mouthful of hay and screamed silently as another tine punctured his buttocks.

Good God, even if he could keep from crying out, they were going to pull out the pitchforks and see blood! His blood. Unless it were wiped free by the hay as it was retracted.

Kilgore waited for a lethal blow into his kidneys, or maybe even the steel would slice between his ribs piercing his heart, his lungs, or his liver.

"Nothin'," a man said. "And I went right to the center of it."

"Me too," another added. "If he were in there and alive, he'd be screamin' like a dog with a face full of porcupine quills."

"Then let's move on. If he's still in Cheyenne, we'll find the murdering sonofabitch."

"Hope I get to put the first bullet in him," a man said, his voice clotted with hatred. "I'll shoot him in the goddamn guts and laugh while he dies slow."

"Enough of that talk," the leader said. "Let's move

along here. Marshal Long and his boys are ahead of us across the tracks and we don't want to get too far behind."

Kilgore understood that to mean that the tall federal marshal had formed two bands of hunters.

Smart.

"He ain't up here in this hayloft!" a voice called. "I checked it good."

"Keep your voice down! We're moving on."

"Wait for me."

"Hurry up then."

Kilgore heard them move off, and he spit the hay out of his mouth and writhed in pain. He reached back as far as he could and laid a hand on his butt. It came away wet and he knew that he'd been stabbed deep. The good part was that he'd wisely decided to expose his backside instead of his front. Had he not, he might have gotten stabbed in his most precious and important parts.

He grimaced and managed a muffled and self-deprecating chuckle. *Now wouldn't that have been a howlin' tragedy for all the lusty women!*

The danger was past for the moment. He was free to rest and even sleep. Kilgore tried to slow the pounding of his heart. He had to rest and gather his strength. He had to live. His revenge against the federal marshal and the Maxwells would be the fire that fueled his recovery and ultimate victory.

The hunted had just become the hunter, and Kilgore knew that time was now on *his* side.

Chapter 11

It was one o'clock in the afternoon before Longarm's discouraged posse gathered at the east end of town and admitted that they had not found any sign that J.D. Kilgore was still in Cheyenne.

"Well," Longarm said, "I'll go to the telegraph office and send a message to the marshal in Laramie to get deputies and carefully search the train to see if Kilgore somehow managed to get on board."

"It doesn't seem possible, does it?" Orvis White asked. "I mean, how could he have done that while being badly hurt and without anyone seeing him go all the way from the jail to the train?"

"I don't know," Longarm replied. "But Kilgore is a desperate man and desperate men can often accomplish things that most of us wouldn't even attempt, much less imagine."

"I guess you're right," the ex-lawman said. "In fact, I

know you're right. I used to work in a penitentiary, and there were some prisoner escapes that seemed impossible yet did happen."

"Then you know what I'm talking about."

"Sure do, Marshal."

Longarm left the discouraged posse, but not before he told them to switch sides of the tracks and go back over the search again, overlooking no place of possible hiding.

Then he hurried over to the telegraph office, which was right beside the train depot, and asked the operator, "What time will the westbound be arriving in Laramie?"

The operator glanced up at a big wall clock with a swinging pendulum. "The westbound should be pulling into Laramie in about half an hour. It's less than fifty miles between us and Laramie, but the train has a couple stops along the way and they have to climb over all those the mountains and navigate dozens of sharp switch-backs."

"I need to send a telegram right now to the marshal in Laramie," Longarm said. "It's urgent."

"I expect it has to do with the secretary of the interior and the death of Marshal Ralston."

"It has everything to do with that," Longarm told him. "Let's get this message over the wire right now."

The telegraph operator sat down over his key. "Marshal, you dictate and I'll tap it out," he instructed. "Talk slow and don't back up or repeat yourself."

Longarm took a moment to compose exactly what he wished to say and thus send. "All right," he began, "here we go.

"Urgent message to Marshal Dwight Pate in Laramie

from Marshal Custis Long, United States deputy marshal from Denver. Emergency. Cheyenne marshal killed by prisoner and fugitive named J.D. Kilgore this morning. Kilgore armed and extremely dangerous. Six feet tall, bloody missing left ear. Bruises on face. May be attempting to assassinate Secretary of the Interior Gordon Maxwell and Mrs. Regina Maxwell on train or upon arrival in Laramie. Arrest and hold. Use all caution. Report search results and possible arrest at once to sender."

"That it?" the telegraph operator asked, lifting his finger from the key and turning to study Longarm.

"That's it," Longarm answered. "I'm going to be continuing my investigation and manhunt here in town. As soon as you get a reply, make sure that I know about it."

"Yes, sir."

Longarm gave the man two dollars. "That ought to pay for your trouble."

Longarm headed for the door, but the telegraph operator called, "I sure hope that Marshal Ralston's killer is on that train!"

"I don't," Longarm said. "I hope he's still right here in Cheyenne so I can find him."

Longarm knew that the men he'd used as deputies had conducted a diligent and thorough search, but he still thought that Kilgore was hiding out somewhere in Cheyenne. The question was, where? Longarm spent the next two hours visiting the side of the tracks that Orvis White had covered with his men, but he didn't find a thing.

"No horses reported stolen today?" he asked everyone he met.

The answer was always the same. No horses stolen.

"Were there any wagons leaving town this morning?" he asked Orvis White later.

"Can't say," White replied. "But I'm guessing that there probably were a few wagons heading out to the homesteads and cattle ranches."

Longarm was thinking the same way. "Orvis, we need to put men on fast horses and follow every road leading out of Cheyenne. If Kilgore was able to get onto a wagon and hide, he might still be overtaken and captured."

"We know the roads out."

"Good," Longarm said. He ordered four armed horsemen to ride out and search the wagons moving on every road. He told them that, if they overtook any wagons, the wagons were to be thoroughly searched. "And make sure that your guns are out and you're ready to shoot," he ended up saying. "Because if Kilgore sees you riding up behind a wagon he's in, he'll try to catch you cold and put you into the grave."

Two hours after he sent the telegram, the answer came back from Laramie that the westbound train had been searched from top to bottom but no one even remotely matching the description of J.D. Kilgore had been found or observed by any of the passengers.

"The secretary of the interior also sent a telegram to you," the telegraph operator reported, handing Longarm a folded message.

Longarm walked away to read it. He didn't know what the Secretary was going to say, but he knew it wouldn't be pleasant.

Unfolding the telegram, Longarm found a short, frantic message that read:

UNTIL YOU FIND AND ARREST OR KILL FUGITIVE OUR LIVES ARE IN GRAVEST DANGER **STOP** FIND FUGITIVE AT ONCE **STOP** WILL REMAIN IN LARAMIE AT ANTELOPE HOTEL WITH NEWLY HIRED ARMED GUARDS UNTIL YOU SUCCEED **STOP** DO NOT FAIL US **END**

Longarm refolded the message and put it into his vest pocket. He could only imagine the fear and tension that the secretary and Regina would be under until Kilgore was captured alive or dead. Longarm was surprised, however, that the secretary and his wife had not remained on the train and traveled as far and as fast from Cheyenne as possible. It told him that the secretary also thought that Kilgore was trapped and hiding out in Cheyenne.

"We must find this man," Longarm muttered to himself. "Since he's not on the train, he's got to be hiding out somewhere in or near this town."

Kathryn found Longarm and said, "I take it from the grim expression on your face that Kilgore wasn't located on the train when it reached Laramie."

"No, he wasn't."

"Is that good news or bad?"

"It's good news for the secretary and his wife. I guess it's also good news for me since it means our man is hiding out here somewhere."

"Maybe he did manage to sneak onto a farm wagon that left early this morning and is miles away by now."

"Maybe," Longarm said, admitting the possibility. "But I doubt it."

"Why?"

"Because Kilgore would have gone to ground as quickly as possible given that it was impossible to hide his bloody ear and the bad shape he was in," Longarm replied. "His first objective would have been to hide and heal. At least, that's my thinking."

"But where?" Kathryn demanded. "You and the men you've deputized have looked under every bed, checked every attic, even every wagon, rooftop, room, and every cellar. Have you checked the outhouses?"

"Yes."

"Caskets at the undertakers?"

"There were only three," Longarm answered. "They were all opened."

"Railroad cars?"

"We checked every last one. Even looked on top and underneath them. Nothing."

"What about trees? He could be hiding—"

"Checked them," Longarm said.

Kathryn frowned in concentration. "Is anyone missing? Maybe the man took a hostage."

"No one in town appears to missing."

"Hmm, then what about our local cemetery?" Kathryn mused out loud. "Perhaps there is an open grave and Kilgore is hiding in it."

Longarm snapped his fingers. "Now that's a fine idea. We'll go check it right now."

"I'll go with you."

"No. If he's hiding in the cemetery, I don't want you anywhere near his line of fire."

She nodded with understanding. "I'll try to think of somewhere else you might have missed where he could be hiding. There are a lot of small hiding places in Cheyenne."

"I don't know," Longarm said, gritting his teeth with frustration. "He's clever and I'm at my wit's end as to where he might be hiding. It's like Kilgore opened up the earth, jumped in, and then covered himself up again."

"Manure piles at the livery?"

"He'd be desperate enough to do that, except that manure is too heavy and he wouldn't be able to breathe. He'd suffocate."

Kathryn snapped her fingers. "What about the hay and straw piles?"

"My men pitchforked them every one right to the center. Nothing concealed in them."

Kathryn shook her head. "This man isn't a ghost, Custis. He has to be hiding somewhere."

"I know," Longarm said. "And that's the scary part. My guess is that he'll hide as long as it takes to recover enough to either slip out of Cheyenne or ambush and kill me. I'll be his first target, and if he gets me, then he'll go after the Maxwells, no matter how far away."

Kathryn heaved a deep sigh. "So it's a case of who finds and surprises whom first?"

"That's a fair way to put it," Longarm admitted.

"Kill or be killed?'

"Yes."

She hugged him tightly. "I can't stand the thought of this man waiting somewhere close and biding his time before he sends an ambusher's bullet into you."

"It's not a thought that appeals to me either," Longarm confessed. "Maybe the men I sent out on the roads will find and take care of Kilgore."

"Maybe," Kathryn said, "but I have the feeling you have your doubts that will happen."

"You're right. That would be too easy. Everything about Kilgore is hard. Secretary Maxwell didn't give me any of the details about what kind of soldier Kilgore was under his command. But I wouldn't be surprised if he wasn't only brave, but also extremely cunning and an expert marksman."

Kathryn looked almost stricken with worry. "You should stay off the streets."

Longarm smiled. "I should stay completely away from you," he decided. "Because if we were standing together, you could very easily get caught in a deadly cross fire."

"Then how about if we were in my bed making passionate love?" she said, trying to make him smile.

Longarm shivered at the thought of being in the act of coupling with this woman and having Kilgore burst through their door to catch him undressed and unarmed. "Kathryn, if we were in the middle of doing it together, it would be even worse."

"I'll take my chances."

"I can't allow that. From now until we get this murderer, you need to stay away from me. And I've got to keep hunting and revisiting every place we've searched. Keep revisiting until I find Kilgore . . . or he finds me."

Longarm raised his hands and dropped them helplessly to his sides. "This man intends to kill the Maxwells. I'd like to go to Laramie and protect them. But I feel deep inside that Kilgore is still right here in Cheyenne . . . waiting to get me into his sights. So I'll stay and hope I get him before he gets me."

"Custis, it's like you're on some kind of a death watch."

"I guess you could say that."

Kathryn placed her hand on his sleeve. "Waiting like this is terrible. Why don't you go to our cemetery and see if this man is hiding in an open grave?"

"I got nothing better to do at the moment," Longarm said. "But I have to tell you that the idea of seeking out an open grave makes the hairs on the back of my neck stand up on end."

Chapter 12

J.D. Kilgore was going crazy in the hay pile fretting about rattlesnakes and rats. He had also discovered that the pile was crawling with biting bugs making his life a constant torment. And finally, he'd realized that he had not accounted for the heat that was generated in the middle of a stack of hay and the mold that would make his nose runny and wheezy. His eyes watered and his throat itched. He was even having a tough time breathing.

"I can't stay in here much longer," he muttered to himself, scratching furiously. "If I do, I'll lose my mind."

So Kilgore began to inch his way out of the hay pile. It was slow going, and he had to keep one hand over his mouth so that he could muffle his constant sneezing.

He had a brass pocket watch, but it had been too dark in the haystack to read the thing. Maybe it had stopped, but he had to find out. If it were nighttime, then he would leave the haystack and try to find a better hiding place. Perhaps

Marshal Long and his hunters had given up or gone searching for him outside Cheyenne.

Kilgore hoped so. He needed a chance to find a better hiding place and to heal just a little longer. After that, he'd be the hunter.

His gun was in his left hand and his right hand held the repeating rifle as he struggled forward choking and sneezing. He'd already drunk one of the canteens dry, and the other he'd slung around his neck with a leather loop.

At the thought of the federal marshal who was replacing him as a bodyguard, Kilgore felt a deep hatred flame anew. Kilgore had already decided that he would pay them all back no matter how long it might take or what it might cost.

He came to the edge of the hay pile, and brushed a small hole open so that he could see without any chance of being seen. It was pitch dark outside, and that was very much to his advantage. Now that sound was not muffled by the heavy hay he'd lain under all day and half the night, Kilgore could hear laughter and the tinkling of a piano coming from one of the saloons.

It made him think that he needed a drink. Rye whiskey. A bottle of it and then he would feel like a new man.

Kilgore lay just inside the hay pile for nearly ten minutes before he was certain that he would have no unexpected guests or surprises. He checked his weapons, took a long pull of water from his canteen, and climbed back into the real world. There was a three-quarters moon and plenty of starlight. The moon and starlight, coupled with the lights from the saloons and businesses, were plenty good enough for Kilgore to see by.

He took in deep gulps of pure night air. Gawd, did it taste good! But dammit, something was biting him ferociously in the crotch, so he unbuckled his pants and wiped out the little sucker, feeling it crunch between his thick thumb and forefinger.

What to do now? Where to go next? Those were the questions that Kilgore considered as he gave himself a last scratch and then lifted and buttoned up his pants.

Once during the war, when he had been a sniper, Kilgore had been on the run in a Johnny Reb town. Hunted and desperate, he had discovered that the safest hiding places were those that were the most unlikely. He'd sneaked into a church, overpowered the minister and his wife, and kept them hostage in their attached house for six days until his pursuers gave up their hunt. He hadn't mistreated the minister, but he had known pleasure with the man's wife. He'd robbed them and then left them both bound, gagged, and praying for mercy.

Custis Long and the others would expect him to try and get as far away from Cheyenne as possible. That was why Kilgore knew he had to stay hidden right under their very noses.

Kilgore studied the train yard, momentarily giving in to the temptation of hiding in a boxcar and then letting it carry him to safety. Instead, he looked past the trains toward the residential part of Cheyenne. Now that, he was certain, was where he really needed to go into hiding.

Kilgore slapped the loose hay from his clothes and tried to make himself as presentable a figure as possible. The ragged cloth he'd tied around his head and missing ear made him easily identifiable, so he tore it off and stuffed it back under the hay pile. If he found a slouch hat, one a little too large for his head, he could pull it low and almost nobody would notice that he was missing that ear.

Looking around, Kilgore saw a pen of horses, and again the temptation to steal one and leave Cheyenne on a flying run was almost irresistible. But instead, he headed back into town, careful to move in the shadows as he avoided the main street and the saloons that held the whiskey he so craved.

There were very few people on the streets and when he came to a gas lamp, he pulled his watch out and saw that it was almost midnight. No doubt the fact that he had not been found had been a deep cause of concern, and the good citizens of Cheyenne would be barricaded behind their locked doors. To Kilgore, that would not create a problem. He would simply scout the dimly lit and mostly shut-down neighborhood until he found a house that looked prosperous and vulnerable.

"That one," he said twenty minutes later, choosing a newly painted yellow house surrounded by a neat, white picket fence, wide front porch and rose garden in bloom. He selected the yellow house for no better reason than it strongly reminded him of one that he had lived in happily as a child.

What Kilgore really wanted was for the house to be occupied by an older couple . . . or a pretty young widow. However, if the home included a husband and children, he would deal with that problem decisively.

He was mostly worried about a yard dog. A big, ferocious dog that would see him enter the front gate and attack. Kilgore drew his bowie knife because he could not risk firing a shot in this quiet residential neighborhood. If he did that, he'd be set upon and caught, if not killed. He figured that Marshal Ralston had probably been a popular officer of the law in Cheyenne. His death or severe head injuries would get the people's blood up, and they might be strongly inclined to fetch a rope and lynch Kilgore from one of the nearby shade trees.

Kilgore vowed that he would not be taken alive.

He opened the front gate and moved quickly to the front porch. The door had a screen on it and when he opened that, the main door was locked tight. No surprise. He moved around the side of the house, tromping through the roses and tearing his pants. Every side window he tested was pulled down and locked from the inside. When Kilgore came to the back door, he also found a screen door and it was only secured by a flimsy little latch, while the main door was standing open to give the people inside fresh night air.

It only took a twist of the blade of his knife to pull the latch free. Kilgore quietly moved through the back door and into a pantry area. Without windows, it was very dark inside, and he waited for several moments until he could see shapes and outlines. He stepped into a kitchen and smelled pea soup, coffee, and vinegar. The kitchen had a glass window over the sink, and that gave him a bit more light. Light enough that he could see his way into the parlor.

Nice, homey room. Big overstuffed horsehair couch. Nice pictures on the wall and a little fireplace beside some floor-to-ceiling bookcases. But no spittoons or ashtrays or smoking pipes. Kilgore reasoned that whoever lived here was educated and doing quite well for themselves. There were doilies on the furniture and lace curtains on the windows. He supposed that a good woman lived here making a nice home for her family.

Kilgore did not see any sign of children's toys or even of their pictures. That was interesting. A childless, well-educated, and prosperous couple.

He saw a bottle of liquor on a cabinet along with several crystal glasses. The temptation to have a drink was so strong that Kilgore poured himself a full glass and took a deep, satisfying drink.

He sighed as the heat of the liquor coursed down his throat and warmed the hearth of his belly. He almost felt human again. With clean clothes, a bath, a shave, good food, and whiskey, Kilgore decided he would be almost back to normal. He needed salve to calm the fiery bites and scratches he'd inflicted upon himself in the hay pile. And he needed some lotion or medicating cream to coat the raw scabs where once he had had a good ear.

Just thinking about the loss of his ear reminded him again of Marshal Custis Long and how much he wanted to repay the favor. If possible, he would take Long alive and then slice off both his ears and shove them down his gullet. Then, he'd slice the man up like a red melon.

As he refilled his glass of whiskey, Kilgore studied two doors leading to what he figured were the bedrooms. Both were closed.

Well, he thought, I might as well get myself acquainted with the family.

With his knife still in his fist, Kilgore chose the door on the right and slowly pushed it open. He saw the dim outline of a figure on the bed. A slight figure that he reckoned was either a child or a woman.

Kilgore tiptoed over to the bed and gazed down at the dim figure. It was a woman, and that made him smile. Maybe she was old and ugly, but maybe she was young and pretty. He'd settle for something in between. He started to raise his hand and clamp it down on her mouth, but had a second thought.

What if there's a man in the other bedroom?

It was best to find out right now.

Kilgore left the sleeping woman and went to investigate the second bedroom. What he found was another woman. But this time, the moon and starlight flowed through the bedroom window and he could see that she was neither young nor old, pretty nor ugly. Just a small, somewhat handsome woman in her forties with streaks of silver in her dark, thick hair.

Kilgore sheathed his knife and went back into the parlor for another taste of whiskey. He sipped the whiskey and considered what to do next. Two women in two different rooms. He didn't want to kill them and saw no need for that . . . unless they began to scream . . . which they surely would if they had the chance.

Silence them quickly, if not permanently, he decided. Then bind them up and use them for whatever good they could provide. If they proved uncooperative, then kill them as a last resort.

Kilgore finished his second glass of whiskey deciding that these two were middle-aged sisters. They might be spinsters or widows. Or, as was more and more common in bigger towns, women who left their abusive husbands and banded together after years of being humiliated, abused, and generally mistreated.

He went into the second bedroom, closed the door, and

then walked over to the bed. The woman was sound asleep when he roughly clamped his hand over her mouth and hissed into her ear, "Make one peep and I'll snap your neck like a chicken bone and then I'll also kill your friend."

The woman stiffened and momentarily struggled. Kilgore used his left hand to wrap his powerful fingers around her slender neck. He slowly began to squeeze until she froze in terror.

"Are you going to be silent?"

She tried to speak but couldn't, so she nodded her head.

"Good. Roll over on your stomach and keep your face buried deep in your pillow."

The woman's eyes widened in fear, so he said, "I'm not going to hurt you in any way. If I wanted to do that, I would have already. Now roll over."

She complied. Kilgore used his knife to slash her sheets into strips, which he used to bind her hands and feet. When she was secured, he used a final strip to gag her mouth.

He stood up next to the bed and inspected his handiwork. There was no way that she was going to get free and cause him problems. "I'm going into the other bedroom to do the same thing to your friend. If you try to get away or make a noise, I'll kill her, then I'll return and kill you. Is that understood?"

Again, the woman nodded, although with great difficulty, into her pillow.

"All right then," he said. "Be still. I'm not here to hurt you. I'm only going to stay a while and heal. Then I'll leave you and your friend in the next bedroom alive and well. But only if you both behave."

She twisted her head sideways and tried to look up at

him. There were tears on her cheeks, and he knew that she was terrified and would do exactly as he ordered.

Taking the second woman was almost as easy as the first. She did try to jam her fingers into his eyes, but he grabbed her hand and nearly broke its fragile bones. When she cried out in pain, he silenced her with a sledgehammer fist to the side of the delicate jaw. He did not think he broke the woman's jaw, but it knocked her out good and cold.

Kilgore picked the unconscious woman up and carried her into kitchen, where he dumped her on the floor. He went back to the first woman and also picked her up and deposited her in the kitchen.

"I'm going to fix myself something to eat," he told the woman who was gagged, bound, and watching him closely. "I'd have you prepare me a meal, but someone might smell it and wonder why you were cooking at this odd hour. So I'll just take what I can find in your icebox and kitchen, and you can cook me breakfast after daybreak."

The woman was staring at her unconscious friend with tears flooding her cheeks.

"Don't worry about her," Kilgore said, finding a nice hunk of cold ham in the icebox and stuffing it into his mouth. "I had to give her a little tap to the jaw. Didn't do any permanent damage. She'll be fine by morning. You'll both be fine so long as you behave yourselves. We'll talk. You'll draw me a bath after breakfast. We'll have a real nice time getting to know each other over the next few days."

The woman began to cry hysterically. Kilgore wondered if she had realized that what he had in mind about a "real nice time" included time in bed with them. Probably so.

"Cheer up," he said. "I know I look rough now, but once you feed me and clean me up, I'm still a hell of a handsome hunk of a man."

In response, the woman cried even harder.

Chapter 13

"Helluva good breakfast," Kilgore said, smacking his lips. "I'll have another cup of coffee and then you'd better start heating water for my bath. Oh, and I had thought I'd shave, but on second thought, I've decided to grow a full beard."

The two women just nodded. The one he'd had to punch in the jaw was acting as if she was about to die. The other, however, seemed to have a lot more spunk. Also, she was the younger and prettier of the pair.

"Are you girls sisters?" he asked, mouth full of eggs and fried potatoes.

They both sullenly shook their heads.

"What are you doing here together then? Don't you like men?"

The spunkier one turned with a spatula in her hand, and Kilgore had the feeling she was going to throw it into his face and then try to grab a kitchen knife and slit his throat from ear to ear.

"I'm Mrs. Ann Walker and I live here. My husband and I own a ranch north of town."

"Is that a fact," Kilgore said, not believing a word of it. "Is it a big ranch?"

"Four thousand acres. We run about eight hundred head of cattle right now. My husband and sons are out working cattle and they could return at any time."

"I'm impressed." Kilgore said. "And what about your friend?"

"She's Mrs. Martha Pollard. She's my older sister."

"Ah, yes. The resemblance is plain to see."

"And you," Ann said, "are the man who killed our marshal by beating in his head, then making your escape from jail."

He nodded, and even tried to look sorry. "I hit him a little harder and more often than I should have. But I hate anyone who carries a badge and throws their weight around." Kilgore smiled regretfully. "You're a pretty nice-looking woman. How old are you and your sister?"

"I'm thirty-seven. Martha is forty-two. Her husband is our foreman and he's coming back soon too."

Kilgore was beginning to think the woman might actually be on the level. "Is that a fact? All your menfolk are coming here to . . . to what? Sit around in the parlor for a while?" He shook his head. "I don't think so, Ann. I think you're *both* spinsters."

Her cheeks flamed. "You're wrong, and when our husbands return, they'll shoot you dead!"

"That I very much doubt." Kilgore finished his breakfast. "Let's take a look around this house and see if there are any signs of a husband."

Ann shot a glance at her sister and said, "Why don't you just leave now. We won't say a word until you're long gone."

"Sure you won't," he told Ann, not bothering to hide his sarcasm. "I'll believe that when hell freezes over. Because you know what? The minute I hit the street you'd both be yelling your fool heads off. So I ain't leaving this house and neither are you. No, ma'am. I'm just going to hole up right here in the lap of comfort and watch you little women do whatever it is that you do."

"My sister has a job and so do I," Ann told him. "Martha works at a millinery shop and I work at Clancy's General Store. If we don't show up, someone will come here asking what is wrong."

"Then someone will get themselves killed."

The sisters exchanged worried glances. "Haven't you done enough to this town already?"

He shrugged his broad shoulders. "Ma'am, I've got nothing against this town. I don't know this town and I never wanted to be in this town. But I was wronged here and I mean to set things right before I leave."

"By terrorizing us?" Martha finally managed to ask.

"Well, it's good to see you do have a tongue, Martha. But you got it all wrong. I'm not going to terrorize you. I'm just going to keep you company for a day or two. Then, when it's safe, I'll sneak out of here and be on my way."

"And you won't hurt us anymore?"

"Not unless you disobey or displease me," he assured them.

"What happened to your ear?" Ann asked. "It looks terrible."

He reached up and tenderly touched what little remained of the ear. "Well, that's one of the reasons I've got some unfinished business here in Cheyenne before leaving. You see, the big federal marshal out of Denver shot it off at the train depot when we had a little disagreement."

"You've killed Marshal Ralston. Are you also meaning to kill the federal marshal?"

"As sure as the sun will rise tomorrow, I am. And you know what?"

"What?" they both asked with alarm.

"I might even think of a way that you ladies can help me."

"Never!" Ann swore, clenching her fists.

Martha tried to look as determined, but failed. Kilgore could see that she was the weak one of the pair.

"Why don't you ladies show me around the place?"

"We'd just as soon not," Ann said tightly.

"Do it anyway," he ordered, his voice turning cold. "You can lead me or I can drag you both by the hair. Which is it to be?"

Martha paled, but Ann's eyes burned with fury. "All right," she said at last, "come along."

She led them into the parlor and he studied the books in the shelves. "Nothing about ranching, cows, horses, or cowboying in here," he observed, turning to watch their faces. "All I see are books on religion, gardening, sewing, and such. I don't see any sign of what a man would read in this library collection."

Ann ignored him, and when she started to return to the kitchen, he pushed her and her sister into the bedrooms saying, "Show me your husband's clothes. Show me something of his so I'll believe you both have husbands."

They couldn't show him anything that belonged to a

man. Nothing. Kilgore laughed mockingly at them. "You're just a couple of spinster sisters. No husbands, sons, or daughters."

Ann glared at him. Martha began to cry.

"I'll need you to start heating me a bath now," he said. "And Martha, cut out that infernal snivelin'. I can't stand a woman who sheds tears at the drop of a damned hat."

" 'Drop of a hat!' " Ann shouted. "You callous brute, look what you did to her poor face!"

He pointed a finger at Ann. "If you don't heat that bathwater and start sounding a whole lot more respectful, then you'll look one hell of a lot worse than your sister."

"I'll never respect a killer and bully like you," Ann vowed as she went into the kitchen to heat water. "And I'll do everything I can to see that you get caught and hanged!"

Kilgore grinned. "That's the first honest thing you've told me. Martha, I want you to wash my clothes. They stink."

Ann said, "That's because *you* stink!"

Kilgore gave the woman the back of his hand so hard that she was knocked up against the kitchen wall. Ann's lip started to bleed and he saw tears well up in her eyes, but she wouldn't cry. He admired that, but he would not abide a woman's sass.

An hour later, the women were tied hand and foot, gagged and seated on the floor while he took his bath. He watched them and they watched him. "My, oh, my," he said, splashing more warm water on his face and gently washing away the dried blood from the side of his head. "If looks could kill, I'd already be a dead man."

Kilgore finished his bath taking his time. When he stood

up to show them what a real man looked like in the nude, they twisted their heads to one side and that made him laugh with derision.

He inspected his filthy clothes and decided to toss them in the bath he'd just vacated. Then he untied Martha and told her to get a bar of soap and scrub the clothes until they were fresh and clean. He ordered her to hang them by an open window where they would dry.

"Martha," he said in a voice all the more threatening because of its quietness, "if you try to go through that window and escape, you might succeed. But you know what? I'll kill your sister quicker than you could blink your eye. So don't even think about calling out for help or jumping through the window. Understand me?"

She nodded, still refusing to look at his nakedness. He turned to Annie, who was still tied and gagged, and said, "You're the one that is formin' bad ideas in your pretty head. But I'll say the same thing to you that I just said to Martha. Try to trick me or escape from this house, and I'll kill your sister before you get to your front gate."

Annie turned and did look at his body, but her eyes did not fill with admiration for his manhood or his muscles. Instead, they filled with something else and he suspected it was loathing.

Kilgore was about to grab Martha and take her to the bedroom to show her what a man could do when there was a knock on the front door.

"Ah, shit," he muttered, reaching for his pistol. "I hate to welcome company without any dry clothes to wear. So what are we going to do now?"

"Don't kill whoever it is, please," Martha begged.

"Everything depends on what you do when you answer the door," he said. "If you let on that I'm here, whoever is at the door dies."

Her hand flew to her swollen face. "But what can—"

"Keep that side of your face hidden from view behind the door. Tell whoever is at the door that you're ill and taking the day off from your job. Tell them that your sister, Ann, is also under the weather. And do it convincingly or someone is going to die in the next minute. Remember, Martha, I have nothing to lose."

He cocked back the hammer on his gun just to emphasize his point. "Is that understood?"

"Yes."

"Then open the door a crack and tell whoever it is that you and your sister are sick, but you don't need a doctor."

Martha was so pale and shaken that she *did* look ill.

He watched her open the door a fraction; then Kilgore heard a man ask why she was not at work and Martha tell the man exactly what she was supposed to tell him.

"I'm sorry to hear that," the man said, sounding concerned. "Is there anything I can do for you and Ann? Anything that I can bring you from the doctor?"

"No," Martha told him, still keeping the damaged side of her face from view. "We'll be all right in a day or two. Please tell Clancy at the general store that Ann is also suffering from the same temporary affliction that I have contracted."

"I'll do that," the man promised. "Good day to you."

"And to you," Martha said, reluctantly closing the door.

"Nice," Kilgore said with genuine approval. "Very nice."

She still would not look at his nakedness, and that made him angry. He grabbed her wrist and bent it up behind her back until Martha cried out in pain. Then he shoved her into her bedroom, clamped a hand over her mouth, and silently ravished her slender body.

That night he bound and gagged Martha and had his way with Ann. She fought him, but he'd expected that and it just made things more interesting.

"I'm going to kill you myself," Ann told him the next morning as she stood in the kitchen cooking his second breakfast. "I'm not waiting for the federal marshal or any of the townspeople to do it. I'm killing you myself."

Her voice was shaking with hatred and Kilgore knew that she was serious. He'd never seen a woman more serious than Ann Walker, but that didn't mean she could carry out the threat. He'd just have to watch her very carefully every minute.

His clothes were clean and dry and he dressed, wondering how he was going to kill that federal marshal before he left Cheyenne and hunted down Gordon Maxwell.

"There has to be some way to do it," he said to himself out loud. "Provided, that is, Custis Long hasn't already left Cheyenne."

The more that he thought about it, the more convinced J.D. Kilgore became that he had to make his move this night. One more day and someone would connect the fact that these two sisters were missing with the possibility that they were being held hostage.

The federal marshal would make the connection. To Kilgore's way of thinking, that meant that he needed to venture out tonight, find and kill the marshal, and then get out of Cheyenne before he was caught and lynched.

It wasn't that big of a town. And more than likely, Marshal Custis Long would be easy to locate . . . although less easy to eliminate.

Kilgore was not in the least bit worried. He had stalked and killed men before during wartime. They had been Confederate officers surrounded by their subordinates in an armed Confederate camp. If he could accomplish that, then he could kill Custis Long in Cheyenne.

"Ann," he said, "after dark, we're going to stroll around town and you're going to act like I'm a longtime friend."

"Don't do it!" Martha blurted. "He's going to murder someone and then he'll murder you."

"Shut up!" Kilgore shouted. "Your sister doesn't have any choice. She either does what I say . . . or I'll slit both your throats before I leave this house. Which is it going to be?"

The shock and then panic in their eyes answered Kilgore's question better than words.

Chapter 14

"There," Kilgore said as he finished tying up Martha and applying a gag. "That ought to hold you until we return."

Ann Walker smiled into the eyes of her sister. "It's going to be all right," she promised. "Just lie still on your bed and I'll be back before long. Everything will be fine."

Martha managed to nod her head, but Ann could see that her sister was terrified. She bent to Martha and touched her face. "Just stay brave and this will be over soon."

Kilgore grabbed Ann by the arm and pulled her roughly to her feet. "I'll decide when this is over. Not you."

Ann said nothing. The sun had gone down and they were going outside. It would be her first chance to do something that would save her life and that of her sister. They had been raped and brutalized, humiliated and imprisoned in their own house. But now, finally, there was a chance to get even. She had managed to slip a butcher knife up her sleeve, and she intended to use it even if that meant her own death. At least Martha would have a chance this way.

"Don't try to escape or make a fuss," Kilgore warned Martha. "Remember, I've got your sister by the arm. Do as we say and this will all work out fine."

"We're going out to kill the federal marshal," Ann said. "That's what this outing is all about, isn't it?"

Kilgore said, "That's right. With you by my side, I can get close to him."

Ann nodded with understanding. "But when you kill the marshal, you will leave town and never return. Right?"

"Of course," he said, shoving her toward the front door. "When I act, it will be fast, and then I'll need to get out of Cheyenne in one hell of a big hurry. You're going to help me do that."

A chill passed the length of Ann's body. "How?"

"I'm not sure," he answered as he slipped his gun into his waistband far back on his right hip where it was hidden from the front. "These things are never predictable."

So they left the house, and Ann breathed in the cool night air and felt the weight of the butcher knife in her sleeve. Kilgore had been right about one thing . . . what was going to happen was totally unpredictable. All she knew with certainty was that she and Martha could not endure another night in their house with this man. One way or the other, J.D. Kilgore had to be stopped at all costs.

They walked slowly into the central business part of town. Kilgore kept his head low and his grip tight on Ann. Thank heavens he wasn't clutching the arm with the butcher knife up her sleeve or he'd have discovered her secret weapon. They passed a group of cowboys standing in front of a saloon, and the cowboys all tipped their hats to Ann.

"This is working," Kilgore said, confidence growing with every step. "We're going to the jail to see if Custis Long is working a little late tonight."

"The moment you step inside he'll recognize you," Ann said, her heart beginning to pound in her chest. "Then—"

"Then I'll get the drop on him and we go from there."

Ann wanted to draw out the butcher knife right then, but that was physically impossible. What was she going to do! She couldn't just let this man murder the officer from Denver.

"All right," he said tersely as they approached the office and jail. "There's a light on in the window and that tells me that Long is probably inside. What we're going to do is . . ."

Kilgore didn't finish because three men moving fast overtook them on the boardwalk.

"Excuse me," one of the men said, not looking at their faces.

Ann's heart was really thumping as the three men barged into the marshal's office and slammed the door behind them.

"That was very close," Kilgore said.

"What now?" she asked.

"We pretend to be looking in the shop windows until those three leave."

And that's what they did. For the next twenty minutes, Kilgore guided Ann by the arm up and down the street. Whenever anyone would pass them, he'd sort of duck his head into his coat or lean close to Ann as if he were telling her an intimate secret. But she knew that, if even one of those passersby had suspected what was going on and confronted Kilgore, he would have shot them dead in an instant. He'd probably kill her too just for the hell of it.

"Okay," Kilgore whispered, glancing down toward the marshal's office. "Here they come again. Lean in close and let's keep ourselves in the shadows or there's going to be the damnedest bloodbath you've ever seen."

Ann did as he ordered. Sure enough, the three men stomped past them talking about how they were getting tired of searching for Bill Ralston's killer when they didn't think he was still in Cheyenne.

"Let's go now," Kilgore ordered, pulling Ann away from the window and heading back toward the jail. "Just keep your trap shut and you'll live."

"All right," she whispered, praying for a solution to this terrible drama that was about to unfold.

Kilgore didn't bother to knock. He just grabbed the doorknob and shoved Ann into the marshal's office ahead of himself.

Longarm had been about to leave the office and lock it up for the night. He'd just had some heated words with Orvis White, who, along with the other men that had been deputized, was quitting the Cheyenne manhunt.

"There's no point left in it," White had declared. "Somehow or other, Kilgore has gotten away from us."

Longarm had told the man that he was probably right and that he and the other deputies were discharged from service.

But right now, Longarm forgot all about that when a small woman and a big man plowed through the front door. And before Longarm could react, the big man had his gun out and pointed at the woman's head.

"One move, Marshal, and I'll kill her where she stands."

Longarm was seated in Ralston's office chair. His gun was on his hip, but not in an easy position for a quick draw. Besides, he knew that J.D. Kilgore wasn't bluffing.

"Put your hands up," Kilgore ordered. "Put 'em up high over your head."

Longarm had no choice but to obey the command.

Kilgore reached around behind his back and turned the lock to the door. He still had the small woman by the arm, and said to her, "Ann, pull the window shades. Do it quick and quiet or I'll shoot the marshal and then I'll shoot you."

Ann was free at last. She thought about trying to yank the butcher knife from her sleeve, but Kilgore had moved just enough so that he could keep them both under his gun. To try and grab the knife now would be tantamount to suicide.

"Good," Kilgore said when the front drapes were pulled down. "Now we can enjoy a private moment or two."

Longarm didn't know what to do. If it had just been him and the killer, he might even have acted in pure desperation and made a play for his gun. But with the woman present, that would be irresponsible. Right now her safety was his primary concern.

"What do you want?" Longarm asked.

"I think you know the answer to that."

Longarm started to climb to his feet, but Kilgore cocked his weapon. "Don't move!"

Longarm froze.

"Ann, get over there by the jail cell," Kilgore ordered.

She hurried over to the cell, realizing that now there was no hope to use her knife.

"Very good," Kilgore said, seeming to relax. "Now, Marshal, I think it's high time I paid you back."

Longarm was desperate to gain a little time so that he could try and figure a way out of what was about to happen. "Tell me one thing, Kilgore. Why did you beat Marshal Ralston to death?"

"Why not? One less officious bastard to deal with. Besides, he tried to fight and that was a bad, bad mistake."

"And who is this woman?" Longarm asked, lowering his hands just a fraction.

"Her name is Ann Walker. She and her spinster sister, Martha, have been mighty hospitable to me while you were combing every nook and cranny in Cheyenne."

Longarm turned his head to look at the woman. Her face was badly bruised, and it made Longarm's blood begin to boil. He tried to judge what strength she had remaining after what she must have suffered so far, but he could not read her expression. The only good thing he could see was that she stood straight and there was hatred burning in her eyes for Kilgore.

Longarm was glad to see that because, had she been a trembling mass of hysteria, Ann Walker would have made what was coming next even more difficult. Longarm decided that the only thing he could do to save their lives was to goad J.D. Kilgore into a fit of anger. The man could not fire his gun without bringing men on the run.

That is my edge, Longarm thought. *He can't use the gun and hope to get away with it. He's got to kill us silently by stabbing or clubbing, and to do that he has to come within my reach.*

Longarm said, "My arms are getting tired."

"Tough. Lower them and I'll shoot you where you stand."

"I don't think so," Longarm replied. "Because if you do that, people will come running."

Kilgore's eyes flicked to the door, then back to Longarm. "Don't bet on that, Marshal."

Longarm lowered his arms until his hands were at his shoulders. "I am going to bet on it because Cheyenne is a powder keg about to explode. If you shoot that gun, people will come swarming around this jail faster than a hive of bees whose honeycomb has just been poked."

Kilgore hissed, "Put those hands back up or I swear that I'll blow a hole in your head!"

"You can go straight to hell," Longarm said, his mouth so dry he could hardly speak as he dropped his hands onto the arms of Ralston's old swivel chair.

The gun shook in Kilgore's fist, but Longarm knew that he had to run this desperate gamble. "Kilgore, there's a way we can all get out of this alive."

"How is that?"

"Lock us up in the jail and take the keys. That way you just might have time to get out of Cheyenne."

"All right, we'll play it your way. Stand up and turn around."

If he did that, Longarm was almost sure that Kilgore would bash his brains in with the barrel of his pistol the same way that he'd done to Bill Ralston.

"No," he decided. "I'll keep facing you."

"Do as I say, damn you!"

Longarm set his jaw and shook his head.

"All right. Use your left hand to get out your gun and toss it on the floor. Do it slow and easy or so help me, God, I'll kill you both right where you stand and take my chances with the town."

This time Longarm obeyed, although he sure hated to give up his side arm. But even without it he still had his ace in the hole, which was his double-barreled derringer resting hidden in his vest pocket and attached to his watch chain.

"Are those the keys to the jail cell?" Kilgore asked, motioning to the desk and a key ring.

"Yep."

"Toss 'em over to me left-handed."

Longarm tossed the keys to the man.

"Get in the jail cell," Kilgore commanded. "You first, Marshal."

Longarm glanced at the small woman before he started carefully backing up in her direction. He really didn't want to be locked up, but he was quickly running out of good choices.

"Inside!" Kilgore shouted.

Longarm backed into the jail cell, and Kilgore rushed over and slammed the door.

"What about her!" Longarm demanded as the man fumbled at the ring of keys. "I thought that you were locking us both up in here."

"Your mistake, Marshal. The truth is that I've got other plans for Miss Ann Walker."

Longarm knew right then that Kilgore was going to take the woman and use her as a shield, if necessary, to pull off his escape from Cheyenne. And from the expression on her face, he also knew that Ann had reached the very limit and was about to crack. So before Kilgore could find the correct cell key, Longarm threw himself at the closed door.

The door slammed into Kilgore's face, and the man howled in pain and reeled back with the gun still in his fist. Longarm tried to reach him before he pulled the trigger, but failed.

The gun exploded close between them, and Longarm

felt a bullet go deep into his shoulder as he fell heavily. He looked up as Kilgore prepared to put the next bullet into his brain.

Ann jumped at the man with a butcher knife, which had miraculously appeared in her fist. She slashed Kilgore across the chest. He howled and clubbed her to the floor with his gun. Then he whirled and ran out the door.

Waves of pain hit Longarm. He could barely stay conscious while he crawled over to the woman, who was lying facedown. He reached for her wrist searching for a heartbeat.

But the effort was too great and he passed out cold.

Chapter 15

Kilgore knew that he was not mortally or even badly wounded. The marshal had slammed the door in his face and his nose was probably broken. At least Kilgore thought that it was because he couldn't breathe through the damned thing and it was bleeding. There was a mirror on the wall, and Kilgore rushed over to inspect his chest wound. That bitch Ann had sliced him a good one across the front, but she hadn't had the strength to really drive the blade of her kitchen knife through his rib cage. Again, the damage looked a lot worse than it actually was.

Kilgore tore off his bloody shirt and saw that Ralston had several coats hanging from a coat rack. He found a sheep-wool-lined leather coat. It was a bit too tight and far too warm for the season, but it would soak up the blood, so he buttoned it up to his neck and wiped his face clean. Then, grabbing a shotgun off a rifle rack and a hat off a wall hook, he barreled out the door intent on getting out of Cheyenne just as fast as possible.

He knew that the bullet that he'd fired into the marshal would bring men running, and so he'd spent only minutes in the jail. Had he been able to fire two more rounds, he would have put both of them out of their misery and given himself a great deal of satisfaction. But there was no time, and so now he was moving as fast as he could down the boardwalk without actually breaking into a run and attracting attention.

Several armed men came racing up the boardwalk to overtake him and one of them shouted at Kilgore. "Where did that shot come from?"

Kilgore kept his face down and away in the darkness and mumbled something unintelligible. The men paused only a moment before they continued running up the street.

There were three horses tied to a hitching rail in front of a saloon just a half block away, and Kilgore meant to have one for his escape. Two would be even better, if he could manage it. There was a lot of noise and confusion going on, but he dared not look back over his shoulder.

The three horses were standing close together, and in the light from the saloon window Kilgore saw they were all ordinary Wyoming cow ponies. He figured that they were probably ridden in from the same cattle ranch. Kilgore was a good judge of horseflesh, and took a quick measure of all three animals by walking around them and bending this way and that to judge their depth of chest and straightness and length of leg. There was just enough lamplight to reveal that they were a bay, a buckskin, and a sorrel. All of them were smaller than Kilgore would have wished for, but he knew that they would be tough and strong.

The sorrel was the tallest, and he saw that the saddle it

bore had the longest length of stirrup. That was good. He'd have no time to adjust the stirrup leathers for hours. Kilgore chose the sorrel. He sauntered over to the animal and untied its reins. Next, he checked the cinch, and was glad that he did because it was loose.

The sorrel smelled the blood on Kilgore's face and chest. It snorted and tried to back away from him.

"Easy, boy," Kilgore crooned, not caring if the animal was a mare or gelding. "Easy there, red boy."

He settled the sorrel horse down, and then he also untied the bay's reins. It would really be to his advantage to have a second animal to relay when the chase began.

Trying to move slowly and deliberately, Kilgore could hear loud shouts coming from the direction of the jail, and that told him he had very little time left before someone spotted him. He would also need to ride south through the train yard before he turned west toward Laramie. The search party would expect him to ride west, and that was unfortunate, but could not be helped. Kilgore meant to get to Laramie and find Gordon Maxwell, that double-crossing sonofabitch. He'd kill the secretary of the interior and then he'd decide if he wanted to kill Regina. Maybe he would simply take his pleasure with her because that was what he'd been fantasizing about for years. Afterward, he'd disappear into thin air. He'd find a safe haven for a few months or even years if that was what it took until things cooled off.

Killing the secretary of the interior was going to create a manhunt like none ever before in the West, and Kilgore knew that he had to be smart or he'd be found and hanged. Since he didn't mean for that to happen, he thought he might even go down and live in Old Mexico.

"Hey, mister, what are you doing with our horses?"

Kilgore had one foot in the sorrel's stirrup and a hand up on the saddle horn when the voice caused him to freeze.

"I said, what are you doin' trying to get on my horse?" the voice repeated, this time more insistently.

Kilgore slowly removed his left boot from the stirrup and released the saddle horn. He was caught, and now he had to do the best he could to get out of this mess before the owner of the sorrel sounded the alarm.

He decided to pretend that he was stinking drunk. "Is tis yore hoarse?" he slurred, careful not to turn around.

The cowboy behind him laughed. "Shit, mister, you're drunker than I am! Hell, yeah, it's my horse. All three of these are Bar B horses. Where is *your* horse?"

Kilgore wondered if the Bar B cowboy was alone or with the two others that owned these horses. If the man was alone, he could be easily dealt with, but if there were three cowboys, even somewhat drunk, that would be far more difficult.

"Hey," another voice demanded. "How come you got my bay's reins in your damned hands?"

Okay, Kilgore thought, dropping the reins to the bay and still not turning around so that they couldn't see his face. *That makes two. Is there a third?*

"Sorry," he mumbled, deciding to move directly across the street and walk another block to where more horses were tied to hitching rails. "Big missake. Ha. Ha."

"Damn big mistake," a third cowboy said in a voice that was anything but forgiving. "Mister, I think that you were going to steal those horses. Stealin' horses in Wyoming is a hangin' offense no matter how damned drunk you might or might not be."

"Sorry," Kilgore muttered, knowing the odds were heavily against him and deciding to leave and find unattended horses to use for his getaway. "Big missake. Too much wiss-key."

He started to leave, but a hand dropped heavily on his shoulder. Kilgore froze with his back still facing the cowboys. He waited, hoping that they would let him go. If they did, then he'd make a real show of staggering across this street. But the hand on his shoulder bit harder into Ralston's leather jacket.

"Turn around."

Kilgore knew that there was no chance to stagger away now. He feigned a coughing fit to give himself time to pull his bowie knife from its sheath. If he used his gun on these three cowboys, he'd draw an avenging crowd and never get into the saddle, much less off the street.

"Turn around, damn you!"

Kilgore stopped coughing and pivoted around in a smooth motion. His bowie knife came up between him and the cowboy who owned the sorrel. Kilgore buried the knife to the hilt in the cowboy's guts, and then he yanked it out and slashed the second cowboy's throat open.

The last cowboy was staring at him with shock and horror. Too late, he tried to turn and run, but slammed into the hitching rail. Kilgore buried his blade deep between the last cowboy's shoulder blades. The man stiffened and hollered, but barely any sound came out. Kilgore yanked his knife free and struck a second time. That was all that was necessary to silence the Bar B cowboys.

Everyone up and about in Cheyenne was still focused on the marshal's office. People were hurrying in that direction, and Kilgore knew that they had no doubt found the marshal from Denver either dead or on his way to the grave along with Ann Walker.

It's all the edge I need, Kilgore thought.

Because of the misdirected focus of the townspeople, Kilgore decided to drag all three of the cowboys across the boardwalk and into the narrow alley between the saloon and the next building. Then he realized that he might as well steal all three cow ponies. He would relay them into the Laramie Mountains so fast that no one would have a prayer of overtaking him.

He mounted the sorrel and led the two spare horses around a corner of the street, and then down past Ann Walker's house with its rose garden and white picket fence.

"So long, Cheyenne," he said with a tight smile as he thought about the hell he'd caused both at this house and at the late town marshal's office. "You'll be singing my legend long after I'm gone!"

Chapter 16

Longarm regained consciousness on the doctor's examining table. The first thing he did was look at the window and see that it was still night. Maybe he'd only lost consciousness for a few minutes. "Where is he? Did they get Kilgore?"

Dr. Evans shook his head and his expression was bleak. "No, Gawdammit! The man slaughtered three Bar B cowboys, then stole their horses right off the main street. Orvis White and the ones you'd deputized formed a posse and went on the chase, but they returned early this morning and admitted that they had lost Kilgore's tracks."

"Early this morning? What time is it?"

"It's a quarter to five."

Longarm realized that he'd been unconscious most of the night. He tried to sit up, but Dr. Evans placed his hand on his chest. "I'd prefer that you stay still for the next day or two. I had to dig a bullet out of your shoulder. Any movement or exertion could open up that wound and start it hemorrhaging again. And take my word for it, Marshal Long; you can't afford to lose any more blood."

"Doctor, you don't understand," Longarm argued. "If Kilgore escaped, then he'll be after Secretary of the Interior Gordon Maxwell and his wife. When he finds them, he will murder them in a way that would make your blood curdle with outrage."

"I don't doubt that for a moment," the doctor agreed. "But I also don't doubt that, if you went after Kilgore now, you'd open your wound and bleed to death. And hasn't that man been the cause of enough death already?"

Longarm was going to object, but Kathryn burst into the examining room. "Custis, I overhead what the doctor told you and you're not going anywhere until it's safe."

Longarm felt light-headed and weak. He knew that they were right, but he couldn't just lie on a bed and do nothing. "Kathryn," he said, "at the very least, I must send a telegram to Laramie and warn the secretary of the interior and his wife. Can you do that for me?"

"Of course."

"Gordon Maxwell is staying at the Antelope Hotel and he must be told that J.D. Kilgore is on his way to Laramie to settle their score. Wire Secretary Maxwell and urge him to use all caution and to keep his new bodyguards close and prepared for anything and everything. Then tell the secretary that I will be arriving in Laramie in two days' time."

"Ahh," Dr. Evans hedged, raising a finger in protest, "I am not sure that you can make good on that promise. As I've said, you've lost a great deal of blood and you might not be able to—"

"Doctor," Longarm said in a flat tone that brooked no

argument, "there is *no choice*. I have to get to Laramie."

"But why?" Kathryn asked. "If the secretary has hired bodyguards, why is it so important that you be there to help protect him? Kilgore is only one man."

"That's true," Longarm admitted. "But I think we've all seen that Kilgore is extremely cunning and dangerous. If the secretary has hired locals, I doubt that they are qualified or capable of protecting him and his wife from a man as skilled and dangerous as J.D. Kilgore."

Kathryn seemed to reluctantly agree. "All right. I'll go to the telegraph office right now and send the message to Laramie."

"Ask for a reply and wait for it," Longarm ordered. "I have to know for certain that the message arrives and the secretary is forewarned."

She left, and the doctor said, "What a mess this is! Marshal Ralston and three innocent cowboys murdered for their horses. Miss Walker and Miss Pollard held hostage in their own house. And are you aware that Miss Walker has taken a terrible blow to the head?"

Longarm remembered that the brave woman had saved his life when she'd drawn her butcher knife and attacked Kilgore. "Yes. How is she doing?"

"She suffered a serious concussion. Both Ann and her sister have undergone a terrible ordeal. I've got them heavily sedated. I can heal the physical damage that those poor sisters suffered, but only God and time can heal the mental damage that Kilgore inflicted."

"Kilgore is coming to a bad end and will reap what he has sowed," Longarm vowed. "I promise that he will before the week is over."

"I know you are sincere," Dr. Evans said, "but I can't

see how that helps those two poor women regain their mental health."

Longarm clamped his jaw shut. The doctor was right. He would take Kilgore's life, but that wouldn't help those unfortunate sisters.

Finally, Longarm asked, "Doc, what time is the train pulling out of town today?"

"Why are you asking?"

"I'm going to be on it."

The doctor reacted with outrage. "Marshal Long, I've already told you that—"

"Put me on a stretcher! Carry me onto the train. Doc, if I don't get to Laramie before Kilgore, two more people are going to die."

"Make that three when you add yourself."

"No!" Longarm snapped. "I can be carried onto and off the train when I get to Laramie. I can then be carried by stretcher to the Antelope Hotel, where the secretary and his wife are staying."

"And what good would you be to them in your condition?" Evans demanded.

"I . . . I could be of some good. I know that. I . . . I believe that I can anticipate what Kilgore will do next. How he will try to get to the secretary and his wife in order to get his revenge."

Dr. Evans raised his eyebrows in question. "Are you telling me that you think that you can read that monster's mind?"

"Not completely. But I've been a federal lawman for years. I've hunted men down, and the reason I've been able to succeed and stay alive is that I can anticipate how they think."

"But have you ever been up against anyone the likes of Kilgore?"

Longarm wanted to be truthful. "I'm not sure," he hedged. "But I've tracked down and either arrested or killed men. Outlaws and murderers like Kilgore who were extremely intelligent and even gifted in dealing out death. A lot of them were survivors of the Civil War. They learned how to kill and how to disguise themselves and stalk an important and protected victim. How to do what seems impossible to an ordinary person. Doctor, not only will the secretary and his wife be overmatched by Kilgore, but so will anyone that he hires. So we are talking about a lot of blood that is going to be spilled in Laramie if I don't go there today."

The doctor turned around and studied his framed medical diploma on the wall. "I can't stop you, Marshal Long. But I can promise that, if you are dropped from your stretcher or forced to defend yourself against Kilgore, you *will* die. Have I made that abundantly clear?"

"You couldn't be more clear," Longarm told the man. "But I have no choice."

The doctor turned around. "Then perhaps I should find Miss Kathryn Hollis and tell her to send a second telegram to Laramie explaining that you will be arriving tomorrow afternoon on a stretcher."

"No," Longarm told the physician. "I don't think that is a good idea."

"Why not?" the doctor asked, looking at him sharply.

"Because I need the element of surprise against Kilgore," Longarm admitted, saying the words even as they came to him. "And because, given my poor physical condition, it's the only edge that I'll have against this man."

Evans slowly nodded his head. "Damn poor edge, Marshal."

"Doc, you know as well as I do that we've all got to play the hand we're dealt."

"Damn poor hand you've been dealt this day."

"I agree." Longarm managed a smile. "Now what time is the train pulling out for Laramie?"

"Two o'clock this afternoon."

"Is there some way that I can be smuggled aboard without anyone knowing?"

"Not that I can think of," Evans said, still obviously very much against Longarm's decision.

"Come on, Doc! Help me out here. Can't we find a few people that will get me over to the train depot and hide me in some corner of the baggage room or something?"

"Are you completely insane!" Evans shouted, momentarily losing his composure. "You're in need of my constant professional attention for the next two days, but now you're talking about being hidden in the baggage room?"

"More precisely," Longarm said, "a box that can be transported to the baggage car."

Evans gave out a groan of dismay. "Marshal Long," he said, "you have to be one of the worst patients I've ever encountered."

"I know," Longarm said. "And I'm also one of the most desperate and determined. Now, can we do it?"

"I suppose."

"Good," Longarm said with as much enthusiasm as he could muster. "Then let's set about it before full daylight. It's important that I get on board that train without being seen by anyone. Will you help me?"

"Do I have any choice?"

"Of course you do, Doctor. But will you help me any-how?"

"Of course I will," the doctor said with a shake of his head. "After all, I've sworn to the Hippocratic oath that I must help all injured fools."

"You're doing the right thing, Doc."

"I sure hope so, Marshal. I really do hope so."

Chapter 17

When the Union Pacific finally pulled into Laramie, Longarm was resting comfortably in a huge and ornately hand-carved armoire imported from France by the wife of a wealthy railroad man. The six-foot-tall armoire had double doors and was wide enough for Longarm to rest on his back. It had been a stroke of luck to have such a huge piece of expensive furniture traveling into Laramie, and although Longarm wasn't sure that the family that had bought it would approve, he was delighted to have had this expensive purchase as his personal conveyance.

Dr. Evans had given Longarm specific instructions as to what he could do and what he could not do, if he wanted to avoid reopening his wounds. Longarm had listened and nodded respectfully, but he knew in his heart that he was going to have to get on his feet and sneak into the Antelope Hotel. Once he had done that, he would get a room adjoining that of Secretary Maxwell and his wife and simply wait until J.D. Kilgore made his move.

"The workmen will be arriving to carry you and the armoire over to Mr. William Dent's home in a few minutes," the conductor whispered. "And I'm tying this thing up right now so that the doors won't accidentally fall open in transport to reveal you in hiding."

"Tie it with a cotton rope," Longarm whispered from within. "That way the outside surface won't be scratched and I can easily cut it away. I sure don't want to be stuck in this thing for hours if the owners don't open it."

"I expect they'll open it the moment it's in place in their home," the conductor said. "And I'm also pretty sure that they're not going to be happy to find a United States marshal inside."

"Can't be helped," Longarm said. "You've heard about all the blood that Kilgore has spilled in Cheyenne."

"Just get him," the conductor whispered as he wrapped the cotton rope around the armoire. "I heard about the three cowboys he slashed to death right on the street before he stole their horses. This whole territory is up in arms, and I don't think you could ever get Kilgore a fair trial."

"A trial is not what I have in mind for him," Longarm admitted.

"Here come the workmen, so no more talking. They're going to have a fit when they try to move this thing with you inside. I bet it'll weigh in close to five hundred pounds."

"It'll take more than two of them, that is for sure," Longarm said.

Longarm heard the grunts of exertion, and then the armoire was laid back down and he knew it was being slid onto a wagon. Moments later, he felt a jerk as the wagon started up the street. He hoped that the Dent house was located close to the Antelope Hotel so that he could make his way there without being seen.

When the armoire finally was placed in the Dent household and the workmen sent off, Longarm breathed a deep sigh of relief. What he expected to do was to have a few minutes alone so that he could slip the blade of his knife between the double doors, slice the sash, then climb out and exit the Dent house without ever being observed.

"Open it, Mommy! Hurry! Will it hold all of our coats?"

"I'm sure it will," the woman said.

"It's so beautiful. It's the most beautiful thing I've ever seen. Hurry. Open it!"

"I should have had the workmen cut the rope," the woman said. "But I'll go find a knife and we'll have it open in a moment."

"Can we play hide-and-seek in it!"

"No because it's not meant to be stood in and you might damage its flooring," the woman said.

Longarm knew the game was up. "No, she won't," he said loud enough to be heard by the woman and her daughter. "I weigh over two hundred pounds and I haven't broken through the flooring yet."

There was a cry of alarm, and Longarm felt he had better sever the cotton rope and step outside the armoire in a hurry unless he wanted two hysterical females to run screaming out of the Dent home.

His pocket knife was sharp and it easily cut the rope. Then, he pushed the doors open to see a very pretty woman in her thirties and her equally attractive young daughter with their mouths hanging open. Longarm was aware that his physical appearance was not reassuring. He was blood-stained, rumpled, and unshaven. Even worse, he probably stank like a wet dog because it had been days since he'd enjoyed the luxury of a hot bath.

"Hello there," he said with as much enthusiasm as he could muster. "My name is—"

"What are you doing in there!" the woman cried.

"Maybe he's from France!" the girl cried, alarm turning to excitement.

"No, he's not a Frenchman! He's . . . he's a stowaway!"

"You mean this isn't my closet?" he asked, looking around as if he were the most surprised person in the room while trying to lighten up the situation.

"Are you *insane*!" the woman cried.

"Ladies," Longarm said, extracting his badge from his coat pocket, "please don't be alarmed. I'm a United States deputy marshal from Denver. I've come to catch a killer, so just relax and be calm. There's no reason to be frightened."

"No reason?" the woman said, still backing away. "What in the world are you doing in my beautiful French armoire!"

Longarm climbed out of it, but as he did, there was a loud and very unwelcome splintering sound under his left boot. "Uh-oh," he said, trying to jump out and get his weight off the flooring. "Sorry about that, but you'll never see the damage from where you're standing because it's taken place inside on the floor."

"You oaf!" the woman cried in outrage. "That rare armoire traveled all the way from Paris, France, without a scratch and now you've *ruined* it!"

In trying to climb out, Longarm tripped on the bottom

lip of the piece of furniture and spilled heavily on the floor, grunting as pain stabbed through his wounded shoulder. Then, he climbed to his feet and returned his badge to his coat pocket.

"I'm wounded," he said with a grimace as he attempted to shrug out of his coat. "I may have just reopened a recent bullet wound. Mrs. Dent, is there a doctor that you could send for who would be discreet? I don't want anyone to know that I'm in Laramie."

"Mother, he *is* bleeding!"

At the sight of his fresh blood, the woman seemed to gain her composure. "You are wounded."

"Yes, I'm afraid so. I was warned not to leave Cheyenne by Dr. Evans there, but the circumstances are so dangerous that I had no choice. It was my hope and full intention to sneak out of this house without even being seen. Now, it looks like I've not only caused you and your lovely daughter a fright, but I've reinjured myself."

"He looks pale, Mommy. We'd better go get a doctor."

"Yes, I guess we should," the woman said, coming forward to lead Longarm over to a couch. "Darling, run and get Dr. Peterson."

"What will I tell him?"

Longarm said, "Tell him your mother had a little accident."

"But she didn't."

"Then tell him a friend had an accident," Longarm said. "Tell him to also please hurry."

The girl nodded, her eyes round with concern. "Don't die on us, please."

"I'll try not to," Longarm promised.

"And don't bleed on that couch or Mommy and Daddy will become very upset."

"All right," Longarm said, pressing his hand to his wound. "Now hurry, child."

The moment the girl was out of the house a groan escaped Longarm's lips. Mrs. Dent knelt on the floor beside him and said, "We've got to try and stop that bleeding right now. I'll go get a blanket and some bandages."

"I'm not cold," Longarm told her.

"I know. The blanket is for you to lie on so you don't ruin my couch."

"Oh."

She returned in a few minutes with the blanket. Longarm struggled back to his feet while she spread it on the couch, and then he lay back down. She unbuttoned his shirt and saw that the bandage he already wore was soaked with fresh blood.

"I don't know how you could be so stupid and inconsiderate as to do this to us," the woman said, clucking her tongue with disapproval. "You should be in a hospital, not hiding in my beautiful French armoire!"

"I know."

"What on earth *can* you be thinking!"

"I really apologize for the inconvenience."

"You've ruined the armoire!"

"No, ma'am. Just its floor, and I'm sure that it can be glued back together so that the damage will never be noticed."

"You don't understand, Marshal. *I* will know of the damage."

"I see," Longarm said through gritted teeth, even though he didn't see at all.

After that he must have fainted, because when he awoke, an old doctor who had to be at least seventy was rebandaging the wound. When Longarm's eyes blinked open, the doctor asked, "What on earth are you doing traveling with this bullet hole in your shoulder?"

"I've come from Cheyenne to try and stop a man named J.D. Kilgore from assassinating Secretary of the Interior Gordon Maxwell and his wife. I believe they are staying at the Antelope Hotel."

"I have heard of this murderer named Kilgore. And yes, they were staying at the Antelope Hotel," the doctor said.

Longarm's spirits sank. "Were?"

"That is correct. Their party quietly left town well before sunrise."

"How could that be!"

The old doctor shrugged his thin shoulders. "They and their party rented a pair of coaches, but this is not common knowledge. I only know this because Mrs. Maxwell was not feeling well so I gave her a medication late last evening. She swore me to secrecy telling me about this terrible man you are after. I got the impression that they are hoping that he comes to the Antelope Hotel and runs into our local marshal, who will arrest and imprison him on the spot."

Longarm couldn't believe what he was hearing!

"Where did the secretary and his wife go?"

The doctor shrugged. "I have no idea. I don't think they told anyone. The secretary and his wife seemed very much upset and in a hurry to disappear."

Longarm tried to sit up, but even the old doctor was strong enough to hold him down. "Marshal, you can't stand up. I'm going to have you taken to the local hospital run by our Sisters of Charity. I'm afraid that it will be quite some time before you are fit to travel . . . if your next stop isn't our local graveyard."

Longarm understood what the man was saying. But he also understood that, if Kilgore got to Mr. and Mrs. Maxwell, they were also going to go directly to a graveyard.

It was enough to make him want to roar with anger and frustration.

Chapter 18

Longarm figured he had one chance to reach J.D. Kilgore before the man slipped out of his grasp and eventually found and slaughtered the Maxwells. And that chance, unfortunately, was slim. It was that he could be taken secretly to the Antelope Hotel, where Kilgore would arrive mistakenly expecting to find the secretary and his wife. At that point, even in his weakened condition, Longarm thought that the element of surprise would allow him to get the drop on Kilgore and either kill or capture the man.

"Doctor," he said, "I'm afraid that I won't be able to use the Sisters of Charity. I'm going to the Antelope Hotel and lie in hiding while I wait for Kilgore. He is hurt and not known for his patience, so I expect him to show up within the next twenty-four hours."

"But our marshal has already—"

"He can be there lying in wait beside me if that is what he wants," Longarm interrupted. "What is your marshal's name?"

"Milton Pope. And although Marshal Pope is young and inexperienced, he seems to be very brave and earnest in his duties. We hired him only last month. He's a local boy and the son of a successful cattle rancher who operates the Double X Ranch just about ten miles south of town."

"Believe me," Longarm said, "J.D. Kilgore would have Pope for breakfast. Your young but earnest marshal would meet the same sad fate as Laramie's marshal. I have to help him."

The doctor raised his shaggy gray eyebrows. "Milton might not be pleased. For you see, I had the impression that he was paid a large bonus by the secretary to go into hiding and then surprise and capture this murderer."

"I'm sure that he was," Longarm said, realizing that paying off the local lawmen was how Gordon Maxwell always handled his most difficult personal problems.

Knowing that Mrs. Dent would never allow him back in her armoire, Longarm allowed himself to be transported to the Antelope Hotel in a simple pine coffin. No one on the street paid any attention to the coffin, and it was carried up the back stairs to the hotel's best room, which also happened to overlook the main street.

"First time I've ever been in one of these things, but I expect it won't be the last," Longarm said when the lid was pried off inside the Antelope Hotel. "Is this the room the secretary and his wife used?"

"It is," Dr. Peterson said. "Quite nice, I'd judge. Can you pay for something this grand, Marshal?"

"Nope," Longarm admitted. "But if I capture or kill J.D. Kilgore, the town will owe me a favor. Besides, I think the hotel will appreciate the publicity . . . given that things work out as I hope and expect."

The doctor helped Longarm out of the coffin and onto the bed saying, "You should rest as much as possible."

"I will. Now I had better see your young Marshal Pope. Get word to him to come alone and not tell anyone that I am here."

"Very well," the old doctor said. "But I don't like this a bit."

"You would like it even less if your boy marshal was shot to death by a far more experienced gunman."

"I suppose that is true." The doctor hesitated a moment beside the bed. "You have really lost far too much blood. Besides rest, you need to eat well, drink plenty of milk or water, and sleep."

"There will time for all that when this is over," Longarm assured the physician. "Now please go get your marshal and tell him that secrecy is very important."

"Do you want the hotel staff to remove that depressing pine coffin?"

Longarm thought only a moment, then answered, "No. I think it will come in handy before this time tomorrow."

"Let's hope that it's not you or Marshal Pope that needs it," the doctor remarked as he left.

A half hour later, there was a soft knock on the door.

"Come in," Longarm said, his gun trained on the doorway.

A tall, gangly young man with close-set eyes and a thin mustache appeared. Around the crown of his flat-brimmed hat was a hatband decorated with silver conchos. Marshal Pope's suit and pants were black and his boots were polished to a high shine. He wore a fancy tie-down holster on each hip that held matching pearl-handled revolvers. He removed his fancy hat, and Longarm saw that his long hair was greased and parted down the middle. If Milton Pope was a day over eighteen, Longarm would have been amazed.

Longarm tried not to show his amusement. "Marshal Pope, I'm Marshal Long."

Pope strode forward with his hand stretched out. They shook and the young lawman said, "I can see that you're in real rough shape, but I still appreciate you being here, Marshal Long. However, you should really go to the hospital because I have everything under control."

"Is that right?"

"Yes, sir! When that killer sneaks into this hotel, I'll fill him full of lead the way he done to the marshal in Cheyenne."

"He didn't shoot the marshal in Cheyenne," Longarm said.

"He didn't?"

"No. He beat Marshal Ralston to death with a gun."

Milton Pope paled, but then recovered to bluster, "Then I'll shoot this sonofabitch and give him a lick of his own damned medicine!"

"Meaning you'll beat him to death with one of those fancy six-guns?"

"That's right!" Milton Pope patted the fancy guns and puffed out his skinny chest. "I can deal out sudden death equally fast with either hand."

"Milton, would you please close the door so we can talk in private?"

"Why, sure."

Longarm shook his head in astonishment. He didn't think he'd ever seen a greener fool. But at least the kid was as earnest as the doctor had promised.

"Milton, pull up a chair," Longarm said.

"I'd prefer to stand."

"Have it your way. I understand that you haven't been a lawman very long."

Milton Pope shrugged off any suggestion that he lacked experience by saying, "I am a crack shot. I am also one of the fastest draws you've ever laid your eyes upon. I'm a shade faster with my right than my left hand, but I am flat-out amazing to witness with either hand. You can ask anyone in Laramie . . . or I can show you right now."

"No. No, that's all right," Longarm said. "I take your word for it. But you see, the man that is coming to this hotel expecting to find and kill Secretary Gordon Maxwell and his wife is—"

"The coward would kill a lady!" Milton exclaimed. "Good God, what kind of jasper is this Kilgore anyway?"

Longarm hardly knew where to begin. He had a feeling that no matter what he told this young marshal, nothing much would register or be understood. But he had to try. "J.D. Kilgore is a killer without conscience. And if that isn't bad enough, he's cunning and experienced from his time in the Civil War. He is totally ruthless and one of the most dangerous men I've ever met."

Pope weighed this carefully, then asked, "Is he taller than me?"

Longarm didn't know what that had to do with anything, but since the question was asked, he answered, "J.D. Kilgore stands about six feet tall."

Pope was relieved. "I'm six-foot-one!"

Kilgore would outweigh you a good seventy-five pounds," Longarm said, "and none of it is fat."

"Oh." Finally, a look of concern touched the young man's face. "He is kinda a brute, huh?"

"You could say that."

"What's he look like?"

"His ear is shot off," Longarm said. "So he's easy to recognize."

"Which ear would that be?"

"Look, Milton, the best thing for you to do would be to go back to your office and just wait and let things unfold here at the hotel."

"Not a chance! Secretary Maxwell paid me to get that man and I mean to do 'er."

"The money isn't worth dying for."

"It ain't only the money," Pope said. "It's the reputation I'll have once I plant a bean in this bastard's gizzard." He looked over at the coffin and nodded with approval. "I should have thought of that myself. You think it will hold this Kilgore fella after I give him lead poisoning?"

"I think it will," Longarm said. "But I really wish you'd go back to your office and let me handle this. You see, I know Kilgore, and that gives me some advantage over someone like yourself who hasn't even seen him before."

"The secretary told me a thing or two about him so I'm up to date."

"We'll need to find the secretary and his wife when this is finished," Longarm said. "Where are they hiding right now?"

Pope folded his skinny arms across his chest, raised his chin, and said, "Sorry, but I can't tell you. They asked me to keep it a secret from everybody."

"But not me," Longarm said with exasperation.

"Sorry, sir. I can only tell you that they aren't going very far from Laramie."

Had Longarm been in better health, he would have jumped up and grabbed Milton Pope by the shirtfront and shaken the information out of him. But given his poor condition, Longarm realized that he needed to show patience and restraint.

"To a local farm or ranch perhaps?"

Milton couldn't help but grin. "You're a real smart one, ain't you, Marshal Long. But I still can't say."

"Did they go to your father's cattle ranch ten miles south of town?"

Milton blinked with surprise. "Golly, Marshal, did Dr. Peterson spill the beans?"

"No, I guessed," Longarm said. "And I wish you would go to your father's ranch and stay there to protect your family and their distinguished guests. That way, if Kilgore should kill me, you'd be there waiting for him at the Double X. It would make you a real hero, Milton."

"I'd rather be a hero right here in this hotel room. And besides, us lawman should stick together. You're going to need my help being as you are almost helpless."

"I'm not helpless," Longarm corrected. "Far from it."

"Well, I ain't goin' no place. I'm going to be here when this killer shows and I'm going to put some lead beans in his bacon. Count on it."

"All right," Longarm said. "Then we sit and wait."

"What about food and something to drink?"

"It will have to wait."

"Shit," Milton grumped. "But all right. Where should I stand? Right here in the middle of the room facin' the door?"

"That would be perfect," Longarm said knowing Milton Pope would stand there like a wooden Indian for hours. "Wake me up if you hear footsteps outside or someone tries our door."

"Would he knock?"

"Not likely," Longarm said.

"And you're going to take a nap right now?"

"Why not?" Longarm asked. "With you standing between me and Kilgore, I don't have a thing to worry about."

"Got that one right," Milton said, easing his pearl-handled Colts up and down a little in their fancy tied-down holsters and spreading his legs wide in what he must have thought was a gunfighter's stance.

Longarm closed his eyes because he had to. Otherwise, he might have started laughing.

Chapter 19

Laramie's Marshal Milton Pope was standing in the Antelope Hotel's best room, ready to draw his fancy Colt pistols, when they heard footsteps outside their door. It was almost midnight.

Longarm was instantly alert. He slipped out of his bed with his gun tight in his fist. There was only one lamp lit in the room, and it was turned down very low, but it gave him just enough vision to see two things. First, the doorknob was slowly turning, and second, Milton's long, skinny legs were shaking.

Longarm couldn't understand it. *Why didn't the young fool draw his two six-guns?* Then, it hit him. Marshal Pope wanted to be a legend, and that meant he had to give his opponent a fighting chance.

Longarm slipped a few feet away from the bed into the deepest shadows of the bedroom, and concealed himself as much as he could behind a heavy oak dresser.

Suddenly, the door flew open. Milton Pope's hands

were amazingly fast as they drew both guns and fired at the man in the doorway. Longarm heard the tremendous blast of the fancy pearl-handled Colts and saw the man in the doorway disappear.

An instant later, as Marshal Pope started to lower his guns, Kilgore slid partially into view and opened fire. Pope was caught flat-footed and off guard. He backed away a few steps, and then he crashed onto the bed with a holler. Longarm had no idea if Pope was alive or dead, but he also knew that he had to hold his fire for one more second.

Up until now Kilgore had only shown a fraction of himself, but that was changing as the man's intense hate and curiosity got the better of his good sense. And when Longarm saw all of Kilgore's shirt buttons, he took deliberate aim and pulled the trigger.

Longarm heard the man's body crash against either a wall or the floor, and he jumped out from behind the oak dresser and moved as fast as he could to the doorway.

Kilgore was down, but not dead. He was crawling down the hallway toward the stairs trying to make an escape. However, something must have told the man that he was about to die, because he rolled over onto his back and opened fire again.

Longarm jumped back inside the room and held his breath. Kilgore was going to run out of bullets soon . . . or else bleed to death. Either way, Longarm knew that it would be crazy to step out and offer himself as a target. So he waited until the shooting stopped.

"Come on out and face me like a man!" Kilgore choked.

Longarm had waited enough. He dove into the hallway knowing that he was going to hit hard floor and that it was going to mess up his shoulder wound all over again. But even before he struck the floor he shot Kilgore again, this time his bullet driving up between Kilgore's thick legs into his crotch.

Kilgore screamed and his gun exploded sending a bullet into the ceiling as Longarm's third bullet caught the man under his chin and blew off the back of his head.

It was over.

Longarm groaned because his shoulder wound had reopened. He managed to sit up in the hallway and lean against the wall, then stared at what was left of J.D. Kilgore. It was all too obvious to Longarm that he'd blasted Kilgore's manhood into a bloody pulp seconds before he'd taken away the man's life. Longarm shook his head, and couldn't help but wonder if Kilgore had known he'd been castrated by a bullet an instant before dying.

Longarm hoped so. He dragged himself to his feet and staggered into the room to see Marshal Milton Pope trying to climb off the mattress.

"You're alive!"

"Yeah," Milton groaned.

Longarm shook his head and turned up the lamp to see a bullet hole in the center of Pope's shirt. "How. . . ."

Milton struggled to remove a flat, thick sheet of metal that he'd hidden under his black frock coat and white shirt. In the exact center of the metal sheet was a deep indentation made by Kilgore's bullet.

"Oh, man," Milton whispered, dropping the metal sheet and massaging his bruised chest. "It hurts like a bugger!"

Longarm couldn't believe his eyes. "Why didn't you tell me that you were wearing armor under your shirt and coat?"

Milton just grinned. "You didn't think I was just going

to stand there like a dumb wooden Indian and get plugged, did you?"

"But I thought you said you were really fast and I figured—"

Pope didn't let Longarm finish. "You figured I was also really *stupid*. Isn't that right?"

"I guess so," Longarm had to admit.

"Well, I ain't all that stupid, Marshal Long." He sighed. "But *you* killed that bastard, not me. You're the one that's going to be famous and have dime novels written about what you did here tonight."

Longarm saw that the young deputy was as hurt by losing his chance at becoming a legend as he was by the bullet that had bruised his bony chest. "Tell you what, Milton. As far as I'm concerned, you killed J.D. Kilgore, not me."

"What!"

"Sure. It was your bullets that hit Kilgore first. I missed."

"You did?"

"Yep," Longarm said with conviction. "You planted two beans in his bacon, not me."

"No shit!"

"No shit."

Milton broke into a wide smile. "Holy cow! Then I really will be famous!"

"That you will be," Longarm said.

"But so will you," Milton quickly added. "I can't take *all* the credit."

"Sure you can," Longarm assured him. "I just staggered out in the hallway to blow off his balls after the man was already dead. As soon as we can rouse help, I'll need a doctor."

Milton went into the hallway. "I shot Kilgore under the chin?"

"Yep."

"But . . ."

Longarm raised a cautioning hand. "Don't think too hard about it, Milton. Just take the credit and whatever bounty Secretary Gordon Maxwell promised for the death of J.D. Kilgore."

But Milton shook his head. "I'm a man of honor as well as being brave," he said. "So we'll share the money."

"No, never mind."

"Listen," Milton insisted. "We were in this together tonight and we'll share two thousand dollars each."

Longarm's eyes widened. "Two thousand *each*?"

"Yep."

Longarm had seriously underestimated Laramie's Marshal Milton Pope. The earnest young marshal wasn't a fool. And neither was Longarm. So he smiled, stuck out his hand, and said, "Put it there, partner!"

Watch for

LONGARM AND THE HORSES OF A DIFFERENT COLOR

the 325th novel in the exciting LONGARM series from Jove

Coming in December!